NUBIA DANCES WITH THE GODS

To Caleb

Dance with Truth & Joy

Lynn & Norman Reed

NUBIA DANCES WITH THE GODS

A NOVEL BY
NORMAN AND
LYNN REED

PRINCIPIA
MEDIA

Nubia Dances with the Gods
©2019 Norman and Lynn Reed

Principia Media, LLC
678 Front Avenue NW
Suite 256
Grand Rapids MI 49504
(www.principiamedia.com)

Scripture quotations marked (NIV) are taken from the Holy Bible, New International Version®, NIV®. Copyright © 1973, 1978, 1984, 2011 by Biblica, Inc.™ Used by permission of Zondervan. All rights reserved worldwide. www.zondervan.com The "NIV" and "New International Version" are trademarks registered in the United States Patent and Trademark Office by Biblica, Inc.™

Scripture quotations marked "KJV" are taken from the Holy Bible, King James Version, Cambridge, 1769.

ISBN 978-1-61485-327-5

Disclaimer
All characters appearing in this work are fictitious. Any resemblance to real persons, living or dead, is purely coincidental.

24 23 22 21 20 19   7 6 5 4 3 2 1

Printed in the United States of America

Cover design and interior layout: Frank Gutbrod
Cover photos: Pixabay

To our children, and grandchildren,
and their children,
for life's purpose and joy is evidenced
in each of them,
and there we find reason to rise.

ACKNOWLEDGEMENTS

I give much thanks to Norman for the daily gifts of love, patience, kindness, gentleness, and a totally unselfish approach to living. He claims I too gift him, but we both know his daily breakfast starts it all. Without it, our book could not have become a reality.

Together, we thank our editor, publisher, proofer, designer, many friends and family who have served to encourage us along the way as we worked to bring forth another dream.

CHARACTERS

Adanna* *(ah-don-nah)* Carnarbrara's sister, Queen of Tungul, Nubian

Adzua* *(ahd-zoo-ah)* Niece of King Tasmeria of Tungul, Nubian

Afolabi* *(ah-foe-lah-bee)* Adonna's husband, Nubian

Amenirdis *(ah-men-neer-dis)* High Priestess of the god Amun-re, Egyptian Nubian

Amun-re *(ah-mahn-ray)* King of the Egyptian gods

Ashur (e*h-sher*) Assyrian god of war

Ashurbanipal *(eh-shur-ban-eh-paal)* Son of Esarhaddon, became Emperor/King, Assyrian

Azbo* *(ah-z-bo)* Tungal shaman, Nubian

Baal *(bahl)* Babylonian king of the gods

Carnarbrara* *(kar-naa-brah-rah)* Mother of Ramtouses II, wife of Dafori, wife of Manni, Nubian

Dafori (dah-fo-ree) Prince of Egypt, son of Pharaoh Shebitku, Egyptian-Nubian

Esarhaddon *(eh-sur-hayd-ahn)* Son of Sennacherib, Emperor/King, Assyrian

Grandfather* Great, great, grandfather of Ramtouses II, Nubian

Isaiah *(ahy-zey-uh)* Prophet of Yahweh, Hebrew

Kobina* *(koh-bee-nah)* Friend of Manni, Egyptian-Nubian

Lillie* *(lehl-lee)* Wife of Manni, Hebrew

Manasseh *(meh-neh-seh)* King of Judah, Hebrew

Manni* *(man-nee)* Father of Ramtouses II, Betrothed/ husband to Carnabrara, Nubian

Menthu *(meh-n-thoo)* Egyptian god of war

Naamity* *(nah-am-eh-tee)* Wife of Ramtouses II, Hebrew

Naqia *(nah-kwee-uh)* Mother of Esarhaddon, rumored to be of Hebrew blood

Necho the First *(nee-koh)* Appointed pharaoh by Esarhaddon, Libyan Egyptian

Pianky *(pee-ank-ee)* First Nubian conqueror of Egypt

Psamtik *(sahl-m-tehk)* Son of Necho I, appointed Pharaoh, Libyan Egyptian

Ramtouses II* *(ram-tu-seez)* Son of Manni and Carnabrara, General of Egyptian/Nubian Armies, Nubian

Sennacherib *(suh-nak-er-ib)* Emperor/King of Assyrian, father of Esarhaddon, Assyrian

Shabaka *(shah-buh-kuh)* Second of three brothers anointed Pharaoh of Egypt, Egyptian Nubian

Shebitku *(sheh-beh-t-kuh)* First of three brothers anointed Pharaoh of Egypt, Egyptian Nubian

Suwanda* *(soo-wahn-duh)* Daughter of Queen Adonna, Wife of Ramtouses I, Nubian

Taharqa *(tah-harg-uh)* Third of three brothers anointed Pharaoh, Egyptian Nubian

Tantamani *(tahn-tah-mah-nee)* Son of Shabaka, Pharaoh of Egypt, Egyptian Nubian

Teushpa *(too-ush-pah)* Cimmerian king

The Old Man* Caretaker of farm near Ekron, Hebrew

Wise woman* Friend of Naamity's mother, Hebrew

Yahweh *(yah-we)* God of the Hebrews

(*) fictional characters

PLACES

Ashkelon (esh-kah-lon) City in the Levant region along the Mediterranean Sea coast

Assyria (uh-seer-ee-uh) Dominant kingdom of the Mesopotamian world

Ekron (eh-krah-n) City allied with Jerusalem and trade center of region

Ell (eh-l) The underworld realm of the Ell people, a tribal superstition in which evil spirits wreck the environment and bring death upon all humans

Israel (iz-rey-uhl) Home to ten northern Hebrew tribes

Jerusalem (ji-roo-suhpluhm) Capital city of Judea

Judea (joo-duh) Home to two southern Hebrew tribes

Lachish (ley-kish) Judean city

Levant (leh-**vant**) Trade and shipping part area

Lower Egypt Region along the Nile River delta on Mediterranean Sea coast

Meroe (mer-oh-ee) A Nubian city and pyramid location

Memphis (mehm-fehs) Capital city of Egypt

Napata (nah-pah-tah) Capital city of Nubia

Nineveh (nin-uh-vuh) Capital of Assyria

Nubia (noo-bee-uh) Country south of Egypt, formerly part of Goshen

Nuri (nur-**ee**) Site of Taharga's pyramid

Thebes (theeb-zeh) Capital of Upper Egypt, Kushite domain

Tungal (tuhn-**gal**) Capital of African nation, Tungul (tuhn-**gul**)

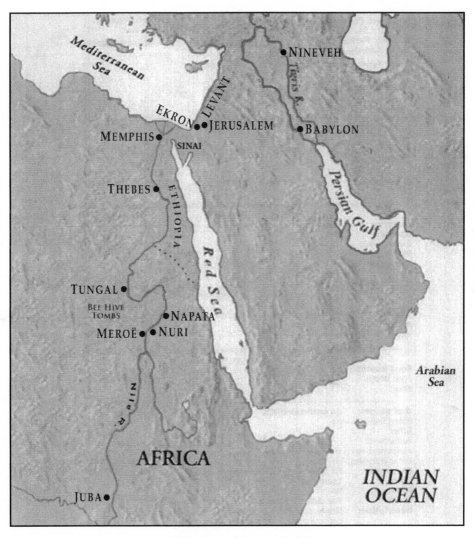

Middle East circa 701 B.C.E.

HISTORIC TIME LINE

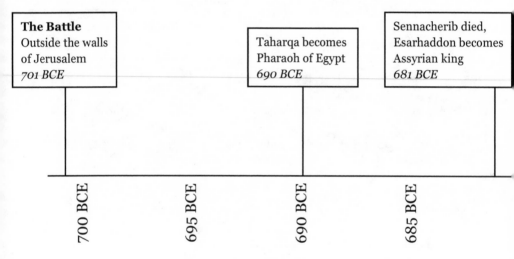

The Battle
Outside the walls
of Jerusalem
701 BCE

Taharqa becomes
Pharaoh of Egypt
690 BCE

Sennacherib died,
Esarhaddon becomes
Assyrian king
681 BCE

700 BCE

695 BCE

690 BCE

685 BCE

Note: Historians do not agree on the actual dates of the events recorded
In our story. The dates we used are those most frequently cited.

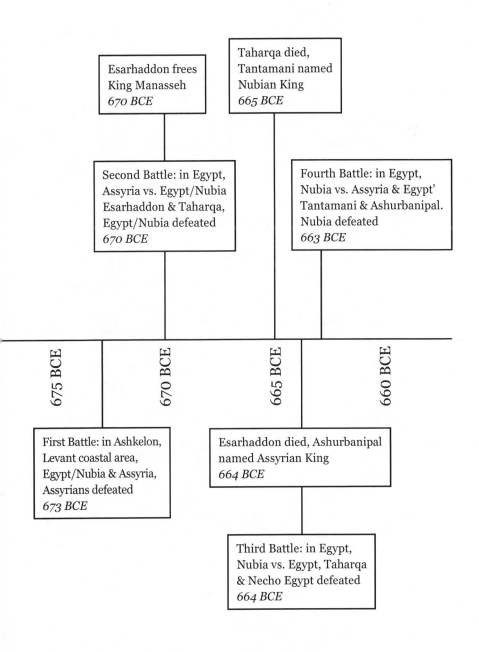

Esarhaddon frees
King Manasseh
670 BCE

Taharqa died,
Tantamani named
Nubian King
665 BCE

Second Battle: in Egypt,
Assyria vs. Egypt/Nubia
Esarhaddon & Taharqa,
Egypt/Nubia defeated
670 BCE

Fourth Battle: in Egypt,
Nubia vs. Assyria & Egypt'
Tantamani & Ashurbanipal.
Nubia defeated
663 BCE

675 BCE

670 BCE

665 BCE

660 BCE

First Battle: in Ashkelon,
Levant coastal area,
Egypt/Nubia & Assyria,
Assyrians defeated
673 BCE

Esarhaddon died, Ashurbanipal
named Assyrian King
664 BCE

Third Battle: in Egypt,
Nubia vs. Egypt, Taharqa
& Necho Egypt defeated
664 BCE

PREAMBLE

The year is 701 B.C.E., and a battle of immense historic importance has just ended.

The great army of Assyria had approached Jerusalem about six months prior to the battle and put a siege upon the city, hoping to instill great fear of their massive war machine in the minds of the Hebrew people. If this had proven unsuccessful in generating surrender, the siege was intended to prevent delivery of food and water into the city, leading to hunger and thirst, and eventually, to a forced surrender.

However, surrender never came. A powerful, unknown army had descended upon the encamped Assyrians in the dead of night. Both armies were destroyed in the ensuing fierce and bloody battle. The only survivors were the leader of the mysterious attacking army and the Assyrian king, Sennacherib, along with a small number of his soldiers.

The wounded leader of the assault lost himself, all memory of his identity, and quite nearly his very life. The defeated Assyrian king lost his peace and was consumed with nightmares.

Thebes, Egypt 701 B.C.E.

The night sky was clear, the air still. Holding her newborn baby, Princess Carnabrara emerged onto the terrace and stood under the darkened sky. She searched the scattered starlight stretching across the great expanse, her eyes on the western horizon, expecting to locate their star. The familiar rush of joy surged through her body upon spotting the brilliant star of her love. She held the baby high up toward the sky, toward the star.

"Are you watching, Ramtouses? Here is your son."

Near Jerusalem

For hours in the dark of night men battled, spilling the blood of others while their own wounds bled and reddened the earth. Ramtouses' arms and legs grew weary as the killing continued. Sweat and blood drenched his body, and it was only the strength of his grasp on the sword's hilt which kept it from slipping in his hand.

He concentrated on the man he believed to be the enemy's leader who loudly urged his people into the battle, demanding they rage on, kill the devils. The enemy spun in circles, swinging his sword wildly high in the air and shouting at everyone around him with a fevered frenzy.

With increasing fury, Ramtouses fought to reach the leader, lunging over the dead and the dying, striking down one soldier after another as they rushed up before him. The leader's screams for his soldiers to fight on never faded—the ferocity in his voice never weakened, and as Ramtouses came closer he looked into the eyes of madness.

He sees me but does not change his stance nor cease his screams. Surely this man is a son of Ell, those who would destroy my people and hold back the rains and have us eat the dust.

Ramtouses drew back his weapon to destroy this monster of Ell and bring an end to the hellish conflict, but at that very moment a terrible blow crashed upon his head sending crushing waves of pain through his body. A ringing in his ears drowned out all other sound.

I'm falling.

The blood-saturated ground rose to meet him, and while he lay there, struggling to move, a senseless darkness claimed him.

No! Do not sleep, Ramtouses.

Ever so slowly, he awakened. Pain slammed into his consciousness and pressed him down like a feared nightmare.

Where am I?

Bit by creeping bit, he reached an awareness of his circumstances.

I'm alive . . . must be if I'm feeling all this pain. But where am I?

The pain struck violently as he opened his eyes.

It's dark. Early morning?

He lifted his head carefully and peered into the darkness.

What has happened here? Are these people around me? Why am I here?

Dazed, weak, and reeling in pain, he slowly rose to his knees, working hard to focus in the shades of night. He managed to stand and scan the earth around him. Bodies lay in all directions, one across another, some with arms and legs twisted and askew.

They lie everywhere. I see no movement. Is anyone alive?
He shouted the question aloud this time, ignoring the soaring pain. "Is anyone alive?"

There was no answer; silence surrounded him.

He touched his throbbing head, feeling blood, and realized a wound still bled, so he tore a piece of his lower garment and wrapped it around his scalp. It slowed the weeping of his wound, but the pain threatened to crush every effort to move or think about the scene that encircled him—bodies, soldiers fallen, already dead or dying.

Can this be real? Who are these people? What happened? Why? Who killed them and nearly killed me?

He stood surrounded by the evidence of violence and death before the dawn of a new day and realized he had to move, had to avoid contact with the bodies and tools of war. *I must leave this place.* The need to move was urgent, but his body was slow to meet the demands of his will.

Begin to walk until you see someone alive and learn what happened here.

He took that first step, faltered, then tripped over a body and nearly fell before regaining balance to continue on through the maze, tripping and righting himself repeatedly.

In his weakened and confused state, the man struggled desperately to push aside piercing pain and continue his stumbling momentum.

I must survive. Why else am I still alive?

The sun's light streaked across the landscape and slowly brought an end to the night. As he walked, he saw fewer bodies sprawled in death. By the time the sun was fully above the horizon, the dead lay in small groups of two or three, spaced farther and farther apart. His thirst grew strong, and he knew the need for water and food would only increase as the day progressed. So with both regret and a thankful heart, the man collected several water bags and food pouches found among

3

the dead. Hours passed, and his journey out of the bleeding land seemed to reach its end.

So utterly tired. I can't go on.

He lay back on the hard earth in a small growth of scrub bushes, partially protected from the late afternoon sun, and contemplated the day's events.

I awoke to pain and the discovery of a hundred—no, many, many more—dead men. I have no memory of who I am or who all those dead people were. What occurred on that field of death? Why? Who?

As daylight faded so did the questions, and he sought a place to sleep against some large rocks. All night, sleep was fitful. His body and head ached, but, come morning, he was eager to continue his search for living people, knowing that even closely rationed, the few supplies gathered from the battlefield would last no more than three or four days.

By high noon on the fourth day, very little of the food and water remained. He spent the remainder of that day looking for water but found none.

Sit, and rest. Then look for water again before nighttime blackens the sky.

But a deep sleep captured him throughout the night. In the morning the search for water resumed, and he fell to his knees with relief when he came to a slow-moving stream. After drinking as much as he could, he filled the bags before washing the dirt, sweat, and blood from his body. The bleeding had stopped from various lesser injuries, but the head wound, swollen and crusted with dried blood, continued to cause intense pain.

When he saw fish moving in the stream and understood he must search for a sharp, straight stick to spear them, he realized he had knowledge of fishing. It caused him to grin.

Well, you may be a fisherman.

As the days passed, the man slowly became aware of his natural attraction to the earth and animals. He saw few trees but many areas of small bushes and large expanses of tall grasses. Occasionally he spotted small animals but had no success catching any of them. His strength slowly ebbed, and after many days of wandering, not knowing who he was or where he was, unsteady, exhausted, and weak beyond comprehension, he finally lay down. The strength to fight for life slipped away.

Maybe I was meant to die back there with the others on that bloody battlefield.

He suspected death would soon find him.

* * *

Two girls walked up and down the gentle hills, calling out and looking for their dog. When at last they heard barking, they rushed in the direction of the sound to find the dog standing over a man lying prone and still on the grass. As the dog continued growling and barking, the girls stood motionless, staring.

Who was this strange man? They saw his injuries. His skin was dark as roasting meat, not reddened from the hot sun. Seeing skin this dark was something one would not easily forget. Thinking back moons ago when a man of this color, so unlike any person they had seen before, had come to their small settlement.

"He's dead," murmured the older girl.

Shadows of birds flying overhead startled the girls out of their trance, and they ran back to their small community, which lay just beyond the reach of a warning call. They yelled as they ran, waving their arms to gain attention.

"There is a man lying on the ground," they shouted, pointing in the direction where they had found him.

"Show me," said an old man.

Rushing ahead, the girls led him to where their dog, still growling and barking, stood guard over the stranger on the open ground.

The old man took a step back in surprise. "I remember seeing this man before. He came by with his men a few weeks ago. Looks badly hurt now. Let's go, we need the cart and donkey to carry him to our settlement."

The settlement was a farm with five wooden houses at the center—two boys and five young girls under the care of an older woman called it home, together with the old man and his wife. All of them accompanied the old man as he led the donkey and cart back to the spot where the stranger had fallen. They lifted his unconscious body onto the cart.

Once at the settlement, they washed and wrapped his wounds with clean cloth, and as consciousness slowly returned, they encouraged the wounded man to drink a little water. For two days he lay there, barely alive, taking a few sips of water when they offered it. His wounds were swollen and his skin feverish. The stranger slept most of the day and night, incoherent the few times he awoke.

On the third day he opened his eyes and realized he was no longer lying on the ground. His head still hurt. His body ached even with no movement. A young girl stood nearby, just watching him.

He glanced around. "Who are you?"

"I am Lillie. I was the one who wanted to touch your skin the first time you visited our home."

The man tried to move but was barely able to raise his head.

Lillie kept talking, "You gave us food. I really liked your food."

Where am I? Who is this girl? And where are her people?

He did not understand a word she said, but he enjoyed listening to her voice and watching the child as she spoke.

Outside the small wooden structure, the old man heard Lillie and the wounded man conversing. He entered the room and quickly realized they could not understand each other's words.

Smiling at Lillie, he said, "Sit and talk some more with our wounded guest. I'll tell the others he is awakened, and the women will fetch some broth for him."

Over the following few weeks, the two village women fed and nursed the stranger back to health. His wounds healed, and he regained lost strength. Lillie came to visit each day and chatted endlessly with him, telling him everything that happened in the village, stopping only when the old man came and sat for a few hours every day teaching him their language. Between the child's and old man's dedication, the stranger learned their language, recognizing many of the Hebrew words along with the rhythm and flow of their communication.

The old man discovered their guest remembered nothing of his past. Because of that he said, "I will call you Manni, for one who has no memory."

Manni grew increasingly restless as the weeks of convalescing passed. His understanding of the Hebrew language improved daily with Lillie's visits, and he enjoyed the attempts to converse with the people who rescued him, but now he needed to move and contribute to his own well-being.

Speaking to the old man, he said, "Allow me to help with the farm work. There is much to do, and my strength has returned."

The old man agreed, and Manni went to work side by side with the old farmer who quickly realized his guest's knowledge of farming equaled his own. Surprised at Manni's understanding of the earth and his natural affinity with plants and animals, the old man concluded a lot of experience growing crops and caring for animals lay hidden in Manni's forgotten past.

Where did he learn such skills? And how long will his memory continue to hide?

They had already determined to start a new field and had selected both the location and which crop to plant. So when morning arrived, both men were eager to begin the work.

Together, they cleared the land of rocks and unwanted brush and tree growth, working it and breaking up the soil to prepare the ground for the seed.

Manni's skin glistened with sweat; he enjoyed the physical demand of digging and turning the dirt to ready it for new seed. Something about the earth and the power of life pushing through the soil energized Manni, and he knew their labor promised a harvest and celebration.

How do I know this? Is it a memory?

The small settlement's survival required long hours working under the hot sun, but each person had specific tasks, and the days moved by with ease as they worked in concert with one another. Laughter and gentle chatter from the children provided a rhythm that boosted cooperation between the adults, and Manni awoke each morning ready to jump into the new day's demands.

He assumed primary care of the sheep and goats and frequently wandered off the little community's self-imposed boundaries to investigate the wildlife of his new environment. For hours, he watched the wild goats traverse steep slopes with amazing ease, their backward arching horns moving up and down with each step. He took note of antelope that preferred to graze on the flat grassland—even with their heads down while grazing, the distinctive long and straight horns gave away their presence in the tall grasses. Manni keenly observed the animals' behavior, and, in time, he successfully hunted the antelope to contribute to the village's food supplies.

The old man was highly religious, a worshipper of Yahweh, and he frequently spoke with Manni about the one and only God who had no beginning and no end, the God of their ancients, Abraham, Isaac, and Jacob. He spoke of the laws of God, who had rescued his people from slavery in Egypt and protected them through the years from warring heathen nations.

Manni listened closely and was quite responsive to the old man's faith. It quieted an inner turmoil, and he often prayed with the old man to this God, giving thanks for his new life, yet always asking for the renewal of his memories.

One day the old man spoke of his own lost family.

"It has been nearly a year since our people went to Ekron to fight the Assyrians. My wife and I promised to be faithful to the children and not leave them for any reason, but now that they are older, I feel compelled to go and see what happened at Ekron. Why did they never come back?"

A long pause filled with silence before the old man spoke again.

"I believe they are all dead. I also believe you were at Ekron, and somewhere in your lost memory you know what happened there. If you return to that city maybe it will nudge your memory."

Again, they sat in silence before the old man said, "It's worth a try. Let's go to Ekron and see what took place."

Manni said, "Yes. Perhaps it will open my memory."

And the two men prepared for a trip to Ekron, a full day's journey.

They arrived close to the city by late evening and selected a spot to spend the night. Come morning, the two men set out climbing the hill that would give them a look down into the city. Just before reaching the hilltop, Manni hesitated, stopping midstride.

"My skin ripples. I'm uneasy. Something tells me you are right, that I have been here before." Manni's reluctance to continue grew heavy, and the weight of his concern shifted into a fear that chilled his body.

The old man held out his arm as if to say, *stay here*, and he moved on toward the hilltop alone. Manni watched.

When the old man reached the hilltop and looked down at the city, he came to a sudden stop. There was a quick intake of breath before he covered his mouth then stood absolutely motionless.

Manni continued the climb and stood beside him. The first thing he saw was a giant statue, standing more than five times

Manni's own height—a mighty monster all weather-beaten and rough, which made it appear even more horrifying than its size alone. The statue towered over its surroundings with an invisible and malevolent force.

He stared at the image, mesmerized by it, before moving down the hill toward the threatening figure. Its possible connection to his lost memory frightened Manni.

"I've seen you before. I've seen you before!" Manni repeated. He yelled, "What are you? Where do you come from?"

The monster's eyes were polished emeralds and seemed to follow Manni's movements. It had the head of a man—a high crown was on its brow, and heavy armor covered its torso. The lower body was that of a muscular lion while wide-spread wings gave it the appearance of a giant bird settling to its perch after flight. Manni stopped a short stone's throw away from it and stared at the monstrous statue, searching his mind for memories, for any information about what stood before the city's entrance, hoping answers would come to him. He could not stop looking into the creature's eyes.

Then from nowhere he heard the cries of men fighting and the sound of clashing weapons. The sounds grew louder and louder within his head, causing Manni to clamp his hands over his ears, but it was futile, for the clamor continued to increase. His body grew cold, and yet beads of sweat collected into little rivulets and slowly slid down his face, chest, and back. The sight of everyone dead, men, women and children, scattered throughout the town, was a sickening sight. The smell of rotting flesh hung like a heavy mist around him.

He began to retreat back up the hill and moved to the other side, where the hill blocked the image of the giant statue. The old man joined him.

"Never did I expect anything like that. I can't trust my own eyes."

Manni heard the old man speak but was silent. The air around him would not give him voice. Finally, he said, "As badly as I want to know my past I will not face that monster again. You can search the town for lost family. I will stay here."

He slowly lowered his body to the ground and sat on the hillside with Ekron to his back and a view of rocky hills and sloping grasslands before him.

"Manni, I must see more."

"I understand," Manni responded.

The old man left him.

Manni remained unmoving on the hillside until he heard footsteps and the old man returned, short of breath and obviously upset. The old man held out his hands in supplication—they shook. His body shuddered at some thought as he clasped his hands tightly against his chest, trying to speak. The sound came out as if choked.

He swallowed, took in a new breath, and started over. "I wanted so badly to know what happened to my loved ones." His eyes brightened with tears. "They are dead. The city looks as if it was torn apart. Much of it is burnt.

"Ah, Manni, such terrible sadness for us both, but now we have some questions answered. That gives us a bit of relief. Right?

"Oh, my Lord, sustain me. How could anyone survive such destruction? What do I tell the others?" He sat down beside Manni and wept.

When the two men returned home, the old man attempted to relate all that he had seen—even the little ones needed to know the truth.

They mourned their loved ones' deaths and prayed to Yahweh for comfort. The women sorrowed within themselves but gave solace to the children, and somehow this provided a measure of comfort for them. Still, sorrow lingered within the settlement for a long time until the day the old man threw away his mourning garments. Life had to go on, and the children deserved the opportunity to grow up without the ever-present face of mourning.

Months later the old man came to Manni with a surprising request.

"As you know, we have dried beans and legumes and freshly shorn wool that must go to the market. Will you accompany me to the city of Jerusalem? There is an annual festival approaching, and families bring their harvested crops to the city for trade with merchants who travel from far away with their goods."

"Jerusalem? Yes, I will go with you. Where is this place, and when do we leave?"

"The third day from Sabbath, it is a short journey."

The little settlement hummed with activity as everyone worked to prepare for the journey. Their excitement altered the routine that had developed at the farm, making the days less tiresome. Manni had no memory of the city but recalled all the stories the old man had shared with him during their many talks. Both the old man and Manni suspected he was somehow involved in the violence put upon Ekron. Now, Manni wondered could it also be true of Jerusalem?

Have I ever been there? Will memories of the city float back to me when I see it? Will my response be like that of the visit to Ekron? But there is no use fretting about it now.

They loaded a cart with the beans, legumes, and bales of sheep's wool, but the donkeys had no difficulty pulling the large load. The old man estimated maybe a three days' journey to Jerusalem, two days of trading, and a bit less than three days back to their people—a welcomed change of scenery and activity. Both men confidently entrusted the care of the farm to the women and children and looked forward to successful trading agreements.

Manni saw the walls as they approached the city, and a strange feeling that he had seen these walls before flickered briefly across his mind. He was taken aback by the huge size of the place. The old man had tried to prepare him for this visit to Jerusalem while they traveled, but he was still amazed to see such a large city and the many people wherever he looked.

"This is the first harvest and trading fair since the Assyrian invasion," the old man had said. "The marketplace activity will overwhelm the city." And the old man was right. Thousands of traders and market-goers lined the road leading up to the city gates.

As they made their way toward the impressive city gates of Jerusalem, both men noticed a skull hanging from a tower above the gate. Its presence sobered their mood, but once they were inside the gates, walking the city streets, their excitement returned. People seemed to be everywhere—no one stood still. Vendors and traders busily moved about promoting their goods and services, people wanting to purchase various items crowded into every square both large and small. The noises, smells, and continuous business of the people awed Manni. He stopped to watch the marvelously chaotic scene before them, and he alone in that crowded market did not move.

The old man stopped and turned back toward him. He said, "Speak to no one. Let me do the talking. Come."

They traded their beans for oil, newly woven cloth, and special candied-date treats for the children. They spent less time in the market than originally expected and chose to roam slowly through the city of Jerusalem before starting back to their village. Both were silent as they walked the streets, leading the donkeys and wagon, watching people move about, going to places they could only surmise, and enjoying the children as they ran around in noisy play, shouting and arguing at points of disagreement in the game.

The two men spoke with no one, each quietly contemplating life. The old man believed Yahweh had given him the task of raising those seven children to adulthood and in the faith of their father Abraham. Manni considered one life lost to memory but another given, and he determined to be a faithful friend to this old man.

13

"We must give praise to our God. We must give Him all thanks for our lives and for His care." The old man turned, and Manni followed him to the great temple built by King Solomon many years past. They stood together at the temple wall and prayed before departing for home, but when they reached the city gates, a soldier came up to Manni.

"Who are you? You don't look like any of the others."

The old man stepped up. "He is a traveler looking to work for food and shelter. He is earning his keep by helping me on my farm."

The soldier looked at Manni. "Are you one of those pagan god worshippers?" Before the old man could answer again for Manni, the soldier shouted, "Let him answer!"

Manni answered with a question. "What is a pagan god?"

The soldier snorted then pointed in the direction of the city gates. "Go." And they left for home within the hour. Once home, the little group settled into life on the farm together and prospered.

Ten Years Later

As he sat beside the old man's body, Manni thought back over the past ten years.

The days creep by slowly. Each morning the sun bursts forth from the Earth and melts back into it when evening comes. Then the moon enjoys dominion over the sky only to be chased away by the new sun. Both the sun and moon carve their paths across the vast expanse of sky, always different from that of the previous day. And each day passes unlike the last.

"Old man,"—he spoke aloud. "I fell in love with this place the first time I saw it.

"The landscape is expansive and beautiful. Hills push up here and there. I see trees and bushes break the straight line to the horizon as I turn around in full circle. We are isolated, away from all the trouble of the world. We made a home here, you and I and our families, like a garden that fills our needs.

"Now and then we traveled to Jerusalem, especially when harvest time came. You shared stories with me on every trip. Even though I carry no past, no memory of another life, you took me in as if I were your own son. We worked the fields together and taught the young boys about the land and the animals. We planned for our future.

"We fished together and ate. There were times when you brought to my mind someone I once knew. And while I searched for memories of him, none came to me. Was there once an older man in my past life?"

The sweet memory made Manni smile.

"Perhaps the greatest thing you did was to offer me the hand of Lillie. Even now, years later, I can hear your laughter when you told me the story. You said that Lillie came to you wanting to know what I was going to do and reminding you she was of age for a husband. You were surprised, and asked her, 'Are you ready for a husband?'

"'I've been ready for quite some time now,' she'd announced. 'Can't you see?'

"You told me it went like this—you said to her, 'I've been waiting for you to ask me. I did not want to rush you into anything.'

"Then she stood straight and came right out and said what was on her mind. 'So you will give me as wife to Manni?'"

Now Manni had to laugh.

"You know, old man, that was both wonderful and scary for me to hear. You told her yes, and then Lillie ran out of the house. I shall never forget what happened after that. She found me in the fields. 'Manni, come to me,' she called. 'Come at once.'

"I thought something was wrong and ran to her, but she only said, 'Don't you want to ask me something?'

"I was surprised and stepped closer. She put her finger on my lips. 'I think you know what you want to ask me.' The way she smiled I knew what she was thinking, told her I wanted her more than anything, and then asked, 'Lillie, will you be my wife?'

"Ah, she surprised me then. 'Manni, you have never given me a passionate kiss. If I like your kiss, I will say yes.'

"I took Lillie in my arms gently but held her tight, very tight. She didn't mind. She threw her head back for the kiss, and I kissed her soft, moist lips. My kiss was returned until she broke away and ran to the house, calling over her shoulder, 'Let's ask the old man to marry us right away.' And so, we were married.

"You know, my old friend, Lillie and I were very happy together for many months, then she came to me one day.

"'Manni,' and I knew she desired a favor. It was that sly little look she gave me. She said, 'I love you greatly, but there is something I must tell you. My younger sister is in love with you also. She is so sad, and I fear she may hurt herself. I can't go near her anymore without feeling her sadness.'

"I said, 'Lillie, what can I do?' And you know how her answer surprised me!

"'Will you ask the old man for her hand in marriage also, so she will not be so lonely?'

"Now I wondered if this was some kind of ruse to test my love for her, so I showed signs of anger and made my voice turn stern and louder. 'Am I hearing you correctly? You are willing to share me?'

"She did not hesitate for a moment. In her mind it was all clear. You remember her spirit. She said, 'Yes, I know it sounds crazy, but you know I love you. You have to promise me I will always be your first love. Manni, do this for me. I'm afraid she may run off, and I will not be able to live with myself for worry.'

"So I tried to calm her fears. I said, 'Lillie, I am very happy and perfectly satisfied with your love. I surely do not need more.' Her shoulders dropped as she turned to walk away, and I could not bear to see her as such. I grabbed her from behind.

"I said, 'I'll do it. We'll be one happy family, but you will always be my first love.'

"Her heart is strong and good. How could I say no? You gave her such strength and compassion, my old friend, and soon both sisters were with child. Lillie was a few months bigger than her sister, but we had become one happy family."

Manni smoothed the covering over the old man's head. "Thank you, old man."

"When we lost your wife five years back, you carried her body to Ekron for burial with her people. You spoke to no one for days. You only prayed, day and night. Now, I shall honor your wishes and carry your body to Ekron for burial beside your wife."

I can never repay all he has done for me during our ten years together.

Thebes, Egypt

Princess Carnabrara's child did not know his father, Ramtouses the lion slayer from Juba for whom he was named, but his mother filled their days and nights with love and protection. Unlike the one hundred virgin girls who'd been kidnapped with her, the princess had not been given as a gift to one of Pharaoh's many supporters. Pharaoh Shebitku had chosen to honor Princess Carnabrara, daughter of King Tasmeria of Tungul, and had withheld her from an unwanted marriage. He had also provided private quarters in the palace for her use only. However, she still had been held there under guard.

Carnabrara knew nothing of Pharaoh Shabaka, who had ruled before Shebitku, nor of his scheme to kidnap her and one hundred other Tungul women, which had been done while all the women had been out gathering reeds for Carnabrara's upcoming royal wedding. Shabaka had hoped to force Carnabrara's father to add his military support against the aggression led by the Assyrian King Sennacherib. However, Shabaka had died before even knowing his plan's success, and his brother, Shebitku, had become the new Nubian pharaoh over Egypt.

When the kidnapped women arrived in Thebes, the new Pharaoh had divided the virgins among wealthy Nubian statesmen and aristocrats but spared Princess Carnabrara.

After the birth of Carnabrara's baby, the Pharaoh's eldest son, Prince Dafori, sought marriage with the Princess of Tungul. She had agreed to the marriage, thinking her son's

18

future was better served with a prince for her husband than no husband at all. Thus, she expected a secure life for herself and young Ramtouses II.

The first two years of marriage proved agreeable. When, in their third year the prince had taken another wife, Carnabrara was not surprised, for she knew most of Pharaoh Shebitku's other sons had many wives and always believed Prince Dafori would follow suit in time. But as there had so far been no sons born from the union between Dafori and Carnabrara, the prospect of other royal children being born to him caused her concern for what might happen to her own son.

Ramtouses II, who though Nubian, was not of Pharaoh's Nubian bloodline. Intrigue existed in all royal families, and Carnabrara suspected she and Ramtouses II might need help and encouragement from people beyond the supporters of her husband's family. With much thought, she devised a plan to protect her son in the years to come.

To facilitate her plan, she needed to contact all one hundred of her Tungul sisters. During the time since their abduction, all had become wives to important Nubians involved in the upper hierarchy of Egypt's leadership and had acquired various degrees of trustworthiness and special privileges from their husbands. This had allowed them some freedom of movement and each was able to meet with Princess Carnabrara in small groups of seven or eight.

Everything had to appear as normal activity, so Carnabrara made no attempt to make the gatherings look secretive. However, she made the importance of secrecy explicitly clear to each woman—no one was ever to learn of their plans.

Early on, each woman pledged secrecy and listened as Carnabrara talked of their homeland Tungul.

"Remember our home villages? Remember our families, our festivals, our strength, and our age-groups? We are Nubian, from Tungul. We must remember how we all came to live in Thebes. We must keep in mind our history; it will strengthen us and our children."

She spoke to the women of the social system within their tribes known as age-groups, which lay at the core of their survival. Age-groups applied primarily to the male children as they moved through the various stages of growth and development together with other boys whose ages fell within the same four-to-five-year span. The bond between the age-group members became strong, respected, and treasured, and it lasted a lifetime.

It established a social environment for each member of the age-group from childhood to youth through adulthood. Participation in structured activities with specific goals to develop physical strength, agility, and prowess and accountability for each member became primary to the survival of the village.

The women all knew of this tribal custom and called out their support as Carnabrara spoke of establishing such a group for their sons.

"We are their village away from home. They will not learn of their heritage if we are silent and do not act. It is time to teach our sons the bond of loyalty. In that way, we will all survive.

"We know we were kidnapped, taken here against our will, and given as gifts to our husbands. To protect our children from believing they are less important than the Egyptian Nubians, tell your children we were given to the Egyptian royal families by the Tungulese king, Tasmeria, in the hope his gift would strengthen the Tungul/Egyptian alliance.

"Training begins today. All our first-born sons will be in one age-group. Later, we will establish another group for the children yet to be born. Ramtouses II, son of the lion slayer, is leader of the first age-group."

One of the youngest of the women whom Carnabrara had selected to participate in her wedding before they were kidnapped rose and stepped forward.

"You chose us for the wedding reed dance because we have courage and good sense, Princess Carnabrara, and today, I believe your plan to unite our sons is the correct approach to promote their success in this place."

Others nodded in agreement or voiced their approval of the idea. The women shared a bond and an allegiance to each other that strengthened in the face of their forced marriages. They discussed plans to begin their sons' training.

"We must arrange times for our sons to be together, to play, and get to know one another," said one young mother.

"Yes," another woman agreed, "and we must meet at different homes with a different mix of the boys, so they all get to know each other very well."

Carnabrara clapped her hands in delight. "Our husbands, the Egyptian Nubians, know we are new to this land, and they will understand that we wish for fellowship within our group. We must present our meetings as visitation opportunities with our sisters, and I invite you and your sons to the palace this day next week. Each visit will be a different group of boys, and you also must initiate gatherings for our sons at your homes. Let no boy be left out of the training."

Carnabrara repeated her strategy until all one hundred of the Tungul virgins who had been kidnapped with her were informed of the formulation of an age-group for their sons and sworn to secrecy. She received total support from each as they worked out plans to unite and train their children. In the process, the women coalesced into their own age-group of committed Tungulese mothers.

They brought the boys together as planned and raised them to love one another, to learn and play together and compete with each other, to respect and honor each other, and to never betray their brotherhood. As time went on, everyone saw the need to let no treachery come to Ramtouses II. The boys were seventy-eight in number and used no identifying mark or symbol to recognize each other. They knew fellow age-group members as well as they knew their right hands from their left.

Years passed. Ramtouses knew Dafori was not his father, yet he respected him as his mother's husband. Carnabrara made up a story and told Ramtouses that his true father had been a prince of Tungal who died shortly before their planned marriage in Tungal. In Thebes, she gave birth to three daughters by Dafori and dedicated her time to them and activities for Ramtouses and his age-group brothers. The Tungulese-Nubian women had successfully established their traditional method of child rearing while living in Egypt, hundreds of miles from their home villages.

One day Carnabrara's youngest daughter ran to her, crying. "I am feeling ill. I want to see my father."

Carnabrara pulled her up close. "Where does it hurt? Maybe I can help."

"No," answered the child, her small chin quivering. "I want to see father. I never see him anymore."

Carnabrara turned to the closest servant. "Go and bring the other girls to me."

The child is correct, she thought. *His other wives and council meetings keep Dafori very busy. He never comes to this part of the palace anymore, so we will go to him.*

Carnabrara walked with her three girls to a different part of the palace, hoping to find Dafori free of any council gathering of statesman and available to visit with them. When she and the girls walked into a large atrium, they clearly heard Prince Dafori's voice as he held the attention of his audience, a group of forty or so young officers and statesmen who would one day govern the great Nubian empire.

Carnabrara said, "Stay here girls. We must wait until he is finished."

They watched and listened as he waved his arms, attempting to emphasize his message.

"Thousands of years ago, the Libyans, who claim they are the true Egyptians, excelled in building many grand monuments and temples. They grew strong and overwhelmed their enemies on the battlefield.

"In time, a great migration of people came, first the Hyksos from the sea, and a few generations later the Hebrews sojourned into this country. The Hyksos became rulers so when the Hebrews multiplied into an astonishing number, the Hyksos moved a multitude of them into Goshen. Others were sent to quarries to cut marble and stone, and a few fortunate ones received servant duties.

"The Hebrews working in Goshen labored to keep the traffic of boats moving north on the great River Nile laden with raw materials and supplies for Lower Egypt. The territory of Goshen was occupied by native black Africans, and the Hebrews lived and worked with them, leading to a great deal of mixing between the two ethnic groups. However, as the Hebrews and Africans continued to coalesce becoming our forefathers, we began to build a culture that demanded development for our own way of life. We became displeased with the treatment showed to us by the Hyksos of Lower Egypt, and hostility grew toward our overseers. This led to a failed rebellion after which our people were subjected to forced labor under military overseers. Thousands escaped the suppression by fleeing westward, some went south; all seeking new homes.

"Sometime later as the burdens became so enormous, a leader rose up among the Hebrews still living in Egypt. He called for his people to follow him to a promised land. The majority of the people working in the quarries became his followers and crossed the Red Sea, but the vast majority of people living in Goshen were not part of that exodus. Eventually Goshen founded a nation, and we called ourselves Nubians."

Dafori stopped, drank a sip of wine, and walked among his constituents who nodded their heads in acceptance of his words.

"The Libyans, who today live under Nubian control, challenged the Hyksos' right to govern. A Libyan prince named Ahmose came to power. He pacified the Nubians, encouraging them to boycott. He enlisted mercenaries from our new nation Nubia. Our superior archery skills and use of deadly poison applied to our arrows made us a handsome commodity, and our support certainly turned out to be a factor in Ahmose's victory over the Hyksos." Dafori pointed his finger, saying, "Listen to my words. When Ahmose became Pharaoh, his policy toward our forefathers who helped him gain control returned to the manner the Hyksos had imposed. But this time we Nubians were stronger and smarter. We built for ourselves a capital, Napata, we cut off all aid to Egypt and used our resources to assemble a massive army."

One by one, Dafori caught the eyes of those he deemed the future leaders of Nubia as he continued. "Never forget our great king Pianky, who led the Nubian forces north into Lower Egypt and Ethiopia, creating the largest Nile-based Empire that ever existed. When Shabaka became Pharaoh, he realized the importance of the Egyptian culture to the people and he liberated the native Libyan Egyptians rather than enslave them, and combined their skills with ours. Together we have built marvelous new cultural centers and homes for Nubians and Libyans to enjoy, as well as spectacular temples to the gods. We Nubian Egyptians must preserve all these accomplishments, and together with your help I, Dafori, will advance our progress to include all nations."

Again, his head moved from side to side as he looked around the room.

"We Nubian Egyptians must consider what it takes to uphold all these accomplishments."

Dafori continued his praise of the Nubian Pharaohs before closing. He said, "We will not gloat in our successes. However, we must continue to strengthen our shared culture and become the most powerful nation in the entire world."

At that he stepped back, and loud murmurs of approval reverberated through the large room. The people slowly left—the meeting was over.

Carnabrara and the girls met Dafori as he began to leave the atrium. She spoke to their daughters knowing he also listened.

"Your father is highly respected. Since our Nubian grandfathers conquered Egypt and became the ruling pharaohs, no Pharaoh has adopted the Egyptian lifestyle, their culture, their art, and beautiful building projects, and above all their gods, as does Pharaoh Shebitku."

"Yes," said Dafori, "and now he is ailing. I am his eldest son and shall follow his lead with just a few changes. We will have greater wealth, for we are masters over all Nubia, Egypt, and Ethiopia."

He reached out his hands for the girls and walked away—Carnabrara followed. She thought of all her friends, the committed mothers who worked and planned for their sons' futures and realized the wisdom of their plan to prepare their sons for success.

Yes, Dafori, you are of the governing Nubians of Egypt, and even though my sisters and I are full-blooded Nubians of Tungul, you are our masters. I am very thankful for our age-group plan for protection.

Months later at another meeting of the mothers, everyone spoke of the death of Pharaoh Shebitku. Tumult had erupted throughout the kingdom. Prince Dafori expected to be named successor to the throne. But Taharqa, the younger brother of Shebitku, brought the army he commanded up from Memphis to Thebes and asked the high priestess to the god Amun-re to announce that he be named the new pharaoh. Taharqa was prepared to take the throne by force, but that proved unnecessary when the high priestess, his younger sister, Amenirdis, agreed to name him as pharaoh. And so it was that Taharqa became Pharaoh Taharqa. The year was 690 B.C.E.

Pharaoh Taharqa of the 25th Dynasty. This statue of Taharqa was found in 2016 in the Sudan desert. Photo by Carolyn Gifford/Flickr

The secret meetings of the age-group boys continued but were scheduled less often to avoid drawing attention from the ruling Nubian Egyptian families. The Tungulese boys also attended various courses of instruction with sons of the upper hierarchy, and by age ten, Ramtouses II found himself in competition with many boys from the ruling families. He and his age-group friends frequently played openly as mates-in-training to be the next generation of leaders in the Nubian nation.

It was unknown to anyone but the Tungul Nubians that some of the boys who were Ramtouses' age-group brothers mixed and even became friends with the Nubian Egyptian boys, without shedding light on their strong connections with their Tungulese brothers. Through their age-group association, the boys grew to know each other extremely well, to the point they often perceived what the others were thinking.

Each year, the competitive intensity increased, and the rivalry became furious. Ramtouses excelled in almost all the required disciplines, and by his eighteenth birthday he was considered a champion with the sword, above his class in military strategy, and a superior horseman who also trained the others. The ability to easily learn languages capped his many skills. He spoke his native tongue as well as the Egyptian and Hebrew languages.

Ramtouses enjoyed his overwhelming popularity, but it was not all friendly. Many of the young men from the royal family, whom Ramtouses considered his half-brothers, grew envious of his success, particularly the oldest son of Dafori whose jealousy became extreme.

He sees himself becoming pharaoh one day, Ramtouses thought, *and maybe rightly so, but why is he so antagonistic toward me?*

⁘

Carnabrara walked slowly through the temple entrance. Amenirdis, the high priestess, watched the face of Prince Dafori's first wife as she greeted her. She stepped close to Carnabrara.

"I remember the first time I saw you—like a wild woman. You stood tall, unafraid, proud, and unbeaten with a strong spirit. I wish more women had that strength."

Carnabrara looked into the high priestess's eyes, trying to read the purpose of this unexpected summons. "I have seen you from afar but never expected to meet you face-to-face."

"I don't like my nephew, your husband, Prince Dafori. He has evolved from a gentle, kind person to a greedy man only wanting power. For that, I would not support his quest to be pharaoh." Her eyes fixed on Carnabrara like arrows. "If he had claimed the throne, your son would be in danger from him or his other sons. I believe you are aware of this."

How much does she know of me? Of Ramtouses?

Carnabrara nodded. "Yes. I feared the danger. I do not know how to answer you this day but with truth. I don't want my son to be pharaoh, never did. I only want him to be respected and safe."

Amenirdis smiled in agreement. "The truth is always a wise approach, and knowledge is useful in all our endeavors."

The high priestess lowered her head. She remained quiet for a long moment and then spoke. "You are aware Pharaoh Taharqa moved his capital to Memphis in Lower Egypt. From there he hopes to gain better control and expand the empire.

"Pharaoh Taharqa received word that King Sennacherib of Assyria is dead. After a six-week civil war, Sennacherib's youngest son, Esarhaddon, emerged victorious and rumors are that he seeks to expand his nation. King Esarhaddon is a man who bears watching."

Carnabrara listened closely to Amenirdis. "May I enquire why you chose to tell me of the Assyrian events?"

"You must be informed. If war comes, your son will be called to fight. Carnabrara, I support you. Know that I have eyes watching and ears listening."

They talked on for a while, recognizing a shared hope for Egypt's secure future. Carnabrara finally felt she had a friend in the kingdom, though she remained unsure how much Amenirdis knew about her and the age-group plan.

Are your eyes and ears pointed in our direction also, High Priestess?

"We will meet again, soon," the high priestess said as she ended their conversation.

Jerusalem

The changing of the guard was not restricted to Egypt and Assyria. In the year 697 B.C.E., King Hezekiah of Judah shared the kingdom with Manasseh, his only son by Queen Hephzibah. When a Hebrew boy reached the age of twelve, he was deemed a "son of the law." Manasseh was twelve. Having passed from the days of childhood to youth, he was considered old enough to concern himself with the serious business of controlling the state.

Judah's relationship with Assyria and King Sennacherib was filled with tension and threats. With this in mind, King Hezekiah worried his life might be cut short and announced, "I would at the earliest moment give the heir-presumptive every advantage of training in leadership." And so it was, Manasseh assisted in ruling Judah with his father.

He grew up studying the neighboring cultures and often wondered why the Assyrian Empire was so successful when they believed in pagan gods, not the one true God of his father. He questioned how the Assyrian gods could be so evil when their followers sat in such high places. Manasseh envied them for having favorable outcomes repeatedly. He questioned who the one true God was, Assyria's pagan gods or his father's one God.

When King Hezekiah died in 687 B.C.E., Manasseh's sole reign began, and he reinstated polytheistic worship, reversing the religious changes made by his father. He restored the worship of Assyrian gods, particularly Baal. He executed the staunch supporters of his father's reform, and innocent blood reddened the streets of Jerusalem. Anyone who sympathized with the prophetic ideas lived in constant peril.

The routines of life on the little settlement outside of Jerusalem where Manni had put down roots continued after the death of the old man. Those who made the periodic journeys to Jerusalem for trading purposes now consisted of Manni and one of the younger men with the young man doing most of the talking. On one such occasion they witnessed soldiers first beat a man then kill him. Manni and the young man looked on in shock.

A soldier yelled, "Is there anyone else among you that believes in this so-called god, Yahweh?"

Manni did not quickly comprehend what he saw and heard. The only god he knew in his current life was the one God the old man had worshipped. Manni had thought everyone believed in Almighty God and worshiped Him, but having just witnessed the death of this man, he now knew the soldiers represented danger for them.

"We are strangers here," he whispered to the youth. They slowly melted back into the crowd, attempting to hide themselves and draw as little attention as possible while they completed their business. As they walked through the gates to leave the great city of Jerusalem, home to Solomon's great temple, a soldier grabbed Manni by the arm.

"Who are you? You don't look Hebrew to me."

The young man with Manni spoke up. "He does chores for my father at harvest time. He means no harm."

"Are you a Yahweh follower?" The soldier stared at Manni.

Manni remembered the last time a soldier stopped him years ago when he'd been with the old man. It had come to nothing that time, so he responded in the same manner. "What is a Yahweh follower?"

The soldier pushed Manni's arm, drew back his whip and struck him, yelling, "Get out of here, and never come back."

Manni and the youth made camp on the way back home. They sat near the fire, puzzled by the hate that now emanated from this beloved city.

"Next time your second brother must come with you to trade. I will stay with the women and girls. It should be less trouble."

The youth understood Manni's decision, but he remained puzzled by the behavior of King Manasseh's soldiers and their attitude against the people of Almighty God. He enjoyed the business of the great city and often day-dreamed about living there with his wife and children.

Each man tossed over the events of their day in Jerusalem as they prepared for sleep . . . it was a long journey back home tomorrow, and they looked forward to the familiar comfort of farm and family.

King Manasseh of Judah, promoted the worship of Assyrian and Babylonian gods such as the one pictured here. This practice was forbidden by the priests of Yahweh but Manasseh persecuted those worshipped Yahweh.
Photo by Wikipedia.org

The Settlement

Manni again knew peace back at the settlement. For many months, the days came and passed like time would never end. However, shortly before the coming harvest, the old caretaker collapsed and died. At the time, she only helped the young women cook meals and watched with delight as the next generation of children, Manni's children, ran about and played. The young people she'd once cared for mourned her death deeply for weeks as though she was their natural parent, but then the two young men determined an end to the time of mourning. The living of life always took over, and harvested goods must be traded.

The two young men loaded the cart with their harvest and finally departed for the markets in Jerusalem. They stayed longer than required for successful trades, and Manni had actually begun to worry, but then everyone rejoiced as the dog announced the boys' arrival home.

"Jerusalem is as busy as ever. The market thrives, and thousands of people flooded the city." The two young men excitedly related their many experiences during the trip, emphasizing the city's good qualities and glancing frequently at their sisters. At the end of their storytelling, they looked toward Manni alone.

"There is something we must tell you."

"Oh," was his response, "what is it?"

One boy spoke while the other hung his head low. "We saved small portions of our earnings over these years, and while in Jerusalem this time, we found a place for us and our sisters to live."

At this point, the boy who spoke also lowered his head. "Manni, we need to lead our own lives. We want to find wives, and our sisters need husbands. We are no longer children."

The other young man spoke. "We discussed the matter with our sisters before we left for Jerusalem. As believers in our Lord, this isolation on the farm can do us no good. We need to marry and have our own families, like you and Lillie and her sister."

Manni rose from his seat and clasped the two youths in his arms. "Yes, you are right. You must go. How selfish we are to expect you to stay here."

He held the two young men at arm's-length away, studying their faces, and knowing how eager they were to move forward in life. "Remember that Jerusalem is not always friendly; dangers exist even there. Be thoughtful and reserved regarding your faith. Remember the soldiers' behavior, and we shall certainly see you again."

He thought of the two brothers and their wives who had left this little settlement to fight the Assyrians in Ekron and had died. Now their sons and daughters, whom he had grown to love, would leave the settlement in search of their future families.

What better reason to venture beyond that which is comfortable? Manni grieved their departure, but he understood their motivation, and he prayed for their safety.

In five days, they finished packing, said their good-byes to Manni and his family, and left the settlement on foot with one donkey and a cart.

Nineveh

The wounds of war are many. Some cause death, leaving children with no father, and mothers without a husband, struggling to feed and provide for the family. Some wounds maim and cripple the body, mobility is challenged and a livelihood denied, the family may still face starvation, certainly life becomes difficult. And some wounds are hidden, deep in the mind where no one sees the injury. Such was the wound that plagued King Sennacherib of Assyria after the great battle outside Jerusalem in 701 B.C.E.

Sennacherib shuddered in his sleep as he struggled to avoid the coming nightmare. His legs twitched and kicked at an unseen barrier while his dream whisked him away to war, to a time recorded in his memory, a time that played over and over, night after night...

He heard the army's encampment sounds on all sides—men talking, sometimes calling out across the campsite, metal clanging as the food provision began and soldiers practiced with weapons, horses stomping and nickering—all the usual sounds and smells of a large army preparing for war. After six months of holding siege around Jerusalem, they were ready for King Manasseh to open his city gates and beg for mercy, but no mercy would be granted. This was war!

Upon hearing soldiers yell and scream, he rushed to the tent opening and looked out only to see the black of night in the middle of the day. There was no light in the sky, no sun, as if something had swallowed it.

"Where is the sun?" he shouted. "What is happening? Oh, mighty Baal, lift this evil curse from the heavens." And slowly light began to enter his world again. "Ah, Baal hears me. Look, he lifts the spell from the sky."

A short while later another great confusion rushed toward him when he heard the shouts of soldiers again. "What is it now?" the king asked.

A soldier answered. "Three strange women have entered our camps. General Holofernes has confined them."

Could these women be part of the same evil spell that took the sun?

He rolled over into the arms of oblivion, of sleep—where the trap of life's wild nightmare resumed . . .

A startling sound assaulted him. Sennacherib covered his ears as the sound grew louder, piercing his eardrums, causing pain.

"I need something to cover my ears. Agh, I still hear it." And he wrapped cloth around his head.

"The evil spirits challenge our presence here. They attempt to drive us away with all these different wicked episodes. I tell you, in the name of Baal, it will not work. We will not leave until this place is destroyed."

An officer entered the king's tent, waving his arms and shouting.

That's my general. What does he want? I do not want to uncover my head.

"Go back outside. Stay outside. Tell me from there what you want."

He unwrapped the cloth just enough to hear the general screaming. "It is the cavalry, my king. Our entire cavalry is lost. In the black of night they were attacked."

Sennacherib burst out of the tent. "What was that about the cavalry?" he roared, knowing the words might not be heard over the constant noise.

The general stood back, yelling at the top of his voice. "The cavalry has been wiped out, every man."

Sennacherib pulled back into the tent. "What kind of nightmare is this? It can't be real. Tell me, Baal, am I dreaming?"

The general yelled again. "Holofernes is in a stupor, my King."

Stay in the safety of your tent.

The maddening sounds stopped suddenly, and the king stepped outside his tent and asked, "What is happening?"

"What is happening?" Over and over I ask, but no one answers. "Why is everyone running? Where are my guards?"

He pulled the cloth from his ears and grabbed the general, who stood waiting as if for instructions.

"What is happening?" the king asked yet again.

"We are in pursuit of the enemy," the general said.

"What kind of enemy would attack us at night? What kind of people can they be? At least we have them on the run."

Then, again, the loud piercing sounds struck. "Oh, no! No! Stop it." He frantically tried to block it, wrapping the cloth back around his head, clamping his hands over his ears. "Who is leading the army?"

"Holofernes is too drunk to lead."

"Where is my uniform? I will lead my men and bring an end to this nonsense once and for all."

He looked out into the night, seeing fighting all around him. *I don't need a uniform,* he thought, and he shrieked, "Kill the uncivilized rats. Enemies of Baal. Enemies of your king. Kill them all."

With those words, all sound ceased. It was quiet. No one fought.

The king approached a nearby officer. "How much evil can there be in one place? Prepare my chariot."

He climbed aboard the chariot and wept, then screamed, "Holofernes, where are you? We cannot leave Holofernes here. Stop. Perhaps he survived in a drunken stupor last night."

The chariot was stopped next to a pile of hay, and the king waited while his men searched for Holofernes. *What's that?* His eyes caught a movement, and when the king turned toward it, a man rose up from the hay and stared at him.

"Get me out of here!" he screamed at the driver. "Holofernes, where are you? Ahikar, in the name of Baal, I will get you. Where is my army?" He continued to scream over and over as the driver raced the chariot across the field over the bodies of the dead and dying.

"WHAT? What is it?" he shouted at the woman who shook him, awakening him.

She was one of his many wives. "Please, King Sennacherib. You are home. You are in your bed. It is a dream. It is your nightmare."

Sennacherib roused and looked slowly around the room, his bedroom quarters in Nineveh, no chariot or bodies of his dead soldiers. His own body glistened in a cool sweat. "Why? Why do I keep reliving that horrible night? Why can't I be left alone?"

Sunlight already shone bright through the window opening, and the king knew his screams had carried from room to room throughout the palace.

Get up, he thought, *and prepare for the day. Get out of the city. Go visit your concubine and let her calm you.*

The Settlement

illie stretched and rolled over. With her eyes still closed, she imagined the morning sunrise and ultimately decided the sun was almost fully risen.

"Manni," she whispered, "it's time to welcome the day . . . but only after you greet me."

"Hmm," he hummed into her ear. "I greet you with pleasure. Good morning."

After nearly twenty years on the little farm, Manni met each new day with joyful anticipation, never knowing exactly what would happen but always expecting to meet it well rested and well loved, happy and confident. His little family now numbered eight since the young people had left to make their futures in Jerusalem. They had five children with another on the way. The fields produced enough food for them all year long with an additional amount to trade at the market in Jerusalem. His small herd of a few sheep and goats had grown ten-fold, and whenever he felt the old urge to wander the hills and woodland, he would take a long walk, sometimes with a child or two and sometimes alone.

What more could a man ask for? He put his arms around Lillie. "I think we need more greeting time."

A full-moon later, Manni awoke hungry early in the morning. He thought, *I want some rabbit for our meal.* There was a special place where he would hunt his favorite food, so after the usual morning chores, he kissed the women and children goodbye, and set out for the woods.

The hunting was good, and soon after the sun rose highest in the sky, he caught a few nice rabbits then headed for home. Just at the edge of the thick vegetation he stopped to rest and enjoyed the quiet of the mid-afternoon. A few animals scurried about, and a soft breeze cooled his face. He fell asleep and began to dream.

He knelt at the bank of a river and ran his hand through the water bringing up fistfuls of sand as if he were searching for something, but not fish. Suddenly, he saw bright and shiny pebbles, nuggets, and as the water dripped from his hand, he continued finding them for a time.

Then he was walking along the road to Thebes. A man in a chariot came riding straight down the road toward him and stopped so close they might have smelled each other had the horse's odor been less strong.

"I am Ramtouses," the man said.

Manni repeated. "Ramtouses."

He turned out to be very wealthy, befriending Manni and giving him a position. Then Manni saw a young girl step into the road before him.

"Grandfather," she said, "you have come for me."

Manni held out his hand to her. "Come, child," he said to her. "Your parents are dead, and you are mine. I will keep you."

The child and Manni traveled from one village to another, and he taught his brothers all the farming skills he knew.

Manni woke up shouting. "Grandfather, my name is Grandfather. I remember my name!" He stood, waving his arms. "Thank you, Almighty God. Wait. I also remember the city. It was Thebes in Egypt."

I have to get home and let my family know.

Manni quickly made his way back to the little group of sheds and buildings he called home. It was dusk when he approached the settlement, but he noticed a door hanging open, and once inside, he saw the house in shambles.

For a moment he could only stand still, just looking, and then he ran outside, yelling. "Lillie! Lillie! Where are you?" Manni raced around the settlement from house to house to storage shed to barn. "Where are you? I must tell you some great news." But fear began to squeeze his heart.

Where is my family? Oh God, please, where are they?

After what seemed an eternity of searching and calling their names, he finally discovered his family—his beloved Lillie, her sister, and all the children—dead. Stabbed and slashed to death out back where the animals were kept.

"Nooo!" Manni yelled as loud as he could, dropping to his knees in disbelief. "No. Oh Lillie. Oh my God. Why? Why would anyone want to hurt them? They are innocent. They are good people asking only to live."

Manni collapsed, sobbing. Great cries of pain that no one heard broke the evening quiet while tears washed his face of the day's dust. He lay there with his wives and children all night, asking why, groaning with sorrow so harsh his chest hurt with each breath.

"There is no breath for my Lillie. No life for my children, my family." He was exhausted, yet he wept.

Early in the morning, Manni rose to his feet, drained of tears, filled with a heavy emptiness, and feeling devastated.

"I ask you, oh God, why am I alive and my people around me dead? Why do you keep me? Life is only pain without the people I love." He heard no answer, yet he listened.

Manni buried his family. All through his moaning he praised God, the God of the old man, of Abraham, Isaac, and Jacob. He would not blame the deaths of his family on Almighty God. God was the final judge, and after several days of feeling lost and alone, contemplating the loss of his family, thinking he had no future in the empty settlement, Manni decided now was the time to uncover his past.

I'll search the springs and streams coming from the mountains for shiny yellow stones. When they called me

Grandfather, I carried them on my travels, and so I will again.

He walked the hills and mountains surrounding Jerusalem for several weeks searching for the shiny stones. Once he collected seven, his search ended.

That's it. This is all I need for my journey to Thebes in Egypt. But where is Thebes?

Manni reasoned the only way to get that information would be to go to Jerusalem and ask someone, even though he feared another encounter with soldiers.

I could offer a nugget in exchange for directions.

Jerusalem

He arrived at the city early one morning and saw soldiers rounding up a family. They shouted, demanding, "Tell us where to find your fellow believers of the one God you call Yahweh."

One soldier scoffed. "Ha, one god. Speak, or you die—we will torture you to death."

Manni trembled. Hearing the soldiers' threats, it suddenly struck him why his family had been killed.

Of course, he thought, *the young people were believers in Almighty God, and if the soldiers found that out they would have tortured them into telling of the settlement. I should never have let them come to this evil place.*

"What are you doing back there?"

Manni turned to see a young boy leaning out a window. "I'm lost. I need help to find my way?"

The boy climbed out the window and jumped to the ground. "Where are you going?"

"To Egypt."

"I don't know where that is, but my father might know," the boy said and disappeared into the house. After a few minutes a man came to the door with the boy. He looked Manni up and down, frowning. "You are a strange one." The man's frown had disappeared, but he remained cautious. "Where do you come from? How did you get here?"

Manni spoke. "I am lost. I want to go to Egypt. Do you know how I can get there?"

The man shook his head. "You are far from home. Again, how did you get here?"

Ignoring the man's question, Manni asked, "Is there anyone around that might know?"

"Yes," he pointed. "There is a stable owner who knows where every town is for thirty days' travel in all directions."

Manni thanked the boy and his father and left to go where the stableman sat. He greeted the man and asked him straight away, "Can I ask you for the route to Egypt?"

The stable owner said, "You are a stranger here. You are not Hebrew, are you?"

Manni answered, "No, I am not. I need directions to Egypt. I can pay for this information."

The man looked at Manni's well-worn robe and sneered. "With what?"

Manni opened his fist and let the horseman see a nugget. The man's eyes widened. "Yes," he said and took a flat, thin piece of wood, some dark coal, and drew the route on the surface of the wood. He took the nugget, saying, "For another one, I will give you a horse."

Manni shrugged. "I can't ride a horse. The animal would be useless to me."

He left the city at once, but it was late. Word spread quickly that the stranger carried valuable nuggets, and when he was about to bed down for the night, three men fell upon him. They took his pouch with nuggets and disappeared into the night. Knowing sleep would not come soon, Manni decided to travel on under the moonlight and put more distance between himself and the city before bedding down again. While preparing for his trip to Jerusalem, he had hidden two of the stones in the hem of his garment. *For safe keeping,* he'd told himself—now he recognized the wisdom of that decision and slept with a bit more assurance all would be well.

On the Road to Thebes

The days rolled by, and the horseman's route led him toward the Mediterranean Sea. Along the way he found an occasional fruit tree and even some nuts. He also used his hunting and fishing skills to keep his body nourished. Traveling day after day, seeing no one, extreme loneliness settled over him.

It's as if my life is over.

"That is not true." He spoke aloud to the world around him . . . the trees, the grasses, rolling mountains, and even the insects that sometimes swarmed around his head. "Your life is opening with each step taken. Keep going, Manni. You must continue.

"I have lost everything, but before I die, I must find out what happened in my past. God Almighty has opened my eyes to know Him. Now it is His strength that wills me to continue this journey. Each breath I take is a gift because there is nothing else left for me."

Talking aloud, hearing his voice in the quiet of the day, in the soft whisper of the breeze, with the occasional rustle of small animals scurrying from his approach, or the whir of insects that seemed too often to delight in his arrival into their space, served to reinforce his intention to discover his past.

One day, several weeks into his journey, Manni walked slowly along a barely visible path, wondering if he remained on the road toward Thebes. He suddenly sensed the need to turn and look back. A figure traveling far behind him, moving in his direction and leading a donkey, grew larger as he neared Manni. The two men eyed each other until they stood face-to-face.

"I am Manni. Who are you?"

"I am Kobina, and I am going to Memphis."

The man's skin color was dark, like Manni's, and he spoke Manni's native tongue. Though slow to understand the language, Manni was immediately put at ease, thinking he might be on the right trail and would possibly have a traveling companion—at least for a time.

"You are travelling to Memphis?" Kobina asked.

"No, I am going to Thebes."

Kobina looked around. "Memphis is this way," he said, looking almost straight ahead, "and Thebes is that way," pointing a quarter turn to their left. "We can travel together until nightfall, but tomorrow you must turn and go the way I pointed."

As the two men continued together, Manni could not stop talking. His excitement over Kobina's companionship overwhelmed the earlier melancholy that had surrounded him, and the opportunity to speak his native language brought more happiness than he had known for months.

At sunrise the following day, he approached Kobina with an offer. "If you go part of the way to Thebes with me, I will give you this." He held out a yellow nugget.

Kobina's eyes opened wide. "Where did you get that, Manni?"

"I found it."

"Do you have more?" asked Kobina.

"No, this is the only one." Kobina reached for it, but Manni closed his hand and drew it away.

"Not until you show me the way to Thebes."

"Well, traveling with someone has many advantages over traveling alone, and my plans are easily changed. I will stay with you for a while, maybe all the way to Thebes."

Kobina had taken a liking to Manni the first day they met and traveling with him was a welcomed diversion from the loneliness of walking the road to Egypt by himself. Manni spoke to Kobina of the one true God of the Hebrews, of life on the small farm outside Jerusalem, and of the many things he knew of plants and animals—and Kobina listened to it all. When an occasional band of merchants caught up with them, the two men moved out of the way and watched the line of camels with riders followed by more camels swaying under their loads of merchandize pass out of sight.

Thebes, Egypt

"Manni," Kobina said late one morning, indicating a view seen far off from their higher elevation. "Look. That is Thebes. It is a grand sight, the capitol city of Egypt, and the seat of Pharaoh Shebitku."

Manni could not look away. "That city will renew my life," he murmured.

As they drew closer, they could see the grand community buildings, the palaces, and beautifully designed temples that stood well above other structures. By late morning they passed through the city gates and became one with the crowds of people moving along busy streets. Manni looked from the market activity to the stone houses and buildings much like those seen in Jerusalem, to people seeking to buy or sell where merchants and vendors called out the praises of their products, to the soldiers standing ready to defend. It was clearly the market section of Thebes.

The two men continued to walk through the city, leaving behind the press of people in the marketplace and observing more buildings with stables or store fronts and temples surrounded by open verandas and large buildings for purposes they could only guess. Manni thought it all marvelous though he could not remember any details from the many years past when he believed that he must have walked these streets. Statues of various gods stood at every corner and beside the beautiful stone buildings. Horses and donkeys with riders caused the people to hurry out of the way. This city was larger and more luxurious than Jerusalem.

Kobina said, "Give me the nugget."

His attention was so absorbed by the city sights Manni gave him the nugget, as promised and without a word.

"I'll break it into smaller pieces." Kobina had no trouble splitting it. "See? No problem. I am a sculptor, you know. This piece will get us a room somewhere." Together they moved on to find an innkeeper willing to put them up for the night.

A short time later, Kobina had talked an innkeeper into an agreement—the gold got them two nights and meals, then they could sleep at his inn if Kobina's little display of carvings would bring people in for a meal and cool drink. The next day Manni left Kobina as he set up his little figures and statues of various Egyptian gods, animals, and pharaohs near the front of the little inn where they had slept, intent on keeping his part of the bargain.

"So we both have some business to see to, Kobina. You must lure the diners, and I must begin my search of the man Ramtouses."

Kobina nodded. "My task is simple. You see? My carvings are lovely, and people enjoy them. May the Hebrew god bless your search."

Smiling, Manni turned to begin his hunt for the man called Ramtouses.

He spoke to several people walking the streets and finally someone said, "Ramtouses? Go that way. He lives in a wing of the palace." And the man turned to continue on his way.

The palace? Why do I have no memory of that? Manni shook his head but spent little time pondering the thought. There was futility in dwelling on it, so he turned in the direction the man had indicated.

Manni eventually found the palace, an impressive, multi-storied building with many wings. He circled the grounds looking for a public entrance, but once he found it the guards would not allow him to enter the gates.

When he made inquiries about a man called Ramtouses, a guard said, "Do not address the prince as Ramtouses. Call him Prince Ramtouses. Besides, he is away right now."

Hoping for Ramtouses' return, Manni decided to wait near the gates but far enough away so as not to gain unwanted attention from the guards. His wait grew long. Throughout the day people came, entered the palace, and left again, their business apparently concluded, and Manni continued his watch.

Across from the palace gates a large open expanse with walkways and statues led to another beautiful building with several tall, thick columns lining the entrance. Close to evening, Manni resolved to investigate the imposing structure. His curiosity led him through the massive entrance into the building where, once inside, he came upon a giant statue of a man looking prominent and proud, even boastful. The figure wore a hat with two ostrich plumes above it and was the same beautiful shine of the stones he found in the mountain streams. Its appearance perplexed Manni—why was it so large and grand, who did the outstanding statue represent?

Suddenly a voice came from behind him. "When entering the temple of Amun-re you must bow down. How dare you not do so?"

The language was very similar to Manni's but the words came fast and loud and he understood only a portion of what the man said.

"Bow down? What do you mean?" answered Manni in his confusion.

The man wore white from head to foot. He spoke again. "You must be a stranger to be ignorant of Egyptian customs. Get out."

Manni turned to leave, but the man spoke again. "Wait. Go to Amun-re and bow down. Kiss his feet and apologize for your error."

Manni felt somewhat angered by the command to make such a gesture. "I will leave as you have asked." He continued to walk away.

The man screamed incredibly loud. "I am a priest in the House of Amun-re. You will come back here and do as I say."

Manni, realizing this could mean trouble for him, returned to the statue, bowed down and kissed the feet of Amun-re. He did it swiftly and with no respect.

Manni hurried out of the place too late for in his rage, the priest had summoned the guards, and they were moving in his direction. He resisted when the guards approached him coming down the stairs, and the soldiers drew their weapons.

The priest yelled, "I want him arrested for insulting Amun-re in his own house."

At that very moment, a man rode up to the palace gates on the largest horse Manni had ever seen.

One of the guards said, "Prince Ramtouses, that man has been looking for you," waving his arm toward the temple steps.

Looking over and seeing the commotion, the prince and his two companions turned their horses to ride over and check out the uproar.

Ramtouses yelled, "Stop it! What is going on here?"

The soldiers lowered their weapons.

The priest shouted his anger. "This dog committed blasphemy to the face of Amun-re. He must pay for his actions."

Ramtouses looked at the man. "What do you have to say for yourself? Is he correct in his charge?"

"I am a stranger here. I do not know the way of your people, and he confuses me. Perhaps the priest is right, and I should not have shown resentment at his request. I am not here to irritate the priest but to find a man named Ramtouses."

Ramtouses looked confused. "Who are you? Does Ramtouses know you?"

Manni gave answer. "I am Grandfather. Ramtouses should know me by that name."

Ramtouses climbed down from his horse. "I am Ramtouses, and I have never seen you before in my life."

Manni responded. "You are too young to be the man I am looking to find. This man would be as old as I am, perhaps older."

The two men considered one another for a few moments.

Manni said, "Does your father carry the same name as you?"

Ramtouses said, "No."

"I worked for a man called Ramtouses a long time ago, before you were born," Manni continued. "Someone should know him. He is powerful, and he employed me because of my knowledge of agriculture. His goal was to safeguard the country from the results of droughts."

Ramtouses shook his head. "I'm sorry, but I know nothing of your story." He climbed back onto his horse. "Ignorance of our laws does not save you from punishment." Turning toward the guards, he ordered, "Arrest him, but do him no harm. See to it he is fairly treated in the dungeon."

Ramtouses galloped away with his two comrades. Actually, the comrades were two of his age-group friends who had accompanied him most of the day. The age-group members rotated daily spending time with Ramtouses, strengthening their friendships and guarding him covertly. One of them was always near him, frequently without Ramtouses' knowledge.

⁙

The sun shone bright and radiated its heat across Carnabrara's veranda, finding every opening in the vines that shaded her, creating a pattern of glittering stars across her morning table. She expected Ramtouses to join her for the morning meal, as he did whenever he spent the night at the palace. He loved his mother and enjoyed their morning discussions, ranging from the mundane issues of their lives to serious concerns within the governing of Egypt. Today's visit did not disappoint him. While speaking to her about the politics of the city, he remembered the man at the temple of Amun-re.

"Mother," he said. "I met a man who questioned me about my name."

She wondered aloud, "Why would anyone question you about that?"

"I don't know. He was an older man, a stranger to our city, searching for a man who would be much older than I. Someone he knew even before I was born."

Carnabrara stood up suddenly, curiosity written all over her face. "What did you say the man's name was?"

Ramtouses said, "Well, I didn't, but he said his name was Grandfather. Strange name. I never heard one like that before."

As soon as he spoke, Carnabrara swallowed, and it led to her choking.

"Are you all right, Mother?" He looked surprised at his mother's reaction.

"I'm fine, something lodged in my throat." She coughed lightly and reached for a cup of water.

Ramtouses waited before he continued. "I didn't think to tell you that same day when the man was arrested. Did you know anyone named Grandfather years ago?"

Holding the cup, she sat quickly in her chair, spilling a little water on herself and feeling agitated by the discussion and her reaction. However, Ramtouses continued to eat, seeming to be unaware of her behavior or appearance.

Nothing was said for a while. Suddenly Carnabrara said, "Arrested?" as if the information had only just been shared. "Where is this man now?"

This time, Ramtouses swallowed his food a bit too quickly and answered her question immediately. "Mother, he disrespected Amun-re and the temple priest wanted him arrested so he is in the dungeon. Don't worry. That's the last I heard of him."

Carnabrara got up and left the room, leaving Ramtouses to finish the meal alone. She returned a short time later with her usual smile and buoyant step. She kissed her son on the cheek and said, "I think I remember a man named Grandfather back in Tungul. I wonder if he has news from our village. Maybe I should see this man."

Ramtouses looked at his mother, pleased to see her happy. "If you wish, I will go and bring him from the dungeon right now. Perhaps you will get an answer to your question." He turned away before she could respond and left to fetch the man called Grandfather.

Ramtouses arrived at the dungeon and found a lone guard. It was not unusual as dungeon duty ranked low on the list of desirable duties for the guards.

"Guard, fetch the man in jail for blasphemy against our god, Amun-re."

"My Prince," the guard said. "That man was released when he paid his fine with a valuable nugget."

Ramtouses moved his hands to his hips. "A nugget? I didn't think he had any valuables. Where did he go?"

"Allow me to check the log for any information given." The guard returned. "A dwelling number is written here, number 2320."

Ramtouses turned and left. Two of his comrades joined him as he rode off to locate number 2320 dwelling. It was a small inn, and Ramtouses did not deign to dismount his horse to inquire of the innkeeper about a man called Grandfather.

"My only guests at this time are that man and his friend." The innkeeper pointed at Kobina, who busily unloaded his figures and statues from large satchels the donkey had carried across the northern dessert. He displayed them in front of the inn and inside.

Prince Ramtouses approached the man outside. "Who are you?"

Looking up at the horsemen and showing no fear, he said, "I am Kobina. Do you want to buy statues? I have more inside."

"I'm not here to buy. I want to know where this man Grandfather is."

Manni overheard the conversation and came out of the inn. He recognized Ramtouses as the young man outside the temple. "Here I am."

"Come with me," Ramtouses said. "You are not in trouble, but we need to talk with you about the first time we met."

Manni tried to contain his excitement. He said, "May my friend, Kobina, come with me?"

"Yes, if you wish."

Everyone waited as Kobina carried his valuables inside, though the horsemen worked to quiet the steeds. Once they left the inn, Manni and Kobina traveled on foot while Ramtouses and his company rode the horses. Upon arriving at the palace, Ramtouses led the two men to the visiting court in his family's wing of the palace and left them to speak with his mother.

"He and his friend wait for you in our courtyard, Mother. I must go to attend other business."

Carnabrara's face appeared flushed, and he realized she had some reservations about meeting this man.

"Go, Ramtouses," she said, "I am fine. My guards are here, and I will call for you later."

He may not be anyone I know. He may not even be from Tungul, but I am reluctant to speak directly with him.

Carnabrara summoned her three personal maids and prepared them to ask questions for her, then she signaled for the man called Grandfather to be brought into the hall and for the questioning to begin. She covered her head with a shawl, placed a veil across her face, and sat in the back of an observation area. She knew nothing for certain of this man, but if he was who she thought he could be, she did not want him to recognize her.

Kobina stood back as Manni walked to the center of the hall. The three women came up to face him. From the recesses of the room, Carnabrara nearly collapsed when she saw him. She had to stifle a sudden intake of breath.

This cannot be real. Wake up! Carnabrara, you must be dreaming. But it was no dream. She was awake, and her eyes did not lie nor did her ears. This was the man she had so dearly loved many years before. This was the man with whom she shared the bright evening star.

She listened closely as one of her maids asked the first of many questions Carnabrara prepared for them. They were instructed to listen to his answers and freely ask any questions of their own.

"Who are you and where do you come from?"

"I am Manni, a name given to me by people living near the town of Ekron in Judah.

"Why did they give you a name?

"Because I was found unconscious on the ground, and I had no memory. I lived with them and farmed for twenty years until I had a dream. When I awakened, I remembered my name to be Grandfather."

"Why did you travel here? And, how did you get here?"

Manni answered each inquiry without hesitation and each answer generated more questions from the three maids. Obviously, they were intrigued with this man and their questions continued well past high noon—by then everyone thirsted for a drink and needed relief from the strain of what was, in actuality, an interrogation. Carnabrara wanted to know everything about his life for the past twenty-three years, but she also realized the unfairness a continuation would be to her maids and the man who had so patiently answered every question put to him. She signaled a halt to the session, and the first maid thanked Manni for his participation and ordered food and drink for both Manni and Kobina.

Carnabrara clearly saw the man had no memory of her. She paced her private rooms, addressing no one, but talking aloud, maybe to the woman she once had been.

"He does not remember me. He thinks he is Grandfather. That makes some sense for he knew all about the travels of that man through the family stories.

"I could reveal myself to him. It might jog his memory . . . and then what? I am a married woman. I have three daughters. And we have a son! Where is his right to know what was? What is?" She threw hers arms up then bent over, tears rushing to escape. "Oh, my love does not remember me."

After a time, the tears dried, and Carnabrara's good sense ruled her emotions again.

His amnesia proves to be both a curse and a protection right now. It keeps us apart, but it also keeps us from Prince Dafori's rage, should he discover the truth.

Every day Princess Carnabrara sent for him, and every day she stayed in a far corner so as to conceal her identity. Each evening she prepped her maids on the questions to ask, communicating her desire to have every possible detail of his life unveiled to her. Once they caught on to the extent of her curiosity, the questioning flowed more smoothly. As for Manni, he spoke freely of his life and appeared to hold back no detail. She yearned to learn of all he experienced in the twenty-three years since she last saw him, but Manni could only recall the last twenty-two years. Before that, he knew nothing.

For Carnabrara, something was reborn deep within her, and she longed for more of his presence, more of his words, just more of him. She arranged improved housing for Manni and Kobina. She sent quality clothing for them and insisted they both be served a meal after each questioning session. She even put out covert word of Kobina's beautiful little pieces of sculpture, and his business grew considerably. As for her husband—Prince Dafori seldom came to her wing of the palace these days, his younger wives keeping him well-occupied, much to Carnabrara's relief.

Carnabrara's days filled with thoughts of Manni. Tears of joy or sorrow would rush to her eyes at any moment, sparked by a memory or a smell. The sounds of daily life, children running, servants talking, rooms being cleaned, food prepped and cooked and served—could give her intense joy or have her curled into a ball, crying. She felt more alive, more alert and in tune to everything around her than she had for a long time. His voice still reminded her of a soft rumble of thunder, and hearing it each day renewed memories of a beautiful time in their life and then the loss of it. Night and day, she dreamt of their time together, coming up with all kinds of ideas—even running away with him back to Tungul or revealing herself to him. She could simply drop the veil and walk to him, welcome him back into her arms, hoping to awaken his past.

She continued to wonder what caused his illness. What happened during that missing year that it blocked out his earlier life so completely? Sleep hid from her, and the desire for food also slipped away. Her usual daily commitments went mostly unmet, and Carnabrara knew she needed her friend, her one confidant outside the Tungul women. She sent word to High Priestess Amenirdis requesting a visit with her in the temple.

Amenirdis and Carnabrara had become close friends sharing each other's thoughts and concerns about many issues. Carnabrara had revealed everything with the high priestess except the age-group society, and, even though it was never spoken of, she suspected the priestess knew something of it.

"I am losing my mind. I'm delusional," Carnabrara said. "I can't think. My life has turned in circles."

Amenirdis said, "Come here, dear child." She spread wide her arms, offering the distressed younger woman a warm welcome and comforting embrace. "Tell me what is wrong."

Now in tears, Carnabrara said, "I will tell you everything." Nothing was withheld, and the high priestess let her vent until she had finished, exhausted.

As Carnabrara's story unfolded, Amenirdis gained a greater appreciation of the far-reaching impact of one's decisions. No one in Egypt ever dreamed someone had survived that war— oh, yes, King Sennacherib and a small band of his army had crept back to Nineveh; but no other person had walked away and lived to tell the tale. That's what Pharaoh Shebitku and all his army had believed; that is what they had reported.

And that is what I believed. Now I must come clean. I must reveal the whole story behind this precious woman's kidnapping. Anger laced with sweet compassion filled the high priestess's heart.

"Carnabrara, I am going to disclose the real reason why you and the young virgins were kidnapped." Amenirdis placed her finger over the younger woman's lips. "You must never tell anyone what I'm going to tell you."

"Never." Carnabrara's dark eyes were large as she whispered her promise.

"Your people were tricked into a war with Assyria. Pharaoh Shabaka led them to believe you and your virgin girls were all dead, killed by the children of Ell. Your father and a mighty warrior grew blind with rage when they heard the report. They assembled a mighty army of warriors and came north to find and destroy the evil Ell.

"But it was not the Ell. It was the Assyrians, the same people who massacred both the Egyptian and Ethiopian forces on the plains of Eltekeh. Pharaoh Shabaka became afraid after that battle. He believed the Assyrians would march on our homeland and everything would be lost, so he designed the ploy to trick your people.

"The mighty Tungul warrior led his army to the camps of the Assyrians. A hellish battle ensued." Amenirdis's slight body trembled at the memory, her voice wavered briefly, and she reached for a cup of water before her words continued.

"To our astonishment, it was said no one survived, but now I believe someone did. I think this mighty warrior was your man, Ramtouses. He may have suffered a head wound that has blocked his memory, concealing that terrible nightmare."

The truth of an old falsehood now lay bare. Amenirdis stood still and silent. Carnabrara reached out to the older woman, the high priestess, her friend, whose sad eyes reflected her regret, and the two women sat. Sorrow for what was lost overwhelmed Carnabrara, and tears ran in steady streams down her cheeks, dripping onto her lovely silken garment. She laid her head in the high priestess's lap. Amenirdis gently stroked Carnabrara's hair while the two women talked for hours, agreeing they lived in a horribly unkind world.

"You are the only Egyptian Nubian I can trust. Thank you for telling me the truth, Amenirdis, and thank you for holding me up when I may have fallen."

As Carnabrara left the temple, she said, "Now I understand why they went through the trouble of stealing us. It never made sense to me before because the Nubians of Egypt have thousands of young girls to fill their desires."

At the closing of another day Manni and Kobina settled down to eat the evening meal brought to them by Carnabrara's servants. Manni shook his head.

"I don't understand what is going on. Every day these women call on me to talk about my past."

Kobina barely stopped filling his mouth as he spoke. "I don't understand what they learn from just talking with you but keep up the good work. I've never had food this good, so let them ask their questions, and you answer. At least we don't have to push the sale of my statues; if the people love them, they buy them."

As Ramtouses mounted his horse, his half-brother rode up fast and pulled hard on the reins to halt his horse.

"Ramtouses, I learned of something very confidential, a secret, and only I know."

Ramtouses looked at the prince, puzzled. "What's going on?" he asked.

"I know I am a better swordsman than you, but everyone believes you are the best, even my father, Prince Dafori."

Ramtouses chuckled a little. "Who cares?" He finished mounting his horse. "Are you going to tell me the secret now after you've excited my curiosity?"

The prince's voice changed to an angry tone. "You laugh, but you do not know how serious this is."

Ramtouses edged his horse closer to his brother's. "I'm waiting."

"What I have to say involves your mother." Ramtouses's half-brother turned his horse. "And if you want to know more, you will meet me in the palace's southwest dungeon. I will be waiting." He rode away, yelling, "Come alone."

"I'm coming." *I better check this out. The fool prince will do anything to destroy my family's reputation.*

Ramtouses rode slowly toward the dungeon unaware that one of his age-group comrades had witnessed the encounter with the boastful young prince and now followed Ramtouses, unseen.

The dungeons never welcomed people. They threatened danger, and Ramtouses walked slowly and with some apprehension into an open space in the center of the cellar. The young prince stepped out from behind a column, smiling.

"Stop the games," Ramtouses said. "What's on your mind?"

"This is no game, my brother." He sneered at the word *brother*. "Your whore mother is sleeping with some strange man."

"Do not slander my mother!" Ramtouses shouted with anger so intense his body shook.

"Ha! As if you didn't know about it."

Ramtouses stepped close to the young man, seething with the insult but very much in control of his emotions. His brother's eyes were dark with a fury that nearly matched his own, yet he too stood resolute and determined.

"What is there to know? My mother has done nothing. Are you mad?"

"Do you think I would bring you down here if I were making this up? Wait until I speak with my father. See if he thinks it is a farce. You know, a crime like this, adultery, is punishable by death. It could cost her life." The young prince almost danced as he said his last words. "Now it is my turn to laugh."

Ramtouses lost the battle of self-control, grabbing the prince by his clothing and shoving him violently to the ground. The young man sprang up, grabbing his sword as he stood snarling.

"I have the proof, so we will see who my father believes." He waved his sword back and forth. "If you slay me, your mother's secret remains safe. If not, all of Egypt will know."

Ramtouses drew his blade as the prince charged and the sound of their weapons rang out, loud and echoing in the hollow of the dungeon. The two men dueled; their deadly dance grew a rhythm with forward charges and clashing of metal as they blocked each other's blows. It seemed an even match for a while, but that illusion soon disappeared. The prince had hidden one of his finest swordsmen in the recesses of the dungeon with orders not to intervene unless Ramtouses got the better of him.

Ramtouses pierced the young prince's body armor, which saved him from receiving a stomach wound, but his left arm received a serious injury and was soon covered with blood. He tripped and fell, but as Ramtouses moved in for the fatal blow, the prince's soldier stepped out of hiding and ambushed Ramtouses. His attack gave the prince time to rise to his feet and come at Ramtouses from behind—two swords against one. Ramtouses lost ground quickly, but at that moment Ramtouses' age-group comrade stepped into the fight. The odds balanced once more—Ramtouses paired against the prince and his comrade against the soldier.

Within a few strikes Ramtouses wounded the prince again— this time a fatal stomach gash. The young prince collapsed to his knees, holding his belly with one hand and his sword still in the other. His head moved upward, and he locked his eyes on Ramtouses, never breaking the connection until he slowly slipped over to the ground and curled up as if going back into his mother's womb. Ramtouses stood motionless, watching the fall, living each moment of his brother's death. It had happened fast, but he saw it all as if time had slowed to a crawl.

Ramtouses turned to aid his age-group companion against his half-brother's swordsman and found both men mortally wounded. The soldier lay already dead, but Ramtouses' comrade and friend held onto his final moments of life. Ramtouses dropped his sword and cradled his age-group friend in his arms.

"Do not die." He wanted to order his friend to live—he had loved him since they were small children.

"Ramtouses, I am honored to have served you. Tell no one what happened here. Let them think we killed each other." His voice faded, but he gripped Ramtouses' arm. "No one," he whispered, "must know you were here. Promise me."

Ramtouses stroked his friend's head and kissed it. "Yes, my friend. I honor you for your loyalty." He remained on the cellar floor, bent over his dying friend and trembled. "You touch my soul with your love." The murmured vow of silence, honor, and love entered his blood stream as surely as the life of his friend slipped away. He kept his word and told no one.

⁘

Ramtouses waited near his mother's court. When he saw Manni approach and enter, he followed him to where his mother sat. "I must speak with you, Mother. Alone." He stood stiffly, his hands open, and knew he was fast losing all composure.

Carnabrara ordered everyone but her son out. "What is this, my son? Why do you come here with a grief-stricken look?"

Ramtouses tried hard to reclaim his self-control and explained that someone on her staff shared private household information—and the result was destructive. "I killed a man, Mother!" With that announcement Ramtouses recounted the entire event with his half-brother, Prince Dafori's eldest son. He left out no detail.

"What is the meaning of this mother? Who is this man, and why do you continue to meet with him?" His voice was rough as he hollered the words.

"If Prince Dafori finds out you have this strange man over daily, it will totally humiliate us. You could even be killed if he suspects you of adultery. What were you thinking, Mother?"

Ramtouses hung his head and repeated, "I killed a man for your honor."

Carnabrara stood alone on the far side of the room looking out across the palace grounds. He had begun to speak with his first step into the room, barely stopping when she had dismissed everyone, and now he was exhausted.

"Mother, I need answers. I must know why. Who is this man, Manni, and why do you meet with him?"

She turned and began to weep.

"Oh Ramtouses, I did not think. I—I made a mistake," she stammered. "I never considered it would come to this. My son, I am so sorry to put you in the middle."

Clearly, she is distraught. However, how does her regret help us now?

Ramtouses made no move to comfort his mother or give any word to ease her distress. He merely waited for the explanation, and it came as a bolt from the skies.

"That man, the 'stranger' as you called him, is your father."

Ramtouses drew back. Neither said a word. She stepped forward, holding out her hands as if trying to grasp some unseen thing.

"I would have told you in time." She moved closer. She needed her son to hear, to say something, to understand, to move . . . to forgive her.

"Ramtouses, Manni has suffered much, and he remembers nothing of me. Nothing!"

"My father? He is my father! How could I have been so blind?" Ramtouses folded his mother in his arms.

Her head pressed against his chest, and he barely heard her speak. "I still love him. I'm so afraid. I don't know what to do. Only the high priestess understands my situation and now, you."

"How did he wind up here if he cannot remember you?" Ramtouses shook his head in confusion. He walked her to the nearest couch, and they sat together. "Tell me all you know."

"He thinks he is his Grandfather, a man he knew only through the stories of his mother and brothers. He has much to say about his life for the past twenty-two years, but nothing before."

"Mother, have him brought back to the palace. I must talk with him. I will not say anything to upset him. I will not reveal your truth."

For the second time in one day Manni arrived in Carnabrara's courtyard believing he faced another series of questions, but this time it was the young man, Ramtouses, who asked the question. "Are you in need to know your past?"

"At first, I dreamed of nothing else, and coming to Thebes gave me hope. But now, I am actually at peace with myself. I believe in Almighty God to guide me in his path of righteousness. I am content with Him and believe He is content with me."

"Of which god do you speak? There are many gods."

"There is but one true Almighty God who watches over those who follow Him."

"Do you want to leave now?"

"No, I must stay in Thebes. Or, do you mean leave the palace? I say maybe, but the people here treat me with courtesy and respect. I feel at ease with them."

"I will leave you to them. However, if you stay in Thebes you must find work, and do not visit the palace as often as you do now. Understand?" Ramtouses waited for Manni's affirmative answer and then left, perhaps more confused than he felt before seeking out his mother.

This man is befuddled. One God?

Ramtouses realized any action to discover the spy had to come from him for his mother was too distraught to attend to such a sensitive issue. Earlier, when he first barged in on his mother, he had ordered his soldiers to guard all exits and entrances to their wing of the palace, allowing no one in or out. Now he consulted with his age-group members on hand and sent word to the others of his suspicion—that a person, thought to be within his mother's service, spied on his family.

Not long after they learned of this deceit, one of the age-group members who tracked personnel information regarding all who worked in Carnabrara's palace wing, recalled that a certain servant was employed at one time by the prince whom Ramtouses had fought earlier in the day. They searched for the perceived spy and found him still in the area closed off by the guards. The servant admitted being an informant and quickly offered to spy for Ramtouses, but the idea a man would so easily turn his allegiances revolted Ramtouses. He ordered the spy be put to death.

The bodies of the young prince, his soldier, and the faithful comrade were found after a few days, and true to Ramtouses' age-group friend, no one suspected him of having any involvement with their deaths. The untimely death of a favored son greatly saddened Prince Dafori. He concluded the three men had some kind of disagreement and, in the end, fatally wounded one another.

The deaths of the three men weighed heavy on Ramtouses' mind. He mourned the loss of his loyal age-group friend, not caring to eat or sleep, unable to put aside the strong feelings of blame and responsibility for his friend's death. His once lively step slowed as if thick, muddy clay was stuck to his feet, and the joy of living faded. His soul grieved.

Ceasing her visits with Manni was not an option for Carnabrara, but she also realized seeing him as she had could no longer be possible.

His visits must be less obvious, and when we meet again, should I use the same pattern of secrecy? If I reveal myself to him, what is the outcome? Would it end his amnesia? And, furthermore, is the time right for that? How do I even evaluate such a move?

Carnabrara resolved to put all the worrying thoughts aside and hoped insight might emerge overnight as she slept. And it did.

She called for Ramtouses. "I have a solution, Ramtouses."

The issue of his father had come as a huge surprise to Ramtouses, and he had no solution for the matter, so he made no response and just listened as his mother spoke.

"Amenirdis, as the high priestess, controls most of the agricultural matters across Egypt. She decides the financial expenses related to farming and food production. If I speak to her about Manni's great talent for farming, she may have a need for his knowledge and experience. She may offer him employment."

"Mother, this could be the solution to the needs of all. I only ask that you be cautious."

"Yes, Ramtouses, I agree caution is required. Please trust me, and do not worry. Now, go on with your day and whatever you have planned. I must contact Amenirdis."

Amenirdis listened closely to Carnabrara's idea and immediately recognized how it could possibly help everyone involved—Carnabrara had to end her many clandestine meetings with this man, and he required a purpose for staying in Thebes. Egypt's agricultural productivity had shown recent reductions, and new ideas were needed to improve crop yield.

"Carnabrara, your plan reveals much promise for all. I must meet him to determine his qualifications. Send him to me tomorrow morning."

Carnabrara left the high priestess and arranged for the guards to escort Manni to Amenirdis.

One of the guards said to Manni, "You will no longer be taken to the palace. You are to be taken to the Temple of Amun."

The Temple of Amun? I hope this does not mean more trouble for me. Maybe they want a proper apology from me? But the high priestess's first words eased his mind.

"So you are Manni? I have been told you are skilled in agriculture—is that true?"

"Indeed it is," replied Manni.

The high priestess spoke with him about his experience, acknowledged his qualifications, and explained to him the recent problems with their yield.

He, in turn, provided possible solutions to the problems she described, leading her to say, "We need a man with your knowledge to manage our farms. Someone who knows all that is needed for healthy, productive plants and animals. Are you this man?"

Manni was taken by surprise, but drew himself up straight, and with no wavering he asked, "When shall I begin?"

"Tomorrow."

Amenirdis provided directions to the places and people with whom Manni would work. It almost overwhelmed him, but he assured the high priestess he could accomplish the task.

Amenirdis ended their meeting by promising to send two donkeys and all the tools he required. She gave him her seal to carry, showing he had official approval should anyone challenge his authority. "You will report to me every new moon," she instructed then dismissed him.

"Thank you for this assignment, High Priestess. I will report each new moon as you instruct. I will not disappoint you."

Manni quivered with delight, barely controlling his elation as he left the meeting with Amenirdis. As he walked down the temple steps into the warm sunshine, the joy of his great fortune escaped, and he jumped into the air with a shout of triumph. *This is wonderful!*

Then he thought of the woman who hid behind her veil in a darkened corner of the interrogation room while the others asked their questions.

No, not their questions, her questions.

Yes, I will report at the new moon to the High Priestess. I will also report everything I do to the mystery woman who hides behind her veil as she attempts to know me.

Thebes, Egypt

Young Ramtouses filled his days training with the army, his age-group comrades always with him or nearby. One day, as they practiced military maneuvers, a group of soldiers approached.

"We have orders from Pharaoh Taharqa commanding you to accompany us to Memphis."

Ramtouses was surprised. In all his years, he'd never spoken to the pharaoh and had no idea why Pharaoh Taharqa would send for him now.

"Be prepared to join us tomorrow morning," said the lead soldier.

Ramtouses left his friends immediately and went to the palace to speak with his mother.

"The pharaoh has summoned me to Memphis, and I leave tomorrow morning with an escort of soldiers. What could he want?"

Carnabrara looked at her son's puzzled face. She caught a brief flicker of fear in his eyes as he questioned the reason for Pharaoh Taharqa's summons.

"Do you suppose he knows anything about the prince's death?"

His mother stepped close and whispered loudly. "No, Ramtouses. If anyone knew that, Dafori would have been the first to express his suspicions." She smiled. "You have developed into a fine leader. Even the Pharaoh has taken notice."

Hearing that, Ramtouses immediately felt at ease. He had worked hard at all his studies, and many knew of his competence in military preparation.

"I have preparations to make," he said. "Thank you, Mother." And he left the palace, walking briskly, with purpose and confidence steering him.

He searched out seven of his age-group comrades and requested that they journey with him to Memphis. His friends eagerly accepted the call and joined him the next morning along with the pharaoh's soldiers as they all departed for Memphis, the capital of Egypt.

A few days passed after their arrival in Memphis before Pharaoh's men called Ramtouses to Taharqa's chambers.

Dressing in his finest military uniform, his shoulders held straight and tall, Ramtouses walked proudly between the two soldiers who accompanied him. He bowed before the pharaoh and then rose when a strong voice ordered him to stand.

A soldier said, "Here stands Ramtouses, as you wished, my Pharaoh."

Pharaoh Taharqa, seated on his throne, looked Ramtouses up and down.

"I have heard only good reports about you. Watched you excel over many fine boys your age."

The pharaoh stood and walked toward Ramtouses, stopping so close that his breath came as a soft puff of air on Ramtouses' face.

"What do you say for yourself?" asked the pharaoh.

"Thank you, Pharaoh Taharqa. All my efforts to become strong and wise have been to better serve you and our people, even to the death."

The pharaoh smiled. "I need fresh, young leaders like you." He pointed his finger at Ramtouses. "I am appointing you a commission in the military. You are now a high-ranking officer."

Taharqa folded his hands behind his back as he continued. "I know you speak more than just our language; you also speak Hebrew. I selected you to make a diplomatic journey to Jerusalem in Judah. You must encourage King Manasseh to join us against our mutual enemy, the Assyrians."

The pharaoh moved closer. "Do you think you can handle such a task?"

Ramtouses answered with confidence. "Yes, I can."

Ramtouses, along with his seven comrades and a company of fine young soldiers, departed soon after Pharaoh's advisors briefed him on all that they knew of King Manasseh of Judah. A messenger traveled ahead of them to inform the Judean people of the group's pending arrival. So when they neared the walls of Jerusalem a few weeks later, the city gates opened and a day of rest after the long journey was graciously offered to the tired travelers.

The day following their arrival in Jerusalem, Ramtouses went before the council of the elders bearing gifts from Pharaoh Taharqa. He bowed before them and then before King Manasseh, offering the gifts.

Ramtouses asked, "May I speak?"

Manasseh waved his arm indicating permission, and Ramtouses continued. "The Assyrians have a new king, and there is no doubt in Pharaoh's mind that he will, like his father, march on the Mediterranean coastal cities. He has a greed for gold and a need to showcase his power over the lesser cities." Ramtouses spoke primarily to the king, but he also turned toward the spectators' stand, hoping to win them to his view as well.

"We will not let the Assyrians destroy our homeland without a fight. We hope you are like your father and will agree to join us in condemning this tyrant's actions toward weaker people."

King Manasseh gave answer. "I have visited Nineveh. It is an extremely beautiful place to look upon, and the people are very hospitable."

Ramtouses moved nearer to the spectators' stands. "I am sure many people from our territory will disagree."

Manasseh cut him off. "But that is only when they resist the Assyrians and their gods."

This surprised and even astounded Ramtouses. "I was under the impression the people of Jerusalem believed in a single god."

The King closed the space between himself and Ramtouses, saying, "Perhaps you were misled, my good fellow." He turned away. "I find the Assyrian gods quite interesting, faithful to the people who believe in them. Don't you see all the power they have given to the Assyrians?"

Ramtouses opened his arms. "I beg you, King Manasseh, to look at their history of aggression. Freedom for all is better than happiness for a mere few. If we stand together as one, it will surely be a deterrent for future hostility against us by the Assyrians."

The conversation continued in this vein for a lengthy time with little or no change in the king's attitude. At the conclusion of the meeting Ramtouses maintained a position of pride even though the outcome caused heavy disappointment. His report to Pharaoh Taharqa would not be what the pharaoh hoped to hear.

A young woman sat in the observation area very close to where Ramtouses stood during the discussions. He noticed her just before the council meeting ended. Her eyes were large and dark, she did not blink as she stared at him. He felt a small quick intake of breath.

She's beautiful!

After she realized he had noticed her, the woman lowered her eyes and bit her lower lip hoping to smother the human desires with self-inflicted pain. Her demure actions served to increase Ramtouses' interest, and his scrutiny, subtle at first, grew less restrained as he exited the council hall.

Ramtouses and his company of men returned to their assigned living spaces and prepared for the long journey home. They were anxious to leave King Manasseh's palace considering his opinion of the Assyrians and his rejection of Pharaoh Taharqa's proposal to unite against Assyrian aggression.

"Pharaoh Taharqa was misinformed," Ramtouses said to the men close to him. "King Manasseh's beliefs are not what he thought, and I hate to carry the sad news back to him."

Traveling through the streets of Jerusalem, they witnessed soldiers rounding up a group of people outside a family home—men and women and several children of varying ages.

"There will be no worship of your one God, Yahweh." The soldier in charge shouted obscenities at them, accusing the family patriarch of betraying the king's orders.

As they rode away, Ramtouses puzzled over the chaotic scene of soldiers shouting, men protesting, and women trying to console both themselves and their children. "What is this one God business? Manni spoke of the same idea," he muttered aloud to no one in particular.

Less than a quarter day's ride away from the city, Ramtouses' contingent became aware of the sound of fearful women crying and shrieking. He called his men to a halt then galloped off in the direction of the commotion.

"Follow me," he yelled.

As they crested a ridge, they saw men on horseback striking down defenseless people on foot.

One of his soldiers yelled to him, "Ramtouses, this is not our affair. We should stay out of this."

Ramtouses ignored the warning. "I cannot stand by and see innocent blood spilled when I can do something about it." And he took off down the hill. "Follow me, men."

After a short but bloody battle, the Nubian Egyptians were victorious. One attacking soldier made an attempt to escape the carnage, but Ramtouses rode him down and put the man to death, shouting, "You will not return to tell your king of what occurred here."

When Ramtouses returned to the attack site his men had gathered all the survivors. He asked, "Is this everyone who was under attack? Including the dead?"

"Yes," answered his second in command.

"Collect all the soldiers' bodies to this spot. Then we'll decide what to do with them."

He rode over to speak with the survivors. The unarmed men and women had formed a tight circle around their children. Many were wounded, maybe ten people in all, and five others lay dead. Suddenly, he noticed a face he had seen earlier. Her eyes were even darker in the daylight and burned with emotion.

Why would anyone attempt to destroy someone so beautiful? He hesitated and then reprimanded himself. *That's not fair of me to even question. Everyone deserves the right to live and I am happy to see her again.*

Ramtouses asked, "What is your name?"

Her eyes moved in the direction of the dead Judeans, and she suddenly looked very sad. "I am Naamity." She spoke in a low voice that required Ramtouses to listen very closely. "We thank you very much for saving our lives. We should also be dead, but your hand was chosen by our Lord God to save us."

"Did the soldiers want to kill you because you believe in the one God?"

"Yes." She looked directly into the eyes of Ramtouses.

Her eyes are honest and pure. I had this same feeling in the council hall when she first stared at me.

"Are you wounded?"

"No," she answered.

"Who is the leader of this group?"

"He was killed in the fight." She glanced again in the direction of the dead.

"You are the new leader. I will come to you with instructions. Your people must stay with us for a few days until we figure out what to do with the dead soldiers. Egypt must not be blamed for their murders."

Ramtouses turned to an age-group friend who served as a healer. "Tend the wounded and report on their conditions."

He turned back to Naamity and asked, "Why are you and your people so far from the city?"

She kept her gaze on the man who was the obvious leader of the small group of Egyptian soldiers and answered the question without hesitation. "We are not allowed to worship our Lord, so the prophet Isaiah set up this alter away from the city. Small groups come out and worship God here."

Ramtouses asked, "What happens now that the altar's hiding place has been compromised?"

"Isaiah will build a new one, and we will continue to worship."

"I see." But Ramtouses did not understand. He rubbed his hand over the stubble that grew across his chin. *Why does their god tolerate so much evil directed toward them? And yet they worship and love him? Even if it should cost a person his life?*

The healer interrupted his thoughts. "Two of the wounded require our constant care. We bound the wounds of the other three. They can travel."

"Can we move them all to another location away from here?" Ramtouses was thinking if more soldiers came from Jerusalem looking for their comrades, everyone would face a greater problem.

"Let's move the wounded and the dead." He ordered his Nubian warriors to clean up the site as if nothing had happened there. The Nubians excelled at covering their trail, and in little time, no evidence of the struggle remained.

Scouts found a rocky place with lots of bushes and small trees, and that evening they laid the bodies on the rocks. Hundreds of birds flew in and feasted on the flesh of the dead throughout the entire night. The next morning they buried the bones and remnants of clothing in the rocks, concealing all evidence of the massacre. The soldiers' weapons were confiscated.

"Now no one will smell the rotting flesh. However, we must move the wounded no matter the risk for the sake of the entire group."

The healer said, "Yes. It will be hard on them, but I'll inform you when they can tolerate no more."

Though he wanted to move the group out as fast as possible, Ramtouses knew they had to consider everyone's ability to travel, the wounded particularly. Two travois were constructed to carry the more seriously injured men behind horses. Those with less severe wounds rode behind one of the soldiers on his horse, while the rest of the Judeans trailed behind, attempting to erase any sign of their movement with long brushes made from the tall grasses. Progress was slow yet steady.

On the first night the Judean group gathered to mourn their dead. Come morning, they continued the journey much like the first day until the sun rose high and signs of slowing down became evident. Ramtouses suggested that the Hebrews able to walk should ride on a horse, each one behind a soldier, to make movement faster. He asked Naamity to ride with him. Again, progress was slow, but they made better time than when walking, trying to put a greater distance between them and the site of the confrontation with the Hebrew soldiers.

On the second evening the group stopped before nightfall and set up camp near a small water source and a heavy concentration of bushes and trees. "We'll spend two nights here then continue to move slowly about the countryside, giving the wounded time to heal." Ramtouses realized he had taken on the protection of this small group of worshippers. The dead soldiers would be missed and others dispatched to find them. The location of their whereabouts depended upon no evidence of their presence ever being found.

"Come walk with me." He gave Naamity no opportunity to respond. "You must make certain your people understand and follow all my orders. It is for the safety of us all. Nothing can be left at any point in our movements to indicate anything other than wildlife was here. No food, no equipment, nothing. Even our waste must be buried. Do you understand?"

She nodded assent. "I will convey all you say to them. They will do what you order."

"Good." Ramtouses was reluctant to dismiss her. He enjoyed her presence in the group, but riding with her, hearing her voice, catching the slightest whiff of her scent, and seeing her face as they walked side-by-side made him think that protecting her was the most important thing he had ever done in all his life. He wanted more. "Tell me something about yourself."

"My mother was one of two women who accompanied Judith on her descent into the Assyrian camps, and with God's help, the women managed to return to the city of Jerusalem unharmed. I was born a few years later, and my father and mother taught me to believe anything is possible through our Lord."

Naamity was silent for a while as they continued to walk around the camp's perimeter. Ramtouses knew nothing of this woman named Judith, but if she entered the Assyrian camp with two other women and they returned unharmed to their home, he knew they were special. And so also would be their children.

He glanced at the young woman beside him and saw her brow furrowed ever so slightly, but it was enough to indicate her sorrow.

"I prayed for our king's heart to soften, that his eyes would open to the one true God before he and my country were swallowed by the Assyrians and their heathen gods."

She touched Ramtouses' arm. "I had just about given up when I saw you in the council hall fighting for the rights of the common men as well as the men of power. I asked God to allow me to come near you. And He did."

Ramtouses turned to look at her. "What a pleasant thing to say." He shook his head. "I must be honest. Egypt has many gods also, like Assyria, but I am not much of a believer in any god or gods."

They stopped walking and faced one another. "Allow me to tell you my history, Naamity."

She nodded, and he began. "Many generations ago, large numbers of Hebrew people migrated into northern Africa. At that time they were fleeing from the mighty Egyptian army. They had escaped to a land occupied by native African tribesmen and lived in union. Together they gave birth to the Nubians who grew rapidly into a powerful nation situated to the south of Upper Egypt. The Nubians expanded their borders to include Ethiopia and Upper Egypt. Eventually they also conquered Lower Egypt. For three generations now, my people, the Nubians, have ruled Egypt as Pharaohs. I am but a messenger for Pharaoh Taharqa."

Naamity said, "Yes, but I can see into your heart. It is pure, not corrupted like so many others."

They stood quietly gazing into each other's eyes. Ramtouses placed his hands on her shoulders and slowly slid them down her back, pulling her close. She was soft. Her hair brushed so gently against his cheek that he thought it might be his imagination. He felt like a child with a new and expensive cloak that he so dearly treasured and dared not to make a move in it. They simply nestled in each other's arms.

Later, as they walked back to the camp, Ramtouses asked, "May I sleep near you tonight? To be certain you are safe."

She was surprised by his request but answered quickly. "Yes, please do."

Evening slipped into night, and the camp quieted for all but a few stirrings from the wounded men. Ramtouses and Naamity lay in their blankets a short distance from others at the campsite, listening to the sound of insects calling their mates. The Earth lay in increasing shades of black with little light from the moon, leaving bright stars exposed.

"Are you looking at the stars?" Ramtouses whispered his question into the night.

"Yes," was her response.

"I have always felt a special love for the night sky." He continued, "You see the stars that look like a trail spanning the entire distance from one horizon to the opposite?"

Ramtouses pointed his finger toward the horizon then slowly raised it the full length across the heaven to the opposite horizon.

"In ancient times before human life, a giant bird carried a blanket in its beak filled with stars and the dust of life. The blanket had a hole in it allowing the dust of life and stars to spill. The stars left this pathway to mark the bird's flight forever."

Naamity sensed the movement of his arm more than she saw it and envisioned the sprinkling of stardust from the bird's blanket. She chuckled a little and asked, "Where did you learn that tale?"

"It's my story of how life was created." They both chuckled and quietly fell asleep.

⁙

Every two or three days the party found a different place to set camp but always near a stream with lots of vegetation, bushes, and low trees nearby to provide good camouflage. Ramtouses had shown his military skill when he insisted no one leave food, clothing, or equipment lying around the campsite. At every campsite, he assigned each person a hiding place in the event of danger. At all times, scouts roamed the area and lookouts were posted at points to spot signs of Hebrew search parties.

The two groups became comfortable with each other as the days passed and easily fell into the routine rhythms of travel, setting up and breaking of camp. By halfway to the coming new moon, the friendship between Ramtouses and Naamity had grown into a relationship where the moments of ease and relaxation were often interrupted with a tension neither expressed, but both felt.

Each day, the two men who had been more seriously wounded showed signs of healing and greater strength, and everyone knew the time to return to Jerusalem would be determined by their ability to travel on foot. One day Naamity approached Ramtouses with purpose and determination, looking straight ahead, and walking faster than normal.

She watched his face for a long moment before speaking. "We must return to the city soon."

He turned his attention to her and saw only sadness in her big, beautiful eyes, but before he could say a word, a camp lookout raced toward them with a warning. "Soldiers are coming."

Ramtouses shouted, "You all know what to do."

No one was surprised. They all knew sentries would be out looking for the soldiers who had never returned. Within a few minutes everything was concealed—no evidence of food, equipment, or people remained. The horses were coaxed to lie down and concealed with thick bushes. Everyone hid in places along the river bank. Even their tracks were invisible.

The Hebrew soldiers rode up— a few looked around, and some dismounted by the water to let their horses drink. One of the horsemen rode his horse into the water, walking the animal very close to the hiding place of two Egyptian soldiers. Ramtouses' men were ready to attack if given the go-ahead, one sharp whistle.

I can't kill these men, Ramtouses thought. *The countryside will be crawling with soldiers if these men come up missing also.*

Suddenly their leader cried, "Come on, let's go. Nothing is here."

At that, all the Hebrew soldiers hurried away, but the people they pursued knew next time they might not be so lucky. As evening approached, the group settled in for what could be their last night together. It was time for the Hebrew worshippers to sneak back into the city.

Naamity walked up behind Ramtouses as he watched a magnificent setting sun. Streaks of red beamed from low dark clouds. Near the horizon the sky shifted from blue to red, the change coming slowly but certainly, like the pain in her chest. She touched his back, and he jerked around as if suddenly awakened from sleep.

She saw the sadness in his face and knew what he was feeling. Tears slowly filled her eyes. "I—" She stopped and simply looked into his eyes as she repeated *I* over and over. Ramtouses gently took her in his arms. "I love you," Naamity whispered.

Time hung motionless about them. The only sounds came from their breaths in and out and from the beat of two hearts signaling one another.

"I love you," she repeated.

Ramtouses whispered. "Run away to Egypt with me. I can't leave you here."

"I want so badly to go with you, but I can't desert my people and my God."

Ramtouses turned her head so they stood face-to-face with barely a breath between them. "I can't leave you here. Don't you understand? I will always take care of you, and together we can believe in your one God."

Their lips met, and they kissed. An intense desire rushed through Naamity. She gasped in surprise and broke out of his embrace. "No. No. This is not the way of God." She turned from him, not caring where she ran. Her thought was to free herself, to put behind her this love and desire for Ramtouses. At one point she slipped on the rough ground-cover and tumbled into the scrub bushes growing in abundance on the hillside. There she lay, breathing heavily, trying to calm her emotions.

Ramtouses followed and found her lying on the ground behind a large bush. He stood over her, looking down at the most beautiful woman he had ever seen. Her chest rose with each breath, and those dark eyes seemed to call his name. He moved down on top of her, so ready to claim her as his only.

She cried, "Take me. Take me if you must, but we will never be happy if this is our beginning. I am a child of Almighty God, and if you take my virginity like this I will never be able to pray to my God with the shame of our sin on my conscious"

Ramtouses drew back, confused by what she said and concerned for her happiness. He listened acutely as she continued speaking.

"The law of our one true God is that a man must take the woman he loves as his wife, otherwise it is fornication. I know these laws are new and strange to you; however, please try to understand."

Ramtouses rose to his knees and then to his feet. "I know you love me as I love you. I believe you would do anything I ask, but I will not ask you to commit blasphemy against your God."

Naamity wept. Her tears washed away the thought of her near betrayal, and peace filled her heart. Looking up, she saw this man whom she loved reach down to help her to her feet. They walked together, side-by-side, back to the camp. A beautiful harmony settled around them, soothing the wild yearning of their love.

"You respect my honor and my God." Naamity's soft, clear voice floated over the two of them that night as they lay beside each other. "You gave strength to our love. You accept me for who I am."

"We are two different people from totally separate worlds, Naamity. Our customs are so unalike, but love can take root in anyone's heart and flourish. If true love is meant to be for us, life will not let it go hungry. Somehow, life will nurture it."

His hand found hers and held it gently as the camp slipped into the quiet of night.

At the light of day, Ramtouses awakened and opened his eyes. He saw Naamity standing at his feet. She stood tall, framed by the morning sun, her thick black hair parted in the middle and hung in waves to her waist. The soft features of her beautiful, unblemished face shone a bright white from the morning sunlight as she looked upward into the heavens. The image of her standing at his feet was splendid and breathtaking, more beautiful than the sunrise itself.

She began to sing, her voice soft and the words clear as they sailed through the air. The notes moved with the words, and then the words moved with notes—not even a lark's trill could have competed with Naamity's lovely song. Nothing could have surprised Ramtouses more.

"God has brought you into my life. He has shown me the beauty of your love

"If only for a moment shall I bear this precious touch of love I feel in my heart."

He sat up, enchanted by her beauty against the morning sunlight and captivated by the song flowing from her lips. The words came free and smooth with no hesitation, as pure as water from a mountain stream—deep, clear, innocent, and powerful.

The melody is more beautiful than the stars at night. Am I going mad? Am I dreaming?

She continued to sing, and Ramtouses wished she would never stop. *Is this the way I am to always remember her? Singing her song? Sharing the heat of her heart.*

But her song did end, and Ramtouses did not know what to say. He reached for her hand, held it firmly in his own, and kissed it—her palm then each finger, one by one—and pressed her hand to his cheek. "I have no words to speak or sing. I am breathless. You are beyond words, and I will remember that song forever."

The rest of the camp slowly awakened and began to gather their things and erase all evidence of their campsite before starting out toward Jerusalem. The previous evening Ramtouses had explained to everyone what to expect of their last day of traveling together. They would start out as usual in one group, but at some point well before the city, all but three of the Nubian-Egyptian soldiers would stop and wait. Ramtouses and two of his age-group comrades would accompany the Judean worshippers on the trek back toward Jerusalem, keeping a considerable distance between them and Naamity's group. He stressed to Naamity that he would maintain visual contact with her.

Before moving out, the two groups acknowledged each other with words and gestures of appreciation and farewell. They represented differing cultures, but having spent close to a full moon's cycle together, day and night, they had learned to respect and honor each other.

The Nubian soldiers rode on horseback at the back of the group, and then Ramtouses and his two comrades, wearing the familiar robes of merchants, rode behind the Judeans who were on foot leading the assembly. Before they merged onto the road leading to Jerusalem, the Nubian soldiers stopped to dismount and settled down to wait for their leader's return. The others continued and soon saw a few merchants and other travelers en route to the monthly market day at Jerusalem. The road became busier with additional travelers, and Ramtouses was challenged to keep the Judeans in sight but still make it appear to any observer that they were not together.

They made good progress, and by mid-morning Naamity's small group of believers mingled with the morning crowd entering the city. Ramtouses turned to his men. "Wait here. I will walk to the city with them."

Ramtouses walked swiftly to catch up to them. As they neared the city's gates, he called her name. "Naamity"

She stopped and slowly turned. He saw her face wet with tears and held his hands out to her.

"If your God has willed for our two worlds to come together as we have, I am sure this is not the end. Take this token, it is my emblem. It will bring you safely to me if you ever get to Egypt."

She took it and began to back away. Ramtouses stood still, watching as she merged with the other foot traffic, until he could see her no more.

There is no place for me in her world. Why must this happen? She is the love of my life, walking from me, farther and farther away. Do the gods play games with us?

Stop. You're an officer. Pull yourself together. Your pharaoh awaits your return.

Ramtouses joined his comrades and rode back to his waiting men.

"We will return to Egypt," he announced.

While riding home, he sang Naamity's song, promising himself to remember the words and melody, to never forget her song.

⁜

They arrived back in Memphis after traveling for nearly the time of one new moon to the next. Pharaoh Taharqa allowed a few days of rest before he sent for Ramtouses to report the outcome of his mission. The Pharaoh anticipated a disappointing report, but he listened to Ramtouses speak of his discussion with King Manasseh of Judah.

"I am not surprised. As a matter of fact, I expected he would not want the alliance."

He bent close to Ramtouses. "Do not worry. I wanted you to gain that experience. Know your enemies and your allies. You will become a fine officer."

"Now, go back home to Thebes. I am making you second in command of my army there, and you will report to me anything out of the ordinary or questionable in the command activities. If war comes, I want people I can trust and rely upon."

Ramtouses returned home where his mother waited to greet him, anxious to hear what Pharaoh Taharqa had told her son.

Her response was jubilant. "Wonderful! I am happy for you, my son. Only the general of Thebes is higher in command than you. I know you are worthy, but I never dreamed you would come back with such honors." She hugged and kissed him.

"That is only part of the story." Ramtouses' head drooped to his chest. "I left my heart in Jerusalem. I met a young Hebrew girl, and I can't get her out of my mind."

Carnabrara's eyes lit up. "Tell me all about her."

"She is beautiful and sweet, like no one I have met. Just the thought of her causes a longing in my heart."

"Don't worry, my son, you will get over it."

"That's just it. I don't want to get over it. You were not there seeing her standing in the sun, singing so intensely. Each word penetrated my very soul."

Ramtouses placed his hands on either side of his head. "I wanted to steal her away but thought she would be in constant misery because of her God. I don't think I'll ever see her again, and I will never love another like this."

He told his mother the whole story.

6

Nineveh

King Sennacherib's dreams haunted his sleep, and he needed the calming love of his sweet Naqia. She alone soothed his ache.

"Servants," he called, "prepare me for a trip outside the city. Someone go and see to it that my chariot is ready."

He arrived at Naqia's estate late morning and found her working in the beautiful gardens surrounding the home he had designed specifically for her and her son, his son. Naqia looked up at Sennacherib with the dark, beautiful eyes he knew could spin webs of delight for him, and he held out his hand. Her smile spread sweetly as she reached for his offer of help and stood to greet him, her king and lover. The sunlight bathed them as one, briefly, before the spell swiftly shifted to the present moment.

"What an honor! You do have time for me." Naqia's voice carried a note of irritation for his last visit had accompanied the previous full moon.

"Too long?" he asked. "I know, but I am here now. How are you?"

"I will live," she answered.

He took her in his arms and kissed her.

"Have your servant dress another dinner place. I will spend the night with you."

His night of rest ended as the dream interrupted his sleep in the early morning hours. The sky remained dark, even before the faintest rays of the promised morning. Accustomed to his nightly rage, Naqia awoke him as gently as possible and wondered if release from the dream demons would ever be granted Sennacherib.

In the morning, after dressing, he said, "I must go to the temple when I leave here. Where is my son?"

"Sometimes he spends the night at the academy," Naqia answered. "I'm sure he's there."

As the king prepared to leave, he said, "You know I love you and Esarhaddon, you are dear to me. I will stop and see how he is doing."

"I know you love me." She frowned. "That is why you hide me and my son away from your Assyrian lords and their wives."

He looked at her. "Don't start that again."

"And why not? It is true." She waved her arms. "I am from Jordan, not of Assyrian blood. They will never look upon me as worthy of you, nor will they respect my son as a royal prince, which he is."

Walking to his chariot, Sennacherib responded, "No one will disrespect you or him, not as long as I am king."

Following him to the door Naqia called back loudly, "You will not live forever."

He pointed toward the academy, and the driver nudged the horse to move.

Sennacherib heard fencing sounds immediately upon arriving at the front steps of the academy building. He climbed down from the chariot and hurried to where the sounds grew louder. A high wall, built to keep out intruders, surrounded the practice fields. He found a crack large enough to peek through and saw his son, Esarhaddon, fencing two opponents, their swords clanging loudly with each thrust and parry.

"Come on!" Esarhaddon yelled. "Try and strike me. No! You're not trying. I can strike you at will."

Sennacherib thought, *He's good, very good.* Esarhaddon's movement was superior by far over his two opponents, his style graceful and fluid. He could strike the two men whenever he wanted. Then it dawned on Sennacherib, and he joyfully shouted, "Of course!" A familiar excitement seized him. *He has the rhythmic motion of Holofernes. How could I not recognize that immediately?*

Sennacherib hurried around to the entrance and located the instructor. "Why have you not told me of my son's progress. I had no idea he could handle a weapon like that."

"You picked me to train him because you know I am one of the best in all the land, and he has learned well. I was just about ready to show you his skills. It would have been a pleasant surprise for you."

"Surprise? I am amazed!"

Sennacherib spent several hours with his son and returned to Nineveh a happy man. *This son makes me proud*, he thought. *He needs advanced training.*

One of his generals worked with Esarhaddon, teaching him the strategies of war, and Sennacherib assigned two more of his top generals to further the boy's education in military matters. The next morning, after awakening from the same horrible nightmare, the king resumed going to the temple to worship the god of curing illnesses.

⁂

About a half year passed, and the king called together the men who instructed his son, Esarhaddon. *I knew what I had to do for Esarhaddon; now I need to be sure my plan has succeeded. Did the generals grow to know and love my son?"*

Standing before the group of his select generals, he asked, "How do you feel about the young man you are teaching?"

They all agreed that this young man was an excellent student. "He could be a great leader if given the opportunity," one general commented. Others nodded agreement, and one said "We love his ability to learn, and there is no one better with the sword."

The king called three more of his most trusted generals into his chamber. He made all six swear before Baal that they would fight to the death to protect the young prince Esarhaddon. Three of the six were more willing than the others. The three newer officers seemed caught by surprise but still gave their alliance.

The king said to them, "You three who do not know him shall get to know him by spending time with him. Do not speak of this meeting. I swear you to secrecy. No one can learn of this oath. I tell you, no one!"

The next day on his way to the oracle council, Sennacherib thought it was Holofernes' spirit that opened his eyes to whom the next king would be to command this mighty empire.

That day has come for me to reveal his name to all.

King Sennacherib strode into the big hall, looking into the eyes of his oracle constituents as he went. They were men of wisdom, intelligent, well-educated, and the acknowledged representatives of the gods in the governing circles. He sat and waited his turn to address the oracles. When the time came for him to speak, he walked to the center of the hall.

"My countrymen,"—he folded his hands behind him—"today I want to anoint my successor to the throne." The hall was quiet, all eyes on the King. "I have chosen Prince Esarhaddon."

The council members' faces registered surprise, their chins dropping as they looked at each other. Some of them did not even know of Prince Esarhaddon. Soon the yelling began. Sennacherib never moved.

The speaker for the oracles rose from his seat and lowered his hands, signaling for quiet.

Once the hall returned to normal, he said, "I don't believe you were joking when you made that remark." He looked around. "We all love you. You are our king. Sometimes it is better to let us know what you are thinking when you make these statements so we will know whether to laugh or cry."

The king yelled, "I want Esarhaddon as my successor because he has a clear mind, one that has not been deluded or corrupted by greed and power."

The spokesmen looked at the king's other sons who were present in the hall. "Are you saying all eleven of your other sons are depraved?"

"No! I am not saying that. I say only that Esarhaddon is the least tampered with."

The oracle leader said, "Will you rethink your decision after I address the seriousness of what you say before your countrymen?"

"I will listen."

The oracle leader walked around the hall, making gestures with his arms and fingers. "Think about this. Is it not true that Holofernes, under your command, ransacked the country of Babylonia in revenge of your brother's assassination in that nation? Is it not true that we, the Assyrians, believe in the same gods as Babylonia? So when General Holofernes burnt down their cities and towns, he also destroyed statues, crushed them under his feet, and then burnt down alters and temples to their gods that happen to be the same gods as ours.

"Everyone knows what happened at Jerusalem. The gods placed a curse on you and Holofernes for your terrible deeds against them, and that is what happened to your army before the walls of the inferior Hebrews. Holofernes was killed, and your whole army was lost. Half the Assyrian population thinks the gods were justified in their actions, even though many sons were lost."

He shook his head and continued. "The other half of the population, including your own sons, thinks your good judgment has deserted you because of your mental illness." He opened his arms to Sennacherib. "Now you come here with some foolish notion that a bastard son by an outsider, a child born from a people inferior to us, should rule over the sons and daughters of our mighty kingdom." He looked around the room at the many faces and heads nodding in agreement. "Come now, can't you see the position you have put us in? We all want the same, a strong nation for all our citizens. Be a wise king. Allow your people who know the needs of the government operations make sound-minded decisions for you. The oracles will vote for the son from your offspring who best holds the right to inherit your throne. Is that not fair for all?"

The room was silent when Sennacherib suddenly cried with a mighty roar, "I declare Esarhaddon will be your next king!"

A groan of disapproval came from all four corners. Many of the oracles walked out before the meeting adjourned. Sennacherib thought as he walked back to his palace, *I will make my own decision. I am king and don't need their approval*

The matter stayed fresh in the king's mind for days. So when he heard a rumor some of his sons might be plotting to kill his favorite son, Esarhaddon, he ordered one of the six generals to secure a hiding place for him.

The general told Sennacherib, "I know of an old deserted palace in southern Babylonia."

"Good. Take him there at once. Provide him with a large protective guard, food, water, and clean clothing. He is to be left alone."

The general raised his brows in question.

Sennacherib responded, "We send a boy and trust a seasoned man returns."

⁑

Esarhaddon found the palace disgusting. The place was in ruins, rubble everywhere. The palace ceilings had rotted and collapsed in many rooms. He slept under the stars many nights. Only a few servants were in residence, and they took up quarter with the numerous soldiers encamped around the property. Esarhaddon found himself alone in the old palace, every day, every night. The servants brought him food daily and clean clothing with other supplies as needed. Most often they quickly departed, not speaking a word. Fresh water was dipped from a nearby spring but the prince bathed a short distance downstream—those times were his rare occasions of freedom.

Most days he wandered around the huge empty shell of a complex. At night the strong winds would speak to him of the passing of time, how this citadel had outlasted the many generations of sovereign lords who occupied this once magnificent mansion.

The march of time had its impact on Esarhaddon. Several seasons of isolation had changed the once carefree youth into a hardened man. He thought of those seeking power and willing to kill for it, of how he and his mother had been despised by the royal families. His hatred grew. He asked out loud, of no one but himself, for he was alone, "Why should I have to hide like a dangerous criminal when I have done nothing to anyone?"

Each time the question was asked a voice in the wind would answer in a hateful revengeful way. "You will prevail."

The King thought of Esarhaddon often. One day he had an idea. *If he is anything like Holofernes, the thing he would most desire is the companionship of women.*

Esarhaddon was sitting on the steps of the ruins when he saw soldiers approaching the palace, escorting four young women who appeared thrilled to have finally arrived. They ran up the many steps toward him. Esarhaddon jumped to his feet, completely surprised. "Why are you here?" he asked.

"The king has sent us to entertain you and stay with you day and night." For the first time in a year and a half, Esarhaddon began to laugh out loud. He jumped for joy and hugged and kissed them repeatedly. "I am so ready for companionship," he shouted.

⁙

King Sennacherib's daily visits to the temple were like clockwork. He hoped the gods would lift the terrible spell that tormented him so. But it wasn't to be.

Two of his sons let jealousies overcome their better judgment, and they plotted to murder their father in hopes one of them would be chosen by the oracles to become king. They felt this had to be done if one of them were to be named King of Assyria since no one even knew if this bastard son, Esarhaddon, was even alive or dead.

At the first opportunity they devised a plan that would cause a giant gargoyle-like statue to topple over and crush their father when he exited the temple, but on second thought the two decided against it. They reasoned that if it missed, a second attempt at their father's life would be impossible, and they chose instead to assassinate him by stabbing him to death inside the very same temple.

This plan might have benefited from second and third thoughts also because a priest witnessed the attack and told others. Word spread like fire and soon everyone knew who had committed the crime, and the two brothers fled for their lives.

Esarhaddon was eating fruit and enjoying the company of his new friends, when a large group of soldiers, headed by the general, suddenly entered his hiding place. It was a total surprise to everyone at the old palace.

The general cried in a loud angry voice, "Prepare yourself, Esarhaddon. We need to act at once. Your father, King Sennacherib, has been murdered."

Esarhaddon sprang to his feet. "What did you say?" Lacing his hands along the sides of his head, he yelled, "Oh no! No!" His face grew pale. He stood with his back to the soldiers for a short while, thinking of the many moons alone in this place and how in time the gods had sent a voice in the winds, with encouragement, saying he shall have his day.

When he turned, his eyes were tight, his lips rolled in. Esarhaddon said, "How do we stand?"

The general answered, "The men are preparing to march. We will merge our troops with those of the other five generals en route to Nineveh.

It was a huge army that approached the capital. King Sennacherib had foreseen this day coming and had recruited well. The royal families had joined forces, not sure what they would be up against. Esarhaddon sent a general to the walls of Nineveh to deliver his message.

"I, Esarhaddon, am the rightful King of Assyria. If anyone wishes to deny me that right, it will mean bloodshed between Assyrians. Let us not fight brother against brother. Open the gate and let Esarhaddon serve his people as king."

The gates did not open, so the civil war began. After a six-week battle Esarhaddon emerged victorious, executed his brothers—families, associates, and all who had joined their cause. Then he took the throne.

Esarhaddon came before the oracles and addressed large crowds of people. "My first duty is to hear the voice of the people." He held his arms up high, his hands open. "I want to right the wrong my father injected so callously upon the gods. Let my actions prove me worthy to be your king and emperor over all Assyria, Babylonia, and our vassal states."

Esarhaddon refurbished existing alters, added new ones, and built new taller, superior statues to the gods all over Babylonia. He converted the old Babylonian palace in which he had cocooned from a boy into a man, into his vacation home, making a fabulous place of it. He made wives of two of the four girls who stayed with him during his final days at the palace, and thereafter they bore him children.

Esarhaddon called upon all his vassal states to come and visit him in Nineveh. He demanded a fair annual payment which now included supplies and materials needed for his many construction projects. Manasseh, King of Judah, often came up short of his payment, which was not in favor of the king.

For a time, no major crisis was at hand until one day, at a meeting of the oracles, a messenger came forward.

"Speak to us," ordered Esarhaddon.

"My lord and king, the Cimmerians again invaded the borders of our trusted allies and Assyria itself."

Esarhaddon spoke without hesitation. "These nomadic tribes who plunder and loot our villages for gold, horses, and women must be addressed. My grandfather, Sargon II, lies slain by the Cimmerians and will never find peace as long as a Cimmerian lives. Make ready our armies."

He would now put his training to the test. One of his six generals was at his side continuously. The Cimmerians received word that the Assyrian army approached their camps. They quickly prepared to meet them.

It was a cool summer morning when the two armies faced one another across the open plains. King Esarhaddon saw a huge cavalry, a number even greater than the Assyrian horsemen, but the Assyrians knew they were the best trained, not the Cimmerians. They had superior equipment, and rode muscular horses that obeyed their every command.

King Esarhaddon asked his general, "Is the cavalry ready?"

"Yes, my king," he answered immediately.

"Wait. Let the Cimmerians charge first. Wearing down their animals gives us a slight advantage."

The Cimmerians did charge first into this immense field of destruction. "Wait," said the king. "Wait."

When they passed the three-quarter mark, he cried, "Charge!"

King Esarhaddon's horsemen galloped at full speed in a tight formation as they'd been taught. The two forces clashed, followed by the screams and cries of dying men and horses. Those sounds dominated the air.

A veil of dust concealed the fighting. King Esarhaddon pulled his sword, holding it high. "Baal is with us. Baal is with us." He repeated it over and over. Then, Assyrian riders could be seen returning to their ranks. They began singing their war song.

The Cimmerian king, Teushpa, a giant of a man himself, wondered what he should do next. The majority of his forces were cavalrymen. The Assyrians stood back as the Cimmerians received their wounded off the field.

The following morning King Teushpa knew the only way to regain the upper hand was to kill the Assyrian king. Teushpa came out before his army and challenged King Esarhaddon to a match in single combat.

The generals advised Esarhaddon against it. "We are winning. You don't need to face him."

Esarhaddon responded, "I know, but I want to avenge my grandfather with the killing of the Cimmerian king with my own hands." He pulled his chariot out into the open fields ahead of his army. The wind blew against his back, fluttering the horse hair on his helmet.

All eyes of the Cimmerians were upon him. Their powerful king, Teushpa, charged out from the midst of his leaders and kept coming across the distant plains.

Esarhaddon brought up his chariot at a slower pace. The two chariots stopped when they neared one another, and the men stepped down. King Esarhaddon waved his sword as he came toward the Cimmerians' leader. The giant king was nearly a head taller than Esarhaddon, and the Assyrian king stood nearly a head taller than his average soldier. As he drew closer, Teushpa began waving his giant sword. The weapon made a whistling sound as it carved its way through the air.

Esarhaddon showed his quickness and agility by avoiding any contact. He knew he had to get in close to strike the big man, so he exchanged a few moments of swordplay, blocking any close swings. He landed two quick blows to Teushpa's chest area. The man's upper body was covered with what looked to be bear skin, and Esarhaddon's strikes did not penetrate his opponent's protection.

He fought his way up close again, this time striking the giant Teushpa below the upper body protection and above his leg greaves. The blood ran down heavily from his thigh. For a few moments, the wound had no effect on his fighting. Esarhaddon's agile movement kept him safe as he waited for the King of the Cimmerians to slow down, and when he did, Esarhaddon went after him for the kill. His sword found flesh along his collar bone, above his protection. The big man fell to his knees. Esarhaddon yelled, "This is for Sargon II."

The Cimmerian king raised his arm to cover his face, but Esarhaddon's sword missed the arm, striking Teushpa on the neck. The giant man fell over, dead.

King Esarhaddon felt the power of Baal and screamed, "After them! Kill them all. Let not one escape our wrath for their crimes against us."

When the fighting ended, King Esarhaddon came home a mighty hero. All Nineveh turned out to welcome him.

Months after his return he began to get reports that Egypt was influencing the territory of Levant to revolt against Assyria. And when their tribute failed to arrive, King Esarhaddon spoke before his oracles. "The Egyptians need to be dealt with more firmly. We cannot let them threaten our power over the vassal states in the coastal region. The territory of Levant is just the beginning." He stood proud, looking around at the many eyes upon him. "We will send an army to Levant and resurrect order as Baal demands. I ask the oracles' blessing before we march."

The Assyrians prepared a military operation quickly to stop the rebellion before it spread to other states. King Esarhaddon did not accompany the forces. He felt his generals were the finest in the world and could find victory without his presence. The army broke camp in the year 673 B.C.E. and headed for the Mediterranean coastal vassal states.

Thebes, Egypt

Ramtouses spent every day, all day, learning his duty as second in command for the Thebes' military. After several months, Prince Dafori sent for Ramtouses. Though he was the Pharaoh's nephew and representative in Thebes, as well as husband to Ramtouses' mother, this was the first time he'd acknowledged Ramtouses' presence in Thebes.

"My son, how proud I am of you." Dafori opened his arms. "Come right up to me; stand beside me." Ramtouses moved forward and the prince put his arms on Ramtouses' shoulders. "So, Taharqa has taken favor of you."

Dafori's summons came as a surprise to Ramtouses, and the prince's effusive greeting was obviously meant to put him at ease. *However,* thought Ramtouses, *it only serves to put me on alert. You never showed any interest in me as a child or young man, Dafori, so why the sudden attention now?* He kept his suspicions hidden and greeted the prince with cordial respect.

Prince Dafori gave little response to Ramtouses' return greeting and kept speaking. "Our general over the army of Thebes has said you have a natural ability to lead, and that is what we need here in Thebes."

He removed his hands from the young man's shoulders and turned his back to walk away as he asked, "What did Pharaoh Taharqa say about Thebes?"

"Nothing," responded Ramtouses, "he only sent me here as second in command of the army."

"He never mentioned my name?" The prince pivoted to face Ramtouses again.

"No."

Prince Dafori smiled and walked back toward Ramtouses. "It is very good to have a loyal son like you, Ramtouses. Still, I need you to swear before the sacred gods Amun-re and Menthu that your loyalty will be to me, and nothing we speak of will leave this room. Swear it now."

Ramtouses nodded his head in consent as the prince spoke. "You will do only as I command. Swear it."

After hearing Ramtouses swear to his every command, Dafori smiled and shifted the conversation to the welfare of Thebes and his dreams of Thebes becoming the capital city of Egypt again with himself as pharaoh. When Dafori later dismissed him, Ramtouses left the prince's palace wondering why he seemed to place so much trust in him after all the years of granting him no recognition.

He informed his mother of the prince's new interest in him, but he did not tell her about the situation Prince Dafori and Pharaoh Taharqa had placed upon him. Instead, he changed the subject. "How is Manni? Have you seen him lately?"

She smiled and cheerfully shifted the discussion with him. "He is so happy with his new job and Princess High Priestess Amenirdis is certainly pleased. He has come up with many new ideas that have made his work beneficial for her."

"That's good, and you sound pleased also. I'd like to see him. When does he report to the high priestess again?"

"In about seven days," his mother answered. "We can show up together, for I am always there to hear him."

On the day of Manni's next report regarding his work for Amenirdis, Carnabrara and Ramtouses walked together to the temple and listened as Manni told of his work with the Egyptian farmers and their acceptance of his new farming methods. Carnabrara veiled her face as she stood toward the rear of the temple room listening to the report. Ramtouses watched his mother while Manni spoke and saw how she never shifted her gaze from him. *She likely could repeat the report word for word if asked,* Ramtouses thought.

They departed the high priestess's temple, and on the walk home to their portion of the palace, Ramtouses confessed his ignorance of love. "Mother," he said, "at first I could not understand why, after all these years, the love you and Manni shared was still alive, but now I know. I will love Naamity forever."

Carnabrara reached up and stroked her son's cheek then took his hand in hers. "Love is a strong force."

For a few months a sweet peace filled the air, and each day resembled the previous as mother and son spent time together working, walking, and listening to each other's stories. For weeks, they experienced no chaos, no commotions, just an ordered ease—until the arrival of a messenger in the year 673 B.C.E. when Ramtouses received word from Prince Dafori.

"Ramtouses," the messenger called out, "Prince Dafori must speak with you immediately. The Assyrians are on the move south and the pharaoh has sent for you to come to Memphis at once."

And Ramtouses knew the quiet, easy days with his mother had ended.

⁕

Prince Dafori pointed his finger at Ramtouses in excitement. "This could be our chance. If Pharaoh Taharqa wins the battle but suffers the loss of most of his army, we have reserves unknown to him who can step up and overtake the throne. Go to Memphis. Keep your ears open. Be wise, my son. I will be in touch."

Ramtouses bowed and left the prince's chambers. That same day he and sixty of his age-group comrades took off for the capital. He arranged for twenty more to follow with the military forces selected to join the pharaoh's army by Dafori.

The remaining age-group comrades were charged to provide care and protection for their mothers and Carnabrara and their siblings.

In a few short weeks, Ramtouses entered the pharaoh's hall and bowed before Pharaoh Taharqa. The pharaoh spent no time on the usual greetings but spoke immediately of the reason for Ramtouses' summons.

"Ramtouses, we are likely to be at war very soon now." He looked around the room where his military generals and officers all stood. "We are aligned with the people of Levant, a people once subjugated to Assyria."

He clinched his fist. "Now we will fight to save these people's right to trade with whomever they please. Their seaports are vital to our naval trade. There are reports Assyria is moving their army south, and the people of Levant have requested our help. Menthu, our god of war, has revealed to me his favor in such an undertaking. I will carry out his pleasure."

The Pharaoh's officers applauded him loudly. The meeting continued on and on as many officers stepped forward to express their ideas to defeat the Assyrians in battle. Each man present voiced great disdain for the aggressive Assyrians, and no one doubted the need for war.

When all had spoken and left the hall, Pharaoh Taharqa called Ramtouses to his private chambers. Immediately after the young officer entered, the pharaoh asked, "Is there anything I need to know?"

"Yes," Ramtouses said. "Your nephew, Prince Dafori, is plotting against you. He has taken me under his wing and confided in me like a favored son. He and his generals are hoping to gain power after this war with Assyria."

Taharqa said, "Tell me everything. Do not leave out a single detail." He invited Ramtouses to sit while they had a long conversation about the matter.

At the conclusion the pharaoh said, "You have served me well. Your loyalty has earned my trust, and because of that, you will be handsomely rewarded." The Pharaoh escorted Ramtouses to the palace's huge entrance. "Someone will come for you at the banquet hour."

Ramtouses smiled and thanked Taharqa for the honor of serving him, then bowed before quickly departing down the long flight of stairs.

He arrived at the dinner dressed very smartly and noticed that the other guests were officers, some from Ethiopia. When the feast ended, Pharaoh Taharqa stood to address his leaders.

"We have a new leader in our midst." He looked over to Ramtouses. "Ramtouses will lead the war effort against Assyria. The other generals will aide him in drawing up the war strategy, but Ramtouses will have the final say."

He raised his goblet to the ceiling. "Almighty Amun has willed it. Menthu will be with him in battle. I know this comes as a surprise for most of you, but do not worry. The gods are with this young man." Taharqa looked at the many faces about him and then asked, "Is everyone pleased? Raise your goblets and drink to Ramtouses."

They all did.

Later, when the officers were departing the hall, one of the generals came up behind Ramtouses. "I will be totally loyal to you, Ramtouses. Believe me, none of the others really care for the pharaoh's decision, yet the Assyrians must be stopped at all costs no matter who leads us in battle."

Ramtouses said. "I had no idea this would happen for me. I have to let this settle in slowly. I am going straight to my quarters to sleep on it." He turned and looked back at the general. "Thank you for your support. I accept all that you give."

The general called out after him. "Savor the moment while you have the opportunity."

When Ramtouses reached his abode, several new guards surrounded his door. Tailors were inside ready to measure him for new clothing befitting an officer of his higher status.

He looked at one of his age-group comrades and winked as if to say, *Can you believe this?*

The next morning Ramtouses inspected his officers. He made special guards of his age-group members. A few weeks before the army began their march, the Ethiopian army joined them. Pharaoh Taharqa wished them well and declared the gods be with them.

Ramtouses' army stayed close to the sea, avoiding the hot desert and keeping a watchful eye on the Assyrian movement toward the territory of Levant through his scouts.

Each day, the generals gathered to review battle strategies with Ramtouses. At first, most of the generals seemed uninterested in his plans, even turned their backs, until his allied general pulled a couple of the officers around to face Ramtouses.

He said, "What is this? Who of you wants to challenge the will of the gods? Didn't Pharaoh Taharqa say Amun-re is with this man? Is not the voice of Menthu uttering words from his lips? Aren't there officers among you who led the army against the Assyrians twenty years ago and failed? Do you really believe you can find victory without the power of the gods?"

The general pointed his finger to the ground. "Come stand here in front of me and tell me I should follow you instead of the power of the gods." He waited. "Hurry up. Come forward."

After no one came forward, he said. "If no one will stand up to the gods, then give this man your full attention."

And they did. And after that day, Ramtouses' ally general stood at his side each time they met.

Now, at the morning meeting, Ramtouses said, "We all agree the battle must take place away from the valuable seaports."

The favored general commented, "But not at Eltekeh. We do not want a repeat of the last battle."

"Correct," responded Ramtouses. "I think the plains at Ashkelon will be best."

So the Egyptian and Ethiopian armies headed for Ashkelon, expecting the Assyrians to follow suit. Each day, Ramtouses went over and over his plan of attack with his generals until the day came when the two armies lay in each other's path.

The Egyptian and Ethiopian men outnumbered the Assyrians three to two. However, the Assyrians were much better equipped, including their fine horses and long lances, iron swords not copper, as well as the pavis wall-of-shields to keep the enemy away from their interior.

Ramtouses said to his men, "Our method of attack will be based upon our failures in the last war. What did not work then, we will not repeat. In the areas where we found some success, we will build upon."

He went on to say, "Our army ran the distance six fold more than a man can throw a stone before reaching the Assyrian's stout wall of shields. Exhaustion will overcome anyone's ability to fight under those conditions. And our cavalry, even though we have the greater number, will not engage the enemy as our first means of attack."

It was a mild and windless morning when the opposing forces came up near one another. Neither army moved forward for a long while. Giving up on patience, the Assyrians began to move forward, singing their war song. Then the march came to a halt, and the singing stopped. After a short period of time, the singing and marching started up again. This continued until the Assyrians' arrow attack could be launched.

Thousands of arrows fell upon the Nubians of Egypt and the Ethiopians. Their shields this time were bigger and stronger, more able to withstand the barrage of iron-tipped arrows. Again and again, the Assyrians repeated their advancement, firing arrows, marching and singing, then stopping.

Ramtouses' army was pounded, but he waited for the right moment to call for a counterattack, not wanting his men drained when their energy was needed the most. Ramtouses' army had built thousands more battering ram chariots upon realizing how well they performed in their first conflict. Each chariot had a long and heavy pole protruding from the front between their horses.

Ramtouses gave the order to charge. The cavalry came out in support of the battering ram chariots. A certain area was targeted for the breach. The Assyrian cavalry came to the front in an attempt to ward off the battering ram chariots. A huge battle ensued, yet the chariots pushed on. Only the driver rode upon the ram chariot for less weight and more speed. The Nubian army rushed up behind them, hoping to find the shields knocked down.

The Assyrians found them an easy target. However, the Nubian-Egyptian forces were so great and their speed so swift that a number of them got past the Assyrian horsemen, plunging their way into the Assyrian interior and crushing the famed pavis wall-of-shields bearers. Ramtouses' order was to kill as many shield bearers as possible, making it impossible for the wall to be reformed again.

The Assyrian cavalry was now forced to retreat and support the areas breached by the ram chariots. Heavy fighting took place as the Nubian foot soldiers moved in. However, remembering how the Assyrians trapped and surrounded them in a similar battle scheme twenty years past, Ramtouses' forces limited their penetration. That mild and windless day witnessed the deaths of thousands of men. Just beyond the exterior of the Assyrian forces, hundreds of pavis wall bearers met death. The high command of officers on both sides did not participate in the slaughter.

As evening approached, the Nubian Egyptians slowly withdrew their forces. Each group aided their wounded, carrying them away from the fighting fields, and removed the bodies of their dead. The only victory went to the Nubian-Egyptians and Ethiopians for literally destroying the Assyrian wall-of- shields. The generals were elated and raised their fists in the air, congratulating Ramtouses on his well-planned battle. The leaders were pleased but not totally happy, knowing the war was not over by far.

The next morning was overcast with a slight rain. The Nubian army found the Assyrian cavalry replacing the wall-of-shields. After the two armies came within range of the arrows, the exchange of arrows rained down upon each army. The Nubians were very skilled when it came to the bow, equaling the Assyrians with that weapon. So at this point there was no advantage. Half the day passed before the Assyrian cavalry charged out, coming right up to the Nubian-Egyptian lines. Bloody fighting escalated. By the end of the day, the Assyrian cavalry retreated, after putting to death many fine Egyptian and Ethiopian horsemen. They won the battle that day but they also suffered heavy losses.

Ramtouses decided to move closer that night and bring the infantry upon them fast with high spirits and agility. Quickly, he moved his army up. The Nubians excelled at moving about without being seen, especially at night.

At sunrise, when the Assyrians were readying to march, Ramtouses' army sprang forth, and with insufficient protection from their previously damaged wall-of-shields, the Assyrians were caught by surprise. The battle surpassed any of the past days. By midday, the Assyrians fled in all haste; Ramtouses' army had defeated the mighty Assyrians. The men of Pharaoh Taharqa had prevailed.

"The gods are with us," both the generals and common soldiers shouted.

The officers praised Ramtouses as if he was the pharaoh. The next two days they buried the bodies of their dead and retrieved the iron weapons abandoned by the Assyrians. On the third day, Ramtouses threw a banquet for the victory. He sent messages back to Memphis with the good news.

During the festivities' dancing and singing, Ramtouses' mind drifted to thoughts of Naamity. "I am so near to her. She is less than a day's ride."

Ramtouses talked to his age-group comrades about her. One of them said, "Let's go see her."

Ramtouses replied. "She won't want to see me. It will restore the feelings of loss neither of us wants to endure."

Another said, "You don't know that. You are a hero, a hero over all heroes. Some of us will go with you. We will pose as merchants."

Ramtouses said, "You don't know how badly I want to follow your idea."

Another one yelled, "Let's go tonight. We can be back in a few days. No one will blame you. You have done something no Egyptian army has been able to do."

Ramtouses threw up his arms, "Let's do it." He left his comrades to speak with the first general who'd allied with him. "I need to make a trip, a personal one. I will return in three to four days."

Puzzled, the general said, "The people will be waiting for you in Egypt. Is there anything more important than seeing their faces?"

"I know," said Ramtouses, "but this is a journey I am compelled to make."

The general studied Ramtouses' face, then he smiled. "Anything you say, Commander."

⁑

So, the four men rode off for Jerusalem. Along the way, they found a caravan headed for the city and traded for new clothing, so they would not be recognized as Egyptian soldiers. After reaching the city, Ramtouses said, "I will do the talking. I understand the language quite well."

Many people were out in the street. It was a market day. They came upon a man selling apples and purchased a few.

"Merchant, are you from the city? We are here to trade and know no one."

The apple seller said, "I just come here to sell my fruit. If you want information about someone, go in that shop. That family knows a lot of people around the city."

Ramtouses walked into the shop alone, not wanting to frighten anyone. He looked at the waistbands and head-wear displayed. "I am looking for a new head cover," he said to the shopkeeper.

"I have many. All different styles," the shopkeeper answered. "Here, come over and look at these."

"That's what I want," said Ramtouses. "I will take this one." He placed his finger on his chin. "You know, long, long ago, my father told me of this woman who became a hero. She went into the Assyrian camp, killing the general and returning to the city. You look old enough to remember that event."

The store owner became very excited. "Yes, yes. I was just a boy then." His eyes lit up. "Never has anyone ever done anything like that in all the history of our fine city."

The store owner continued to talk about that terrible time. After a long while, he finally stopped.

"What a great story!" Ramtouses said. "Are these women still around? I surely would like to meet them."

"Which one?" the shopkeeper asked. "There were three. Judith, what a woman! I have no idea where she went off to live. She withdrew and lives in seclusion. The other two still have families here in the city."

Ramtouses asked, "I believe one of the two died five years after her daughter was born, is that right?"

The shopkeeper said, "Yes, you are correct."

"I really would like to meet the daughter."

"Well, here is where you go." The shopkeeper walked over to the door. He pointed his finger. "Go down to the statue. Turn right. Follow the street to the end. Their house will be to the right."

Ramtouses thanked the man over and over. The keeper watched Ramtouses walking. He became suspicious when he saw three other men join him. He thought, *Maybe I should not have told them where she lives.*

He called his son from the back. "Go down to Naamity's house and tell them strangers are coming."

The boy ran down to the house before Ramtouses arrived.

Their house was well kept and had a wall around it in order to keep intruders out. This family was loved by all. Even the king, Manasseh, gave them respect. He could never be sure of their belief, so he did not press the matter.

The boy banged on the door. Naamity opened the door. "What is wrong?"

The boy, catching his breath, said, "Strangers are coming. In error, my father told them where you live."

Looking toward the front gate, Naamity did not see anyone come up to the front gate. She pulled the boy inside.

Her uncle heard the chatter. "Naamity," he said, "these could be agents from the king. Go over to your friend's house down the street."

Naamity and the boy exited the rear door.

Ramtouses alone approached the gates. He saw a man standing at the door of the house. "Hello, good man," he said. "My name is Ramtouses. I am looking for a young lady named Naamity. Do you know of her? Is she here?" Ramtouses looked in both directions then entered the gates.

"Naamity has left the city. I have no knowledge of her return."

"Who are you?" asked Ramtouses.

"I am her uncle."

Ramtouses looked very disappointed. "Are you sure she has left? I have traveled from far away to see her." He shook his head. "If you know anything, please tell me, I implore."

The uncle held his hands open. "I know nothing. I am so sorry."

Suddenly there was a lot of commotion in the streets. Ramtouses walked back to the gate and looked out. Some of the people were yelling. "The Egyptians have defeated the Assyrians."

Ramtouses stopped a man. He said to him, "What is the problem? That should be good news."

"Oh no," said the man. "The Egyptians hate us for siding with the Assyrians. They may come here next. Look. Soldiers are gathering. The gates will be closed."

Ramtouses ran to his comrades. The four of them got to their horses, hoping to flee the city before the soldiers locked the gates.

Naamity, out of curiosity, returned to the house to get a look at the strangers. At this point the commotion had started. "Where are the strangers?" she asked her uncle.

The uncle said, "They have just left. One was very upset not finding you."

It suddenly struck her. "Did he say his name?"

"I believe he said Ramtouses."

Naamity screamed. "Ramtouses!" She took off running toward the gates. "Ramtouses, I am here."

She ran all the way to the gates; they were closed. She found a peep hole and saw a group of men riding away. "Ramtouses! I am here."

Over and over she screamed to no avail. Ramtouses did not hear her.

She curled up on the ground. Her uncle walked up to her. She was shaking all over. She looked up at him. "Uncle, why does love have to hurt so much? What have I done to deserve this? Is this a test of my faith? Do I have to live this kind of life?"

She cried and cried. Her uncle said nothing. He finally helped her up from the ground and led her home.

Ramtouses returned to his command, they had waited for his return and everyone looked anxious to begin the journey home. For Ramtouses, the ride home was somber, but what a sight it was to see the army march into Memphis between the giant monuments and statues of the gods. He and his generals walked toward the palace. The people were all cheering and yelling.

Ramtouses was at the center and forward of the others. When they came near to Taharqa, they bowed down. Pharaoh Taharqa raised his hand, and the people all raised their hands, continuing to cheer. The Pharaoh approached Ramtouses and gave him his hand to kiss. Thousands of Egyptians jumped for joy. What a wonderful time it was to be an Egyptian, Nubian-Egyptian, or Ethiopian Nubian.

The army turned over thousands of iron weapons, including a huge pile of iron tips for arrows, gold and silver coins that could be melted and remolded into Egyptian coins, horses and other equipment—all spoils of war were collected.

⁜

Carnabrara sat with Ramtouses' age-group associates and thousands of others who had made the trip from Thebes. Pharaoh Taharqa held a banquet that night for Ramtouses and his generals. When Ramtouses and Carnabrara returned to Thebes, a second celebration awaited them with Dafori during the honors.

After all these wonderful happenings Ramtouses was not happy—his heart was longing for Naamity, and each time he sat alone her song would come to him. Carnabrara recognized his sorrow.

She asked him, "What is wrong, my champion?"

Ramtouses tried to hold his head high. "I met this young Hebrew girl for only a short period of time. Now I cannot get her out of my mind."

His mother embraced him. "You were really bitten."

110

She went on to say, "You are on top of the world. No one has ever done what you accomplished. Only the pharaoh's light shines brighter than yours."

Ramtouses smiled. She pointed her finger. "I think I have a solution to your problem."

She nodded her head. "I will let you know tomorrow."

That evening, Carnabrara showed up at the high priestess's temple. When Amenirdis received her, the two women came close together.

"Carnabrara, my child, I am so happy to see you again." She gestured with her hand. "Come. Sit down and tell me what is on your mind."

"Well, it is my son. He feels heartbroken over a young woman he met."

Amenirdis rose up with excitement. "Oh, that Ramtouses, the hero of all the land? How could anything be troubling a young man in his position?"

Carnabrara placed a slight smile on her face.

The high priestess continued. "I have it. I will be joyful to see him again. I am surprised you did not bring him to meet me when you and he returned from Memphis." Amenirdis rose, holding Carnabrara's hand. "Come. I have to make ready for his visit." Together they walked to the hall entrance. "Bring him after his morning meal. I have the cure for him."

Ramtouses and Carnabrara went to the temple the next day and were warmly greeted by the high priestess. "I am so happy to see you, the big general now, Ramtouses. The people are saying many wonderful things about you."

The three talked for a while about Ramtouses' military success. Finally, the priestess said, "I have a pleasant surprise for you, a gift for your unbelievable victory, for saving our people from utter disaster."

She clapped her hands and ten veiled young women came out into the hall. The high priestess took Ramtouses by the arm and escorted him over to the young ladies. "Pick the three you want. You can ask them to lower their veils before you select."

As Ramtouses walked along, looking at the girls one by one, he remembered that, on his eighteenth birthday, his age-group comrades brought a few unwedded sisters over to entertain him. What a wonderful birthday gift.

After carefully studying the group, he picked three of the young girls. The three would obey his every command and serve him without question. If he chose to, he could even take one or more for a wife.

He walked away, thinking, *I will never see Naamity again, so maybe I can will myself to be happy surrounded by these beautiful women.*

8

Thebes, Egypt

Carnabrara wondered if she would ever find happiness again for herself. She knew how painful love could be and understood completely what Ramtouses, her son, was going through. Dafori never came to her anymore, and there was no love in her heart for him anyway. She had three daughters by a man she had come to despise.

Pushing her troubles to the back of her mind, Carnabrara prepared to visit Amenirdis—this was the day Manni was to report to the priestess on his agricultural findings.

Before Manni was led into the temple hall, Carnabrara entered from another door and went to her usual sitting place. When Amenirdis saw the princess sit down, she raised her hand for the servants to let Manni enter. The report began. Carnabrara sat there, listening.

This is ridiculous! Here is the man I love. I am torturing myself, sitting here, listening to him every time he comes in to present his report to Amenirdis, just watching, and listening. I need more. I need to touch him, feel his strength.

Carnabrara rose to her feet just as Amenirdis concluded her business with Manni, causing the priestess to hold her hand in dismissal of him. She moved quietly across the floor, aware that Amenirdis had turned to watch her approach Manni.

Manni also noticed the high priestess's hesitation to dismiss him and looked in the direction she had turned. He saw a woman moving in his direction. *That is the woman who always watches from afar. What is she doing? She is walking toward me, ah, so slow and graceful.*

Manni looked back toward Amenirdis who kept her eyes on the woman.

Do I go? Stay? What is happening here?

He could not move even should the priestess dismiss him. His eyes fixed on the woman who had always secreted herself to the back of the room.

Is this the day she will reveal herself? I only see her eyes above the veil she wears.

She stopped within an arm's reach of him and just stood there, no movement, no words. Her veil fluttered with each breath taken, her eyes glistened as if she was about to cry.

What is it that makes you sad, beautiful woman? My own heart is beating fast, my mouth feels dry. He raised his hand to his throat, twice. *This woman seems to awaken strange feelings in me.*

She reached out and touched the arm he had raised, running her fingers along it. Manni suddenly began to feel aroused. *There is something about her I recognize.*

He said, "Do I know you? Please tell me." She quickly withdrew her hand and began to move away. Manni reached for her. He whispered, "Please, tell me, what is all this."

Amenirdis rose from her seat and pointed to the door. "Thank you for your report, and I will see you next time." He left the temple.

Amenirdis went to Carnabrara and embraced her. She stood there and covered her face and said, "I am so sorry. You have been so good to me. I do not want to do anything foolish."

"Don't worry, my child. When the time is right for you to reveal yourself to him, I want to be there. You and Manni have become symbols of a life I can never have. I can never have a mortal man. I am the wife of the god, Amun. And it gives me pleasure to watch your story unfold."

The two women walked around the temple in prayer.

Kobina witnessed the entire event—the report, the approach to Manni made by the veiled woman, Amenirdis' observation—he had stood by the door mesmerized, watching.

She's a special woman, he thought, *there must be something between them.*

Ramtouses' duties with the army in Thebes kept him busy most of the time. One day, a few months after his return home when he and some of his men were eating their meal, a messenger delivered a note to him—orders from the Pharaoh Taharqa for him to return to Memphis at once.

Ramtouses packed his things, bid farewell to everyone, and began another trip to Lower Egypt, along with several age-group comrades.

When he entered the palace hall, Ramtouses found other leaders and generals already present.

He bowed and said, "I am at your service, Pharaoh Taharqa."

The pharaoh glanced around the room. "I brought you all here to remind you that Assyria is not dead. That defeat only opened their eyes to how vulnerable they can be. They are home now, licking their wounds and reassessing the war, but as sure as I am standing here, they will return with vengeance in their eyes." He yelled, "We must be ready."

He began to move among his military leaders. "This time when we win, there will be no other return. We will destroy their armies, press on to Nineveh, and burn down their homeland. We will become masters of their empire."

Taharqa continued to talk about war planning. At the conclusion of the meeting he spoke with Ramtouses alone. "What is Dafori planning?" he asked.

"After your stunning victory, it is very unlikely he will call up the hidden reserve forces he has in hibernation awaiting a great loss of your manpower. Because we did not sustain a greater casualty number, he will once again wait for the right opportunity—perhaps after a big battle when thousands will be lost."

Pharaoh Taharqa wrapped his arms around Ramtouses' shoulders, and together they walked onto the terrace. "Do not fret. Dafori will never be pharaoh, thanks to the trusted information I have received from you."

The Egyptian Nubians kept patrols as far away as a day's ride from their borders, guarding against enemy forces. They had spies traveling up and down the Mediterranean and toward Assyria. Pharaoh Taharqa's military personnel covered vast distances, as far away as Ethiopia, where the men were ready to move out to Memphis at the pharaoh's calling.

After the Assyrian army returned to Nineveh, humiliated by their defeat, Esarhaddon assembled his military officers for the debriefing.

In a calm voice, he said, "I just departed the temple of Baal. He revealed to me his forgiveness for the error his loyal subjects inflicted upon his glory by blindly running off to war without examining the enemy's strengths, weaknesses, or asking his blessing. 'Do not panic. I will not desert you in the face of your enemies,' he said to me. 'Prepare to march down there with the greatest army the world has ever seen. Build superior weapons and, above all, know your enemy. Hold your heads high. There is no doubt you will return my glory to me, more excellent than before.'"

The discussion went to planning a new invasion, where the Nubians had found success in their attacks, and where their strategies failed. Esarhaddon announced, "We have the best weapon building skills in the world. We designed the composite bow, a bow capable of striking its victim at a distance of 350-fold a man's height. We used it effectively at Lachish, but because it takes patience to make and requires excellent craftsmanship, we shied away from building it. Our god of war, Ashur, did not teach us to be victorious in war by sitting on our hands. Do the work that is hard, train thousands to make the composite bow."

Emperor Esarhaddon confessed he chose to stay behind during the conflict because he had not taken the enemy seriously. He walked around, shaking his head, and stopped near a window opening, pointing his finger to the south. "We know how to stop a chariot attack—the catapult sling. It's our offense against this kind of aggression. Where was the sling?"

His face reflected a puzzled look. "I understand we had only a few with us. Why do we have these weapons if we are not going to use them? I want thousands of catapults built—thousands. This time we must remember we face a sophisticated army, one not to be taken lightly, but one whom only Ashur can defeat."

The congregation of generals and military officers made not a sound. Silence filled the room. Esarhaddon watched the officers stand taller than they had when the meeting first began—shoulders held back, their heads lifted higher, convincing the king that their confidence and self-esteem had risen. Esarhaddon walked past them, looking into their eyes. The toughness of their gazes convinced him the will of Ashur was upon them—nothing less than victory.

Later, when the meeting was adjourned, the emperor stood with three of his top generals. "Now I will go and consult with the oracles regarding their support and blessing from the gods." As he expected, the oracles rendered him their blessings and full support.

King Esarhaddon recruited thousands, speaking to all, including able-bodied women and older people, beseeching them to put forth their efforts in the design and building of the composite bow, the construction of large and improved catapult slings, and the creation of large chariots able to carry three or more bowmen and a driver.

Again Esarhaddon demanded large tributes from his vassal states. This time, not to rebuild Babylonia, but to supply the raw materials needed to build weapons. Even the provinces made contributions. Esarhaddon reviewed each state payment and discovered Judah had once again failed to meet the quota demanded from them.

Esarhaddon determined to visit Judah. "I will send Manasseh a message informing him of my arrival."

Manasseh, upon hearing the news, declared the city would receive the emperor with warm welcome.

In early spring of 670 B.C.E., King Esarhaddon prepared to meet with several of his generals and officers. He asked them, "I understand my armies are eager for retaliation. Is what I am hearing correct?"

One officer stepped forward. "We have completed the building of thousands of catapults, bigger and stouter than ever before."

Another spoke up. "We have hundreds of new chariots capable of carrying up to five bowmen."

Yet another officer said in a loud voice, "The composite bow is now the fashion of all the bows."

Esarhaddon listened as the checklist of improvements continued. He concluded by asking, "Are we ready to march?"

A unanimous agreement encompassed the hall as the men waved their arms, shouting the call of war, confirming that war was ready to begin.

King Esarhaddon raised his hands. "Quiet. Listen to me."

Everyone stood still.

"I am going to lead this army to avenge the insults placed upon Baal and his brother, the god of war, Ashur." His eyes were large as he looked around with his arms now akimbo. "The gods have entrusted their desires to me. I will be there to ensure their wishes are fulfilled. Leave this building and prepare—tomorrow morning we march."

With that, the meeting ended.

That night, Esarhaddon had all his military effects brought out to the camp of the generals where he slept. The next morning, he led the way as the army broke camp while thousands of Nineveh spectators waved and watched. Later that evening when the army movement for the day came to a halt, the generals met again to review their strategy.

Esarhaddon announced, "We will first recapture our vassal cities in the territory of Levant and severely punish them for their lack of judgment in choosing to abandon us for the likes of Pharaoh Taharqa. We shall kill the leaders of the rebellion and take the people back under our wing, as a bird would do for her chick that was lost then found again. Their seaports are invaluable to us. We will not destroy them."

Esarhaddon marched along the military road running across Syria and along the coast of Palestine. He conquered Sidon. This ancient Phoenician city was situated on a promontory jutting into the sea. Esarhaddon cut off the Sidonian king's head and sent back to Assyria a rich bounty—the king's wife, his children, gold, silver, precious stones, elephant hides, ivory, maple and boxwood. Following the fall of Sidon, he called for all the vassal states to send tribute to Nineveh—even those now rebellious. He threatened to attack Tyre, another state that had conspired with Pharaoh Taharqa. The King of Tyre gave all their treasures to save his city from destruction.

Emperor Esarhaddon thought, *this is the time to pay King Manasseh a visit. That vassal state never pays its full tribute. I will have no more of it. I am not my father. Manasseh will have no special privileges from me as he enjoyed in dealing with my father. I will send another message of my coming.*

Manasseh was sitting on his balcony when the messenger arrived. He worried whether or not Esarhaddon was now threatening Jerusalem, and nervously he read the message. A smile came to his face.

He said in a loud voice, "Emperor Esarhaddon is coming to Jerusalem."

The queen asked, "Is he coming to honor our beautiful city?" Manasseh ignored her inquiry and announced, "We will begin preparing the city at once for the Assyrian king. I must call together the elders. We ought to make Esarhaddon completely welcome." He rushed out.

119

The elders suggested ways to brighten their already lovely town by hanging flowers from buildings and walls. A great feast was planned. Soldiers rode around passing the news, making everyone aware of the mighty king coming in three days. People were expected to come in from near and far throughout the country to hail Emperor Esarhaddon.

Naamity's eldest brother was standing in front of his house when he heard the news and quickly turned to enter the house, only to hear his brother arguing with Naamity. "You must marry, my sister. You need a husband, someone who will protect you. Our brother will marry soon, as will I, and only our uncle will be left to care for you. He is old and needs help himself."

She sat with her hands in her lap. "I understand, but none of these suiters are men I wish to spend the rest of my life with. No man has made my heart flutter like the man from Egypt. I must have been out of my mind to let him walk out of my life as I did. Maybe the Lord was telling me he was the one. I sometimes hate myself for that one moment in time." She held her head low and continued. "I can only hope he will try again to find me. I pray to the Lord that he will."

"Don't be silly. That man will never come back; I only want to do what is right for you."

The older brother interrupted. "The king has sent word that Emperor Esarhaddon will be here in three days. We must turn out in our best clothing."

Naamity scowled. "King Manasseh is of two minds. He treats his people like dirt and then wants us to act as if things are delightful because his beloved Assyrian emperor is coming."

Her younger brother who argued with her now agreed with the one who had delivered the message. "The king has at the least saved our nation from destruction in a war we cannot win." He walked around the room and continued. "I will join those who greet the Assyrian emperor."

"It seems like he has given us a choice," the older brother responded. "So, Naamity and I choose not to be there."

"And you too speak for me?" Naamity shook her head slowly, and sighed.

On the day of Esarhaddon's arrival, Manasseh waited on his throne above the steps leading up to the palace. Assyrian soldiers marched into the city before King Esarhaddon while thousands of onlookers lined the main street leading to the palace. When Esarhaddon's chariot, drawn by four golden horses, stopped at the foot of the staircase, the Judean king stood, walked down the steps, and came before the Emperor of Nations. Esarhaddon put out his hand. Manasseh knelt and kissed it. A load roar came from the crowd and Assyrian military personal.

King Manasseh lead the way as the two men climbed the steps to enter his beautiful palace with gold and silver around the base of each column and floors tiled with ivory.

A lavish banquet feast in honor of Esarhaddon was well attended by all that evening, including the emperor's generals and military officers present. It lasted late into the night.

The next day, from Manasseh's balcony, the king of nations addressed the Judean people gathered in the huge courtyard beneath it. His speech was short and to the point.

"Jerusalem is similar to my beloved Nineveh in splendor and beauty. You are fine, upstanding citizens. It is your hard work that keeps your country among the elite. It is a joy to know that you have a choice to worship Baal and all the Assyrian gods."

When he withdrew, cheering and screams of his name were long lasting.

The next day when the Emperor and Manasseh were alone, Esarhaddon let the Judean king know just how he really felt. "What do you think of me as ruler of the entire world? Have you ever taken the time to know my mannerisms? My likes and dislikes? Ha."

Manasseh had a surprised look on his face and said nothing.

The Emperor continued. "You think because you have adopted our gods and aligned with us, manifesting yourself above others in this area of the world, you can fall short on your tribute. I am not like my father. You will learn as you get to know me. I am a man of my word. If I say to you I desire the timber of one thousand trees, I will expect that amount— nothing more and nothing less. Do you understand?"

Manasseh dropped to one knee. "It will never happen again, my master."

Thinking of his obligation to his men of war, Emperor Esarhaddon departed early the next morning. While travelling, he contemplated the time spent in Jerusalem.

The kingdom of Judah is well recognized in this region. When I was speaking to the Judeans, the streets and courtyards should have been overflowing with people, but they were not. I have never been so humiliated, not that I can remember. Does he think I am blind? Many of his people still worship their one God. I need to make an example of him, make it clear to all in the region that no one is exempt from my power. I will stop there on my return—this time to reprimand him severely.

⁂

The spies and scouts of Pharaoh Taharqa had been watching the Assyrian army's every move. Upon realizing the size and sophistication of Esarhaddon's command, Taharqa had second thoughts of going out to meet them and determined it best to fight the Assyrians in their homeland at a favorable location.

King Esarhaddon expected the Nubians of Egypt to meet him before he reached their homeland. When he did not locate them coming up from Egypt, he continued across the desert.

Pharaoh Taharqa knew the desert well. Thinking the Assyrians would come straight toward them once they knew their location, he set up camp just inside his borders across from an area known to be inhabited by deadly scorpions and highly poisonous snakes.

The Assyrian scouts found the Egyptian Nubian camps, and Esarhaddon moved his army straight for them. With only two days' travel left in the hot desert, the Assyrians elected to hurry their pace in hopes of reaching a terrain with less dryness. Without warning, dreadful and dangerous vermin attacked them. They now found themselves fighting an unforeseen war with the environment, stomping the scorpions and slicing the snakes into pieces with their long swords. It appeared the hot ground was covered with them like ants.

It was a short battle the Assyrians won but not without a costly payment, losing well over a hundred soldiers. Any man who'd been bitten by these killers had to be left behind, dead or dying.

Taharqa's plan was successful, but it served only to slow down the aggression of Esarhaddon, not stop it. His forces gave way to the marching men of Assyria, and left them unopposed only as far as a place called Ishupri, where Taharqa commanded the Nubian and Ethiopian forces himself. Ramtouses commanded the troops from Upper Egypt.

It is a warm morning, Ramtouses thought to himself, *no breeze in the air. Our Nubian army is posed for the fight along a slightly elevated plane, forcing the opposition to come up after us.*

As the morning mist slowly lifted, the Assyrians' gray shields could be seen faintly in the far distance, moving uninterrupted toward them. Ramtouses and his men watched as they drew closer, singing the Assyrian song of war.

The Egyptians had discussed their strategy knowing the Assyrians would be aware of the results from their last meeting in war. The first phase of the operation was to exchange arrow attacks and irritate the enemy before any serious maneuvers.

However, to the Nubians' surprise, the Assyrians stopped long before coming into the Nubian arrow range.

For a short time, an eerie quiet hung in the air. Animals fell silent, knowing instinctively danger was lurking, so the silence of nature added to the stillness as the two military mights stood before each other unmoving. Abruptly, first one then hundreds then thousands of arrows came raining down on the Nubians from a shooting distance much farther away than anything the Nubians could manage. The composite bows made it clear who had the advantage. It was an agonizing type of attack, one that left the Nubians and their Ethiopian comrades protecting themselves at all times—adding to the terror, an occasional cry from a mortally wounded soldier was heard. This was a psychological victory for the Assyrians. When men are fighting, fear has little time to enter one's thoughts—training and skill prevail in their minds. However, when they are continually defending, they cannot mount an offense, or attack and fight—their training and skill remain untried.

Ramtouses quickly recognized the impact made on his forces and went to the Pharaoh. "We must attack even from this great distance, not to challenge the pavis walls but to get within range to exchange arrows."

"Go ahead," commanded Taharqa.

"I will signal for the ramming chariots and cavalry to fake a charge in order to draw attention and give the infantry a chance to move up." Ramtouses left to implement his ploy.

The false maneuver began with the cavalry leading the way. Then ramming chariots mixed in with the cavalry, followed by thousands of brave fighting men charging toward the Assyrian lines of defense.

The Assyrians expected a full attack and readied their pavis linkage. Esarhaddon gave the command to let fly the large stones mounted on the catapult slings. This weapon was designed to stop the ram chariot warfare; Ramtouses watched from his vantage point as the boulders rained down from the sky as deadly obstacles on his chariots and cavalry. He halted the charge after the Assyrian army showed its hand with the catapult slings; he now knew what they would do the next time they were faced with a ram chariot assault from Egypt.

The maneuver to move his Nubian archers within bow range was successful, though they suffered many casualties in the process. However, they now equaled their opponent's capability of delivering a barrage of arrows. It was like swarms of fireflies darting past one another in the evening sky, only it was daylight. This type of fighting continued for the rest of the day. The Nubian Egyptians and Ethiopians had the larger number of bowmen. Still, with their composite bows and catapult slings, the first day of battle clearly went to Esarhaddon's forces.

The pharaoh's army had to endure a heavy bombardment of arrows and sling boulders just to get within range of their adversary. By the end of the third day, the Nubians looked humiliated and demoralized. Everyone knew their forces could not repeat the first three days. That night, Ramtouses and his generals gathered in the presence of the pharaoh.

"How do we correct this dilemma we find ourselves in?" Taharqa asked.

Ramtouses spoke first. "This time when we bring our cavalry into the fight, we will not withdraw but continue the attack until they bring up their cavalry in full force to keep us away from their front lines.

"The ram chariots will follow and concentrate their attack on the center wall. The aerial assault will have to slack off to keep from striking their own men. Our infantry will move up and throw flaming spears into the center of the wall of shields."

No one knew whether or not this strategy would prove successful, but no other battle strategy was voiced, and Ramtouses' battle plan was accepted.

The center of the pavis wall was breached, allowing Pharaoh's fighters to enter. It stalled not long after, and a lot of fighting occurred in that area the rest of the day. Surely this day went to the Nubians. However, Esarhaddon's men were prepared for further attacks resembling that day's battle and brought in several units of heavy spear personnel the following day to increase the protection of the center wall area. The heavy spears provided greater defense against attackers rushing the pavis wall. When the Nubians came within range, the Assyrians let fly their heavy spears, the large iron shafts were meant to disable the protective shields of the enemy.

Even though the Nubians and Ethiopians carried big and thick shields, the heavy spears did not lose their effectiveness. Thousands of these weapons sailed over from the Assyrian lines, randomly lodging into war shields of the charging men. Because of the additional weight of the heavy spear now protruding, the shields proved to be more burden than protection.

The battle favored Esarhaddon that day.

Ramtouses and the generals gathered again that evening to devise another plan for bringing down the wall of shields— instead of pushing against it in hopes of physically pushing it down, they would pull it down.

This time Taharqa's men threw hooks attached to long ropes, hooking the shields and pulling them over. The Assyrians, not expecting this, fell vulnerable to the hook and pull maneuver. When several areas left the interior exposed, the Nubians were able to penetrate the Assyrian line of defense, but quickly reached a point where their advance stalled again. The carnage was intense and carried over into late evening before the two forces withdrew, helping many wounded off the fields.

The Nubians suffered the greater losses that day even though they breached the pavis wall—the Assyrians had deployed too many weapons.

The following days were a repeat of the same action, concluding with similar results. Pharaoh Taharqa's army could only briefly engage the Assyrians within their ranks. Pavis shield bearers quickly cut the ropes of the hooks, avoiding the collapse of their wall of shields and sealing the victory of that day's battle. Esarhaddon succeeded in slaughtering thousands with arrows, slings, heavy spears, and his cavalry horsemen with a furious battle at their pavis wall late in the day.

The brave men of Nubia lost so many that when war began the next day, the Assyrians were able to force them into a retreat to the point they lost their advantage on the sloping hills.

That day the two armies paced off on flat ground. Assyria moved to within range of the composite bows and opened fire. This continued for hours while the Nubians of Egypt and Ethiopia could only attempt to protect themselves as the arrows continued to rain down.

At the meeting that evening, Pharaoh Taharqa asked, "What can we do to slow down or stop them? I have run out of options."

Ramtouses stood slowly. "Perhaps there is something we can do that will have a dramatic impact on their morale."

Ramtouses walked over near the pharaoh with a confident posture. Facing him, he said, "I have to kill their Emperor Esarhaddon." All eyes were on Ramtouses. "I will face him in single combat."

The generals murmured their surprise.

Ramtouses raised his hand to quiet them. "The moment he goes down, we must rally and charge them, give them no time to absorb the shock of their fallen king, their god among men." Ramtouses' eyes grew large. "We will drive them from our lands then annihilate them all."

Loud, boastful reactions ignited among the officers.

The pharaoh welcomed him with open arms. "I wondered about such a match, knowing we have the best swordsman

127

in the world. It is your choice, not my command." Taharqa embraced Ramtouses and said, "I love this man as if he were my own son."

The Nubians displayed a swagger not seen in recent days as word spread throughout the entire camp.

After things settled down and Ramtouses sat alone in his tent, he began to wonder about the possibility he could go down the next day.

Ha, how often do I think of Naamity, so beautiful and so peaceful, singing with joy of her God and her love for me. If misfortune comes to me, I want to ask my father's and Naamity's God for aid in the hope that I, my friends, and family might be with them in His kingdom.

The next morning, after preparing for another day of hostilities, the Nubians crowded together, and Pharaoh Taharqa together with five generals stepped forward from within their ranks, stopping at a short stone's throw from their men.

The Assyrian officers saw them dressed in full military uniforms and assumed Pharaoh Taharqa wanted a consultation. Their army came to a halt.

Three of Esarhaddon's officers walked forward toward the Nubian force to hear the pharaoh's offer.

Taharqa said, "The time has come for the gods to reveal whom they have selected among men to be champion over all in the art of war."

The Assyrian generals frowned. "Is that your best offer? We will deliver your message."

They hurried back into their ranks.

Quiet ruled—no sound of dying men, no arrows zipping through the air, or horses galloping to the fight. The morning seemed peaceful.

King Esarhaddon received the message, remarking, "I am called upon once again to prove that I am master in all arenas of warfare. It is the gods' will that I demonstrate their gift bestowed upon me. Let it be known it is Baal who has granted me the wisdom and Ashur the strength to overcome our enemies."

He rode his chariot toward his tent "I will dress in a uniform more fitting a king when butchering an adversary who opposes our gods."

The generals knew Emperor Esarhaddon's character would not let him pass up this opportunity, even if they advised against it. The Assyrians were winning the war—a personal duel was not needed, especially considering it could affect the army's morale.

Both forces moved up closer, each expecting to see their leader achieve glory.

Esarhaddon was first to break ranks, riding his chariot drawn by four golden horses. He stopped between the two armies, waited for a few minutes, and looked back at his men with a big smile on his face. He raised his arm before demanding, "Where is your hero? I am waiting."

Ramtouses came forth parading two black and two white horses before his chariot. Every eye was on him as the soldiers created an opening while he rode through the thick crowd of Nubians. He felt proud and confident thinking this fight was larger than two men clashing in battle. *My nation shall fall if I don't find victory. There is not a man alive who can win over me with the sword. I am invincible. Now I shall prove it.*

Ramtouses' horses broke ranks toward Esarhaddon. In no hurry, the two men moved toward one another, each sizing the other up as they approached. When they came within a spear's throw, they turned their chariots to form a diminishing circle that brought them ever closer to each other.

Now they could see the other's stature—Esarhaddon had dressed completely in black body armor covered with highly polished iron plating, the squares sewn into the garment like a checkerboard. He was very tall. His helmet sported a white column of horse hair from front to back with a long, white horse tail protruding from the lower back of the helmet. Truly, his appearance made him look indomitable.

Ramtouses wore a jacket and skirt made from tough animal hide with gold and silver plating sewn upon it and surrounded by an assortment of sparkling adornments that reflected the rays of sunlight. Ostrich feathers encircled his waist over his lower armor skirt. His helmet spouted ostrich feathers in all directions. He was a fearsome slight to behold.

At a short walking distance, they stopped and climbed down from their chariots. Ramtouses noticed the horse to his near side quivered as if he sensed danger. He rubbed and patted the steed as he walked by. The two men of war circled each other on foot, closing in until they stopped and stood staring into each other's eyes.

Esarhaddon spoke. "What is your name, so I will know what to write when I add you to my trophy collection?"

Ramtouses understood enough of the Assyrian language to answer, but Esarhaddon did not understand Nubian Egyptian. "I am Ramtouses," he said. "Let the armies bear witness to which of us is greater in battle."

With those words both men drew their swords and slowly closed the gap between them.

Ramtouses had armed himself with an iron sword from among the spoils of the previous engagement with Assyria. After practicing with the new weapon, it had become easier to handle, familiar in his grip.

The swordsmen charged one another, and the clash of the iron blades rang out so loudly all could hear. The soldiers of both armies moved in closer, hoping for a quick victory for their hero.

The two experts danced and sparred with lightning speed, taking vicious whacks at each another. Esarhaddon's sword whistled as it sliced through the air again and again until it finally struck the shield of Ramtouses who retaliated with swings, first one way then the other. Esarhaddon's agility aided him in avoiding his enemy's sharp-edged sword.

The fight went on and on with no advantage to either, and it appeared stamina would choose who would be triumphant.

When the two skilled fighters saw there was no upper hand to be had, they changed their method of attack. They stood their ground, standing toe to toe, exchanging mighty whacks, banging their two deadly weapons in an effort to wound the other. Ramtouses was struck on the helmet but continued to fight. Esarhaddon took a blow to his body armor that dislodged some of the iron plates.

Both men began to display signs of tiring, and their skills showed the strain. Each man knew he had to stay the course, for death would come to the one not able to move or strike his powerful sword.

The armies moved in even closer.

Pharaoh Taharqa spoke to his nearby officers. "I am truly amazed at the great battle these two men have demonstrated here today."

A short time later, the agony of weariness dominated the limbs of both—Esarhaddon lunged, and Ramtouses swung his sword at the same time, blocking the blow. Then he pulled away and thrust at Esarhaddon, his weapon penetrating flesh where the iron plates of armor had been knocked away. The point sank into the Assyrian king's side. Ramtouses withdrew the sword, seeing the tip covered with blood. He followed up with his assault, lunging at Esarhaddon, hoping to finish him off.

Esarhaddon was still swift enough to evade the next blow, and when Ramtouses moved past him, the king jabbed his mighty sword. The fearless Ramtouses was struck in his back in an area not protected by metal plates.

Ramtouses felt the sharp pain as the sword found its mark. As he was unsure of his opponent's situation, he staggered away as quickly as he could. His legs buckled beneath him, and he fell to the ground. Looking back, he expected to see

Esarhaddon bearing down on him—but instead Esarhaddon had also fallen and lay collapsed on the ground.

Ramtouses began to crawl toward this mighty man of war. Every reach, every movement brought Ramtouses sharp pain. His exhaustion was overwhelming, and the strain weighed on him so heavily, he felt as if his own weakness might defeat him.

The two military groups saw their leaders go down and broke ranks to race across the open plane. Ramtouses cried out with each movement. "Oh, most high God of Naamity and my father, give me the strength to reach this Assyrian dog to destroy him and save my people."

He could see both armies coming at all speed. And suddenly, a hail of arrows and spears blackened the skies as a mass of humanity collided at the dueling site.

Emperor Esarhaddon was shielded and moved away from the impact of the desperate soldiers. Ramtouses lost consciousness from being tugged and banged in so many directions. The two leaders were taken away from the melee as war raged on, more intense than ever.

At the midst of the fury there was no organized fighting, and the bodies piled up like fish caught in a net.

The grand total of fighting men lost in this one battle surpassed all the deaths sustained in the entire war effort—a massacre. As the sun hid its face beyond the horizon, the armies withdrew.

One general commented. "This is why it is advised against kings engaging in personal combat on the field."

King Esarhaddon felt responsible for the lives of so many fine soldiers lost in the killing brawl. His attendants constructed a bed that would tilt him upright in order to address his officers, without aggravating his tender wound.

They gathered next morning, and he said to them, "We are a strategically trained army with fighting skills that can be matched by no other. If I am willing to go into combat for the sake of my country and my men, then let it be for the right reason, meaning, when we have utilized all other tactics and fail, then I will gladly stand up again and face our enemy. I will not do battle for the glory of it in the future."

The officers felt proud to hear his words.

Ramtouses received the highest honor from Pharaoh when he announced, "I place you in command over all my Egyptian and Ethiopian forces. But, you must rest and recuperate now. Go back to Thebes. Be in the company of family as your wounds heal."

Taharqa granted Ramtouses' request to take his loyal comrades and other Nubians from Thebes with him on leave, and the following morning they watched their Egyptian Nubian brothers march away to continue the war effort. When the two military forces came near, an Assyrian general at the forefront of the troops called out to his enemies, "Let there be a four-day grace from the cry of war. Let us bury the dead and give homage to the many brave men who fought and died on this site."

The Nubians agreed.

Over the next four days the men of Assyria, Ethiopia, and Nubia-Egypt became aware of the wind, still blowing softly, and the chirping of birds expressing life around them. Their battling had smothered all signs of life other than that of the enemy, and too soon, the next day found them preparing for the resumption of hostilities.

An Assyrian general came to inform King Esarhaddon that the men were ready again for war, but upon entering the king's tent, he stopped mid-step, alarmed by what he saw. "My king, what are you doing?" he asked.

The king's dressers were preparing him in the uniform for war.

Esarhaddon responded, "I want the men to see me alive and well. Building their morale will give them more valor in the fight for victory."

The general pleaded "Your wound is freshly stitched. Movement at this time could cost you your life."

"Have no fear," he responded in a loud voice. "I'm fine and will only stand on my chariot and point the way."

King Esarhaddon's chariot could be seen among his officers high on a ridge. He waved his sword toward Egypt. The shield bearers looked proud as they marched forward, singing the Assyrian song of war.

Pharaoh Taharqa expected a stalemate between the two forces, because during the truce his men had built bigger and thicker shields to protect against the barrage of arrows from the Assyrian bowmen. A stalemate would work in his favor, considering the fact that he had the greater number of Egyptians and Ethiopian personnel, but after the war resumed, Pharaoh Taharqa's army was driven back to the walled city of Memphis.

An officer soon reported to King Esarhaddon. "Thousands are evacuating the city."

The king's expression hardened. "Go after them. Bring only the women and children back as slaves. Kill the others."

Thousands escaped the Assyrians' round-up as they fled south to Thebes, but one of Taharqa's many wives and her children were captured. They witnessed the mighty Assyrian army surround their beloved capital city as the soldiers brought up powerful catapult slings.

While observing the situation from the walls, Pharaoh Taharqa was grazed in the face by an Assyrian arrow. That night, following the battle, Taharqa and his top officers escaped through an underground tunnel built especially for the pharaoh's secret departure.

In the morning, five siege ramps made it to the high walls, allowing thousands of Assyrians to plow their way into the once beautiful city. They flung open the gates, and the slaughter escalated. The Nubian Egyptians were shown no mercy. Thousands died attempting to defend their precious city

Pharaoh Taharqa escaped with less than seven thousand of his once magnificent army. Thoughts of the certain deaths of many loyal companions refused to leave their minds as Pharaoh's men encouraged their horses to gallop faster on the flight from battle.

Taharqa spoke to his leaders. "Our only hope is to reach Thebes."

As they rode, he thought of the reserves Prince Dafori hid from him. *The Assyrians were able to defeat my mighty army in fifteen days. What might the outcome be like with Dafori's full support?*

Moving south toward Thebes, thousands of Nubian civilians joined them—older men and boys expressing their will to fight. Women and children too young to fight found refuge traveling with the men of war.

Thebes, Egypt

Prince Ramtouses, the commander of the Nubian armies, reached home while the war raged on in Lower Egypt.

Carnabrara came out to greet her son. "Oh, Ramtouses, I thought I would never see you again. There is no news of what is happening, and Dafori will tell no one of the war situation. I have been so afraid for you." She hugged and kissed her son. "I just learned yesterday of your being wounded and returning home. How badly are you hurt?"

"I was stabbed in the back, but I will recover, Mother." He moved slowly, his brow was dry and furrowed from the weeks of war and harsh living conditions, and when he spoke, Carnabrara heard deep concern for the country. "Worse than my wound, we are losing the war. If the fighting comes south, which I believe it will, we may all be killed."

Ramtouses and the princess sat together, both worried about the Nubian future. Carnabrara reached for his hand, it was hard and held numerous cuts and scrapes in varying stages of healing. "Tomorrow we will go to the temple and pray to Amun-re to stand by us in our time of need."

⁙

Manni and his friend Kobina were talking to a group of farmers about their irrigation systems when a houseman rode up shouting, "We all must leave. The Assyrians are winning the war and may be headed south toward us. All able men must join for a final stand."

The farmers quickly dispersed.

Manni looked to Kobina, "We must return to Thebes as soon as possible."

The gates were closed when they arrived at the city entrance.

The guard asked, "Who are you?"

"I am Manni. I bear the seal of the high priestess, Amenirdis."

The guard opened the gates and inspected the seal. "Come inside, hurry."

Manni turned to Kobina. "It is late," he said. "We will go to our abode and send a message to the high priestess of our early arrival before going to the temple tomorrow."

When the high priestess received the message, she immediately informed Princess Carnabrara of Manni's return and his planned report at the temple.

Carnabrara contemplated the recent events regarding the war and Ramtouses' injuries. She thought of seeing Manni give his report to Princess Amenirdis in the morning. *Is now the time to find out if I can bring you back to me?*

She entered her son's rooms. "Ramtouses, your father is here and will be at the temple tomorrow morning."

Ramtouses rose from his bed where he'd been recovering, focused on his mother as she walked across the room. "Will you see him?"

"Yes," she said in a low voice. "I will, but this time it will be different. He will want to see you after I tell him of your wound from the vicious dual between you and the Assyrian king." And she left the room, allowing no opportunity for discussion of her decision.

Carnabrara walked onto the balcony of her rooms and looked up to the western skies, finding the star of Ramtouses, or Manni, as he was now known.

She stood still for a long time looking at the star, feeling the chilly breeze swaying her gown back and forth, remembering the time she first met him—his pronouncement of love, his persistence to win her, her insistence to refuse him. Then, he had left. The pain of her deception which caused him to leave made her double over, even now, so many years later. But she searched for him and found him, and they had become one.

"Yet forces behind powers greater than us interfered with our lives." Carnabrara spoke aloud, surprising herself, then turned to re-enter her rooms.

She retired for the night, thinking. *If the Assyrians defeat the Nubian Egyptians, I want to be with Manni either in life or death.*

The next morning she dressed in her native Tungul Nubian clothing and arranged her hair to look as it had in years past, hoping Manni would remember it. She made her way to the temple at the hour she knew Manni would arrive. Inside she approached Amenirdis.

When Amenirdis saw the princess, her eyes grew large with surprise.

"What a difference! You are magnificent. I have never seen you in your native clothing."

The princess asked, "Do you think he will recognize me?"

"Carnabrara, don't worry. The gods are with you. Time will change us all, but looking at clothing from yesteryear can reflect as a mirror to our forgotten past." She answered quickly, knowing Manni might enter the hall at any moment. "And, yes I believe he will recognize you." High Priestess Amenirdis walked over to her seat of authority, her cathedra, and sat, leaving Carnabrara standing in the very spot where she last addressed Manni.

Moments later Amenirdis's guard entered, announcing, "Manni is here, and he wishes your audience."

"Send him in," Amenirdis replied.

Manni and Kobina entered the chamber. Kobina stood near the door, while Manni kept walking until he was within an arm's reach of Carnabrara who stood with her back to the entrance.

She heard him stop behind her. With her face held down, she turned around tentatively, like a cautious child. When she stopped and slowly raised her head, confidence began to build within her. Her eyes moved up to meet his, and she caught the first brief glimpse that swiftly changed when their eyes met.

Manni looked curiously at the woman, and then abruptly drew back his head, placing his hands to his temples. His mouth opened, then clamped shut, he ground his teeth, never taking his eyes from hers.

Her eyes glistened with tears.

In a quiet, whispered voice he said, "I see myself sitting on a low cliff watching hippopotami, I hear water flowing, women screaming." His voice became more intense. "'Ramtouses'...a woman is calling for me. I know her. It is Carnabrara, looking for me with great intensity. She is running toward me.

"She arrives where I stand and punches my chest with both fists over and over, wild with torment."

He paused and looked around the room. "What is happening to me?" Then the memory continued, and he relayed it aloud to the woman who stood before him in the center of the temple chamber. He saw only her.

"I catch Carnabrara's arms; she weeps loudly and says, 'Why have you done this to me? I love you. I love you, Ramtouses. Please forgive me.'" His voice was now loud. His anguish echoed around the room.

Manni pounded the sides of his head and turned in a circle, trying to understand what was happening to him. The two women and Kobina watched the transformation of Manni becoming Ramtouses, the father of Prince Ramtouses. Carnabrara's face was covered with tears as she held her hands together on her abdomen.

Manni spoke again. "She frees her hands and wraps her arms around my waist, then slowly slides to her knees, her cheek rests on the side of my thigh. I can say nothing. I know her pain. Love can hurt deeply. Her cries continue, and I hear her words 'Do with me whatever you want. I will never leave you.' I feel her trembling, and the weeping persists as I pry her hands from my legs and lift her up in my arms.

"She wraps her arms around my neck and rests her head against my chest. The loud cries subside into soft whimpers as I carry her. I say, 'I am here with you my love. There is nothing to forgive.' I kiss the tears on her wet cheeks. She turns and looks into my eyes, saying, 'I love you, Ramtouses. I will love you for all eternity.'"

Manni appeared uncertain when his eyes found her eyes again, but his voice was soft, yet firm, when he spoke.

"The spirit that brought us together has awakened in me."

He stepped close to her and placed his hands upon her shoulders. "When a person is open for love he must be willing to accept the consequences, which can lead to heartache."

The High Priestess said, "You are free to show her what has been hidden away in your heart."

Ramtouses' eyes were now glassy from tears. He gently lowered his arms, placing them around the princess's waist. She wrapped her arms around his neck—both wept. He rocked her from side to side.

"Can this be real? After all these years, can this be real?" he whispered to her. "How can you be alive and in my embrace?"

He gently began to kiss her wet face and neck and buried his face in her hair, recognizing her scent immediately. His kisses became more aggressive but amazingly passionate to her. Low groans escaped his throat.

Amenirdis watched, mesmerized by the change in her friend Carnabrara, as Manni's arms encircled her, holding her tight against his body, as if he would never let her go.

"Love her. She is yours," the priestess said. "Kobina and I shall leave the room. Stay as long as you wish."

She looked at Kobina and glanced toward the entryway with a slight tilt of her head to indicate their departure.

"We will leave them here. You can make his report to me in another chamber."

Kobina followed her out of the chamber into the back recesses of the temple and gave the account of Manni's activities—after all, he worked side by side with Manni and knew the farming projects well. At the conclusion of the report, the priestess asked him, "What is your story? I see you with Manni each time he has council with me."

Kobina smiled. "I have to say Manni is a comfortable person to be around. I met him one year ago, and I feel as if I have known him my whole life. His honesty is something you don't find every day. As for myself, I love the art of sculpture, making things with my hands. I am not a man who believes in the gods as you do. After my wife died, I did a lot of migrating. I didn't know which way to turn until I met Manni, a real friend."

They continued their conversation for a long time.

When the high priestess and Kobina left the chamber, the reunited couple stood looking at each other, moving their hands along the other's body as if feeling a need to prove their existence, to confirm their reality. He kissed her lips, her neck and earlobes, running his tongue inside them, pressing his face into her hair. She wore it bound down her back and shivered slightly as he undid the ties that held her hair captive, remembering the days of their courtship when she had worn her hair loose and free and he had loved it.

His kisses grew in ardor when she returned two for his one. She pressed her body tighter against him but soon pulled back and slowly removed his outer garment. Together, they gradually slid to the floor, and the soft sounds of love increased. His affection rose like the awakening of a sleeping volcano before it erupts, and Carnabrara had no control over her own feelings.

They lay together on the floor until late that evening when Carnabrara rose and led him to her quarters in the west wing of the palace, where again they found love. The servants brought dinner in, and for hours Carnabrara explained to him how her life had developed over the many years. They held one another as if their new reality might somehow be lost also, and finally, in the early morning hours, they fell asleep in each other's arms.

Carnabrara's love blinded her to the consequences if they were discovered. Caution should have been taken at all times, for spies were everywhere.

One of her servants saw the princess lying with the outlandish man and hurried to inform Prince Dafori. The servant said to Dafori, "Forgive me, my lord, for what I'm about to say."

"Speak up," yelled the prince.

"Your wife, the queen, is keeping the company of a strange man."

The Prince replied, "Is that so? Ha-a,"—rubbing his chin—"return to your duties. I will reward you later if it is true. Otherwise, I will have your head."

Manni awakened late that morning. "Carnabrara, let's leave this place and return to our home in Tungal. There is nothing for you here."

Carnabrara rose slowly and answered. "That sounds like a wonderful idea. The trouble is Ramtouses is loyal to his Nubian countrymen, and he will never leave them, and I can't leave him behind. He knows very little of the world you and I once knew." She lowered her head for a brief moment before raising it again sharply. "There must be another way for I will not give you up. Nothing will destroy our love this time. I will go to the prince and beg him to give me my freedom."

"And if he says no? He has the power."

Carnabrara stood. "Dafori has no use for me. It has been years since he has shown any affection to me."

Manni took her in his arms, and she curled into his warmth. "I feel so alive now. The love that has been in hibernation all these years has come forth."

Neither said anything further but held each other tightly.

At midday Ramtouses joined his parents for a light meal. This was the first time Ramtouses would see his father since Manni awakened from amnesia, and he was excited to become acquainted as father and son.

Ramtouses' wound had partially healed, but he still experienced considerable back pain. The two men met in a strong embrace for a long moment until Manni pressed his son away to look directly into his face. "Here I have a powerful son in the Egyptian army. What an honor."

They smiled at each other and sat down to eat. Just as the meal began, a commotion could be heard coming from outside her chambers.

A maiden ran in, screaming, "The prince is here with several of his men."

Ramtouses stood, immediately alarmed. "I did not bring my sword."

"But I have mine." Manni stepped in front of Carnabrara. "You are not yet fully healed and in no condition to fight."

Six of Ramtouses' age-group comrades were near the door when Prince Dafori arrived; he knew they were loyal guards of Carnabrara and immediately initiated a short skirmish, catching the guards by surprise. Three of them went down quickly. The other three ran inside and stood guard before Ramtouses next to Manni.

Dafori's men banged open the door and rushed in. Dafori strode in, looking as if he were a child with a new toy, sporting a very big grin on his face, but his voice sounded angry.

"Who are you?" he shouted at Manni. When no one answered, he continued. "How dare you come into my palace and sleep with my wife." He threw open his arms. "And to do it openly?"

He nodded, as if he had total control over the situation, and looking around at his men he said, "I can have my men cut you down with the clap of my hands." And as he said it, he raised his finger up high. "But I will not put you to death—just yet. Any man brave enough or stupid enough to insult me like this must have a powerful reason for this act."

Manni stepped forward and said, "I am the man who was to marry Princess Carnabrara when your people stole her away from me years ago."

Dafori laughed. "So you are the bush man who thinks he should marry a princess."

Ramtouses moved forward. "The pharaoh will have your head if you kill me and my family."

"I don't worry about Pharaoh Taharqa. He has his hands full trying to stop the Assyrians." He laughed again. "I have no anxiety when it comes to that dog who stole the throne from me. He will get what he deserves."

Carnabrara pleaded, "Please, Dafori, let them go. I will do anything you ask. I have devoted my life to you. What more do you want?"

Ramtouses said, "Don't beg, Mother. He is like a mad man full of hate."

Dafori walked around waving his sword. "I will tell you what I am going to do."

He pointed his sword at Manni. "I will fight you, just you. If you win, you have your freedom, Carnabrara, and your son. After all he's not mine. Ha, he's your son."

"I have no armor," Manni said.

The prince chuckled again. "What more do you want? Would you like for me to lay down my sword?" He said looking at his to his men, "If I lose, let them go. Swear it before the gods."

They swore and drew their swords to hold Manni's family and the comrades at bay.

Not being a trained swordsman, Manni realized his only hope would be to wear down the gifted Dafori. Dafori ran at Manni, swinging his sword left and right. Manni blocked the blow but could only put up a defensive fight. The match seemed endless as the prince hacked away at maximum speed, trying to wound or strike Manni.

When the prince showed signs of weariness, Manni came alive, suddenly exchanging hard clashes of iron on iron. Dafori tripped over his own feet and fell. Manni swiftly came above him, but before he could raise his sword for the kill, the prince yelled, "Kill him, kill him now."

One of his soldiers drew back a long spear.

A few days earlier Taharqa and his small army had traveled at top speed to get as far away from Memphis as possible. At a safe distance, they watched the red skies near the horizon reflecting the flames coming from their beloved capital. The pharaoh worried over the terrible trouble that he knew lay ahead for his nation. Each night as they traveled south to Thebes, he prayed to the God of War, Menthu, for help.

Taharqa hauled his army to less than a day's march to Thebes. Alone in his tent, he channeled his thoughts to a more pleasant time and how good it would be to see Ramtouses again. The pharaoh remembered when the brave officer first came to Memphis—*a bright young man with a happy face, eager to do my bidding. I knew I could trust him when he corroborated the information my spies and high-ranking officers had already delivered to me concerning Prince Dafori.*

The pharaoh's mind then returned to the moment at hand. He sent for a messenger. "Take this scroll to my officer in Thebes. Hurry."

The general who received the message from Taharqa read it. *Myself and twenty others will meet you at the city gates in one sunrise. We will be dressed as merchants—make sure the prince does not know of our coming.*

The messenger returned to the camp with his reply—*Dafori has not made an attempt to call up his reserves as yet. See you when you arrive, my pharaoh.*

Taharqa knew the reserves were loyal to him. His general had communicated to the other officers that there would be no fighting, Nubian against Nubian. Dafori had no knowledge of this.

The next morning the general arrived at the gate to meet Pharaoh and his party. The gatekeepers would often let one or two enter the city without a challenge but never this many during a time of war.

The general ordered, "Let the travelers in. The prince awaits them."

The gateman opened the gates.

The twenty were Pharaoh's most trusted and skilled fighters.

As they walked the streets, the people did not know them. Taharqa's undercover officer escorted them to the palace. When the high-ranking officer questioned the palace guards concerning Prince Dafori's whereabouts, no one seemed to know. The guards joined in on the search when it became clear he was not in the palace.

Pharaoh Taharqa removed his cloak, revealing his royal dress and soon everyone in the building knew the pharaoh's presence.

He instructed one of his men, "Place on my head my crown of war, the Khepresh. Then let us return to the streets of Thebes so everyone can see their living god, Pharaoh Taharqa."

He exited the palace with the guards as well as his military companions behind him.

When people saw him, they quickly fell face down on the ground, extending their arms out to him. They expressed praise in seeing Taharqa. At the foot of the stairs he turned and walked onto the street near the palace grounds.

Kobina worried about Manni, his close friend, spending so much time in Carnabrara's company. Feeling the danger, he decided to find him and tell him of his concerns. As he approached the west wing of the palace, he saw armed soldiers led by Dafori himself headed his way.

Kobina suspected he was too late, and, assuming the worst, he went no farther but sat down on the steps of the royal structure. He pondered—*What can I do? There must be something. I know—I will pray to Manni's one God.*

"Please, oh Mighty God of Manni, please save your true follower and his family. Only your miracle can save them."

During Kobina's plea for help he looked up, envisioning a figure dressed in the clothing of the pharaoh coming toward him.

Is this real? I have to find out for sure.

He ran to the figure, throwing himself on the ground at his feet.

He said, "My pharaoh, will you please save my friend Manni, his son Ramtouses, and Princess Carnabrara from Dafori? In his anger, he has come to kill them."

Taharqa yelled, "Get up. Show me where they are. Hurry"

Kobina rose from the ground quickly and ran into the palace with the pharaoh and his men hurrying after. Kobina pointed to the door as he ran, and Pharaoh's men burst it open.

Taharqa moved in immediately, took a spear from one of his soldiers, and just as Dafori's man was about to let fly his spear to kill Manni, the pharaoh's weapon struck the man in the back. He fell forward, mortally wounded.

Prince Dafori rose to his feet, yelling, "I am so glad you arrived in time, dear Uncle. Ramtouses and his father were plotting to assassinate me. I learned of the conspiracy and took action first."

Ramtouses was about to speak, but Pharaoh stopped him by raising his hand. "Don't say a word Ramtouses." Taharqa pointed at Dafori. "Take him."

He addressed Dafori's men. "You men will not be held accountable for your actions. You were only following orders from your master. Now that I am here you will obey my commands as you were sworn to as Nubian Egyptians soldiers."

Dafori's men joined with Pharaoh's. He went on to say, "Take Dafori to his chambers, and keep him under heavy security." He then turned to Ramtouses. "It appears as though I arrived just in time."

Ramtouses smiled. "That was a narrow escape. Never have I been so happy to see anyone."

The pharaoh embraced him.

"Pharaoh Taharqa, this is my father, Manni, and I believe you know my mother, the Princess Carnabrara. This man is Kobina, Manni's close friend."

Looking at Kobina, Taharqa said, "You should thank Kobina. It was he who showed me where to find you." Manni put his arm around Kobina's shoulder.

Carnabrara asked, "What will happen to Dafori? After a few tolerable years with him, he turned out to be such a hateful man."

"Power can turn to greed, and that can change anyone. I cannot have him killed outright. It would create a bad precedent—pharaohs killing relatives whenever they wish in order to remove any threat. I will leave it up to the high priestess, Amenirdis."

More of Pharaoh's army entered the city.

Most of the officers, without Dafori's knowledge, had remained loyal to Pharaoh Taharqa. The few who had not met a swift execution.

They called up the reserves of some fifty thousand fighting men, mostly cavalry. The total number of Nubians joining Taharqa on his retreat south, including the Ethiopians and Egyptians, added up to seventy thousand.

Taharqa discovered that thousands of refugees were flooding into Thebes. Many of them had traveled from as far away as Ethiopia, trying to escape the marching Assyrians.

Pharaoh had all the women and children, as well as those men who were unfit for war, diverted to the south toward Napata, the former capital of Nubia. Another ten thousand, mostly boys and older men, were gathered from the refugees.

While Taharqa was mustering his army and devising a plan of attack, Prince Dafori came before the high priestess, and she informed him of the charges.

"You are accused of conspiracy, plotting to unlawfully overthrow Taharqa's position as pharaoh. Also, you are accused of blasphemy, disrespecting the gods, choosing one as pharaoh, and not upholding the laws sworn by you to carry out Pharaoh's command, even with your life."

She then asked, "What have you to say to these charges?"

"Please let me live. I can go away, live in exile. Just don't kill me," he cried.

"The penalty is death, not exile."

Nothing was said for several moments. Then she said, "You have been found guilty. You knew the risk. Dafori, you will be beheaded first thing tomorrow morning. Take him away."

Pharaoh Taharga was told of the execution the next morning and he personally informed Princess Carnabrara. He knew the story well of how his brother had deceived the Tungul people into war, something that had to be done to save Egypt, but now the deception was over for the Tungul women.

"Dafori is dead. After all these years of being forced to live away from your kingdom, you are a free woman."

She hugged Manni and wept. Manni nodded to the pharaoh and said, "Thank you. You are a kind man. We will never forget what you have done for us."

Taharqa then said to Ramtouses, "I am sending you with your parents back to Tungul."

Ramtouses answered, "No," with a straight face. "I am a Nubian Egyptian. I know little of Tungul. Let my mother and father return there, but I want to fight and, if necessary, die with my countrymen."

Pharaoh responded, "I understand your feelings and would love to have you here fighting with your people, but you are wounded and can help very little. If you were in good health, we know where you would be,"—he opened his arms to Ramtouses—"of course with your men."

Ramtouses' voice was filled with disappointment. "I have comrades who are loyal to me, the sons of the virgins who accompanied my mother years ago."

Taharqa made answer, "If that will make you happy, yes, take your conrades along and all the maidens and their children who want to return to their homeland. I have no objections to that. Go with my approval."

When Ramtouses and his caravan made camp with less than a day remaining on their journey to the territory of Tungul, he asked his father. "Manni, my father, there is one thing I am most curious about. How is it you thought your past was that of a man called Grandfather? Mother knew right away upon hearing that name it was somehow connected to you."

Carnabrara smiled, adding, "Come on, tell him. My knowledge of Grandfather is limited, so I want to hear it too."

Manni sat back and begin to talk. "To tell you the truth, I don't understand how that happened, but as a child I grew up hearing many tales of my great-grandfather. My mother, your grandmother, told me many stories about her grandfather, and that was the only name we ever knew. The tales never seemed to end. I knew nearly as much about him as I did myself."

Manni raised his head and for a few moments seemed to be in deep thought. He shook his finger up toward the dark night sky and continued. "I have a story that all Nubians should know."

Kobina and some of Ramtouses' age-group comrades were nearby to hear.

"A long time ago,"—Manni spoke so all could hear—"my great-grandfather was a farmer, a very good one. He experienced years of good crop growth and periods of drought as well when he worked very hard to save his crop. He learned how to irrigate fields, fertilize the earth, and identified which crops grew better with less water.

"During his journey in the north, he found some shiny yellow nuggets that he discovered could be traded for just about anything. While walking on a road leading to Thebes, he encountered a caravan and when it was less than a large stone's throw away, he noticed a well-dressed man, whom he presumed was in charge, sitting on a beautiful, large horse-drawn chariot.

"He crossed the road and attempted to stop the prominent man's chariot by waving his arms, but one of the armed soldiers accompanying the caravan blocked him, yelling, 'Do not disturb my master.' But his master heard the commotion and directed his driver to prance the powerful horses close to mother's grandfather.

"'You, stranger,' the man said, 'why are you trying to approach me?'

"Grandfather answered the man directly. 'I travel through your land and to this grand city that I may understand more of your ways. Today, I respectfully declared my desire to trade some of my yellow stones for food, water, and a sorely needed bath—or, I would work for the same.'

"The man ordered a soldier to get one of the nuggets and bring it to him. He rolled it in his hand as if appraising it. He nodded his head of approval 'I am Ramtouses. Who are you?'

"'They call me Grandfather.'

"The man named Ramtouses invited him to have dinner with him that evening and stay with his servants for the night. Grandfather stayed with the caravan for several days and held many conversations with the nobleman, Ramtouses, sharing his extensive understanding of weather and crops. The man took a liking to Grandfather, and recognizing Grandfather's agricultural knowledge, he hired him without hesitation as an observer and adviser of his country's farming system.

"Grandfather earned many privileges though this powerful Egyptian nobleman. Ramtouses gave him a signet ring to identify himself as his official representative while he traveled through the land. He became a wealthy man and employed many people to journey and study with him. When he returned to his homeland many years later, he spent his time traveling from village to village and tribe to tribe, teaching farmers about the care of our land, including tools for easier and faster working of the soil.

"When Nutombi, my mother, became an orphan, Grandfather came back to his home village of Juba, claimed her as his own, and then resumed his teaching with her at his side. As Nutombi grew, her knowledge and wisdom of Mother Earth grew greatly also, and when Grandfather left the year she married, she passed down to her children all she had learned from her grandfather. This was a huge contribution to Nutombi and her children for they were known throughout Northern Africa, thanks to Grandfather's adventures. His skills saved the lives of thousands who may have died of starvation from the prolonged drought.

"The name Ramtouses was always kept sacred in her heart. However, after ten children I received the name. But as you all know, I'm today known as Manni and the bearer of that name is my son.

"When war came after the abduction of then Princess Carnabrara, most of Northern Africa was willing to join me in fighting the Ell. I earned some creditability when I became known as a lion slayer.

"And there you have it as I was told by my mother."

After hearing that story, Ramtouses said, "I want to learn more of my distant grandfather."

"You will." Manni smiled at his son and, with that, the camp turned in for the night.

The ruins of Dungola, Sudan, formerly known as Tungal.
Photo by Nubian Image Archive/Flickr

Tungul, below Egypt

A few weeks passed, and the travelers noticed an increase in vegetation as they came nearer to their destination. Abruptly, a faint sound of drums beating in the distance could be heard, and, immediately, there was a change in the air as Carnabrara, Manni, and the sixty-six surviving former maidens remembered Tungul, their home. Most of them were children from Tungal and all of them knew what the drums were saying.

Ramtouses heard his mother say, "We are within Tungul territory, and they think we are a band of strangers looking to trade."

Manni replied, "What a surprise we will have for them."

Carnabrara held her upper arms with her hands. "I feel so nervous but yet happy."

Manni walked over close to her and put his arm around her waist. "Our home will be a different place than the one we left so many years ago."

The caravan made camp that night, hoping to reach the capital city of Tungal by the next day.

As they drew closer, the drums grew louder and more frequent. By late afternoon, warriors could be seen walking at a distance trailing the Nubians from Egypt.

Ramtouses decided to make camp rather then enter this unfamiliar place. The warriors camped close to them without making contact, but before the sun fell below the hills and tall trees, a group of them came up and stopped.

Ramtouses accompanied his parents as they went to address them. He stood back and watched the interaction between his mother and father with the villagers.

"This is your moment," said Manni. "Tell them who you are."

Carnabrara stepped forward. "I am Princess Carnabrara of Tungul."

The guardians were perplexed, looking at one another. Finally, one said, "Princess Carnabrara is dead. Everyone in Tungul knows that."

Carnabrara went on. "I was kidnapped by Egyptians twenty-seven years ago,"—she pointed at Manni—"just before my marriage to Ramtouses. None of you were born then."

The leader of the group thought to himself this woman's knowledge of the Tungul language is too fluent for her to be an outsider.

He cried in a loud voice, "Princess Carnabrara."

He then collapsed to the ground, reaching out with his hands to her. The others immediately did the same.

"Get up. You men will camp here with us tonight. I don't want anyone to know I am here. Report on your drums that you will escort the strangers into the city at first light tomorrow morning. I don't want any preparation. Just as I will be vigilant to them, so also will they be vigilant to me. I want to see their reaction without warning."

The warriors were very excited and constantly bowed down to her. Early the next morning, Carnabrara and Manni led the way toward the cluster of villages making up the town of Tungal. Ramtouses followed closely, looking on. The chief guardian met them at the outskirts. He was an older man near the age of Carnabrara. One of the warriors ran up to him, pointing his finger at Carnabrara.

"This is our lost princess, Carnabrara."

The chief guardian tightened his eyes and held his hand up to shield the sunlight. He began walking to get a better look and when he drew close, he examined her up and down. After a few moments, a look of excitement crept over his face as he remembered the days of the zealous, carefree princess. His eyes grew large.

He turned and shouted, "Princess Carnabrara has returned."

He ran in the direction of the royal grounds. The people began to gather near them until soon hundreds were surrounding them. The princess raised her hands, and people began bowing to her.

Ramtouses, who had not seen anything like this before, looked on with amazement. *Never did I realize how important my mother is.*

Carnabrara made small waving movements with her hands, trying to indicate silence, and then asked, "Where is the king? Is my father still alive?"

The king, after being informed, quickly led a party of family members and elders to their location. He quieted everyone down before speaking to the princess. "I understand you to be the long-lost daughter of King Tasmeria. Is that right?"

"Yes. I am Princess Carnabrara. My father is dead?"

"Yes. Your father died ten years ago."

A strong voice from behind the king said, "I am Queen Adanna the daughter of king Tasmeria. I remember the story of what happened to you but can't remember what you looked like." The queen moved out to the opening between the two groups. "How can you still be alive after all this time? Your story must be a fascinating tale—it can only be beyond belief."

The Shaman called to Carnabrara, "My dear Princess, it is you."

He spoke with confidence. "How could anyone forget the love between you and Ramtouses, a legendary story I have talked about for years? I am Azbo, the errand boy for King Tasmeria back then."

"Yes," shouted Carnabrara. "I remember you."

He continued. "I will let you settle in. We will discuss this matter further later."

The Queen ordered the guardians to escort the princess's caravan to the visiting area on the royal grounds.

Still looking at Carnabrara, she said "We will talk without end." She held a big smile on her face as she continued. "We will discover each other's journey through life."

The drums relayed a message signifying the return of their lost children of years past. Word spread, and the surviving relatives of the hundred virgins who were also taken began to gather. People were coming from all around, congregating at the foot of the royal grounds.

Carnabrara's cousin Adzua was sleeping when she heard the commotion and drums; she came from her abode and asked a woman on the road, "Is what I'm hearing true?"

The woman threw her hands up with excitement. "The princess has returned to us."

Hearing these words, Adzua nearly fainted. She dropped to her knees, thinking this cannot be. *It cannot be—she is dead.* She climbed to her feet. *I have to see for myself.* "Where is she?" Adzua yelled.

She ran as fast as she could, and when she saw her, Adzua threw herself at Carnabrara's feet, and wept with joy.

At first Carnabrara appeared to be startled. *Is this Adzua?* she wondered. The princess pulled at her clothing. "Get up from there. Let me look at you."

They looked into each other's eyes then joyfully embraced. Manni happily looked on, smiling. Ramtouses had no idea of what was going on but smiled anyway.

Carnabrara said in a loud, happy voice, "Adzua! I am so delighted to see you."

Adzua answered, "I asked the Ell to bring misfortune upon you, cast an evil spell on you. I wished I would never see you again, and then you were gone. I felt like it was my fault. For years I carried that burden and expected to die with it."

As she was speaking, so also was Carnabrara. "I am so sorry for the unkindly deeds I put you through. I was so imprudent, only thinking of my own selfish needs. No cousin can be as close as we were. We were more like sisters."

They both wept openly and without restraint, holding one another.

The king said, "I want the travelers to rest after their long, exhausting trip. In two suns we will reunite the families."

Carnabrara said to Adzua, "Until I become familiar with my surroundings, you will accompany me everywhere."

Adzua took her hand. "I will, gladly."

Two of Ramtouses' female cousins led him away to meet a large group of relatives. Manni found himself surrounded by young members of the royal family. They had heard stories of the man who came to Tungal and slew the man-eating lion.

On the third day, the women who were taken with Carnabrara were reunited with their loved ones. This brought about a happy time in Tungul the nation. Ramtouses felt out of place but enjoyed the constant attention.

Thebes, Egypt

In the north, Nubia prepared for a final stand. All males who were able to fight were gathered from all over Egypt and Ethiopia.

Meanwhile, the Assyrians found no obstacles before them as they marched south to Thebes. Emperor Esarhaddon felt obligated to remain with his forces. On a hot and muggy day, the two armies came near one another. Taharqa knew the landscape while he dictated the location for the battle. The terrain was littered with stones, but the Nubian horsemen were trained to fight under these conditions.

Taharqa hoped his cavalry would have the advantage, so the cavalry went out first. The Assyrians filled the air with iron arrowheads. The charge was executed with such speed and numbers, the Assyrians decided to oppose them with their own horsemen.

At first the Nubians had the edge on the rocky surface but could not sustain the attack because of so many lost in the arrow barrage, which was followed with the Assyrian long lances. The Nubian chariots came up to support. The battle went on all day before both forces finally withdrew.

King Taharqa realized his cavalry had suffered a terrible rout, but he still had one more feather to pull from his hat. The next morning the Assyrians could not find the Egyptian Nubians anywhere and assumed Taharqa had fled for his life. Surveying the countryside, they came upon a large forest. In order to get a better look, Esarhaddon camped near it overnight.

That morning he sent in a patrol. When they did not return, the Emperor moved in with full force.

The Nubians were hidden deep in among the trees when Taharqa gave orders to attack. Savage fighting went on for hours. A large number of Nubians were perched in trees, which gave them a slight advantage.

The Assyrian losses numbered in the thousands, yet Esarhaddon did not give up the fight. In the end, Pharaoh Taharqa's army was defeated. Even Pharaoh Taharqa received minor wounds, and only the few accompanying him were able to escape a second time.

The Assyrian losses on this day surpassed the total they'd sustained thus far over the entire campaign.

When the battle was over, less than a hundred of Taharqa's top officers and skilled fighters remained to make the journey south to Napata, Nubia's former capital. Over seventy thousand brave men were lost.

Emperor Esarhaddon and his generals felt masterful digesting their triumph, while at the same time, they sorrowed for the fallen.

Esarhaddon spoke to these officers. "I want patrols sent out to all parts of Egypt to make sure no forces of Taharqa remain."

The Assyrian king then returned to Memphis. He met with the native Egyptians, the Libyans, ancient Egyptians who had ruled their country for hundreds of years before the Nubians came to power.

"I need strong Egyptian leaders of men. I cannot govern this country and my vast empire. I will expect the people in charge to be loyal and trustworthy. There will be an agreement to become a vassal state and make annual payments to Assyria. I have people who will discuss the arrangements with you."

King of kings, Esarhaddon then withdrew and prepared to return to Nineveh.

Thebes, Egypt

While in the process of leaving, King Esarhaddon received information of a Libyan living in Saia, a territory of Egypt, who was considered a descendant of the once royal clan of Egyptian rulers. Esarhaddon traveled to the territories, met with him, and after a conference with him, was convinced Necho the First was his man.

"I want you to assume the position as head of state, pharaonic titular. I am also adding in the rebuilding of your capital, Memphis. You will follow my bidding."

Necho bowed. "It will be an honor to serve you."

Weeks later, Necho entered Memphis while the palace was still under restoration, and called for a meeting between Libyan leaders and aristocrats throughout the country.

He spoke before them. "Here is what we shall do. I want all Nubian works destroyed. Knock them down, take them apart stone by stone, and demolish all Nubian monuments."

Before continuing, he waited for his command to resonate with his audience. "The Nubians tried to imitate us, but we will not let their memory be that of Egypt."

The search went forth that any Nubian statues or hieroglyphics would be reduced to rubble or burned, leaving no trace of their rule or influence.

He continued. "Because Amenirdis was not an Egyptian native and fled with the Nubian population when evacuation came, our god Amun-re has no wife."

The priests came together in discussion. "We must select a Libyan wife for our great god Amun-re, who heard our prayers during the hours of darkness."

One of the priests suggested, "Let us go to the surviving Libyan royal clan and select a virgin from among them to be his new bride."

The priests sent out the word. "Bring all your virgins before us. One will be chosen for the honor of becoming Amun-re's new wife."

The brotherhood expressed their joy with singing to Amun-re, a bride was soon chosen, and the ceremony began at the temple of Amun-re.

Necho came out to the people and spoke these words. "This is not a pleasant time for Egyptians. The fear of a future Nubian invasion weighs heavy on our minds, and we must prepare now—every body and soul. Men, women, and children shall work feverishly to build a wall to protect our borders."

This gathering was held outside the temple, and thousands of people lined the streets, crowded the courtyards and buildings. He looked around in a slow, continuous movement.

"We will not be vulnerable to attack from the south. To guard the wall, a large number of sentry towers need to be built."

This photo depicts the ruins of a fortress wall built by the Egyptians to keep out invaders from the south, particularly, the Nubians. It gives us an idea of the sophistication of these fortresses for it was built on the remains of an even earlier structure. Photo by Institute for the Study of the Ancient World/Flickr

With his last words, Necho withdrew into the temple for days, praying for guidance, and throughout the city efforts to reclaim Thebes began.

Over the next few weeks, Necho went about the task of seeking recruits, and no matter how feeble or how stout, all boys and men found themselves in camps, training for war. He selected men from the ranks with military backgrounds to serve as leaders and officers.

Necho counseled with the new leaders. "I am assigning you men a very important and difficult commission, which is to identify the people who are defiled by Nubian blood. These people destroy the purity of Egypt. I have been informed that nearly a quarter of the population is of mixed blood. Those who are most like the Nubians will be taken into slavery. They will labor to assemble our weapons and work our fields as farming help. Furthermore, we shall bring in workers from Ethiopia to strengthen the work force. Listen to me—anyone suspected of even having some part of Nubian blood, even if it cannot be proven, shall not be taken as wives or husbands."

The Egyptian plan to expunge the Twenty-fifth Dynasty from their history became more of a reality with the passing of each day.

⁕

Taharqa was no longer Pharaoh over Egypt, but he remained King over Nubia. As King, he directed a trusted messenger who knew the territory well to go to the town of Tungal. "Deliver this scroll to General Ramtouses."

The message read, *Ramtouses, I send you bad news. The Nubians of Egypt are defeated. I, Taharqa, suffered minor wounds, and now dwell in Napata with thousands of refugees who retreated here. I planned a meeting that will include all remaining officers. Come at once to share your knowledge on the situation.*

Ramtouses received the message and prepared for his departure to Napata immediately. Upon seeing the chief general arrive, soldiers lined up to escort him to the palace to meet with Taharqa.

The general approached Taharqa and bowed deeply in respect. "Come close, my valued countryman," the king said.

When Ramtouses stepped forward, the king lowered his head and placed his arm across Ramtouses' shoulders. "We are a defeated people," he said, his voice was subdued as he continued to speak.

"For the moment, the gods have turned their backs on us. There are only a few high-ranking Nubian officers remaining." He shook his head slowly, sadly. "Thousands of our Nubian brothers lie dead on the bloody planes of Egypt.

"The Assyrians have decimated our world, yet we will return."

Listening to the king's words, Ramtouses' body posture reflected his feelings of anguish. "King Taharqa, what can we do?"

The king replied, "For now, nothing—our army is depleted."

To hold the discussion the next evening, the king made arrangements for a banquet that he'd been delaying while waiting for the arrival of Ramtouses. It was a wonderful meal and served to reignite some of the old enthusiasm to conquer the enemy, and afterward, Taharqa talked about the current dilemma in which they found themselves.

During the discussion, Ramtouses stood. "It is likely that war could come to us again. Without the production of raw materials, Egypt will struggle. Their greed for power shall dictate their actions, and with the support of Assyria, our home land could be invaded. We have no resistance to stop them; they will defeat us and make of us a nation of slaves."

Another officer stood. "It will take ten years or more before we have enough young warriors to nurture a formidable war conglomerate."

King Taharqa now stood. "Hear me!" And all eyes turned to him. "I declare that Nubia will rise again. The gods have spoken to me, saying they will be with us. In two years, we shall be ready to march. This was just a test to measure our faith. We will be back in Memphis sooner than you may think." He smiled. "When the gods favor us yet again, we shall be invincible."

He then adjourned the meeting. Most of the officers certainly did not believe Taharqa's words. Dumbfounded, they glared at each other, wondering if there was any sincerity in his statement. Two years seemed impossible. Within a short time and with very little conversation, the men cleared the hall.

Two days later as Ramtouses prepared to leave, Taharqa bade him farewell.

On his return home Ramtouses questioned his king's behavior, suspecting him of being tyrannical or even mad, but he did not consider anything other than giving his faithful support.

⋄

Nearing the territory of Tungul, tribesmen followed Ramtouses to the village where another group led him to the royal grounds. There, he discovered an unexpected situation. It seemed the royal family had gathered, and all the elders were present.

When Ramtouses approach the crowd, the shaman was speaking. "The laws of Tungul are clear. The oldest living offspring of the deceased king shall rule our nation. I have spoken to our ancestors, and they expressed to me, 'Go out and declare to the people that Princess Carnabrara, the oldest living daughter of King Tasmeria, should be named queen.'"

The king rose up to speak, but before he could, the queen put her arm before him and whispered. "Wait. This is my fight."

Already standing, she said, "I am Queen." She had an angry look on her face as she glared around her. "I, Adanna, have devoted my life to insure every citizen of Tungul the right to an orderly and healthy life. I choose Afolabi, an honest man with outstanding leadership qualities, to be my husband—your king. Why put our trust in the hands of a stranger—a person we know nothing about and a person who knows very little about us?"

The shaman responded. "Wait. We cannot ignore the laws set down by our ancestors in order to satisfy our own egos. Without them we will lose our heritage."

The queen placed her hands akimbo, shouting, "When the last shaman died, I was first to name you as his successor, and this is the way you repay me?"

Carnabrara jumped up. "Stop it. Stop it." She opened her arms. "I don't want to be queen." She wore a sad look on her face. "I would not know the first thing about governing our country." She paused again, looking over at Manni. "Ramtouses—Manni." When he stood, she placed her arm around him. "All Ramtouses, er, Manni and I want is peace and happiness, withdrawal from the troubles of the world. That is why we returned."

The shaman yelled, "I will not give up my crusade. Princess Carnabrara will be queen to respect the honor of our ancestors who demand their laws be observed. You will step down Queen Adanna."

The meeting ended with those words.

Ramtouses rubbed his chin in wonder after hearing the intense commotion. He later said to his mother, "Can the shaman force the queen to step down, even if you have no desire to be queen?"

"I don't know. I guess he can appeal to the people and create such an uproar demanding that I be queen that Adanna might step down. As you heard me say, I have no interest in becoming queen. My interest lies completely in my upcoming marriage to your father, Manni.

"In a few days, the queen will call upon the young virgins of marrying age, women who have never been picked, and those who have lost their husbands through death, to come before me. I will choose those who will participate in the wedding ceremony from that group. The reed gathering can start as many as seven days before the celebration and continue until the night of the new moon and the marriage."

Ramtouses looked at her in question, and she realized he did not understand.

"Reeds that are grown domestically cannot be used, my son. The virgins and I will locate and harvest the reed grass growing wild in the swamps or marshes and bring them back while singing our traditional songs of love. The girls will place them at my feet, before the festivities and dancing begin."

Ramtouses asked, "What have the reed grasses to do with the marriage?"

She answered, "This ancient ritual is how our virgins find husbands. Also, widows can re-marry if still in their child-bearing years but cannot participate in the gathering of the reeds. A husband may pick as many wives for whom he can provide shelter. The reeds guarantee longevity and a fruitful life of happiness. They also keep away evil spirits. Furthermore, the golden reeds, like the ones we were harvesting upon my kidnapping, are the crown jewels of the reeds. They add to good fortune and wealth and are also said to symbolize the power vested in life that reflects a deep spiritual connection between man and nature. From a multitude of earlier generations, our forefathers passed down how our original ancestor emerged from a bed of golden reeds deep in the bush where wild virgin girls were dancing. He mated with them, creating humankind—the Nubians."

Ramtouses responded, "I never heard that story of our ancestors. Do you actually believe it?"

She smiled. "After living in Egypt for such a long time and coming in contact with so many different gods, it is hard for me to know what to believe. One thing is certain, after what happened to me when seeking the golden reeds, it is hard for me to believe anything could be sacred about them. I must confess though, I was not a virgin at the time. I was already carrying you. Perhaps that is why terrible misfortune fell upon me."

"Mother, there is so much about this Tungal life I don't know," he said as he walked away to his hut. "But I must tell you I do not believe it all happened because you and my father lay down together before the reeds were gathered. Love does not work that way."

The next day Ramtouses heard singing as the young girls returned from their search carrying long stalks of reeds. He went to his father's hut. Manni was standing outside, watching the girls. When Ramtouses stood next to him, he smiled and put his arm across his son's shoulders.

"Tonight is the night, and you will have your first opportunity to see a new moon wedding ceremony."

Ramtouses repeated, "New moon? I heard mother use that term."

Manni explained. "Each new moon, Tungul holds a celebration, lots of feasting with everyone in the many towns attending. There is a burnt offering sacrifice. It is a spiritual renewal welcoming the first day of the new cycle. Traditional singing and dancing also play a major part in new moon celebrations, whether for a good harvest, a beginning of the growing season, honoring our ancestors, dead heroes, even newborns. Twice a year the new moon celebration observes a wedding dance.

"Your mother asked the older women who returned from Egypt with her to dance during the ceremony also, thinking perhaps some men might still want them if only to help with the work." Manni was smiling when he spoke again, "More than half the women accepted. It will be a wonderful celebration!"

And indeed, the celebration was spectacular and went on for hours. Finally, Princess Carnabrara danced in front of Manni who returned the honor by getting up and dancing with her until the music stopped, and the food was all eaten, and the fire's embers grew dark. After a short ceremony in the morning, Manni took Carnabrara for his bride and all the maidens who found a husband were received as brides.

The moon cycled from crescent to full again, and again, and the days were filled with many new activities, but Ramtouses never seemed to be happy. During this time, others throughout Tungal, including many of his age-group brothers, appeared full of joy.

One evening, after Ramtouses finished instructing the young village men on the proper use of the sword, Manni invited him to dinner. When Carnabrara had stepped away, Manni said, "You seem so unhappy here. Is there something I can do to help?"

Ramtouses looked down to the ground. "I know, Father, you and Mother want the best for me, but I must tell you I am not happy here. You and Mother grew up here, but I am not a part of this world. I feel so out of place." He paced with his hands behind him. "I don't want to hurt Mother or have her worried about me."

"Son, I understand. You are a lot like I was years ago. You need to be your own man." Manni came up close to him "What is it you want, to join your brothers in Nubia?"

"I am a soldier. I want to be with them. Mother wants me to take a new wife and give her a grandson who will one day be king." Ramtouses looked his father in the eyes. "Will you explain to her if I decide to leave?"

"I will. I will. She will give you her blessings."

After a few days Ramtouses had rounded up his age-group comrades who all wanted to join him. He was preparing to leave when Kobina came to him asking, "May I join you?"

Ramtouses looked surprised "What about Manni? Is he all right with this?"

"No," replied Kobina. "He was highly upset and demanded I stay here, but when he realized it was selfish of him, he wished me well."

Ramtouses smiled, shaking his head, and said, "Yes, we each need our own road to travel. Of course you may join us."

And the next morning Ramtouses' company rode away as Carnabrara and Manni looked on.

King Taharqa was happy to see them and arranged for special quarters in the palace for his chief general. He talked almost non-stop about conquering Egypt again and crushing Assyria beneath his feet.

"Ramtouses, you will lead the army," he said. "You will kill that dog of a king, Esarhaddon, and run his men all the way back to Nineveh. This is only the beginning—you shall see."

The king laughed and laughed. Each day Taharqa revisited the same victory, but while Ramtouses enjoyed the humor, he did not take Taharqa seriously. Still, he felt at home commanding what was left of the Nubian army and watching a trickle of new recruits from Ethiopia and the Nubian territory join the ranks.

Amenirdis discovered that Kobina had made the trip to Napata with Ramtouses. She summoned him to her palace, anxious to learn of Carnabrara and Manni's wellbeing.

When he entered her court, she asked him, "How are you? I am pleased to see you again. And how is the exultant couple doing in Tungal? Are they enjoying life there?"

Her questions came fast and almost hid the "pleased to see you again" comment, but that was the part which thrilled Kobina. He answered, "The princess bade me tell you they are well and asks you to visit them."

Amenirdis responded, "An excellent idea, and perhaps I will someday. Oh, what would life be like to live in the bush,

NUBIA DANCES WITH THE GODS

outside our fair city? But tell me, Kobina, what brings you to Napata."

"I am not part of their way of life and would rather live in Napata."

They had a long conversation and spoke of many things before he departed. On the walk back to his quarters, Kobina felt more content than he had in years.

After settling in, Ramtouses sat down to compose a message to his father.

I am reestablished as commanding general. We are comfortable here and miss being with family, but we trained to serve in the military and we share this common identity with other Nubian soldiers. There is one perturbing problem— King Taharqa has visions of upcoming war with Egypt and Assyria where he is the victor. We do not have the manpower or weapons for such a confrontation, and I fear he may act foolishly and relinquish what little status we yet have.

I tell you, Father, I am doing all that I can to brace our frontiers in Nubia and southern Ethiopia against an attack from Egypt. My fear is their greed for the raw materials trade, and the wealth and power it brings, will force Egypt to march south. They have the support of Assyria with arms and manpower if necessary. When an attack does come, not only will Nubia face destruction, but Tungul will be threatened as well. Assyria would like nothing more than to have all the riches of your territory and your people as slaves to import their goods. So you see the dilemma I face.

Your friend Kobina is doing well. I arranged an abode for him where he makes his sculptures to sell for food and clothing. He is lonely, so I visit him often.

When learning of Ramtouses' concerns, Manni began to wonder if there was something he could do to help improve Nubia's outlook. He agreed with Ramtouses' perception that if war came to Nubia, Assyria would not stop there—Tungul would also be threatened. That was why, when he read the message to Carnabrara, he shared an idea that might lead to strengthen the Tungul position.

"My love," he said, "perhaps we can build an army just as I did years ago. I don't have the influence to persuade enough warriors to come to fight, but there is another option. What if you were queen and all Tungul men were under your command?"

The princess listened closely, and then said, "Maybe I can convince my sister of the danger, and she can recruit the tribesman."

"What if she does not? Can we take that chance?"

Carnabrara looked Manni in the eye. "The people have been loyal to her for ten years. What makes you or Azbo the shaman think they will gravitate to me, a stranger?"

Manni stood before his wife and placed his hands on each side of her waist. "Without trying, you cannot know."

"Truthfully speaking," he said, "you have learned much over the years. Talk to the people with a powerful voice. Speak with passion. Make them understand your sincerity as well as the severity of what could happen to them. You have a much better understanding of the evil men in Assyria than anyone else here."

Carnabrara smiled. "I don't know how I ever lived without you." She kissed Manni and said, "First, before I wage war against Queen Adanna, let me go to her and get a better understanding of who she really is and what she would do if war comes."

That afternoon the two sisters, a queen and a princess, spent a lengthy time talking of shared experiences and discussing the needs of their people and the nation. When the meeting ended, the princess appeared quite angry as she walked away from the royal compound in long strides, her arms swinging back and forth.

I am ready to meet with the shaman, she thought.

Arriving at his abode, she said to him, "I remember you better as Azbo, the boy who always delivered messages for my father."

The shaman laughed and greeted her. "How may I serve you, dear Princess?"

"I have changed my mind, I want to be queen."

The shaman's face lit up. "That is good news indeed."

Carnabrara hesitated for a moment. "What do I need to win the queenship?"

"First, let me tell you of Adanna's weaknesses—she is out of touch with the people. She keeps her distance from the farmers and livestock workers, never seeing them, even when the Ell strikes destroyed the crops and animals. Most of the common villagers do not see her in present times, unless it is at a new moon celebration."

"Hmm," replied Carnabrara. "That could place me in good favor." She paced the open space before him, deep in thought, considering her options and a potential plan of action to win over the people of Tungul began to emerge.

Much later, after he and Carnabrara talked deep into the night while the moon journeyed through the darkened sky, Manni sat outside the doorway and contemplated a plan to recruit a mercenary army from the vast territory around them. He recalled how he and Carnabrara's father used the relay drum system to organize an army to fight the Ell years ago.

As a common language understood by all the tribes throughout North Africa and Ethiopia, even if their spoken tongues differed, the drums provided a method of contact between tribes as they had expanded into broader areas through the many years. It was essential in the building of the first great Tungul/Nubian army that Manni had led many years past.

A lifetime ago, he thought, *and in the morning we will attempt to repeat that plan.*

Manni trusted the young man who relayed his messages to Ramtouses, but now he focused on the importance of accuracy and caution for that day's communication.

"Deliver this message directly to General Ramtouses," he instructed.

Ramtouses, your mother has decided to do battle for the throne. It will be a contest between her and Queen Adanna for the king is like a puppet with no direct right to the throne. If your mother becomes queen, she will control all the fighting men of Tungul, and I will send messages through the drum system, asking for all young warriors to join us. We will trade their fighting skills for grain, animals for meat and milk, and clothing.

Ramtouses, with the drums, we can bring in thousands of mercenaries.

Ramtouses went to Kobina and shared the message. "My parents are going to have a confrontation with the ruling powers of Tungul in order to save our people. Maybe the gods have answered King Taharqa's cries for help. And maybe I should pray to the Egyptian God of War, Menthu."

Kobina said, "I have never known you to pray, Ramtouses."

"There is no greater reason than now to start," responded the general.

In Tungal, unrest began to mount. The shaman informed the elders that Carnabrara demanded her title and that the ancestors willed it. Word was spread among the people and tensions continued to build as tribesman were divided on who should be queen.

Adanna was forced to address the people, and speaking before a crowd of villagers comprised mostly of women from Tungal, the queen talked about things the people already knew—an abundance of good food and better living conditions than anywhere else in the territory. It was out of respect that most cheered her at the end.

Princess Carnabrara had her opportunity to speak a day later. The shaman brought in people from all over Tungul, a massive crowd who gathered mostly out of curiosity to hear her.

Manni sent three messengers to Ramtouses, each with a portion of his message, including the speech Carnabrara made before her people. Ramtouses gathered his comrades and Kobina to hear the three messengers—they all cheered once he had finished reading.

"I am no different from any of you," she said. Your mother stood straight and spoke clearly, with a full voice. "We all have the capability of thought—what we do with it is up to us— be it good and honest or evil and destructive. Sometimes we cannot control which way life will take us. When the thoughts of evil people confront us, if evil is stronger than good it will prevail, and those who are trapped within will suffer as I did suffer twenty-seven years ago. Look at me, my people. My virgin sisters and I were kidnapped and compelled to serve evil people, but we have returned to you after overcoming our enemies.

"See me. The laws of the ancestors say I should be the rightful ruler of this land as the oldest of King Tasmeria's offspring with no remaining males. I have proven my strength just by returning here alive. Come to me. Tell me your problems. Just as I have dissolved my problems, so also will I dissolve yours. I will not be an invisible monarch. I will come to you as did my father before me. We will move forward together, no matter what the cost."

My son, when she finished speaking a thunderous roar erupted, and to my surprise the people started chanting, "Carnabrara Queen of Tungul," over and over. They thought of her as a hero overcoming her misfortune, and returning to her people.

Following Carnabrara's speech, the people had marched around the royal grounds asking Queen Adanna to give up her position as alpha of the Tungul people. All town activity came to a halt as the warriors and guardians joined the dispute and more and more people came in from villages near and far joining the Carnabrara campaign. After five days, Adanna called Carnabrara into her abode to discuss the terms desired in surrendering the throne.

When the agreement was complete, the elders gave the ceremony for Princess Carnabrara, certifying her position as hereditary ruler of the Tungul nation.

In less than the span of one new moon to the next the Queen was ready to address her people once again.

"Thank you for supporting me, your rightful queen. However, all is not well in our land, for we live in dangerous times. I can say this because I have seen and experienced a great deal more of the affairs between great nations beyond our territory. Evil men are out there, and if given the opportunity, they will whip our backs, take all that is ours, rape your wives and daughters, and enslave us to labor for them.

"In years past we thought we fought against the sons of Ell, but today we know they are only men, as we are men. The one difference is they are extremely evil men who have a heavy drive for greed, at our expense.

"Hear me. I will not allow what my virgins and I experienced to happen to my people when there is something we can do to stop it before it occurs. We must build an army and go out to face our enemies before they come here and attack our homeland. Make no mistake. If we do not act now, it will surely come to be. That is why I call young men of adult age to prepare for war."

There were people who stood in silence, most were mothers and grandmothers, but many more called out shouts of approval for the proposed preparation against intrusion.

Manni watched the crowd respond to Carnabrara's speech and hoped the tribesman had stellar memories of how the Ell had smothered the land with drought for many years, and that they had shared the stories with the young men. He wondered if the youth had learned of the deaths of their fathers and grandfathers before them due to the evil of the Ell. Now was the time they all needed the powerful motivation revenge can provide.

Even with the recruitment of thousands of Tungul warriors, Manni knew that defeating the Egyptian and Assyrians would be no easy task. Additional thousands needed to be recruited from the large surrounding tribal lands. They too were plagued with severe drought for many years, and he proposed that Carnabrara arrange a substantial payment of goods for the families of each recruited tribesman. The opportunity for revenge and payment in the form of food and supplies for their families would provide abundant inducement for many to come forward and join the new army.

Ramtouses thought it time for King Taharqa to be made aware of the positive information he had received from his family. He found the king leaving the temple of Menthu, the war god.

"I have some exciting news for you."

The king said, "Walk with me. I want to hear it, if any news can be good."

His general revealed to him all that had transpired between him and his family in Tungal.

Taharqa looked up into the heavens. "I knew you would answer my prayers, Menthu. I will be Pharaoh of Egypt again and rule all the land that is Assyria. No one will equal me in greatness." The king stepped up his pace. "Come with me, Ramtouses. We must inventory our financial capability in order to aid in the recruitment."

Ramtouses responded, "Yes, we are expected to contribute to the remuneration, including a large portion of the weapons."

Kobina met with High Priestess Amenirdis to inform her of the events taking place in Tungal and she laughed with happiness when he told her Carnabrara was now queen over the entire nation. "I am so delighted and I am not surprised. She is brave and wise, and a queen needs to be both." Kobina watched her smile enliven her entire face, her eyes twinkled with delight and he chatted with ease about Manni and the new queen's happiness in marriage.

Eventually, she asked him about his own happiness. "How did you like Tungul? Were you happy? Could you advance your beautiful sculpture skills?"

Kobina said, "There is not a lot of trade in it, there or here, but I love the work."

She responded, "Perhaps you shall make a bust of me. I will pay you handsomely."

Kobina's eyes grew large. "That sounds like a wonderful challenge. My work is usually limited to smaller figurines of the gods but the thought of working on a larger piece is exciting. When shall we begin?"

The High Priestess thought for a moment. "Tomorrow morning, if that's all right with you?"

"Yes! I will arrive with the sun." answered Kobina.

The next morning, Amenirdis walked him to a large space behind her living area. Two armed guards stood outside. When they entered the room, she said, "I think I want a full body statue."

Kobina looked surprised. "That will take much longer to complete than a figurine."

She waved her hands over empty space and shrugged, "I have little else to do."

So Kobina explained the process to execute such a large design. It required sketches and drawings of the subject, Amenirdis herself. The selection of stone was critical for success. Measurements were needed, and most of all, long hours of her posing while he drew and, later, while he hammered and chiseled. "You need not be present every hour I work, but there will be many days when you must be available to pose for the sculpture. I want this work to be perfect."

She promised to cooperate with him. "It is my idea," she said, "and I too want it to be wonderful." Kobina walked around the room and chose a spot close to an open space where sunlight spilled into the room. "Here," he said. "Please stand in the sunlight and I will begin at once." He removed and unfurled small squares of papyrus from his satchel along with pieces of charcoal, and they began a process that took seven full moons to complete.

He sketched Amenirdis from multiple angles for many days before taking time away from her to travel to the quarries, searching for the perfect stone that he would transform into a likeness of the high priestess. This required many trips before the right piece was located and transferred to their working space.

When it was finally found and moved, Amenirdis looked at it with huge hesitation. He saw the crease of her brow and tilt of her head. "This?" she asked. But he was ecstatic. It was a beautiful rock and he knew it was exactly what they needed.

"Let's get to work." He practically danced on the balls of his feet, so ready was he to execute his vision.

While Kobina worked on the sculpture Amenirdis chatted freely. She was inquisitive and asked unlimited questions of him. "Where did you live as a child? Are you a father? Did you study with the elders? What did you learn? Or, did you run wild? Were you ever married? Who is your god of all gods? Have you slept with many young girls? Why have you no wife now?"

Often Kobina was totally involved and absorbed with his work and if his answers were not readily given, Amenirdis would reply as though the question was directed to her, not by her. In the process, they became more acquainted with one another than many two people who have spent years together are. The sessions ate up most of the daylight and nearly every evening ended with a shared meal served by her house staff before Kobina left to walk home.

He had erected a screen separating the emerging statue from his model, Amenirdis. It served to protect her from any errant chips of marble, and also functioned to shield the statue from curious onlookers. No one was to view the sculpture before Amenirdis. At the close of each day, he draped a heavy cloth over the stone.

The project consumed their days and near the end of the finished work she asked, "Have you not been gentle with your partner, is that why you have no one now?"

Through the many long days Kobina had answered all her questions and he did not avoid this last one, but he took some time to set down his tools and then looked directly into her eyes as he spoke.

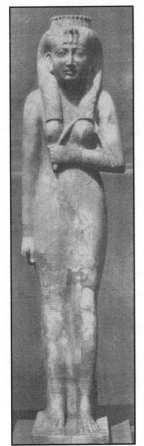

"Yes, I am gentle and very experienced in knowing how to please my companion. I don't have a mate now because I cannot accept ancillary positions at this time in my life."

His eyes never left her gaze and they seemed to shimmer in the soft light of the approaching evening. He watched as she pursed her lips, and said. "Oh."

"My work is finished." His sudden announcement startled her. "Come, look at yourself." And he unveiled the sculpture before her.

She cried out, "Oh, oh, that is so very much in my likeness. You are a master. I love it. I love it." She turned to face him. He was looking at her, not the sculpture,

A statue of Amenirdis, Nubian
High Priestess to the god Amun-re.
Photo by Travelers in the Middle
East Archive/Wikipedia.org

and moved ever so little when the high priestess hugged him, saying, "My image will last forever."

Kobina was proud of his art. "It is the best work I have ever done."

Walking to her temple, Amenirdis' eyes began to fill with tears.

Why? Why, Amun-re, am I bound to a marriage with you that has no rewards, not even a hint of recognition for the pure sacrifice I honor you with? My prayers go unanswered. Do they mean nothing? I feel love for a human, and if he wants me as I want him, I must make it possible for my feelings to be realized by him. What shall I do to reveal my love for him? I am ignorant to the ways of love. I must find a way.

She arrived at the temple still consumed with her ache, thinking an answer must be found. *I know! I have an idea—he must make the first move but I need to nudge him toward it. If Amun-re wants to take my life for this, then let it be so. I would rather be dead than continue living this way.*

A guard came to Kobina's living quarters a short time later. "The high priestess has requested your presence at her palace."

Kobina followed the guard into a large hall in the palace. The guard indicated he should wait there, and then he left, leaving Kobina alone.

Some time passed and seeing no one within the hall, Kobina started moving around. Wondering if she would enter soon, he called out to her. "High Priestess Amenirdis, are you here?" It was unusual for her to make him wait.

Looking along the walls he saw an open door. He went to it, pushed it open farther, and saw the priestess lying on a large couch. He stopped. Completely stopped all movement. In his surprise and amazement even his breath was held.

She was covered with a beautiful silken cloth. An opening high above Kobina's head let sunlight beam down upon her, creating a golden shimmer that covered her body. The garment was thin and almost transparent, and he thought it difficult to discern which was sunlight, fabric or her flesh in the scene before him.

So lovely, he thought, *I am unable to move. My tongue locks in my throat. I can't move my eyes from her. She is beautiful—a woman of near fifty years, yet she has the body of a young woman.*

He did not want to turn away, but felt he should. He wanted to move closer, to keep his eyes upon her, but he felt he ought not. Then, suddenly, a thought screamed inside his head—*Is she dead?*

He watched intently and saw the rise and fall of her chest. Great relief slipped through his body, and he breathed with her—in, out, in, out. *Maybe she is just sleeping. I should leave. But, wait, just to touch her leg, to know how wonderful that one moment might be.*

His heart beat faster with each small step forward and when he slowly, silently, raised his hand to touch her foot, he dropped to his knees in near exhaustion. The tension in his body screeched for release. His heart raced, his hand trembled, and softly, so softly, he whispered her name—and time paused. His heartbeat faded.

Amenirdis lay with her eyes closed and, though he made no sound, she knew when he pushed open the door, she heard his slight intake of breath when he first saw her, she felt his eyes upon her, knew his tension, wanted his touch, and heard the soft, loving call of her name—but she could not move. She waited, torturing herself, wondering if he too felt tortured by the silence.

Then, she opened her eyes and saw his bowed head. Her hand moved to touch him and she slowly ran her fingers through his hair. Kobina's heart began to beat again.

His hand moved effortlessly to her foot, over the silk garment, slowly up her leg and to her thigh; his touch was so tender that their skin barely met and yet the sparks they shared nearly lifted him from the floor, and still his hand moved, resting ever so slightly on her belly before it reached her arm. Her skin was soft and on fire. He felt the warmth of her fingers in his hair, the slightest movement of her hand sent promises no one could, or would, ignore.

Kobina lifted his head, he saw her face, and heard her say "Yes." It set in motion a slow melting of fears and concerns, of oughts and ought nots, while their hands moved over hills and curves not traveled before, revealing secrets not known but suspected, giving joy and delight long denied.

Kobina exhausted himself loving this magnificent, noble Nubian woman. He fell asleep beside her. In the early morning hours he was awakened by Amenirdis sitting beside him. He nearly jumped off the couch.

"Don't be alarmed," she said. "You were the man I knew you would be. You have given me a happiness I have never known—I finally feel whole." She took his hand. "Everything will be all right. Go now, I will call on you later for dinner."

Kobina hurried and dressed, then departed. When he left, Amenirdis walked around thinking of her position in life. *I have betrayed my husband, the god Amun-re. I have felt the urge and desire to lie with a man over the years, but my faithfulness and belief in Amun-re was too strong. I would have continued to be loyal to my master if he had not deserted me in the face of our enemies.*

The people came to me, asking for Amun-re to save them from the Assyrians, and I prayed day and night. When he did not grant us safety, I threw myself on the floor before his image, pleading with him. I knew then that he had turned his back on me and for what reason? I have been obedient to him from my earliest years. It was the worst feeling I have ever experienced.

Without direction, she found herself before his statue, speaking aloud to it.

"I am a woman of flesh and blood who was willing to sacrifice all, even my life for your love. Always doing your bidding, always obedient and for what? Now I understand your thoughts when it comes to our thirty-four years of alliance. For you to spit on me when our enemies are on the horizon? For leaving me to fend for myself with my people who look at me as if I was the enemy for not persuading you to show mercy? They think I am not a fit wife for you. Am I so wrong to ask for something in exchange for my loyalty? Are the Assyrian gods stronger than you? Is this a way of testing my love? Are you just a statue with no real power at all? Shall I have died not knowing if you care anything for me? An old woman denied the right to know physical love as others do?"

On her knees she bent her body forward, to the floor, as she had once bowed in honor to Amon-re, and wept.

As the months passed, thousands of new recruits from the greater Nubian area and thousands of Tungul warriors gathered and bivouacked on the old training grounds used by that first army Ramtouses from Juba trained so many years past. Manni sent his son a final message saying the men were assembled.

With that message in hand, Ramtouses went to the king.

"King Taharqa, it is time to go see your new fighting men."

The king responded, "Good. Are the officers and men who are to train these people ready?"

Ramtouses acknowledged the king. "Yes, at day break we will move out for Tungul."

Hundreds of Nubians who fought against the Assyrians in Egypt now prepared to train this new army. Kobina noticed the commotion and realized the time had come for the journey to Tungul. He sought out Ramtouses, and asked if he could join them.

The general said, "Of course." And Kobina went to tell Amenirdis.

"You are leaving me?" she said. The surprised look on her face caused Kobina to falter. "I thought you said you love me," she shouted.

"I do," declared Kobina. "I will come back to you."

"When?" Her voice was harsh. "A month from now, a year, many years?"

Kobina could only stand there.

"If you love me, how can you leave me?" She moved close to him "No one knows we are lovers. Go to Tungul. I will keep your secret safe."

Kobina tried to smile; he was just beginning to understand her angst. "It's all right. I will stay here with you. Who am I? A warrior? I should have known you would not be happy to see me leave."

Early the next morning just before their departure, the High Priestess Amenirdis came to Kobina's abode. "Kobina, please forgive me. I want you to be free to leave whenever you want. I am so jealous. First Amun-re has left me, and now you want to leave. I feel abandoned."

She began to cry, and Kobina took her in his arms. "It's all right. I understand. Maybe I should have asked if you wanted to come."

"No, no," she answered. "You must go, or I will always feel as if I held you by force."

"No. I will stay here with you. I was not thinking properly. I do love you and will never leave you. Anything we do will be together."

That same morning the Nubian tutors of war departed for Tungul, a journey that would take no more than seven days.

Ramtouses was excited to see his parents again. He envisioned their greeting with great joy—hugs, smiles, rejoicing, feasting and dancing. They would arrive in time to see his father crowned King of Tungul, even though it was in title only, with little or no authority. A large family assembly would gather the first evening, in Manni's honor, and his mother would arrange another gathering to celebrate the arrival of King Taharqa for all who wanted to pay homage to him. Most people knew him as a powerful Nubian king from another land and anxiously awaited their entire party.

Such were the thoughts of Ramtouses—for the next seven days.

Jerusalem

King Manasseh was furious with his people for such a poor reception honoring King Esarhaddon. He yelled at his elders. "They will not get away with this. I—I alone am king. I will make them pay."

He later spoke to the captain of his guard. "Go out and arrest a hundred people from all parts of the city."

The captain of the guard made the king's decree known to his soldiers. "We are arresting people who are suspected of being believers in the one God. If someone strongly insists to be falsely accused, tell them to give the name of someone they know is of that faith."

The soldiers began their roundup, and the accused were arrested, beaten, and tortured.

In the end, the brutality caused the surrender of many names—in some cases, the names of those not even belonging to the faith. Due to the confessions and betrayals, the cycle of arrests continued and resulted in yet additional torture. Many more than a hundred people suffered unjustly.

The elders spoke on behalf of the people. "When will this stop? Everyone is not of the faith of the one God."

King Manasseh made answer. "You are right. This is fruitless. My desire is to punish those who follow Isaiah."

He considered what was happening around his great city of Jerusalem and decided to take a new approach to right the wrong of their lukewarm reception given the Assyrian king.

He fumed silently. *I will have my revenge!* And again, Manasseh went to the captain of his guard. "Bring the prophet Isaiah to me—alive. Go now. Find him."

The search for the prophet went on for more than the length of a new moon before he was found and brought before the king—not because he was hiding but because no one truly knew of his whereabouts.

Manasseh stood before Isaiah and said, "I accuse you of inciting the people against the will of their king. What say you in your own defense?"

The prophet said, "I teach the word of the Lord not the word of man."

The king walked around him, measuring Isaiah's worth, knowing he dare not kill the prophet without a justifiable reason. Such actions had been known to bring misfortune to rulers in the past.

"I have heard that you claim to have seen God. Is that true?"

Isaiah then said, "I saw the Lord sitting on a lofty throne and situated up above him were six seraphs—each having six wings, two wings covering their faces, two wings covering their feet, and two held the throne aloft. All six took turns calling to one another, uncovering and recovering their bright faces. The callings came closer and closer together then ended in one prodigious simultaneous utterance. The Temple was shaken to its foundation, and the sanctuary became filled with a vaporous substance as the Lord rose into the heavens."

The council hall was quiet, and all eyes were on Isaiah. King Manasseh walked up within a few hand widths in front of him, and then raised his hand for his scribe to read from the scripture.

The scribe began, "Moses thy master said no man shall see God and live."

Manasseh then said, "Why are you not dead? You appear very alive to me." He looked over to his scribe. "There is a contradiction here." Manasseh turned his head and yelled into the prophet's face. "Why are you not dead?"

Without hesitation Isaiah said, "I dwell in the midst of people with unclean lips. My life was spared when one of the seraphs returned from the heavens and flew down to the holy alter. There, it picked out a burning coal with a pair of tongs and touched my lips with it, saying, 'Your sins are removed.'"

Manasseh pointed at the door. "Get him out of here. You are guilty of statements contrary to the teaching of Moses. Blasphemy. The punishment is death."

The captain of the guard asked, "How shall he be executed?"

"In the worst manner—the cedar tree."

As the officer turned away, the king called out. "Wait. Carry out the order in an area of the city where most citizens can see his fate."

On the morning of a market day when hundreds of people moved about the streets, soldiers brought Isaiah out from the dungeon, placed him inside a hollow cedar tree, and sawed the tree in half. Isaiah did not cry out. Most all the Hebrew people were appalled at such a gruesome sight and, as ordered, the soldiers arrested anyone who screamed or begged for mercy for Isaiah. That was thought to be a signal they would surely be followers.

Naamity and her uncle did not go out into the street, and by chance, on that very day, an official from the palace walked into their shop, looked at Naamity, and said, "Are you Naamity?"

"Yes, I am." She was puzzled.

He went on. "Our records indicate that you are twenty years old. Are you not?" He smiled shrewdly.

"Yes, I am twenty. Why do you ask?"

"It is most unusual for a woman of twenty to have not found a husband. Is there any reason why you have not married?"

Naamity couldn't hide her anger. "Why does the palace concern itself with why I am not married?"

"The king can concern himself with what pleases him, and it may please him to choose a husband for you. Have I made myself clear?"

"My mother is honored by this whole country. May I not be patient about whom I pick in marriage?"

The captain raised his arms in a gesture of goodwill. "Calm down my good lady. A relative of the king is interested in taking you as his wife, but because of your heritage, it is only fitting that you have a say in the marriage. It is not every day a woman has a chance to marry into royalty. Perhaps a meeting between the two of you should be arranged. He is a tall, handsome young officer."

She fought for composure, struggling to maintain a pleasant appearance. "And if he does not please me and I choose not to marry him?"

"We will not concern ourselves with that now. Let us move forward slowly."

With that he turned to the door but paused to look back at her. "Someone will come for you in a few days. Smile."

Naamity was highly disturbed by this. She knew of a certain captain whose duties were to change guards at the main gates of the city. He was also one of those who quietly believed in the God of Isaiah, and he spread the word that in two nights at midnight, the gates would be opened and all of Isaiah's followers would have an opportunity to escape the madness of Manasseh.

At first Naamity thought this could be a trap, but she understood and trusted that only believers would know whom to contact when invoking such a request. Her two brothers had moved away after finding wives, and for quite some time she and her uncle had been running the store.

"What are my options—stay here and have a marriage forced upon me, or escape to an unknown fate?"

On the night of the escape opportunity, her uncle said, "Perhaps you would be better off traveling alone without the burden of an old man to hamper your journey. Please don't try to talk me into leaving with you; my place is here in Jerusalem.

Take only the necessary essentials, my child. It is approaching midnight. Go. Hurry."

Naamity zigzagged through the city streets and alleys toward the main gates under the cover of night. At the stroke of midnight, a flood of people crept through the unlocked gate. They all knew the meeting place would be where the altar was hidden.

Countryside Outside Jerusalem

A spokesman emerged, saying, "Isaiah is no longer with us. Someone must stand up and take charge, and for the moment that person will be me. This is a very large group, nearly two hundred people. There is no doubt Manasseh's soldiers will come after us. Perhaps it would be best if we divide into two groups."

Many voiced nervous agreement. The spokesman walked to the center of the assemblage, pointed in opposite directions, and said, "All standing to the north of me shall go north, and the others travel south."

For a few minutes there was confusion because families were divided, but this was remedied by quickly switching a few people here and there, and the two parties began moving in opposite directions.

Naamity traveled with the group headed north. While both parties wanted to reach Egypt as their final destination, traveling south meant crossing the hot desert. The soldiers might think those who went south faced doom in such an undertaking and perhaps not even pursue them. On the contrary, the northern route, which reached the Mediterranean, meant a much safer journey to Egypt. This band of people had to hasten. The longer it took for Manasseh's men to discover the missing people, the better chance they would have.

It was a race against time—Naamity and the group fleeing north found themselves continually running, knowing the soldiers would be on horseback. By the fifth day they were exhausted, and one of the believers said, "I think I know a way to the Mediterranean over this field of stones. Plus, the soldiers will not be able to trail us on horseback."

On the night of the escape, three guards were on duty standing watch over the main gate. The captain of the guard, being a follower of the one God himself, had to make sure the people could safely make their getaway, so he drugged all three himself.

Later that night, the three were discovered sleeping but were only reprimanded mildly. The captain hoped it would take some time before the truth of the matter came to light, but on the third day after the believers' flight from the city, people began to realize certain citizens were missing. When officers who out-ranked the captain learned of the matter, in an attempt to protect his involvement, the captain accused the three sleepers and ordered their execution. No trial, no defense; only charged and executed. The captain believed God directed his actions.

Manasseh was certain this would be his opportunity to stamp out the believers in the one God for good.

"Find them," he ordered. "Bring as many back alive as possible. I want to see their faces before I have them stoned to death. Make haste. This is the chance I've been waiting for."

The captain of the guard was one of the officers sent out to hunt the fleeing Hebrew believers. The soldiers came to the place where the assembly had first gathered then divided.

The lead officer yelled, "You men go to the south, and if you discover they entered the desert, stay there a few days to make sure they do not return. The rest of you follow me north."

King Manasseh's men looked for them for three days without a trace.

On the fourth day, the soldiers searching to the north came upon a rocky area covered with thousands of large boulders. Riding with the search party was the captain who had aided the believers' escape.

He called to the officer in charge, "Dismounting and searching this whole area could take weeks on foot, and there is no real proof they traveled this way."

The lead officer agreed. "We will dismount and search for any evidence suggesting they took this route. Otherwise, we will have to abandon the search here and hope we can pick up their trail farther north."

All day they ventured over the sea of rocks that seemed to never end. As midnight approached, they were totally exhausted, needing food and sleep.

While lying on a large stone, Naamity looked up at the sky remembering what Ramtouses had told her about the trail of glittering stars across the heavens having been caused by a bird carrying a blanket in its beak and the sprinklings from a hole in it created life upon the earth. *I cannot wait to see him. Will he be glad to see me?* She held his emblem tight in her fist.

An old woman resting near her said, "My child, I remember when you were born. I thought you were the most beautiful baby I had ever seen."

Naamity looked at her. "I know you, but I have not seen you in many years. Did you live on the other side of Jerusalem?"

She smiled. "Yes. Your mother and I were the best of friends, but in time we drifted apart."

They were quiet for a while before the older woman said, "If you need me for anything, just let me know—even if it's for just a bit of advice."

They exited the rocky terrain late the next day and saw the Mediterranean before the setting sun. Their spirits soared, and they burst into songs of praise to the Lord as they walked along the sea shore. Traveling at a comfortable pace for the next two days was peaceful, with only the sound of men hunting for food, until someone called out, "Look! A cloud of dust comes from the horizon."

He pointed in the direction ahead of them. "It comes toward us. Do they chase us?"

They ran to find hiding places in the abundance of tall grass and bushes nearby, and quietly lay hiding, watching as an immense army of horses and men approached.

At first, they thought the army must be Egyptians. Naamity wondered if perhaps it was even Ramtouses going to fight Manasseh, but on closer examination it became clear they were Assyrians, and it took the rest of the day and late evening for the army to pass. Everyone had time to think about their situation as they remained hidden during the day. It wasn't until the dark of night covered them that they slowly emerged from their various hiding places.

Only a few Hebrews spoke enough Egyptian for acceptable communication, and seeing this Assyrian war machine traveling from the direction of Egypt, they worried how they would be received by the Egyptians.

Naamity came to the man leading her group and said, "When the Egyptian ambassadors were in Jerusalem two years ago, the leader left me with his emblem and told me if ever I traveled to his country, I was to show his emblem. It will assure safe passage to him."

"That could be just the bit of luck we need. When we get to an Egyptian city, you come forward with me and show the emblem," he responded.

Esarhaddon still felt discomfort from his wound. "Where are my physicians? I have much pain."

After reexamining the wound, they said, "Great King, we can do you no good if you continue to be so active." They threw up their hands in anguish. "It will never heal if you don't rest and give it time."

"Perhaps I will follow your advice for a time," Esarhaddon responded and retired to his tent for the remainder of the day and all through the night.

The next morning he arose and dressed for travel, informing his generals, "We leave for Jerusalem. I have some unfinished work to do there."

He stood on his chariot watching the crowded terrain around him filled with men, horses, and war machines, and contemplated his decision to visit Jerusalem on the way home to Nineveh. *I am the closest these men will get to the gods in their lifetimes. I cause the men to feel a vanity when they see me among them. It is my duty to give them pride in sacrificing their lives for the good of Assyria.*

Jerusalem

Hoping to please the Assyrian emperor with a greater welcome than he received at his last visit, Manasseh gave a decree that all citizens must attend the emperor's arrival, and a crowd of people awaited Esarhaddon's entry into Jerusalem. However, Esarhaddon rejected any ceremony and demanded Manasseh lead him directly to his palace.

He pointed his finger at Manasseh. "You must think me ignorant as to how your people feel about me."

Manasseh looked surprised as the emperor walked right up to him. "Manasseh, I know a great number of your people still love and fellow their one God. It was made clear when I was here months ago just how much your people love me— so much love that thousands stayed at home rather than even come out to greet me."

He placed his fist on Manasseh chest. "Yet there is one other thing even more offensive and despicable to the Assyrian nation than that." He pushed his fist against Manasseh's chest a few times before continuing. "You forget that your country is a vassal state of Assyria. When I ask payment, I expect full tribute, no less. Other vassals meet their requirements without delay, without complaint, without deficiencies. You are no different yet somehow perhaps you feel you are?"

Manasseh threw himself on the floor at the emperor's feet. "Please," he cried. "I will never let that happen again. Can you forgive me, this one time?"

Esarhaddon demanded, "Get to your feet. Because I am convinced you are a true believer in Baal, I will not have your life for this. However, there must be some reprimand for your behavior. Go. Gather what you may need and report to my officer of the guard. You are my prisoner. No tricks or I will burn down your city."

The officer of the guard brought him out before the whole city for all to watch as Manasseh was led away in chains.

Nineveh

On his way to Nineveh, Esarhaddon halted in Babylon, at the old palace where his father had once sent him as a young man in training. As emperor, he had beautifully re-designed and rebuilt the old structure, and his family now enjoyed it as a leisure retreat site. He brought Manasseh into the great hall and the King of Judah was astounded by its luxury.

The emperor warned, "Don't feel your lodgings will be thus. You shall be confined in the dark, old space beneath these rooms."

Esarhaddon enjoyed the lovely palace for a few days, resting and recuperating, while Manasseh adjusted to his stark and gloomy dwelling below.

After several days, the Assyrian forces moved quickly to their beloved city of Nineveh where a magnificent reception awaited them. The enthusiastic crowd came from not only Assyria but from all the different provinces to honor Emperor Esarhaddon, for he had done something no other Assyrian king had been able to do—he had conquered Egypt.

In the coming days, Esarhaddon basked in the attention he received, regularly hosting gatherings for aristocrats and men of the government to bargain for his many slaves and valuable exotic merchandise from faraway places in exchange for gold and silver.

His physicians once again warned him of too much activity. Again and again, the emperor promised to slow down.

Egypt

Naamity and the people with whom she traveled finally reached the city of Memphis in Egypt. Standing atop a long, sloping hill, they watched from a distance as a network of traffic ventured in and out of the city gates, and thinking it wise to make a reconnaissance effort before bringing the entire group into the city, their leader decided that only a few should attempt to enter the city and mingle with the crowd. A few could pass by the guards without notice more likely than twenty or thirty.

Naamity spoke to the leader, "Because Ramtouses is a soldier, maybe it would be best if I come along to show the emblem, if necessary."

The leader responded, "Yes, for that reason you should be one of the first to enter. One other thing—who can speak the language?"

He pointed, "You there." When the man stepped forward, he asked, "Did you say you may be able to understand and translate some of the words?"

The man answered, "Yes, I will gladly go along."

As the three prepared to leave, the older woman who had befriended Naamity on their journey called to them. "Wait. Wait."

Naamity turned to her. "What is it?"

"You are a jewel amongst stones. Anyone seeing you will be diverted by your beauty, and that could be a problem—the world is very cruel."

She walked toward them and wisely counselled the leader and Naamity. "We need a plan before approaching any of these people."

Naamity looked interested. "What do you have in mind?"

The wise woman continued, "First, you should look different."

She suggested they proceed by cutting most of Naamity's long hair. "Unmarried women are held in great esteem and do not cut their hair. It is considered part of their beauty. However, because our lives may be threatened, I believe it is wise to disguise your female appearance. It is a deceit, but I pray the Lord will forgive us this one time."

They cut her hair, changed her clothes to those of a boy, and placed a turban on her head. When Naamity's disguise was complete, she asked, "How do I look?"

The leader of the party responded with a smile. "That's better. The old woman's advice may save us all. You are inconspicuous for now, an ordinary boy."

Mingling with other travelers, they entered the city successfully and walked among the street vendors looking at all the merchandise, attempting to fade into the crowd. Their worn-out sandals from the long trip to Egypt needed replacement so they purchased new ones, as many pairs of sandals as they could carry.

The interpreter asked the shop attendant, "Have you any knowledge of an officer named Ramtouses?" The shopkeeper did not fully understand what he was asking and pointed down the street where several soldiers stood near what looked to be a military building.

"Go down there. The soldiers will help you."

Naamity said, "I will give you the emblem to show the soldiers."

The translator took it and walked toward the soldiers with Naamity and their leader following him.

One soldier saw them coming and moved to meet them. "What do you people want?"

In his somewhat deficient language skills, their interpreter said, "We are here to see Ramtouses." He held out the emblem in his hand. The soldier came closer to get a better look.

The three of them had no way of knowing the Nubians had been defeated and driven out of the country so when the soldier chuckled a bit disrespectfully and took the emblem from his hand, the three Hebrew travelers immediately stepped back as if reproached.

The soldier asked, "Where did you get this?"

"An Egyptian officer gave it to my friend here," he answered, nodding to indicate Naamity.

The soldier seemed to doubt the interpreter's answer as he looked reproachfully at them and sneered, "You people don't look Egyptian. Why would an officer give this to you?"

The translator answered, "We are from Jerusalem. The officer, Ramtouses, made friends with this boy here."

The soldier walked back to where other soldiers stood, and after a short conversation with them, he returned with another. The new one seemed to understand some Hebrew. "How did you get here? Are there others with you?"

No one said a word.

The soldier continued. "Show me where the others are, and I will take the lot of you to Ramtouses."

Naamity and the translator stayed in the marketplace while the leader left and several soldiers followed him. After a long stint, all the Hebrews were within the walls of the city where many more soldiers gathered and surrounded them, leading the way to a weapons depot. It was a camp where many slaves labored, assembling all manner of war equipment.

The officer in charge of the depot had been notified of the new group of workers and came out looking for the three who had first come into the city. He asked, "Which one of you carried the emblem?"

The interpreter told Naamity to nod, and when she did, the officer looked around at his men, and turned to the soldier who had gathered them. "Well done," he said. "Seize them. We need them all to build and store our weapons."

The soldiers drew their swords and took aim with their bows to make sure no one tried to flee.

Before the officer walked away, he threw the emblem at the feet of Naamity and yelled, "No Nubian dog resides in the kingdom of Egypt."

She silently bent to retrieve Ramtouses' emblem.

The Hebrews cried for mercy, but the soldiers forced them into a fenced area and left them heavily guarded. Their hope lay in the one true God, Yahweh, but their cries seemed unheard. The wise woman sat next to Naamity.

"You are dressed as a boy. Thank the Lord; otherwise you would be among the many daughters who will be raped tonight."

Naamity cried out in an agonizing voice. "Oh my Lord, what have I done? This is my fault. I deserve the worst."

She twisted back and forth, screaming loudly. Two men held her, one covering her mouth in an attempt to avoid drawing the guard's attention.

"Come to your senses. Adding another victim for their pleasure will not help any of us," said one of the men.

The wise woman put her arms around Naamity and lightly massaged her back. "Be still. You could not have known. Calm down, my child. The Lord has spared you for now—be thankful. You must be strong and follow the will of the Lord."

She continued to rock her gently, while Naamity whimpered, trying to gather some sense of the situation.

In the coming days, the people were sorted for different types of work—some to assemble weapons, while others were sent to forging mills. The wise woman and Naamity stayed together and worked in the assembly building, at night they slept near one another.

One night she said to Naamity, "I have prepared a solution from vegetation we encountered on our way here, for I worried that something awful may happen to you. The Lord has a plan for you, and I must help you whenever I can."

Naamity responded, "We are going to die here. We should have stayed in Jerusalem. At least we would be in our own country and be buried with our people, not in a strange land of idols. It was senseless to think I could find Ramtouses after all this time."

The wise woman spoke again. "Where is your faith, my child? The Lord has not brought you here without reason."

Naamity held her head up. "You are right. I will never lose faith in our Lord, no matter what occurs. I am a child of Almighty God, and from now on I will act as one. Showing weakness in my words also shows weakness in my faith. Thank you, my Lord, for bringing this wise woman into my life to help me receive your strength to move forward."

The woman passed her a pouch filled with a powder. "If you are discovered, use this powder to discourage your attacker. Wet your fingers, dip them into the solution in the pouch, and then rub the wet mix between your legs. Cover the complete outer surface. Don't put your fingers on any other part of your body after you have inserted them into the solution. It is more effective if you shave your hair from this part of the body, but again, though it is not our custom to remove this hair, our lives are in danger and it may become necessary to save us. Your skin will turn red, you will develop small bumps and sores, and you will be in abundant discomfort."

Naamity asked, "How long will it stay that way?"

"About ten days."

Naamity had more questions. "What if I don't have time to use it?"

"Naamity, it starts to work as soon as you apply it. Keep the area shaved. Be prepared." Beginning the next day, she shaved regularly, using a tool smuggled from her work station, and kept the pouch close at all times.

Several months later, Egyptian officers from the quarry came to the depot.

"We need more slave labor. We understand you have found additional workers. Give us all the males you can spare."

Except for the old, most of the Hebrew men were rounded up, including Naamity, and marched to the quarry within the city walls. She remembered the wise woman's words and quickly concealed a sharpened arrowhead to cut her hair from both her head and lower part of the body. The pouch holding the prepared powder was tied at her waist beneath her garment.

Unlike the guards at the depot who did not pay much attention to the workers, at the quarry the guards were continually watching, and whipping them for the least infraction—not moving fast enough, not working hard enough, taking too long for a drink of the rationed water. Work at the quarry was long and hard, and the only chance she had for cutting hair was at night when she found a private corner under cover. This proved difficult, and she dared not enlist help from anyone.

At the munition assembly site, men, women, and children worked together in relatively close quarters. They wore lightweight over-garments that served them both day and night. At the quarry, the men worked hard under the hot sun, and soon after arrival most everyone discarded the long garment in favor of aprons covering their lower bodies. Naamity knew she could not discard her upper body wrap but was essentially compelled, after many days of hot and sweaty work, to remove her top garment, leaving her to labor with her chest wrapped tightly and wearing the full-torso apron like the men.

Her hope was that among the hundreds of men and boys, she would not attract attention, but one day she noticed a guard watching her closely. He left but later returned with the officer in charge and pointed at her.

The officer called out an order, "Come here," he demanded.

When she ignored him, he ran over and snatched the turban from her head, revealing that the hair on her head had grown longer because the small arrowhead was ineffective cutting that much hair. Then grasped her top wrapping and pulled it away. Naamity immediately covered her breasts with both hands. Her ruse was now exposed.

The officer grabbed and then shoved her over to one of his men.

"Take her to my quarters. Tie her up and stand guard over her until I arrive. And don't touch her, or I'll have your life," he warned.

Oh Lord, she thought. *Save me from this horrible nightmare.* To her good fortune, the man had tied her hands in front of her, and the pouch was attached to the lower half of her garment. Naamity told herself, *Control your nerves, and use your head. The Lord has given you a way to save yourself.*

While the guards were outside the doors, she was able to recover her pouch; she wet her fingers with saliva and dipped them into the pouch before rubbing the solution between her legs a second and third time. By the third application her fingers stung, they were red and tender. She felt sore between her legs. She crawled to a corner and sat, waiting.

Later that evening the officer came in, he looked around the room, and upon seeing her, he yelled, "Rise!"

He pointed his finger at the floor near to him. "Come and stand next to me."

Naamity slowly moved over to where he stood. He took her by the chin, raised her head, and looked her over.

He said, "How did you get this far before being discovered? You could even be beautiful."

He led her to his sleeping area. "Lie down on the bed. I could make life easy for you here."

He quickly started removing his uniform. "Take off that piece of garment," he demanded.

Naamity did, and then lay back on his bed with her legs closed and hands covering her breasts and lower torso.

The light of the evening dusk shone through many slatted openings of his dwelling, and he could clearly see the softly-bronzed tone of her olive skin. Thinking her truly resplendent, his eyes grew large. A romantic mood came over him, and he began to lightly rub her legs. Moving his hand upward, he said, "Remove your hands."

She did, slowly, and upon seeing between her legs what appeared to be a flagrant infection, his hand withdrew quickly, and he shouted as he jumped to his feet.

"You have been cursed by the gods." He hurried back into his clothing and ran out.

The quarry officer was a strong believer in punishment being placed upon humans by the gods. He went to the newly constructed temple of Baal and voiced the matter before the high priest.

"Listen to my words," he pleaded. "Baal, king of all gods, has found female humankind most pleasurable to mate with, and he is often caught by his wife, Anat. She punishes the human females with horrible curses."

"Yes, that is correct," said the priest. "If you have such a female amongst you, it would be wise to stay out of her company. Do not kill her, for if you do, the curse will pass on to you."

The officer left the temple wondering what he should do with the woman if not kill her, and the answer quickly came to him. *Rid her from my camp.*

The next morning he returned and said to Naamity, "The captain at the weapons depot despises me and would do anything to cause me misery."

He kept his distance from her "My thoughts are that no one at the depot knows you have been tampered with by the gods, thinking you to be a boy. So, when I return you to the depot, you shall spread the curse of Anat amongst those people,"—he snickered a bit—"my most hated adversary."

Two soldiers entered. "Remove her immediately, and don't touch her. She has a curse bestowed upon her by the gods."

That same day he had everything in the room burned and replaced, and Naamity found herself back at the depot. When the wise woman saw her, she began to cry with joy and took Naamity's hands and kissed them. "The Lord has returned you to us. I am filled with praises for our Lord. He loves you so."

Naamity held her head high. "Why the Lord saved me I may never know."

She returned to work in the munition depot without further incident.

Tungul

When Taharqa arrived at the territory of Tungul, his party was met by nearly a thousand warriors sent by the new queen, Carnabrara, expressing the magnitude of her power.

Ramtouses smiled proudly. "My mother has sent a convoy of elite warriors to escort us to her royal grounds."

The warriors kept their distance all the way to the vicinity of the main village of Tungal. As they approached the village, hundreds of people gathered along either side of the visitors' path. Some even bowed down to Taharqa, surprising him with their attention. The drums beat at a quick and loud rhythm.

Taharqa asked Ramtouses, "What are the drums saying?"

Ramtouses called for one of their escorts to translate their meaning.

"They welcome the Nubian King Taharqa and also express full acceptance of Queen Carnabrara as the ruling monarch of our nation."

The long parade of mules delivering tons of supplies—clothing for combat, food, metal arrowheads, swords, shields, horses for a new cavalry, and chariots by the hundreds—with the hundreds of Nubian officers prepared to aid the training of the new army, were on display as Queen Carnabrara's warriors escorted them to the training grounds.

Taharqa and Ramtouses, along with their highest accompanying officers, were led to an area of the royal grounds designated for special guests of the royal family and given a hospitable greeting by everyone in attendance.

The queen hosted a banquet that night in honor of the Nubian king, giving the travelers a late night before they retired, very exhausted.

Around noon the next day, Ramtouses came before his king, saying, "King Taharqa, it is time to inspect your newest recruits."

From behind a bamboo wall, Taharqa answered, "I will be ready shortly."

While walking away from their dwellings, Ramtouses reported to the king regarding the day's planned activities. The time for serious, intensive training had arrived.

"Most of the Tungul tribesmen live with their families in Tungal, and the mercenary tribesmen have temporary campsites in an old training field across the Nile River. In time, we will have all the men living together as one fighting unit," said Ramtouses. "As of now, all the men are in that area awaiting your inspection, including our Nubian officers."

When they crossed the river, the officers greeted their king respectfully before Ramtouses and Taharqa led the way to the tribesmen lined up according to their ethnic background. The king took his time, nodding approval as he looked into the eyes of many of them before moving on to the next long row of men. There were many rows of men willing to take part in the coming battles for Nubia, and the inspection continued well into the day.

When the tour ended, Taharqa commented to his officers, "There is no reason a fine army can't be assembled from these brave men. Begin your duties."

Manni awaited them at the end of the review.

King Taharqa said, "We will forever be indebted to you. I am overwhelmed at your success in recruiting so many strong, young warriors."

The king walked close to Manni and took his hand. "Manni, there is one other thing I must say to you." He paused. "I want to ask you to forgive your Nubian relatives, namely my brother

Pharaoh Shabaka, for causing you so much misery all these years. Can you find it in your heart to accept my apology?"

"We cannot go back and change the past," said Manni. "It is the future we look to. Further, it was you who saved my family from the hands of Dafori. For without your intervention, I would be dead. It seems we are even."

Taharqa responded. "I'm glad you think of it as so."

Manni put his arm across Ramtouses' shoulder. "I will work with my son to train his warriors in utilizing the techniques I used so successfully. With his existing knowledge of warfare strategies, he may have the best army in the world when training is complete."

Training began right away. Manni reviewed the methods he used many years ago—this time it would be his son's venture. He discussed with Ramtouses the maneuvers he found most effective while fighting the Assyrians, and together they considered which tactics he might want to incorporate into the training.

"Daylight fighting has been the model for war. It is overwhelmingly predictable and expected, so I changed the rules by attacking at night, creating confusion and an element of surprise. This I learned from watching lions because they do most of their fighting and hunting at night, surprising their prey."

Manni went on to say, "Another way to confuse the enemy is to employ an agonizing and irritable noise which can disrupt a person's normal way of thinking. Certain animals use sound to ward off enemies. I found a shrill sound that could be maintained for a long period of time and proved highly successful."

Manni held his finger up. "But my most effective weapon proved to be the poisons we utilized—one type is liquid, the other powder."

Some Nubian tribes who lived in the drought area isolated from the general population knew how to make the poison. The poison for the arrowhead was made from milkweed plants. It caused a quick death from heart seizure. The slightest contact with blood would be fatal. The powdered poison used on the tip of darts came from the skin of a curtain frog and was strong enough to easily take down an elephant. These poisons were not accessible nearby, and they would have to recruit people who knew how to handle the poisons from the warriors who came in to fight. Like the tribesmen of Manni's day, they could train the villagers to help make and store that poison.

Manni only gave advice when needed and did not spend much time training the men, rather, he left it up to his son and his officers to prepare this new army. He spent most of his time teaching the village elders of the one God of the Hebrews, talking about the similarity between the circumcision of their own infants and those of the Hebrews, also of the celebration of the new moon with the sacrifice of sheep and young lamb, and the strong love of both their ancestors and the one true Almighty God for His people.

After finishing training one day, Ramtouses came to where his father was speaking of the one God. He stood back, listening.

"There is a holy temple in their magnificent city where the believers go to worship the one God. Much of their history supports this belief, just as we have a long history of our ancestors. I challenge you in the creation story of the golden reeds being the source of the beginning of mankind.

"The Lord alone created all things, by giving a bit of himself when he blew the breath of life into a human's nostrils, and man became a living soul. As children of God, we must follow his commandments. If his commandments are not kept, we must pray for forgiveness."

Manni said nothing for a few moments, then continued. "The one God is a selfish God. He tolerates no other God in any fashion. I am not saying our ancestors do not deserve recognition, but not equal to God Almighty."

He raised his arms and gestured in all directions. "God Almighty is the Father of all life. He alone offers an opportunity of forgiveness for our sins. We need only to pray for forgiveness when we have sinned and for mercy when trouble or evil happens to us or others."

Ramtouses thought of the time he was in Jerusalem and of the faith those people had in their Lord. He wondered what Naamity might be doing at this moment.

Maybe she is happily married to someone of her faith. Then again, the Hebrew king, Manasseh, hates the followers of the one God. Maybe Naamity is dead now. I should have done more to persuade her to leave with me. I feel this regret could haunt me for the rest of my life. It is a terrible feeling, living with this remorse.

A voice awakened him from his daydream. "Prince Ramtouses, the queen is requesting your presence."

When the prince entered his mother's royal hut, she looked up. "Sit down, my son, we need to discuss some important information concerning the arrangement I made with my sister Adanna.

"First of all, I am sole ruler over our people. The same authority as my sister had, I have. It is the final word. Manni can only express my will, which he accepts without question, because, as you know, Manni is not a native of Tungul. He settled here from Juba.

"Part of Adanna's and my agreement is for you not to be able to inherit the throne. However, if you marry a daughter of Tungul, of my father Tasmeria's lineage, that child will inherit the throne. If, Ramtouses, you elect not to marry a Tungul female, then Adanna's oldest child shall inherit the throne."

Ramtouses stood up with a curious look "I have two wives given to me in Thebes, sisters of my comrades. Their mothers are from Tungul."

"Yes, I know," answered Carnabrara. "But their fathers are of Nubian Egyptian blood, not full-blooded Tungul. Think about it. You do not have to decide right away."

I don't want to make the decision, he thought, but he said, "What do you want, Mother?"

"Of course I would want my grandchild to be ruler. But again, it is your decision, Ramtouses."

Ramtouses excused himself and walked out, stopping to survey the view to his front and sides. Everyone was busy doing their chores. He felt more like an outsider than ever. The whole town seemed happy and peaceful. *Yet I feel so miserable. Why can't I be happy? What is wrong with my thinking? Why cannot I feel the joy of life? I can't wait until we conquer Egypt again, and when it is done, I will go straight to Jerusalem, find Naamity, and carry her off. That is the only solution to my pain, and she must be feeling the same as I. Why else is my heart still longing for her?*

Egypt

After her near rape from the Egyptian officer at the quarry, Naamity went back to her pervious labors, and each day became a pattern of the day before it. One day, the overseer of the weapons depot, who periodically inspected his staff and workplace, noticed a young girl whose appearance led him to believe she could be very beautiful underneath the clutter and dirt that covered her.

He asked one of his guards, "Who is that slave? I don't remember seeing that one before." He pointed at Naamity.

The guard said, "That is the worker who was returned to us from the quarry."

The overseer responded, "Something is not right. Why would he return such a beauty? The quarry master would never send a slave back to me. Does anyone know why he did not want her?"

The men looked at one another until the chief of the guards answered, "No, he did not give reason, except to say not to fondle her."

The overseer thought for a few moments. *The officer down at the quarry despises me.* He became full of suspicion. "She may be possessed by an evil spirit. Remove her from my depot."

The chief guard asked, "Where shall I send her?"

"I don't care. Just rid us of her. Today. Now."

The chief guard had two soldiers report to him. "Come. A short journey is required of you."

The overseer approached Naamity, yelling, "Gather your things, and go with these men."

Naamity said to the wise woman, "Don't worry about me. If the Lord is willing, we will meet again."

The chief of guards spoke to his men. "Take her to the farm, and don't touch her. We don't want any curse brought back to us."

When Naamity arrived at the farm, she was put to work helping to dig trenches for irrigation. The labor in the hot sun made the work miserable and strenuous for anyone without the strength to endure, but Naamity proved her worth in keeping the whip away.

One day as she worked, she decided to sing, thinking it might help her to feel better about the situation. Song had always been a joy to her mother also, and remembering a particular tune of praise and thanksgiving, Naamity started to sing softly, and then with more exuberance. Her voice was sweet and pure—it carried in the gentle wind and lightened the hearts of all who heard. The workers around her felt a joy move about them and started humming softly in the background of her singing.

A guard heard the singing and went to tell the chief. When the chief heard it, he followed the sound and located the source, Naamity. Even though he could not understand Hebrew he enjoyed the beauty of the song.

He gestured to her. "Come out of that trench."

He called upon his interpreter. "Tell her I enjoy her singing and want to have her assigned a new task." He thought for a moment, smiling, something seldom seen in the work camp. "I want her to sing in the morning to start the work day, at noon, and in the evening after work. Her lovely voice will strengthen the morale for all."

One of the guards declared, "This woman has an evil curse on her. That is why she was sent here."

The overseer of the farm said, "Good, then that should keep lustful hands away from her, so she can concentrate on her singing." He thought, *As long as the curse does not affect her voice, I am happy. She shall receive instructions on how to sing Egyptian songs as well as her Hebrew songs.*

Tungul

Ramtouses' army continued to grow as more and more tribesman found their way into Tungal. The new men would be used exclusively for infantry. Horse riders required time not only to learn to ride the horse but also how to maneuver the animal in combat. Only the early recruits and Tungul warriors were given that honor. Chariot driving took excellent skills and would be the second longest process.

Time played an important role in training the army. Ramtouses was mostly in charge of training the tribesman. King Taharqa showed up on fewer and fewer occasions. Each day was fully scheduled. After finally, committing to give his mother a Tungulese grandchild, Ramtouses managed to delegate some time to meet eligible young Tungul girls. Unlike most grooms, he wanted to get to know the person he would marry, and fortunately he had ample time because the next new moon wedding ceremony was three moons away.

He often went down near the river where the girls returned from their daily bath and met with a few to determine a similarity in their thinking and his own because their lives in Tungul and his in Egypt were so different. He was talking with one young woman when an officer approached him.

"My general, the king is asking for you."

Ramtouses answered, "Take me to him."

Ramtouses thought King Taharqa had not been feeling well since for weeks he had missed a lot of the training.

Arriving, Ramtouses walked into the royal living space and bowed. "I am happy to see you, King Taharqa. Are you feeling better?"

"Sit down, here beside me, Ramtouses. My body weakens. It grows worse each week. The healers can do nothing but mix tonics for me to relieve the pain."

"What can I do to help?" Ramtouses could hear the sadness in his own voice.

"You can do nothing but continue to build an army superior to that of any other nation in the world. That will make me happy. I will fight through this thing at home in Napata where I will go to the temple of Amun-re and pray there with my sister."

He continued, "Ramtouses, the one thing Amun-re can do for me that is an answer to my prayer, is let me live long enough to see Egypt under my rule once again. That may be possible through your hand. How long before the men are ready?"

"In three months we are expected to bring the new war machine to Napata and from there, Egypt."

"I will go to Napata for healing and await our army with great anticipation."

In less than four days King Taharqa's party was ready to break camp, and Ramtouses watched as they made their way across the open plains. The whole country of Tungul, along with Ramtouses and his officers, was sad to see Taharqa leave under these circumstances, but renewed their commitment to the task at hand—to prepare this new army for war. Ramtouses consulted with his officers, and they all agreed that the training was on schedule, progressing well.

In his private time, Ramtouses continued to search for a mate among the eligible young virgins. One day, a young woman came to his hut.

She said, "Can you come out and talk to me? I am an unwed virgin and can't enter a man's living quarters."

Out of curiosity, Ramtouses came out.

She began, "I have noticed you talking to several girls. Have you anyone in mind yet?"

Ramtouses smiled. "No, I do not."

She then said, "Why do you wait? Only ten days remain before the big event. You are the fortunate one. Girls from everywhere in Tungul will want to marry you."

Ramtouses looked at her from her head to her feet. "Why haven't I seen you before?"

She answered. "I have been avoiding you. I have seen you down near the bathing area, talking to the prime of the picks. I stayed back and only watched."

Ramtouses, even more curious, asked, "Who are you? What is your name?"

"I am Suwanda," she replied.

Ramtouses turned his head from one side to the other, looking in both directions. "If you avoided me all this time, why are you here now? Is there something I should know?"

Suwanda then said, "I wanted you first to see the others, so when you see me, you will have knowledge for comparison."

Ramtouses said, "I must confess you stand head and shoulders above the others. But I don't want a woman solely because she is beautiful. She must be honest, smart, kind, patient, loving, good natured, and witty."

She turned and started walking away but did not get far before Ramtouses called and ran after her.

"One more question. How old are you? You girls look so young."

"I'm sixteen, and I need to marry now. Next year I will be too old to be considered amongst the top choices."

Ramtouses watched as she walked away, disappearing in a crowd of villagers.

Later that evening while having dinner with his parents, he mentioned the encounter to them.

"You know, Mother, most of the girls here look very young, much younger than sixteen. I don't want to marry someone who looks like my little sister. Still, I have to admit the one I met today looks more like a woman."

The queen asked, "From those you have seen so far is there anyone you would consider?"

Ramtouses held his silence as the meal continued until he finally said, "It does not please me to marry and then in a few days run off to war."

The queen pressed him again. "Who was the young virgin you met today?"

He replied, "Her name is Suwanda."

"Suwanda," said the queen, "Adanna's oldest daughter. Maybe Adanna put her on you. Is she your preference?"

"She sounds very honest. I don't think her mother has anything to do with her behavior, and yes, I prefer her over the others."

Ramtouses met with Suwanda several times before the day of the big event. On the last occasion he said to her, "Suwanda, before I select you at the new moon wedding ceremony, I want you to understand that there is another woman in my life, and if I find her and bring her back, she will be the only woman in my life. Also, because I am a soldier, I will be leaving in a few weeks. Will you accept all of this and still marry me?"

She closed her eyes and said, "Yes, Ramtouses, any moment with you I shall preserve and cherish for my lifetime."

Ramtouses was surprised to hear her words.

During the ceremony, the two of them danced with each other the whole evening, certifying their union in marriage.

Adanna came to Queen Carnabrara. "You should know I had nothing to do with our children's decision to marry. In truth, I was against it because Ramtouses is so different from the men of Tungul and he's a soldier leaving to fight at any time now. She may never see him again."

The queen responded. "Ramtouses is a survivor. If anyone returns, he will."

Three weeks passed, and Ramtouses and his officers organized the different units for marching to Napata. Ramtouses rode out on his monstrous chariot to address his soldiers before the departure. He looked to his right—men as far as he could see, likewise to the left.

It was too far for all to hear his words, so men with strong voices were placed at spaced intervals along the fields of the newly trained soldiers to relay his message to everyone. Manni had prepared the speech to motivate Ramtouses' men for war.

He said to Ramtouses, "Our tribesmen like to be reminded of the fight and encouraged by their leader. It builds morale."

Ramtouses began to talk loudly to his Nubian countrymen.

"A generation ago, our fathers fought and died so that we could have a more productive life. That did not happen. Our crops continued failing for lack of water. I want to be clear about one thing—our fathers thought they were fighting the Ell and believed if they won, the rain would return to the sky and water their lands. Perhaps the one thing we gained from that experience was preserving our freedom. My brothers, it is not the Ell we fight, it is evil men who want to kill us and take away our freedom, making us slaves to labor and stripping our land of its values for their pleasure."

Ramtouses raised his fist and shook it.

"We must strike first before they invade our land, find us unprepared, and win over us. We will conquer Egypt first. This time we will make new homes for our families in Egypt, Nubia, and Ethiopia. Drought-stricken areas will not support us. We need more for our victory, and we shall have it."

Ramtouses pumped his fist up and down as he turned his chariot and rejoined his officers behind him. Thousands upon thousands made the war cry in a deep, heavy, loud voice, pumping their fists over and over in response to Ramtouses' brave words.

In high spirits, the men marched to war, now singing a Nubian war song. With the queen beside him, Manni bid them farewell. He remembered the day when he led a Nubian army such as this one to war and carried the faith of his ancestors in his heart. Today his prayer was sent to God Almighty.

Napata

For a man who was very ill, the trip back to Napata was long and painful. King Taharqa decided he should go to the temple of Amun-re to pray. After all that had happened to him, he hoped his prayer might soften Amun-re's heart toward him. Taharqa could hardly walk without support.

He asked his sister Amenirdis, the high priestess, to join him.

He said to her, "Amenirdis, I think I am dying. Please pray with me to Amun that he might save me long enough for me to see my throne once again in Egypt."

Amenirdis began to cry, her voice weak and shaky. "Amun-re has deserted me, and I no longer honor our marriage."

The king was dumbfounded. His jaw dropped, and he desperately hoped he had misunderstood her words. "What have you done?"

She got down on her knees. "I have slept with a man." She paused. "One whom I love."

Her brother, who once was named Pharaoh of Egypt, knelt onto one knee in front of her. In a more understanding voice, he said, "Are you mad? How could you do such a thing? Has it crossed your mind what kind of action Amun-re might take in retribution for your behavior? Has it occurred to you that Amun-re may have caused my illness in order to punish you for your crime against him? You know as well as I the gods

217

often take their anger out on those close to the one offending them. Don't you know this?"

Taharqa covered his face. Amenirdis reminded her brother, "Amun-re turned his back on us long before my violation. Don't you see that? Look at the whole situation. He ignored my prayers when we needed him the most. What crime had you or I committed when he handed our kingdom to the Assyrian dogs? He has chosen the Libyans, the so-called native Egyptians, to rule in place of us."

The two prayed for hours and before Taharqa finally exited the temple, he told her, "Amun-re will never forgive you for that particular insult."

Weeks later the king called his sister and her lover to his bedside.

"I had hoped it was you, Kobina, and I will not allow the two of you to live in shame. I want it to be known that the palace has no objections to your relationship. But I cannot change Amenirdis's status with Amun-re. I am too weak to find another virgin to replace you. That will come with the new king."

At the end of the first day of travel, while Ramtouses was inspecting his four chariot horses, a messenger approached him and bowed down. "I have urgent news."

"What is it, man? Speak up."

"King Taharqa is asking for you. He is gravely ill."

Ramtouses went to his generals. "I must go ahead. The king needs me now. Bring the army up as planned."

He traveled day and night without stop, drove his chariot straight to the palace gate, and turned over his lathered horses to an attendant. Ramtouses walked quickly up the high staircase, keenly aware of the large group of nobles, family members, and others gathered at the top. He spoke to a high-ranking officer.

"Take me to King Taharqa."

The military man said in a sad voice, "The king is dead. You are too late."

The officer led the way, still talking. "Come. You may view the body."

After spending a few last moments with his king, Ramtouses offered his respects to the queen and other family members and exited the palace, feeling unfathomably weary and sad.

No one really knows the bond we had between us. I will miss him dearly.

It was a three-day journey with mourners, day and night, to the king's burial place. Ramtouses was asked to accompany the procession, and he now spoke to the priest in charge. "Tell me the procedure for burying the king."

"Long ago," the chief priest said, "when King Pianky, the first Nubian pharaoh, ruled Egypt, he adopted the Egyptian customs to promote peace throughout the land. That you may know. What you may not know is Pharaoh Pianky loved our homeland so dearly that he moved the burial practices, building pyramids to house the sleeping pharaohs, to our homeland. All Nubian pharaohs' now rest near the town of Meroë, but Taharqa requested that his pyramid be built across the River Nile near a Nubian town called Nuri.

"King Taharqa designed and built a pyramid in which his body would reside on the east side of the great River Nile and a pinnacle on the west side. The two structures were situated so that when observed from the west side, standing before the pinnacle on the beginning of the annual flooding of the Nile, the sun would rise from the horizon directly over the great pyramid's high point. Four months later at the end of the inundation of water, one would observe from the pyramid the sun set directly over the pinnacle's high point. Such was the extent of King Taharqa's understanding of his place on Earth."

It was abundantly clear to Ramtouses that a great man had slipped from their lives. He waited the seven days for

King Taharqa's body to be wrapped, mummified, and prayed over, bidding the gods' acceptances into their kingdom. His pyramid was sealed, and the reign of Pharaoh Taharqa, loved by Ramtouses, came to an end. The entire congregation returned to Napata where the debate began on who would be his successor to the throne. King Taharqa had not named anyone to be anointed king after his death.

Taharqa, Pharaoh of Egypt and King of Nubia, died in 664 BCE.
His pyramid was erected near the Nubian town of Nuri.
Photo by Hans Birger Nilsen/Flickr.

One officer said, "Ramtouses, you should be king of all Nubia and pharaoh of Egypt once we rule the land. The entire military supports that."

Ramtouses took the comments as a compliment and smiled to the soldiers and guards who saw him in the palace.

However, the royal family had different ideas as to who should be the new king. The family went to High Priestess Amenirdis and told her of the king's failure to name a successor.

"Who is best suited to be king?" they asked.

Amenirdis would not select among the male aspirant hopefuls, and declaring herself unfit, she said, "The god Amun-re has abandoned me, turned his back when our people were in stress before the Assyrians and their gods."

She confessed her adulterous behavior.

The family was stunned to learn of her unholy activities, unknowing and afraid of what Amun-re might do in retaliation to her but also to the family. Much bickering erupted into screaming and yelling until the anger was such that the family asked Amenirdis to leave the temple. Some wanted her to be severely punished, even put to death, but the majority did not agree with that. After all, she had been a loved and respected family member who helped them when they needed her. Besides, she had not been wrong when she'd said Amun-re had left them and allowed the Assyrians to drive them from their homes in Egypt.

In the end, they determined the task to select a virgin from the family line to replace Amenirdis belonged to the new king. That night after she moved from the temple, Amun-re came to her while she slept, saying, "Prince Tantamani is to be your new king."

Amenirdis arose and immediately went to the young man's quarters in the palace.

"I want to see the prince at once."

The prince's guard replied, "He is sleeping."

"Awaken him. I have important news for him."

Tantamani invited her in. "What brings you here this time of night?"

"While I was sleeping Amun-re spoke to me. I was completely surprised after all that has happened. However, he instructed me to tell you that you are to be named the new King of Nubia. He said you must go out and declare it before your kin and Nubian countrymen, without rebuke."

The prince was a little hesitant, thinking, *How can I believe anything she says?* Still, he wanted badly to be king and was willing to accept her foretelling.

The next day, guards rushed into Ramtouses' quarters. "Prince Tantamani wants an audience with you."

"Let him in," Ramtouses said with a gesture.

The prince walked in with his arms folded behind him.

Ramtouses stood. "What is it, my prince?"

The prince said, "I am going to announce to the world that I am King of Nubia, but I need you and the new army behind me."

"What makes you believe they will accept you as the new king?"

"Because I am the best fit to rule our nation and Egypt. Amun-re has told me so. The two others are too old and will not be around long. We need a young, strong leader who will govern for decades."

Ramtouses looked him in the eyes. "How old are you, Prince Tantamani?"

"I am nineteen."

Ramtouses turned his back to him. "I have no knowledge of who would make the best king, but I have to admit I like your spirit—a man who knows what he wants and sees that it happens."

The two men talked for a long time. Ramtouses wanted to understand what the young man's policies would be as king, he did not want to be riding a losing horse. At the end of the conversation Ramtouses committed, saying, "Yes, you have my support. The army will march into the city in two days, and I will lead them. When you emerge, I will come before you and recognize you as King of Nubia."

Within a few days, Prince Tantamani was proclaimed King of Nubia, and a teenage virgin became the new high priestess.

King Tantamani came to General Ramtouses. "I want to be with the army every step of the way to Memphis. I want to set Taharqa's crown, the Khepresh, upon the throne."

"As you wish," responded Ramtouses.

Before I leave, thought Ramtouses, *I should go see my father's dear friend Kobina.*

He found the place and entered. "How are you? I just want to make sure you are not having problems here because of the talk going around. If any man confronts you, show them my seal."

He handed his father's friend his emblem. "And here are some funds you may need." He gave him some gold coins then asked, "Is Amenirdis here?"

"No, she has her own place, a building much like the temple but smaller. I have declined to dwell there as yet."

"As you know, I'm off to war but could not leave without coming to you first. My father would never forgive me. Tell Amenirdis I wish the both of you good fortune until I see you again. Farewell."

Tungul

The war campaign set forth for Egypt in early spring 664 B.C.E.

King Tantamani informed Ramtouses, "I want to learn everything there is to know about techniques and strategies for fighting a war. Leave out nothing."

Ramtouses responded with confidence and authority as the head General of the army. "First, you must have knowledge of your enemy's activities. We send out spies and scouts often months before the army makes any attacks. This helps us understand the strengths and capabilities of the opposing forces."

The king focused on Ramtouses and asked, "So what have we learned that will better help in this operation?"

His chief general replied. "The information provided by our people led us to discover where huge walls have been built along strategic avenues needed to move a large army into Egypt. However, in their haste not all the structure is composed of brick. There was just too much territory for them to barricade in the given time at hand. In many places, they had to settle for heavy timber."

Ramtouses walked up close to the king and showed him a clay tablet with markings on it. "Look. Here is a map locating the walls. The timber shows a weakness in the barricade. We can burn it down then tramp our way through."

Tantamani looked up to the heavens when he said, "The gods are with us. I had a dream last night. Goddesses huddled close to me, one on each side. The one holding my left arm never left me, but the one holding my right arm departed for a while and then returned. I interpreted the dream to mean the one on my left arm was Nubia, and the one on my right arm was Egypt."

After leaving Tantamani's presence, Ramtouses wondered if he could really trust that this new king had the temperament to oversee and make the final decision in critical situations.

The Egyptians had grouped large patrols serving as sentries at different locations along the walls. Concealed by darkness, Ramtouses brought his army up. The Egyptians did not venture beyond their borders into Nubia.

Ramtouses said to his officers, "It appears our presence has not been detected by their sentries. First light of day, our arrows will burn down the timber walls and open a passage for our army to trample through."

The Egyptians were alerted when flocks of flaming arrows buried themselves into the timber defensive walls. They were not totally unprepared for an attack; their main forces lay in wait beyond this weak area of the wall. Messengers were sent to alert Necho of a Nubian invasion and their army, like a great magnet, mustered from all directions to the flaming timber.

Ramtouses told his king, "The dense timbers will take days to cool off. We must wait until it does. I suspect their army will also be waiting."

Two mornings passed before the Nubians were able to march over the now cooled cinders.

The Egyptians, thinking the Nubian infantry would be first to cross over and therefore easy victims for their superior Egyptian cavalry, galloped their well-trained horsemen out first.

Not knowing what to expect in spite of freshly trained horsemen, Ramtouses said to the king, "I'm moving the cavalry through first."

A vicious battle ensued, and after a short fight, the Egyptians withdrew. Ramtouses' suspicion had proven correct.

The attack was meant to cut down infantry coming across into Egypt, not be a full-scale cavalry conflict. The Nubians moved their forces into Egypt.

Ramtouses informed his king, "We will camp on the flat terrain ahead. From there we can see anything approaching us from all directions. When the battle starts, the conditions for fighting there are more suitable."

In less than two days, the opposing men of war stood facing each other.

Necho paraded around his men and officers. "We will win over the Nubian dogs, destroy their army, enslave their people, and take from their land the raw material we need as it has been foretold by the gods."

He looked around at his fine army and continued. "Thanks to our alliance with Assyria, we have superior weapons." He pointed his sword toward the Nubians, and the Egyptian army started its march.

The armies of Ramtouses came to meet them. The Egyptians' powerful composite bows gave them the early advantage and when the arrows came raining down, Ramtouses said to King Tantamani, "The only way to address this type of attack is to counterattack."

He ordered the chariots to charge the Egyptian wall of shields, knowing if the horse-driven vehicles made it to the wall, they would demolish their first line of defense.

Ramtouses said, "I expected the cavalry to engage our offensive move."

Instead, their chariots were first to meet them, and as the battle raged among the chariots, the Nubian archers moved within firing range. The arrows flowed overhead as the mêlée continued beneath.

Ramtouses addressed King Tantamani yet again. "I put my heart and all my faith in my chariot command. If that huge weapon doesn't win, this can be a long war."

The king replied. "I put my faith in the gods. Menthu will stand beside us."

Ramtouses rolled his eyes and said nothing more.

Sometime later in the day, the Nubian chariots returned victorious after slaughtering the Egyptian fleet of wheeled vehicles. The general in command had called off the attack to recuperate and fight another day before they reached the shields.

Ramtouses' face told the whole story as he watched with pride while his general gave the victory sign. Ramtouses knew now that the only protection the Egyptian wall of shields would have was their cavalry. As the day came to an end, the two war machines moved away from each other.

Ramtouses spoke again to Tantamani. "We achieved a major victory today. Only their cavalry remains to defend their wall of shields. This favors our forces as we outnumber their cavalry two to one."

He paused for a moment, thinking of the triumph. "I must congratulate my generals for proving once again that intense training pays off, not to mention numbers—they do help. Something to remember—I have always believed a strong chariot force could dictate the outcome of a battle. Tomorrow they will try to immobilize us with their powerful bows, but we will send forth our cavalry to draw out their horsemen who protect their shield bearers. Our archers will move within range and return the fire. The outcome should be a repeat of today's contest, only this time their cavalry will suffer the defeat."

The king nodded. "I must say you have put together a fine army and fully understand the strategy and principles needed for victory. I see now why my uncle loved you so."

The next day, the fighting went as Ramtouses had predicted. After the cavalry engaged, the Egyptians counterattacked with their riders. The charging forces clashed in the open fields between the two armies. The Egyptian bowmen had to refocus their arrowheads to the oncoming infantry for fear of targeting their own cavalrymen. Before the end of the day, the Egyptians had retreated for fear of losing their whole cavalry.

Though the Egyptians were far better horsemen, the Nubian numbers were too great and they won the battle. However, unlike the chariot battle, this time their losses were extremely high and Ramtouses lamented the number of cavalrymen lost. Still, he had good news for the king as he recounted the victory.

He said to Tantamani, "It takes just too long training successful horsemen to be superior fighters."

Necho considered the war results, thinking, *I am totally disappointed. The big surprise for me is the massive army the Nubians have put together after the humiliating defeat they suffered just a few years ago at the hands of the Assyrians. I will order my men to give up the aerial attack.*

"Every arrow counts," he said. "Save your fire until the infantry is near enough so every arrow can find its mark." Necho yelled to his generals, "Must I dress for battle and show my army how fighting is done?"

The next morning Necho pondered, *Perhaps I should wear my war uniform and call for my elite fighters to gather around me. If the Nubians penetrate our lines and fighting erupts in our interior, I will be ready to fight with my men.*

He screamed, "I will not let these wretched people control Egypt again."

The Nubian army moved toward the waiting shields of the Egyptians. "Have the men stand fast. We must be ready to withstand their impact," Necho called to his generals.

The Nubians kept coming, expecting a rain of arrows upon their heads. When none came, Ramtouses' men continued their advances. However, when the two armies were within a stone's throw of one another, the Egyptians' arrows began to whistle through the air. The percentage of Nubian victims was greatly increased as men dropped to the ground in great numbers. Ramtouses gave the order to charge the Egyptian line of defense and within a short time, the shield bearers found themselves struggling to hold back the wave of Nubian infantrymen.

Thousands pressed against the wall but without success in breaching it because the Egyptian spearmen had slain many, jabbing their long spears into the wedges between the shields. Ramtouses withdrew his forces long before evening.

General Ramtouses said to Tantamani, "This was an unexpected turn of events. I wanted to test their ability to protect their interior but did not expect it to be so stout. I suppose I was drawn into that because of our early success. Don't worry, my king. This is merely a temporary advantage for them. Tomorrow we will send in the ramming chariots, this will aid our infantry in bursting through."

The king responded, "The execution of war can be viewed as masterful when the outcome is in your favor."

"Yes, that is true," Ramtouses agreed, "and tomorrow, with our new design for the ramming chariots, we shall see it in our favor once again."

Large tree trunks were attached to the center of the chariots between the horses, protruding out five to seven feet beyond the horses—some had the image of a ram carved at the end. It was a powerful weapon against men holding shields.

However, the next morning when the Nubians approached the battleground, it became clear the Egyptians had retreated during the night.

Ramtouses said to his generals, "There is no doubt the Egyptians knew today we would overrun their wall of shields with the ramming chariots since we damaged all means they had to protect them. I don't know what they are planning, but they have not given up the fight."

He looked around in several directions. "Find them. They cannot move very fast with an entire army."

The Nubian army stalked the Egyptians for the next six days.

At first the Nubians thought they were headed for Memphis which was one and a half days' journey from where they were, but the scouts soon discovered a large Assyrian garrison in the area.

The Assyrians had established various outposts along their far extended borders as a first defense against invaders and to serve as a base from which they could monitor surrounding activity. Necho spoke to the Assyrian officer commanding the outpost. "I need your horsemen. We cannot defend against these Nubian dogs without a cavalry."

The officer responded, "We have but a thousand men here. It would be suicide to go up against a Nubian army."

Necho pressed him. "If you do not aid us, the Nubians will overrun this garrison anyway. You will lose either way. If we are to have any chance, it is best we fight together. We have a little over a hundred well-trained horsemen remaining. During the battle with their horsemen, we nearly had the better of them, but there were too many. The Nubians are not well-trained. With your elite riders we could win over their depleted cavalry."

The Nubian scouts reported the location of the Assyrian outpost to Ramtouses. He planned his strategy—an all-out attack to obliterate the Egyptian army once and for all. The addition of the Assyrian cavalry did not change Ramtouses' mind.

The next morning, he brought out his cavalry and ramming chariots with the infantry bringing up the rear. He said to his officers, "I don't want any more surprises. We will bring this war to an end today."

Their outnumbered opponent met them. While the cavalries from both armies did battle, the Nubian chariots continued toward the wall of shields. Egyptian archers took aim at the charging vehicles—more than half were disabled, but the rest collided with the walls and burst through.

The remainder of both the Assyrian and Egyptian cavalry withdrew into the Egyptian ranks when the Nubian infantry came slicing their way in. The fighting was furious. There was a total breakdown in the shield bearer protection and Necho the First dressed for battle, giving the order for his elite fighters to move up.

"We must drive them out of our country," he screamed.

Ramtouses moved closer to the fighting, standing alert on his chariot, occasionally shifting his shield to block arrows that came his way.

Since Necho had joined the fighting, he and his special unit cut down Nubians coming up before them from all directions. When Ramtouses saw this, he focused his attention on the group.

"Look." He pointed. "Their leader has now entered the battle."

Other officers noticed the aggressive move also, and Ramtouses said, "I will go up against this hateful ruler."

Ramtouses began to move through the ranks of Nubian men, his first general coming up after him. The general called for the men to fall back and stand fast. The fighting was so fierce, it took some time, but as word was passed along, a short distance was cleared. Ramtouses climbed down from his chariot and entered the open space.

King Tantamani asked one of the generals, "Why is Ramtouses fighting alone?"

The general made an answer. "Sometimes when leaders fight, a sign is given to stand down, and war will cease to give the lords of war a moment of glory. In close quarters, it may be necessary to protect the back of the leader to prevent interference, and the ceased fighting can be halted."

Necho saw him, recognizing him by his dress of ostrich feathers and shiny armor as the same leader who had fought against King Esarhaddon.

Necho wore a silver uniform with many gems. He climbed down from his chariot and yelled. The armies became aware their leaders were about to duel and grew quiet.

"I, Necho the First, will spill the blood of this wretched Nubian dog who thinks his sword skills equal to that of an Egyptian."

He shifted his feet and swiftly came at Ramtouses. The Nubian hero ignored the comments and advanced to meet him.

Necho let out a cry of anger when he swung the first blow. He continued to shriek curses as he again and again hammered Ramtouses' iron sword. He hoped the insults would anger his opponent and cause him to make mistakes. Ramtouses went on the offensive and drove back the Egyptian leader of men.

Necho would not let that stop him and came forward again, waving his powerful sword. Ramtouses met his blow with a prevailing swing, creating a mighty impact. He rushed him, banging his shield against Necho and knocking him to the ground. Before Ramtouses could strike a final fatal blow, Necho found a rock and hurled it at his rushing opponent, who ducked away as it sailed pass him. This gave Necho time to scramble to his feet. Still Ramtouses came up fast, striking him on the helmet. Necho covered his head with his shield, while Ramtouses banged on it twice. He took a wild swing at Ramtouses, trying to ward off the attack but missed badly.

Ramtouses struck again—this time his sword swept across the king's midsection, the iron blade knocking loose several metal plates of body armor. The next blow landed on the back of Necho's neck as he turned to reposition himself for better fighting. Necho's body slammed flat onto the ground and lay still. The Nubian army erupted with a victory cry.

Ramtouses raised his sword high in the air, looking toward his enemies. "Your Egyptian king has been defeated. Take the necessary days for his burial."

As Ramtouses walked back to his Nubian ranks there was a roar of pride and joy amongst his men.

King Tantamani approached him. "That was a magnificent duel. The gods are surely with you."

Ramtouses replied, "I credit it to skill and intense training."

He headed for the healers to attend his minor cuts while the men closest to him reached out, trying to touch him while praising his skills and courage.

The Egyptians moved slowly in defeat as they wrapped the body of Necho in cloth and carried it into their ranks in a state of bereavement.

After five days Tantamani came to Ramtouses. "What is going on in their camp? How much longer do we wait? We must attack now while we can impose our dominance over them."

His chief general's answer came to him slowly, with deliberation. "My king, our spies and scouts have been observing their daily movements. They have returned the body of Necho to Memphis for the final ceremony. Perhaps during this time they shall also select a new leader or pharaoh to lead them."

The king had a curious look about him. "What else have you not told me?"

Ramtouses then said, "I believe they are planning to retreat back to the city and make a last stand there."

The king threw open his arms and in an impatient voice said, "And meanwhile we sit here and do nothing?"

Ramtouses quickly responded. "No, my king, during this time we are building siege towers needed to elevate us over the high walls, and a battering ram to knock down the gates. The towers are wooden so we cover them with thick animal hides to inhibit fires. We expect to receive flaming arrows from the enemy. The battering ram must be many times heavier than those used with our chariots."

Tantamani, satisfied with this information, turned and walked away. After five more days, just as Ramtouses had predicted, the Egyptian camps had been evacuated and their troops had retreated back to Memphis.

One of the general's scouts said to him, "Most of the civilian population has been displaced to make room for the soldiers."

Ramtouses ordered his generals to move the army to the city.

A few weeks had passed since the slaying of Necho, and during that time Prince Psamtik, the son of Necho, emerged as their ruler.

He spoke to his officers. "Go declare this to the men." He looked around at each man. "In giving me the authority to lead our people, I, the son of Necho the First, will not surrender our precious city of Memphis to our enemies, the Nubians. I will preserve this wonderful place where our kingdom was founded in remembrance of my father, and I shall dedicate each spear or arrow that brings down a Nubian to him."

Ramtouses stood poised to attack Memphis.

King Tantamani stood ready to give the command. "Before I give the order to attack, I want it understood the city must be recaptured with minimal amount of destruction. I want Nubia to return to the city as it was before we left."

He took in a deep breath and yelled, "Now go with the hand of Menthu and bring Memphis back to its rightful rulers."

It was a very dark and gloomy morning when the four huge siege towers and the giant battering ram crept toward the city walls with thousands of Nubians troops around them. To the Egyptians, it signified the coming of death. Bringing war to the city walls seemed like a few moments to the Egyptians, but for the Nubians the task of moving these war machines took all morning. Suddenly, the sun burst through the cloudy overcast, and just as it did, fighting began.

Ramtouses looked on, watching thousands of Nubians crowd behind the tall war weapons while arrows flew back and forth. The Egyptians shot flaming arrows to burn down the siege towers, but the covering protected them. At close range, the Nubians employed the battering rams but failed to open the gates, as hot tar and large boulders assaulted them from atop the city walls.

Before the four towers reached the walls, one was pushed over, crushing and injuring a crowd of Nubians. But the general smiled as the other three succeeded in reaching the walls. Ramtouses gave credit to his enemy, as the Egyptians fought with all their might. In the end, the Nubian numbers were too great.

The influx of fierce and brutal Nubians slaughtered all who stood before them throughout the rest of the day. Before night fell, Memphis was taken. During the battle, the Nubians were careful not to overly damage the city's monuments.

Ramtouses said to Tantamani, "The nation once again belongs to Nubia. There is one thing left to do—the new ruler and what is left of his elite force are barricaded within the palace."

The king answered, "I don't want the palace demolished under any circumstance. How do we negotiate with them?"

"I will offer them their lives."

Ramtouses and two of his officers positioned at the foot of the long flight of stairs leading to the palace main doors.

He shouted, "Can you hear me?" When no answer came, Ramtouses continued. "I am the Chief General of the Nubian army, and my loyalties lie with my king and the gods. May my word be my keeper if I declare a statement before them to witness, I will not forfeit their trust in me by uttering lies in their name. So I say to those of you within the palace, if you come out peacefully, you will not be put to death. You have my word before the gods. I cannot promise your freedom, but you will live."

Ramtouses waited a long time, and when no one responded, he slowly moved away.

The next morning, Prince Psamtik opened the doors and asked for Ramtouses.

When Ramtouses returned to the palace, the prince said to him, "I am holding you to your word. We are coming out."

They were immediately taken as prisoners of war. Before King Tantamani entered the building, he had it rearranged to look as it had when his uncle Taharqa last saw it. Once the work was completed on the interior of the magnificent royal home, he walked proudly in with Ramtouses escorting him.

When they came into the pharaoh's court, Ramtouses stopped and watched as the king gracefully walked up to the throne and knelt.

He said, "Honorable Taharqa, I know you are watching from the Kingdom of the Gods. I vowed to reestablish the Nubians as the rightful rulers of Egypt. Today that promise is fulfilled."

He stood.

Ramtouses witnessed a complete change in his demeanor. His eyes were fixed, staring straight ahead. His face showed no expression. A collection of pharaoh's crowns set nearby and choosing one, Tantamani moved back to the throne. This time he sat down and placed the Pschent crown that represented a unified Egypt on his head. It displayed a large, golden serpent. He folded his arms across his chest holding the crook in one hand, the flail in the other, representing kingship and fertility of the land, then whispered. "I am now ruler of Egypt, Ethiopia, and Nubia."

A few other officers had joined Ramtouses and stood next to him. After the new pharaoh's words, Ramtouses approached the throne with his companions and knelt on one knee, bowing his head.

⁖

In Nineveh, King Esarhaddon came before his oracles. He vowed to continue the commitment in his restoration of Babylon. His goal was to divert some of the blame from his father.

Standing before them, he said, "Because of the war in Egypt, the progress in Babylon was stifled, but now I have returned and am focused on fulfilling my promise."

He reminded them. "In the reign of an earlier king, there were evil omens in Babylon—their crimes were injustices, lies. The inhabitants mistreated the gods by not making regular offerings and worship. They took the temple treasures to pay debts. For this, Baal became angry with Babylon. He caused the Euphrates to overflow and turn the city into a ruin."

His explanation of how the gods' divine anger had set in motion the events leading to the destruction of the once beautiful Babylon served to offer an alternate premise to the truth of how the riches of Babylon had been hauled off by his father.

It also explained why Baal had turned his back when danger came.

King Esarhaddon added, "Whoever is responsible, let it be known among the gods that I brought back the glory of Babylon."

The project again started as before, but this time thousands more slaves were added to the labor force, mostly Egyptian and Ethiopian Nubians.

For the next two years, the burden on the slaves was tremendous. If one failed to keep up with the work, he was beaten or killed and replaced with another.

Esarhaddon came before the oracles again. "I have done wonders in Babylon. I have restored the status of the gods, built new alters and temples. The city of Babylonia is magnificent—the great temple complex restored, also the structure known as the tower of Babel. I have made the processional way of Babylon shine with baked bricks from a ritually pure kiln, so that anyone seeing the radiant brick pathway leading to the temple of the gods will remember my contribution."

More than most kings of Assyria, Esarhaddon trusted the oracles' opinions and accepted them gladly.

The speaker for the oracles responded. "It is honorable that you take on such a task of healing the wounds, making restitution for the transgressions of your father as suggested by the Court of Oracles. It is right that your family should not be held totally responsible."

The speaker went on to say, "Remember, our people are very resentful. If they think you are doing more for the beautification of Babylon then for Nineveh, it could cause a problem."

Esarhaddon pointed out, "Don't forget Merodach-Baladan's son who collected his tribesmen and marched up to claim his father's old Babylonian Territory. I went down to meet him. I defeated his army then sacked his villages of their gold and silver. I brought the treasure back to Nineveh. In addition, I went down to the potent country of Egypt, brought back as much booty as we could bear, and returned that to Nineveh as well. Nineveh has no reason to feel slighted."

After the meeting came to adjournment and he descended from the building steps, Esarhaddon thought of the rumors of war brewing in Egypt. Suddenly a messenger approached him with a script that read, *Egypt has fallen under Nubian control once again.*

Nineveh, Assyria

Emperor Esarhaddon called his officers to counsel. "You know why we are here." He paced the floor. "The Nubians must be stopped before they decide to infiltrate other vassal states in the area."

He addressed his highest ranking general. "How soon can we be ready to march?"

The general answered, "The army has been preparing for months because the Nubian uprising was expected. We can be ready in fourteen days."

"You will be ready in seven. March the infantry out first. The cavalry can overtake them later on horseback. My son, Prince Ashurbanipal, will stay with the generals to learn the ways of a king and military leader."

The meeting continued; the only topics discussed involved war preparation.

Following his war council, Esarhaddon went directly to his wives and younger children. "We leave immediately. Gather what you will. We are going to our retreat in Babylon."

When they arrived at Babylon, Emperor Esarhaddon spoke to his first wife. "The armies are passing this way, and when they arrive, I will join them. War with the Nubians is inevitable, and as king I must lead them."

He looked around at the well-kept vegetation before him with wonderfully designed flowing green spaces, waterfalls, and landscaped with trees and bushes in various states of bloom. "This is a beautiful place. I want to enjoy a few days of happiness here with you."

For two days, Esarhaddon did nothing but entertain his children—they ran races and wrestled, rolling freely in the grasses. They enjoyed laughter and food, always talking. The children kept his mind off the serious matters demanded of him by the kingdom and the army, but by the third morning, he began to think about Manasseh, wondering how the deposed king was doing after two years of confinement.

I should go down to the prison and see him.

That day the King of Nations addressed his palace guard. "Take me to the dungeon. I want to see the prisoner."

The interior of the prison was dark and musty. A large, heavy door enclosed the prisoner in a windowless space with an earthen floor that barely allowed for a two-step pace in any direction. A small opening was cut into the door for passage of food and water to the prisoner.

"Open the door," said Esarhaddon to the guard.

Once the guard had done as ordered, an offensive odor wafted out the dark space beyond. The emperor called, "Manasseh, come out. It is I, your king." Hearing no response, the king looked at the guard again. "Does he ever come out?"

"At times we allow him out into the corridor to determine his health," answered his guard.

Esarhaddon pushed the guard aside, saying, "Move. I'm going in."

He took the lit a torch from the guard's hand and walked inside the cell. He found Manassas lying in a far corner but could not see what his condition might be.

"Guards," he yelled. "Come, take this man out into the light, so I can see him better."

Manassas was covered in filth, the old kingly garments hung from his thin body in wide empty folds that once were filled with muscled arms and legs, legs that now could barely hold his weight. Manassas was in poor health, and Esarhaddon felt his ire rise immediately, and intensely.

He crossed over to the head guard. "What is the meaning of this? Your prisoner is a king. Unless I give orders for harsh treatment, you will honor his dignity—confinement, that is all."

The emperor took another look at his prisoner. "Send for a healer. And move him upstairs. Feed him, bathe him, and clothe him in fine garments worthy a king."

After two days, he went to the healer and asked, "How is Manasseh?"

"Better—he's sitting up today." The healer answered.

The king wanted to see him. When he entered the room, he asked. "How are you today?"

Manasseh said, "I feel as if I'm awaking from a nightmare."

The king said, "I did not expect my men to treat you as they did. Your future confinement will be much less severe."

Manasseh looked steadily at the emperor, not wavering his gaze with his head slightly tilted to the left. He said, "I received a punishment far less fitting me for my crimes against the Lord. I am not an Assyrian, I am not Babylonian. Worshiping your gods is a façade that was not for me; one cannot change who he or she is."

Esarhaddon rolled his eyes, waiting to hear what Manasseh would say next.

"For years I have been unreasonably cruel to my people. I have put thousands to death in the name of Baal, shunning the one true Lord and all the blessings he has bestowed on me and my people."

Esarhaddon walked closer to him, his dark eyes narrowed as he spoke. "Baal is the king of the gods. Don't you see that? He controls the world through me and chooses who will live and who may not live. It is I who placed you in the dungeon. The Assyrians rule all lands, and do not ever forget it."

Silence held the room captive for a few moments, and then Manasseh said, "What is it to be alive? Is it a test for those who have much and a test for those who have nothing, a test to measure their worth by their deeds?

"The wealthy man will hold onto his fortune even when God dictates that he should share with his brother. He will say, 'No, I will not share it with the fatherless or poor. I will rather turn my back on God.' The unfortunate person shall hate God, blaming him for his poor conditions.

"Some of us will be born with many loaves of bread, fleece from the sheep, higher learning and powerful influence in court. I knew certain ways were not right in the eyes of the Lord, but because I both feared and idolized the Assyrians, I put my faith in their power and wealth. I did not speak against them. I said 'I will put my trust in gold. Pure gold, you are my security.'

"If a man came to my court with a grievance and I ignored him, what then? What will I do when the Lord confronts me? What will I answer when called to account? To love God, I must fear him more than any earthly value, for I dread the mighty destruction and frightful splendor my God may wield the day I stand in judgement."

King Esarhaddon placed his hands akimbo and said in a loud voice, "What does that mean? Everyone has a story to tell. Shall I open my doors to the weak and feeble and let chaos rule?"

The emperor turned to leave. "Enjoy your time up here away from the dungeon."

Esarhaddon considered Manasseh's words all that night and wondered what the deposed king would do if given the opportunity to return to his beloved Jerusalem. The next morning, immediately after he had finished his morning meal, the king returned to Manasseh's bedside.

With a slight smile he said, "It seems I will not bury you here after all. I think you have had enough. Would it please you to return to Jerusalem and rule your people?"

He expected a sign of relief, or joy, or even thankfulness, but Manasseh's face did not register any happiness when he spoke. "If you return me to Jerusalem, I will try to reverse the wrong I have done. I will sway my people back to the one true God, our Lord."

Esarhaddon stamped his foot. "You must be mad. You tell me this to my face, knowing I have the power to return you to the dungeon."

Manasseh leaned forward in his bed, tears collected in his eyes. "Return me to the dungeon if you must. I will never betray my people again."

The king thought for a moment. *Did he find divine solitude behind the walls of this enchanted place as I did? Is that what drives his words now?*

Manasseh interrupted the emperor's thoughts when he spoke again. "The divine glory of God has found me inside these walls, and I will never lose Him again."

Esarhaddon whispered to himself, "Divine glory?" A calming spirit seemed to encircle him. "I respect your honesty. There are not many men who will speak their true feelings to my face. Because of that, I will not interfere with whatever you and your people believe in. Just remember to pay all your tributes on time."

By the time the army arrived from Nineveh for Esarhaddon to join them, Manasseh was strong enough to ride.

The morning they approached Jerusalem was a market day and the city bustled with activity. The army of Assyria was miles away as King Esarhaddon and a large convoy of soldiers met Hebrew soldiers coming up from the city. When they realized Manasseh was with them, a rider hurried back to the city while the others escorted the elite party up to the main gates.

243

Word of the arrival of King Manasseh escorted by Emperor Esarhaddon traveled fast across the city, and hundreds of people came out and swarmed around them, some calling to Manasseh by name. No king had been selected from his family as everyone believed he would return. However, the people of Jerusalem had very mixed feelings for the man who had put so many to death. Scores of families had lost loved ones because of his brutality. Still, the majority remained loyal to him. Manasseh raised his hand as the procession made its way to the palace where his family members hurried out to meet them—but not all.

In order to control them, the Manasseh of old had divided his relatives into opposing camps that overflowed with jealousy and animosity toward each other.

Esarhaddon and his officers stayed at the palace that night and enjoyed a hefty feast.

In the morning, Manasseh made it known that his intention was to heal the wounds that had been buried deep in some of his family members. It took all day to convince them of his good intent, and in the end, Manasseh realized that healing could take years. He also wanted to address the nation, so he announced he would deliver a speech from his balcony on his second day.

A number of rumors circulated among the people regarding Manasseh's coming announcements. Both fear and happiness vibrated throughout the city. Not even his family knew what he would say. As early evening approached, Manasseh gathered himself to emerge onto the open deck of the palace. Thousands of people were crowded in every available spot with and without a view of the king.

Emperor Esarhaddon, selecting to stay another night in Jerusalem just to hear what the king would say, stood behind a large column where the people outside could not see him. He watched as the Hebrew king slowly walked out, gazing around the crowd.

Manasseh began to speak. "I ask you, my countrymen, listen to my words before passing judgment. In the past, I decreed the defilement of the Holy Temple of our Lord. I ordered the execution of many of my people. There are no excuses for my violent behavior. By right, I should be dead, but the Lord in his anger took me and locked me away in a dungeon, and in my darkest hour, hidden from the eyes of the world, I humbled myself before the Lord Almighty.

"There was no way of telling day from night, new moon to the next new moon, and then, after what seemed an eternity of soundlessness in the deep darkness of my confinement, I began to feel that someone else was there with me.

"And then I heard a voice in a vision speak to me; it said, 'The Lord has placed redemption next to your name among the kings of Judah and has granted you a second chance to rule your people for many years.' I saw no one but often heard the voice speaking to me about the days to come in my life. Without the voice, I don't know if I would have survived in that place. If the Lord can hear the sobbing of a corrupt soul whose hands have spilled a thick trail of innocent blood for many years, including turning his back to the true God to worship other gods and in the process desecrating His holy temple, then any man, no matter what sin has been committed, God can forgive for the asking. As of this day, the purpose of my life will be to bring back the glory of God to Judah. The Lord is willing to give me a second chance."

He opened his arms to his people, adding, "Will you?"

With those words, he departed.

Esarhaddon left also, with no additional word to Manasseh, and returned to his waiting army. They broke camp and proceeded to Egypt.

Memphis, Egypt

Ramtouses was quite aware of the Assyrian movements. He was busy reinforcing Memphis' resistance to attack—improving the structure of the walls, building sophisticated devices designed to kill hundreds of invaders unexpectedly. A large number of the army personnel were out scouring the territory searching for runaway Nubian slaves held by the Egyptians, in an effort to recruit them. Extra manpower was necessary to replace the thousands lost fighting the Egyptian army.

During the search across the countryside, Ramtouses' men encountered many Egyptian soldiers who held Nubian people captive, and in the process the Egyptians themselves became prisoners. One of the Egyptian soldiers kept yelling, "Please, I must see your General Ramtouses."

After a Nubian soldier became irritated by his demands, he yelled with an angry voice, "Silence. I have no concern what business you may have with our General Ramtouses."

When he would not stop asking, the Nubian soldier struck him in the face.

An Egyptian officer overhearing his own soldier's plea, curiously asked, "Why is it you keep demanding to see Ramtouses? Why should he give you any of his time?"

He came close to the officer and said, "I have something of great value to the man."

The officer's curiosity continued to grow. "What is it you have?"

The soldier showed him a large bronze coin and quickly returned it to his sarong.

"Wait. Let me see that again. What was that?"

The soldiers said, "We are prisoners, and I don't have to obey your orders."

Another Nubian soldier approached and drew back his whip in a threatening manner. "Shut up," he yelled.

From then on, the Egyptian officer used every opportunity possible to question the soldier, asking, "Why would the masterful General Ramtouses be interested in the emblem you carry?"

The soldier made sure no one else could overhear him and finally said, "I am trying to gain the freedom for my family. This seal can make that happen."

"I am an officer. If you know something that can help us, please tell me. I have a better chance of getting the attention of the prisoner guards."

The bearer of the coin said, "I will tell you. Accordingly, we will work together, and I will keep the emblem. You can do the talking; the value of this information is wealth more than one man or even a dozen."

The soldier told the officer of the young woman from Jerusalem who had the seal originally and had been looking for Ramtouses. "I knew it was very important for her to find him after such a dangerous journey."

The officer asked, "Where is she now?"

"That, I will not tell you. First, let us see if we can get the attention of the Nubians."

The following morning while they marched en route to Memphis, the officer considered how he could find a guard who would listen. In training men to be soldiers over the years, the officer had developed a strong sense of the character of others. He chose a soldier whom he had observed to hold many brief interactions with other soldiers. He might be willing to converse with the captives.

He waited for the right opportunity. "I need to relieve myself," the Egyptian officer said to the one he had selected.

The Nubian soldier said, "Let it out as you walk."

He did but slowed down and began falling behind. The Nubian came up to strike him.

The officer covered his head. "I fell behind on purpose, so you can hear the words I have for you. Do you desire to be only a guard when I have a gift from the gods that could lift you from this situation, make you an honored man among the officers and Ramtouses himself? Strike me as much as you like if my words are not all that I have said." He spoke rapidly, believing this might be his only opportunity to be heard.

The soldier lowered his whip. "Just how can you do that? And it better be convincing."

The Egyptian told the guard about the seal and how important it was to their chief general, Ramtouses.

The Nubian soldier thought for a moment. "How can you be sure she is still alive?"

"We are not sure, but Ramtouses would want to know."

The Nubian asked, "Where is the other man?"

"He is in the crowd of prisoners," said the Egyptian.

"I must see this emblem—take me to him," ordered the Nubian.

The two men walked over to the one carrying the intriguing object.

The Nubian guard demanded, "Where is the emblem? I need to see it now."

As the soldier showed it to him, the Nubian snatched it and felt it with his fingers. After a few moments he said, "This looks and feels genuine."

He looked the Egyptian soldier up and down. "How did you come across something like this?"

The Egyptian soldier told him the story of the young woman from Jerusalem and her efforts to find Ramtouses.

"You have the coin, but where is she?"

The prisoner spoke again, "For this knowledge I should receive reward. If this emblem is as precious as we think it is, there will be plenty of compensation for the three of us. It is better that I save the location of the girl until we see Ramtouses."

The Nubian guard said, "I could torture you and get the answers I need." *But that could work against me,* he thought. *It would be to my advantage to keep this between us for now.* "But no torture today," he said the prisoners. "No one else needs to know until we arrive at Memphis."

The Nubian soldier removed his helmet and walked around rubbing his head. "Meanwhile, I will keep the coin to show General Ramtouses, and I will come for you two as soon as I know more."

They reached the capital and all the prisoners were assigned to labor camps. For three days, the Egyptian soldier and officer worked day and night, they were fed a single daily meal, and guarded closely. The fourth day brought a surprise when the Nubian soldier, accompanied by an officer, came searching for them. On the way out of the labor camp, he said, "I delivered the seal to the general today, and he sent this officer for us."

They entered the palace and Ramtouses met them at the vestibule. He held the seal in his hand.

"Where did you get this?" His voice was firm, his eyes were large, and there was no doubt in the mind of anyone who heard or saw him that the situation demanded serious attention. "Tell me now."

The Nubian guard said, "I recovered it from these two."

He pointed at the Egyptians with him. Ramtouses drew his sword screaming, "Where is she? I will cut off your heads right now if what you say is not the truth."

The Egyptian officer answered, "If you do that, you will never be able to find her."

After hearing that, Ramtouses struck the man with his fist, knocking him to the floor. The general then turned and walked away, pressing his hands against the sides of his head as the memory of her allure came lovingly back. *Control your emotions,* he counseled himself, and took a deep breath before he slowly turned back toward the people waiting at the palace entrance. He stood before them showing little, if any, emotion. His words were, "What is it you want? Name it."

The three men started talking all at the same time.

Ramtouses shouted angrily. "Wait—this will get us nowhere. First, I need all the information you have concerning this young woman."

He motioned for his officer to come closer. "This officer will make a record of whatever your needs are. If your information is valid, compensation will be paid. If not, I will execute the three of you myself."

The Egyptian soldier who carried the coin started talking. "Longer than two years ago, a group of people from Egypt came to me asking if anyone knew how to find Ramtouses. They had no idea the Nubians were no longer governing this country. They were taken prisoner, the coin discarded. I retrieved the coin, thinking of its bronze value. The girl was disguised as a boy and later taken away to work at another site. When her identity was discovered, for some reason she was returned to the weapons depot, and that is where she remains."

Ramtouses interrupted. "That's enough. Bring my horse and three mounts for these men. Do you know where the depot is from here?" Ramtouses looked at the Egyptian prisoner who'd told the story.

"Yes, I do, sir," he answered.

Ramtouses called to some of his soldiers, "You men, come with me."

He pointed at another one. "You," he yelled. "Go and alert the comrades. I might need their assistance."

Ramtouses and his party rode toward the depot. Before long the group came upon the depository building, which showed signs of war everywhere.

When Ramtouses saw the place, he cried, "I am too late."

He waved his arms. "Dismount and search the entire area, every inch. We are looking for a young woman of Hebrew descent with pale skin."

Dead bodies were scattered here and there across the whole site. Ramtouses looked at the three men accompanying him. "You three, stay with me. I don't want you out of my sight."

The company of men looked until most of the grounds were covered.

The bodies of several girls were found but not Naamity. Suddenly, the Nubian soldier who had accompanied the two of the Egyptians prisoners yelled, "This one is still alive."

It was the wise woman who helped Naamity during their imprisonment, but Ramtouses knew nothing of her.

He ran to the soldier who knelt beside an old woman and dropped to one knee beside her. "Can you speak?"

The woman began to smile. "I would not die because I knew that child would need my help again." Her voice was a weak murmur.

Ramtouses asked, "Naamity—is she here among the dead?"

Lowering his ear to her face, he heard, "God is with that child."

The general grew impatient. "Do you know if she is alive? We cannot find her here."

The dying woman took Ramtouses' hand. "You are the one she has been looking for. They took her away to a large farm south of the city."

"Farm south of the city," Ramtouses repeated. He looked around. "Get someone over here to help this woman."

"No, no," she said. "I will sleep now." She released his hand and died.

Ramtouses sent a rider to inform his comrades that he would meet them south of the city. He left a detail at the munition depot with orders to bury the Nubian and Hebrew slaves. That night, he camped outside the city and waited for his comrades to join them. Ramtouses sat in his tent alone as if he could not wait until dawn. *What was she doing in Egypt, and how did she get here?*

At sunrise, Ramtouses was first to rise. "Up now, men. We must leave. We will eat when we find the farm." He walked through the camp giving instructions. "I want to divide the men into four groups."

He pointed at some. "Go that way."

He continued to point. "You men, go down there, you men this way. The rest of you will ride with me. If anyone finds a very large farm, send a rider to me."

They rode off in four different southerly directions. All day they searched but only found a few small farms. Early that evening a rider who had been searching in another area came to Ramtouses.

"General, I think we may have found the farm."

"Where?" Ramtouses responded.

"East of this location, but less than a quarter of a day's ride."

Although Ramtouses and his men had already dismounted, he called to them. "Mount."

Another officer said to him "General, the men are exhausted, the horses worn out. Would it not be best to have a fresh start early morning?"

Ramtouses hesitated, knowing his officer was right. "Yes, that is best. Care for the horses' needs, prepare a meal, and rest for the night. We will continue the search come sunrise."

At dawn, they were off with haste. When Ramtouses and his men arrived, it was late morning. Unlike the weapons depot, there were no bodies lying anywhere. Ramtouses looked around the huge place. He thought, *Even with a hundred men it could take days to search.*

He picked three riders. "Find the other search parties and have them join us here." To the three that carried the emblem, he said again, "Again, you three stay with me. I don't want you out of my sight."

The search was now focused on one location, the farm, albeit, a large farm.

Back in Memphis, King Tantamani asked for his chief general. "Where is Ramtouses? Find him."

One of the officers reported to the king "Ramtouses has left the city and is expected to return before the end of the day."

When he did not return, the king wondered why. *What kind of an army do I command? Where anyone can do as they please? Have not the gods elected to give the glory to me alone for crushing the Assyrian army? This is my moment in history—Menthu is standing beside me.*

King Tantamani said to his next general in command, "Come to me with all the updates on the Assyrian movements."

I have learned much from Ramtouses and can lead the war campaign myself.

The general later reported to him. "The Assyrians are fourteen days away from our border. Shall we remain in the city or move our armies up to the border to meet them? If we don't act with haste, it will be too late to get there in time."

Tantamani said, "What do you think Ramtouses would do?"

The general was quiet as if in thought. Finally he said, "Are you certain you don't want me to lead our forces?"

Thinking of the elaborate defense system Ramtouses had designed for the city, one that could change the tide of battle, the king responded, "Never mind. Move the men out. We will meet them at our border. The city will be our haven if we fail to stop them."

Ramtouses directed the men to branch out in groups of ten and search the large farm, including the buildings, the tilled fields, and rolling hillsides left to grow wild.

"Blow your horn if you find anything."

It was early evening when Ramtouses suddenly stopped. "Quiet, everyone—I heard something."

Only the group accompanying him could hear his voice and they froze as if time itself had stopped. It was so still only the rustle of a warm breeze interrupted the silence.

Not far from Ramtouses one of his comrades whispered, "Over here. I heard a sound."

Ramtouses moved toward the man, listening intently. They heard it again and the men moved in the direction it seemed to be coming from, following the faint sound, weaving their way through the vegetation as the sound grew louder.

Suddenly Ramtouses said, "That sounds like singing."

The sound was slow and sorrowful, reaching deep into the heart where loss and grief resided. It attracted them like a magnet draws opposite poles, for they all had suffered the sadness of war.

They stepped from the bushes into a clearing, and stopped. Ramtouses alone walked further into the open space and then, he too stopped. Less than a stone's throw away, a woman stood on a mound of earth with several people seated on the ground in front of her. His body went limp, almost causing him to stumble and forcing him to take a few deep breaths to compose himself. He shook his head, trying to clear the vision that appeared to be a dream. Then, not moving his eyes from her, he said in a voice so soft only he could hear the words. "No, no. It can't be. Can it be?"

He started walking, taking each step slowly, and hoping not to awaken himself from this reverie. The last brilliant rays of the sun highlighted her face and bright clothing.

Naamity turned and saw him coming toward her. The song that was soft and mournful ended, replaced with a strong and powerful tune, expressing exuberance and energy, full of emotion.

"I will never lose the love I have for my God.

My God who walked with me through many dreadful days.

My God who leads me to my destiny in life."

Ramtouses wove his way past the onlookers, mesmerized by her song, and stopped at the foot of the mound. He and Naamity gazed at one another, two lost souls reuniting. Naamity's tears ran down her cheeks like water rolling off a petal during a rain storm. She ended the song by singing these words, "God has redeemed my tormented soul."

She held the note for as long as she could and then, without hesitation, she hurled herself forward. A bewildered Ramtouses reached out as she fell upon him, surrounding her precious body with his powerful arms.

Naamity cried out with joy, and Ramtouses held her tight, not wanting to lose her if he should awaken from this dream, yet knowing it was reality.

"How can this be?" They stood there as if frozen in time, embracing.

Ramtouses repeated, "How can this be? I found you—I found you. Your God is very powerful and has sealed our love for this breathtaking moment."

Naamity said between sobs, "I have not been able to find peace without you."

She buried her face against his chest. "How can one person love another so much, and yet here I am preserved for you as I was the many moons ago."

She began weeping again.

More and more of his comrades gathered at the site.

Ramtouses finally looked at his men. "We will make camp here tonight."

He turned and led Naamity to a spot where he and she would bed for the night. "Tomorrow we will head back to Memphis."

The Egyptian officer thought as he watched the Nubian general gently kiss her wet face over and over.

This is more than I expected. This man's whole world revolves around this beautiful young woman. I am an Egyptian officer sworn to defend my country with my life if need be. I have an opportunity to do just that now."

As they prepared to bed down, he said to his fellow Egyptian soldier, "You are a soldier and like myself are sworn to defend your country. You will do as I say. Otherwise you can be executed for treason—we are prisoners at a time of war."

The soldier, unhappy with his comments, spoke. "What are you talking about? We can soon be free men joined with our families with fists full of gold."

"Did you not hear my words?" he said in a very angry low voice, grabbing him by the upper garment. "I will wake you when everyone has fallen asleep."

The soldier said no more and lay down.

Later that night when the camp was totally motionless, the officer awakened his Egyptian countryman. "Don't make a sound."

The man wiped his face several times, waking himself up.

"I have a plan that will make us both heroes."

The three men who made the search for Naamity possible slept near one another. The officer and his companion crawled over to the third man, the Egyptian Nubian. The officer turned and whispered in his fellow Egyptian's ear.

"If he wakes up, cover his mouth."

The officer slowly removed the Nubian soldier's dagger, but the man turned over, making it impossible to recover his sword. The officer put the dagger to his throat and slowly awakened him. When he opened his eyes, he discovered a hand over his mouth and a blade's sharp point pressed against his neck.

The officer looked him in the eyes, at the same time placing a finger to his own lips indicating the Nubian should remain quiet. The officer then removed his enemy's sword and gave it to the Egyptian soldier.

He said in a low voice, "Put this sword point against his back. If he tries to alert the others, run him through with it."

The soldier continued to cover the Nubian's mouth, as he listened to the officer whisper, "I will return in a few moments."

The officer placed the dagger into his upper garment and went off into the night crawling quietly along the ground. He came near to where Ramtouses and Naamity lay sleeping. His eyes had completely adjusted to the dark. He watched as the two slept very close to one another. He waited until one of them moved, putting a slight space between them. When there was space for him, he lay down beside the precious maiden.

He uttered a silent prayer. *Please, Amun-re, stand beside me in my hour of need.*

With that, his hands stopped shaking, and he collected the dagger, slowly placing it near the throat of Naamity. As she turned towards him, he laid the point against her throat and covered her mouth with his other hand. Startled, Naamity opened her eyes.

Am I dreaming?

The officer lay so close he could whisper in her ear, "Quiet or I'll kill you with this knife. I have nothing to lose."

He removed his hand from her mouth and lowered the dagger to her side pressing it hard enough so that the pointed tip nearly punctured her skin.

The officer whispered again. "Crawl with me, and remember if you try to scream for help I will kill you, and you will never see Ramtouses again."

The two gradually moved away from Ramtouses. When they joined the waiting men, the officer said, "Follow me, and keep the sword to his back." They continued to crawl.

All four people rose to their feet after exiting the camp.

They saw a guard, but he faced the opposite direction. They moved soundlessly away. As the distance from the camp grew greater and they hadn't been seen, their self-assuredness increased. They sped up and in a few hours were completely exhausted.

The officer decided to stop. "We will rest for a few moments. Then we will head down toward the river."

They watch as the skies were beginning to brighten.

Naamity looked around at the three men with her—one the obvious leader, one his subservient, and the last man was evidently her co-captive, for he was prodded forward with a sword at his back for most of their flight through the night.

Cautiously, she spoke to the officer in charge. "You will never get away with this. From what I was told, Ramtouses has granted you whatever you wish, something anyone would be thankful to receive. Why do you want to spoil it for yourself and your companion? This just doesn't make sense."

He answered, "The bargain we made with him was before I understood your real value to him."

Naamity shook her head. "You are foolish. What do you plan to do with me?"

"Stop talking," he shouted.

"I will not. Ramtouses is a good man. He will give you what you want. Why put him through this?"

"No more. Bind her hands and silence her with a gag." He looked at the Nubian. "Him also. It will be much easier traveling with them bound."

By daylight they reached the river. "Get in the water, and start walking against the flow," he demanded.

Near midday they came to a fork in the river where it divided into four smaller ones. The officer looked around as if he were trying to determine where they were.

"We will follow the second stream to the north. Ramtouses will never know which way we've gone."

The officer knew that by staying in the water, their trail would be much harder to follow, even on houseback, and now it would be impossible because of the branching off. That evening, they stopped to rest and find food. The four slept along the river's edge while the two Egyptians took turns guarding the other two.

The next morning, they came upon a small Egyptian village. The officer approached one of the buildings and knocked, calling for entrance, while the others stood back. A man came to the door.

The officer addressed him. "I am a soldier looking for refuge from the hated Nubians."

The villager saw the others waiting. "Who are these people with you? One looks like a Nubian."

"I have a soldier with me and two prisoners. The woman is from Jerusalem. The man is Nubian. Can you tell me where we can go into hiding for a few days?"

The man answered, "Yes, I can help. Come in. I have friends who are looking for an officer to lead them."

The four entered. The prisoners were unbound when the villager gave everyone food, and then left to counsel with his neighbors. He returned with three other Egyptian men, all looking very worried. One joined the soldier in guarding their prisoners who had been restrained once again. The others and the Egyptian officer quietly retreated to another room.

There, the officer explained his plan to trade Naamity for their prince, Psamtik, who had been captured by the Nubian general, Ramtouses. After a long while, they returned, each with the countenance of assurance, as men with a sound plan of action after being presented with a problem. The Egyptian officer, a captain in Necho's defeated army, addressed the soldier who had escaped with him. "They tell me they have a hut where the prisoners can be kept. No one will find them there. Two village women will accompany us to carry our prize possession Naamity."

Two villagers arrived, accompanied by two women, and led the way into a wooded area where the captives were to be kept. They treated Naamity with a semblance of respect but showed no compassion to the Nubian soldier captured with her. The villagers assured the captain that there were many loyal Egyptians in the area who would be willing to join his cause in freeing Prince Psamtik. The thought of an exchange of Prince Psamtik for this woman whom Ramtouses held dear appeared wise, and they were pleased to play a role in the scheme.

When Ramtouses awakened, he assumed Naamity had gone for water. Suddenly, it struck him that she was gone. At first, he felt frantic, then moments later his heart felt crushed, as if this had all been an evil trick played on him by the gods, tearing away his heart for destroying the Egyptian army. *Do the gods want my soul to know more agony and despair?*

A comrade called out, "The three who delivered the seal to you are also missing."

Another of his comrades said, "Take your sword and cut off my head. I and two others were watching the camp last night. When it came my watch, I was careless with my duties thinking we were free from harm."

Ramtouses placed his arm across his comrade's shoulder. "I will not hold anyone accountable for this dreadful situation. It is my fault as well. I did not keep her safe as I should have. Regret is worthless. It will not bring her back."

Ramtouses sat down and lowered his head.

Another of his men yelled, "We can yet find them—we must hurry." He looked at Ramtouses sitting there. "Don't you want to go after them?"

"No," said Ramtouses. "How could I have trusted enemy soldiers? What was I thinking?"

Ramtouses walked about in the camp all day in a trance, talking to no one. It seemed as if he were a thousand miles away.

At the end of the day he finally spoke. "The officer is a military man and will have thoughts of making some kind of a trade in exchange for Naamity. We will wait here to see if he tries to contact us."

They waited four agonizing days with no contact. On the morning of the fifth day, they were preparing to break camp when one of the comrades ran toward Ramtouses, calling, "There is a rider coming this way."

Ramtouses joined his comrade for a better vantage point, and after a few moments, he recognized the rider as the

Egyptian officer who had taken Naamity. Ramtouses stood waiting as he rode up and dismounted, walked up to him, and looked him in the eye. Ramtouses drew back and punched him in the face—the officer went down. Ramtouses waited until he'd risen to his feet.

The officer said, "Your anger is warranted, but for the sake of the woman, you should hear my proposition."

"I struck you for lying to me."

Ramtouses lashed out a second time, sending the officer to the ground again. When he got up, this time holding his bloody nose, he threatened in a low voice. "If I don't come back alive, they will kill her."

Ramtouses said, "I struck you this time for betraying my trust. Now you can tell me what business you have come to conduct."

The man regained his composure before speaking. "First, know that the woman is unharmed and will remain that way."

Ramtouses cut him off. "What do you want?"

The officer continued. "We want Prince Psamtik released and returned to us unharmed."

With a surprised look on his face, Ramtouses answered, "I am not the Nubian king. I have no such power." Ramtouses shook his head. "Was my deep love for Naamity so obvious that you think I would do anything?"

The officer answered, "You conquered the whole of Egypt for your pharaoh. What does one prince matter to him?"

Ramtouses aimlessly walked around in deep thought. At last, he placed his hands akimbo, coming close to the officer again.

"You are an officer and well understand the pride in the trophies that come with victory. Your Prince Psamtik is a trophy for King Tantamani. I am his general, a tool for his purposes. Naamity is no one to him. You know a king will never have it said he surrendered an enemy prince for the sake of a commoner." Ramtouses left the man standing there. "I shall think on this matter more. Wait for me. I will return to you."

When the commander entered his tent, he sat, wondering. *What would Carnabrara advise me to do? I can't just leave Naamity at the mercy of the enemy, not now that I know she is alive and well. In truth, not ever. Manni, tell me. How do I persuade Pharaoh to give up the Egyptian prince, a sworn enemy and supreme trophy of Tantamani?* Ramtouses covered his ears. *I hear her calling to me in her song.* "How happy I am with you at last, the man I love, the man my God has saved me for." *I had no faults—because of Naamity have I shown weakness before the world?*

He heard a voice deep within him—his mother's voice. *Hear me, my son, this does not reflect weakness in you, just the opposite. You are stronger now, showing your ability to distinguish right from wrong and act upon it.* Ramtouses then wondered, *If this prince is freed, he could instigate more wars and cause the death of thousands. Will that lie on my shoulders?*

His mother's voice answered, "If Naamity is lost, it will alter generations of unborn righteous men and women."

After a long while, Ramtouses emerged from his tent and returned to the officer sitting on the ground. The officer rose when he saw the general coming.

"I am going to Memphis. I will return in less than seven suns, with or without the prince." He pointed to one of his men. "Bring the officer's horse." He looked at the officer. "I will meet you at noon seven suns from today. Where is the meeting place?"

The Officer drew a map showing Ramtouses directions to a place at a bridge near a small village.

"I have it," said the general. He pointed at two of his soldiers. "You two will ride with me. The rest of you will wait here."

When he arrived at Memphis, he discovered Pharaoh Tantamani had already left, and the army was now at the Egyptian border waiting to face the Assyrians."

While in the capital, out of curiosity, Ramtouses decided to visit Prince Psamtik.

He said to him, "Do you know who I am?"

"Yes, you are the one with whom I negotiated ending the war. You also are the man who killed my father. Why are you here now?"

While he was talking, the general looked him up and down. Ramtouses walked away without answering. He spoke to the head guard before leaving.

"The prisoner looks somewhat frail. Make certain he is fed well—he is a prince. We need him in good health."

"As you say, General," answered the guard.

Ramtouses then departed, on his way to reach Pharaoh's camp.

Near Egypt's Northwest Border

Ramtouses arrived at Tantamani's war conglomerate of fighting men approximately one day after leaving Psamtik in his prison cell. The whole army was happy to see him. Waving and boasting was all around. He found the pharaoh and bowed before him. Tantamani raised his arm for him to rise. He looked at his chief general as if puzzled.

"I don't know what to make of a man like you, so gifted in the art of war but with a hidden side unrecognizable to others. Perhaps the gods have fumbled with your mind and decided not to share their amusement with me."

Ramtouses said, "I apologize for my heedless behavior."

Before he could say more, Pharaoh interjected these words. "All is forgiven if you are now ready to serve your pharaoh and country. Your achievements immensely outweigh this minor incident of absenteeism."

Ramtouses said nothing, deciding to wait until they were alone.

Tantamani then said, "The generals will bring you up to date on our situation."

Ramtouses spoke to one of his Tungul generals. "What are the Assyrians up to?"

The officer informed him, "We have been here for ten days, and the Assyrians moved their armies down to the foot of the desert around the same time. An aggressive army like the Assyrians should have waged war by now. The scouts and spies say something very important is going on in their camp—perhaps the death of a leader or something similar to cause this kind of delay."

General Ramtouses said, "I will not be here when war does come. There is a terrible situation going on in my life."

He lowered his head and continued. "As soon as I conclude my business with the pharaoh I will be leaving. I am extremely sorry, but my position right now is just too complicated to explain. You understand the same strategies and technics I do. You must somehow convince Tantamani that you need to make the final decisions while letting him believe the choices are his."

The spies were watching the Assyrian camp, and from the appearance of their activity, they were still not preparing for battle.

Prince Ashurbanipal, oldest son of King Esarhaddon of Assyria, walked up to the chief Assyrian healer. "What is his condition? Has it improved?"

The healer said, "No, it has not. If only he had listened to me long ago. His old wound never healed properly. Now, it has putrefied and spread throughout his body. He is dying."

Prince Ashurbanipal walked into his father's large tent.

When Esarhaddon saw him, he said, "I am so happy to see you. I need to discuss something with you." He paused for a few moments. "I am going to die. I know that now. I will join the gods in the kingdom of the gods. You will be king and may the skills you have learned make you a great king as I tried to be."

The prince spoke. "You must not die. The gods will make you well again if you believe that Baal will hear our prayers."

Esarhaddon raised his hand from his bed. "No, no, my son, it is too late for that. I have been living with this nagging pain for quite some time. There is something else I want to talk to you about. I have tried to save you from knowing that my mother, your grandmother, was rumored to be a concubine, a gift from a Hebrew king. Since I have become king no one would dare mention it."

Ashurbanipal responded, "I remember Grandmother Naqia telling a story of her past to me. But because it was never clear to me, I did not pursue it further."

The king waved his arm. "Wait, wait, there is something else I want to say while I can. The King of Judah, Manasseh, has taken up the belief in a single god. Give his country the freedom to worship whatever god they choose. I don't think you will have a problem with the tribute."

The King of Nations lay still when he concluded with these words.

"I keep thinking about what he said in his speech to his people. His god came to him in the dark prison and forgave him for all his years of blasphemy against him. What god would do such a thing?"

Ashurbanipal just stood there with a sad look on his face. The next morning with the prince kneeling at his bedside, King Esarhaddon died.

The healers confirmed his passing, after which the priest came in to begin the ceremony necessary for him to be offered up to the kingdom of the gods. This ritual could last many days. Prince Ashurbanipal went out and assembled his generals.

"The emperor is dead. Let the sad news be spread throughout the empire. Because we are at war, my reign begins now. When we return to Nineveh, we will have the spiritual indoctrination performed by the priest." With these words, Ashurbanipal bent to one knee and continued. "Kneel and ask our god to give pleasure to his servant King Esarhaddon and stand beside us to face our enemies in battle."

Within days, the king's death was known throughout the many territories to the north, south, east, and west. Even the Nubians received the message. During the ritual, a giant hill of timber had been gathered, and when the timber was lit, smoke could be seen from far away. The cremation of Esarhaddon signified the end of an era.

Ashurbanipal again came before his generals. "We will carry out my father's desire to crush the Nubian forces. We will again show them the power of our war god, Ashur. And for each Nubian who falls, we shall give homage to Esarhaddon who will be watching from above. We march first light of day tomorrow."

The officers repeated his words to their men.

King Ashurbanipal had been well groomed for the duties of leading his countrymen through vigorous training from the time he was a very young boy.

So now the stage was set for the confrontation as the Assyrians moved across the hot desert.

Ramtouses walked slowly toward the king's tent. *I must bring my situation to the King quickly. Each moment Naamity's life is in danger, and I only have a few more days left before the meeting with the Egyptian officer.*

He reached Tantamani's tent quarters and entreated permission to enter. The king acknowledged his request. Ramtouses entered with a quick bow. "I have a matter that needs your immediate attention."

The king looked surprised. "Oh," he said. "What is it? I could see something was troubling you from the moment you returned. I had hoped it would go away with my forgiveness."

Ramtouses spoke in a respectful manner. "First I must tell you I did not return to take command of the army. Our generals can do that as well as I if you give them the opportunity."

The king came closer. "Then why did you come back?"

"Years ago, while I was in Jerusalem, there was a Hebrew woman to whom I gave my seal and my word that if she ever came to Egypt, I would see to it she would have a better life. When life became intolerable for her in Jerusalem, she sought me out. Because of the turmoil in Egypt at her arrival, she has fallen into malicious hands and now I am responsible for her being in an even more perilous position. When I came to help, the situation grew worse. Egyptian rebels kidnapped her. Now they demand a ransom."

The king rubbed his chin. "Ransom you say. I understand your concern, but we don't make bargains with our enemies." After a few moments of thought, the king then added, "Break the rules. I am with you—give them what they want. You have the power to meet their demands."

Ramtouses held his head low. "What they demand is the freedom of Prince Psamtik."

The king had turned his back and was moving away from his general, but when those words pierced his ears, he stopped in his tracks.

"What? They must be mad! What kind of an exchange is that? The prince for a Hebrew maiden? Don't make me laugh." He chuckled a little. "How could they muster up such a ludicrous idea?" Tantamani suddenly realized. "Wait. You are here." The king's eyes grew large. He yelled, "I can't believe you are here with this mad notion. What has come over you?"

The two men stood looking at each other.

Ramtouses finally said, "I gave my word. My word is my life—without it I would have nothing."

Tantamani showed increased anger. "I don't care about your word. Sometimes your given word cannot be kept. It is just a fact of life. You, of all people, know we are in the middle of a war. Think about it. You want me to give up our most valuable prize possession for . . . for some peasant girl?"

He placed his hands akimbo. "This is the most ridiculous nonsense I have ever heard. Ramtouses, where is your head? You know me well enough to know I would never, ever make such a trade."

Ramtouses held his anger and departed.

If I return without the Prince, Naamity will die. There is but one other thing I can do.

He called the general of the Tungul Nubians. "Have the Tungul contribution to the war effort ready to ride as soon as possible. We are breaking camp. Hurry."

Yes, sir," said the general.

He thought, *if Naamity is to die I must be ready to retaliate with force. The Tungul army makes up one fifth of the Nubian fighting strength—70,000, nearly all cavalry and chariot drivers.*

Ramtouses addressed his generals. "I only want the tribesman of my country. The Nubians of Egypt and Nubia along with the mercenaries can wage war beside the pharaoh. You officers must stay here to command them. However, the Tungul generals will ride with me."

Ramtouses and his men rode away.

Pharaoh Tantamani said to the remaining generals, "Let him go. I believe him to be a brilliant leader because of his wonderful war skills, but yet he's foolish in other ways. I can lead my army. Thousands join us daily, former soldiers who were held as slaves by the Egyptians. After being liberated, they want to fight and preserve Egypt for Nubians and their families. I will achieve a great victory that will last forever in history and become the most powerful king in the world."

He yelled, holding his sword up toward the heavens.

"Stand beside me great God of War, Menthu. The slaughter is yet to come. Ramtouses will beg me for forgiveness, but I shall not give it."

The generals were troubled at his remarks.

One of the generals called out, "The Assyrians are on the move, crossing the desert as we speak."

In two days, a cloud of dust marked the approach of the Assyrian army coming out of the desert. They made camp within sight of the Nubian opposition.

Tantamani gave the order. "Have the army ready to attack at dawn."

The new Assyrian king, Ashurbanipal, had his men on the march early the next morning. Led by the pavis wall of shields, they sang the Assyrian song of war, and when the men of

Nineveh came within range, they opened fire with their long-distance composite bows.

The Nubians were forced to cover their heads to protect themselves from the barrage of arrows. The Nubians had no weapons that were a match at this distance. The Assyrians continued to press on, shortening the distance between the two armies.

Pharaoh Tantamani's general said, "If they keep coming, it will give us an opportunity to exchange arrow attacks. Even closer should allow us a chance to hit them with a wave of infantry to test the strength of the shield walls."

Tantamani said, "A wave of infantry against that kind of arsenal may be a waste of fighting men!"

"War is the loss of life," said the general. He paused. "My Pharaoh," he continued, "testing the wall will save lives later once we know the strength of their shield protection. Any damage will weaken its strength for whatever we do afterwards."

The pharaoh paused then ordered, "Just as I thought. Do it."

"Yes, my Pharaoh."

The general executed the order and Nubian arrows soared into the sky as they moved forward. The distance between the two armies continued to decrease until the order for the Nubians to charge was given. Thousands of tribesmen raced across the open fields.

The Assyrians were ready for an attack like this, and when the Nubians came within range of the Assyrians' heavy spears, the big spears were thrown and came crashing into the shields of the Nubians, weighing them down and making the shields difficult to use for protection. Most were rendered useless and eventually abandoned.

This was a double attack by the Nubians—half the attackers stopped, dropping to one knee once their dart weapons were in range, and began to blow poison darts into the Assyrian secondary. The rest kept charging toward the Assyrian wall.

Thousands made it to the pavis wall but were met by long iron spears jabbed through the grooves between the shields. The Nubians who had lost their shields due to the heavy spears were easy targets.

The tribesmen who had stayed back to blow poison darts into the Assyrian interior did not have the expected success. The Assyrians had new uniforms with long sleeves and pant legs purposely designed to repel the darts. The fighting was savage, and hundreds of bodies of the brave Nubians lay before the stout pavis shields.

Then suddenly the wall was breached, and the Nubians concentrated their efforts to that area. Their generals sent out a second wave focusing on the breached area, including replacements for the poison dart men, whose numbers had been severely reduced by a bombardment of arrows. Again they sent flurry after flurry of poisoned darts into the Assyrian interior over the breached shall area. The Nubians were fighting just inside the Assyrian lines.

Ashurbanipal's men of war concentrated their efforts on sealing the gaping hole. The loud cries of battle equaled the swift movement of the men attempting to kill or to avoid being killed. Each moment seemed like perpetuity for the dictators of war from both sides. It was a hellish event that did not end well for the Nubians. The generals had to halt the attack because of the great numbers of men lost in what seem to be a stalemate just inside the Assyrian interior. No matter how hard they fought, no farther penetration could be accomplished.

It was evening, and the two armies moved away from each other, carrying their wounded.

The generals came to the pharaoh.

The first in command said, "Pharaoh, if the battle tomorrow is a repeat of the one today, we will not be able to stand up against them on the battlefield. Even though we have greater numbers, they are well trained, and have more experience and superior equipment. We need the Tungul cavalry if we are to have a chance. I beg of you give Ramtouses what he wants before it is too late."

Tantamani screamed, "Who am I now?" He looked at the faces of his officers. "I am to blame for this?" He screamed again. "I'm the villain? You believe it is my entire fault we are in this predicament?"

Pharaoh Tantamani was boiling with anger. "Get out. I will not give up an enemy prince for a peasant. If that makes me unreasonable, then so be it. Get out."

The generals joined their men and bedded down for the night.

Later that same night, the first general was awakened by a guard. "What is it?"

He was told, "Pharaoh is here."

"Let him in at once."

The pharaoh entered looking humble. "How much difference would it make should Ramtouses return with the Tungul cavalry?"

The first general responded, "It isn't possible to know for certain, possibly no difference. But without them we have no chance."

Tantamani answered, "I have been wrestling with this all night. I cannot ask the Nubians to die with no chance of winning. I've changed my mind. Send word to Ramtouses that I'm willing to make the exchange."

The general hurried outside where a rider stood ready to carry Pharaoh's message. Tantamani emerged from the tent and stood next to the general as they both watched the messenger gallop away into the night.

"We will withdraw tomorrow to delay further fighting for the next few days."

Ramtouses arrived at the huge farm well into the evening, too late for his noon meeting as agreed, and was now intent to meet danger with its death, if so needed. He spoke to his countrymen.

"With the rising sun tomorrow morning comes a test of fortitudes. Will the Egyptian rebels impose their desires on us, their masters, or will we stand up to their demands and show them who dictates the rules? Because they have stolen someone precious to us, we will respond with a terror greater than their treachery."

His comrades and the men of Tungul agreed with a show of clenched fists.

With the rising sun, Ramtouses and three others rode to the meeting place located near a small bridge just outside of a village. There, they waited and waited until finally the officer emerged from the midst of the houses with a few other men. They stopped within talking distance.

"You are a day late, and I see no prince. Do you need more time?"

Ramtouses said in a loud voice, "I regret that my Nubian pharaoh does not make transactions with the enemy. But I do have an arrangement you must consider for the sake of your people. If you don't release Naamity, my Tungul cavalry will burn this village down to the ground and all nearby villages with it, kill all the men young and old, and take all the females as slaves for my men. I will give you four days to think about that ultimatum."

The captain laughed. "You wouldn't risk it."

Like a lion Ramtouses roared. "Play the game, and we will see who will win. I tell you if Naamity is not returned to me in four days, unharmed in any way, I will assume you have killed her. Then I will show you the butchery in me." Ramtouses mounted and road away.

The people of the village became very nervous and pleaded with the rebels to give up their crusade.

They said, "This Ramtouses is a mad man. Dying for king and country is one thing, but to see our loved ones, our wives and children slaughtered, is another. We are in a no-win situation. Our rebel brothers will never let her go, and the Nubian king will not release Prince Psamtik."

Fear collected around the villagers. It stuck to their skin, gripped their hands and hung to their feet in clumps, immobilizing them. Their pleas to the rebels increased.

The very next morning, a rider galloped into Ramtouses' camp shouting for the general. He jumped from his sweaty horse and ran amongst the men until he found and respectfully addressed Ramtouses. "General, the pharaoh has recanted. He is releasing Prince Psamtik to you."

It was as if a heavy timber had been lifted off Ramtouses' shoulders. He placed his hands on top of his head and walked in a small circle. "I presume the war has not gone in the favor of the Nubians."

The messenger said, "The generals need the Tungul cavalry if we are to have any chance for victory."

Ramtouses pointed to some of his men. "Get this man a fresh horse. Accompany him to Memphis and escort the prince back here to me safely. Make the journey as swiftly as you can. Hurry." Ramtouses spoke to his generals, "Prepare the Tungul cavalry to return to Tantamani."

Simultaneously, Ramtouses and three others mounted up to return to the meeting place so the rebel captain could be told of the surprising news. They waited for a while trying to determine if anyone in the village noticed them.

"The village looks deserted, not a soul anywhere," said Ramtouses. "Perhaps they are afraid and think I mean to kill them." He thought for a moment. "I will walk in to see if anyone is still hiding someplace. Stay here. I am going across unarmed."

Ramtouses walked over the bridge holding his hands up high. He continued to walk toward the nearby houses, venturing close to see inside. He heard a noise and looked around at another building. Out came the Egyptian officer, stopping near the door as if unsure as to Ramtouses' intentions.

"I am here with great news. The Nubian pharaoh has decided to exchange the prince for Naamity."

The Egyptian captain was still not sure how to react and just stood there.

Ramtouses said in a gentle voice, "I am here only for Naamity, nothing else. Let's talk about the exchange."

The captain said, "You are earnest!" The captain smiled and waved for two of his companions to join them. They all walked back toward the bridge where the general's cohorts were waiting.

The captain said, "Can you trust the word of your pharaoh? Is he one to go back on his word?"

"No, he is a firm believer in the gods and would do anything to please them. If he believes the gods favor his decision, he stands by his word. The Tungul cavalry is his remuneration for favoring such a trade, and for him the gods have foretold this need."

This pleased the captain as he clapped his hands and picked up the pace. "It is too late for the prince to be returned to us. The Nubians and Assyrians are already fighting. It would be wise to have Prince Psamtik released to the Assyrians."

Ramtouses answered, "It shall be arranged."

"We have spies everywhere who will let us know when he is safely in the hands of the Assyrians. Meanwhile, Naamity is a half-day's ride from here and will be brought to this village to be returned to you."

Ramtouses looked surprised. "She is not here? Is she being well cared for?"

The captain quickly answered, "When you threatened us with fire and death, we moved all our families, along with Naamity. She is safely hidden away and well cared for, I promise you that. She is immensely valuable to us both."

"It could take days for the prisoner to be moved from Memphis to the front lines," was Ramtouses' reply. "We understand," said the captain.

Ramtouses nodded. "Let us go now, and fulfill our obligations to meet exchange." The two men each turned and departed in opposite directions.

Ramtouses hurried back to the camp to have another rider intersect the first group of riders with the change of plans. In less than two full days, guards came to Prince Psamtik of Egypt and said, "Arise. You are being released to the Assyrians."

The prince rose to his feet. "What is this, some kind of Nubian fallacy?"

"No, it is not," expressed the guard, angrily.

The prince looked around outside the gates. "I don't believe you." He then backed away.

"Come on." yelled the guard. "This is a matter of urgency."

When they were outside the building, another soldier said, "Mount up. We haven't a moment to waste."

The prince rode away with nine heavily armed soldiers.

Meanwhile at the front, each day the Nubians moved away rather than fight.

The Assyrian king Ashurbanipal had no knowledge of the transaction developing. He said to his generals, "They believe we will allow them to retreat until they reach Memphis, but they are sadly mistaken."

The next morning, before the Nubians could continue their routine of moving toward the city, they found that the Assyrians had marched during the night and now were within range of their long-distance composite bows. The scouts had not reported such a move. The arrows came down like a locust cloud before many of the Nubians could protect themselves with shields.

The Assyrians pushed forward at a faster pace than before. The leaders were hoping they could provoke the Nubians into a fight, and indeed they did.

The first general of the Nubians said to Pharaoh, "If we are to have any chance, we need to get into their interior."

He called for his ram chariots. "Knock down the shields so the infantry can break through."

It had been dry for several days when the large number of chariots and horses trampled across through the dusty fields, creating a huge, thick cloud of dust. The cloud could be seen from far off, and concealed the infantry coming up behind.

The Nubians chanted a shrill cry, a noisy, irritating sound meant to annoy and confuse an unsuspecting adversary. The Assyrians were aware of the sound and did not allow it to inhibit their war effort. The ram attack came as no surprise to them. Their catapults were up near the pavis wall of shields to stop a ram chariot attack and reserve the use of their cavalry. The catapults could hurl a boulder ten times as far as a man could throw a stone. Boulders large enough to completely demolish a chariot came crashing down upon the Nubians. Ramtouses believed the ram chariots were the lifeblood of the Nubian forces. He'd had thousands built and plenty of drivers trained to maneuver them. The fields were covered with the wheeled vehicles. Because of this, the catapult bombardment was not able to halt the attack, and nearly half the chariots made it to the shield walls.

In not attempting to send out their cavalry, the Assyrians had clearly underestimated their numbers. In a desperate attempt to stop the approaching chariots, the Assyrians flung spears and shot arrows. Yet a few were able to breach the shields, allowing the tribesmen to reach into the Assyrian interior. Agonizing fighting took place, but the breakthrough bogged down, and for a second time the Nubians had to retreat. This withdrawal was a terrible blow for the Nubians who now showed signs of distress.

Prince Psamtik arrived in the Nubian camp the next day and Pharaoh Tantamani asked the Assyrians for a truce to give them time to deliver the Egyptian leader to them. The pharaoh stood on a chariot before his army with a few of his generals beside him. Psamtik dismounted his horse and climbed aboard a chariot waiting for him. The driver alerted his horses to head out into the dry soil separating the two enemy forces.

The prince had a silly smirk on his face when the chariot pulled away. He yelled, "Goodbye, you Nubian dogs."

The prince was driven close to King Ashurbanipal's chariot that set out in front of his men. The king said, "Why on Earth did the Nubians release you? What do they hope to accomplish?"

Prince Psamtik said, "My emperor, I have no idea why I am here, but I will be at your service whenever you need me."

The king had a puzzled look. "Take him to the rear. I will figure this out later."

A messenger came to Tantamani with a note. It read, *The Tungul men of war are on their way but cannot get here in time to participate in any upcoming battles. They will meet you at the capital.*

One of the generals said, "I have a thought that could greatly improve our chances for victory. Let us create the impression that we are fleeing to the safety of the walled city of Memphis, but before we enter the city, we make one last stand. The Tungul cavalry will have time to approach from the south and hit them at the rear where they will be the most vulnerable."

The generals gathered together and drew up a map with plans of how the attack would proceed.

"Hurry," said one of the officers. "Take this message to the Tungul cavalry command without delay."

The next day Tantamani's Nubian forces mounted a full retreat, lengthening the distance between the two armies. The Assyrians had expected such a move and continued to advance.

Near the end of the second day of withdrawal, a rider informed the first general, "The cavalry is near, and it does not appear the Assyrians have seen them yet."

The general came to the king. "We are ready to carry out our plan."

"Go," said the king. "May Menthu be with us."

The Nubian general gave the order to commence the attack. The Assyrians did not expect this sudden move and were puzzled to see the weakened Nubian cavalry and their depleted chariots stream out across the fields. Upon seeing this late strategy move, the Assyrians force had little time to consider it and they did not attempt to position the catapults but instead swiftly mounted a cavalry counterattack. Overhead arrows flew from one side to the other. The Nubians were able to cross the fields and approach the Assyrian wall of shields.

The Assyrians scrambled to defensively align their wall of shields and avoid falling prey to the swarming Nubians. As the armies were engaging, the Tungul cavalry came up from the rear, creating a second front. The battle to the front was decisively controlled by the Assyrians, but the tables were reversed at the rear where there was little support from the Assyrian cavalry and none from the Assyrian catapult.

The pavis wall in this area was very susceptible to a full-scale aggressive maneuver. Before they had time to adjust, a wave of Tungul cavalrymen burst through their lines, and the interior Assyrian fighters were no match for the men on horseback. Hundreds were cut down.

To the front, the Nubian cavalry and chariots were nearly wiped out before the Assyrian cavalry was alerted of the disaster taking place at the rear. Soon their cavalry entered the battle. It was a hellish battle with both sides suffering heavy losses. The Assyrians had the assistance of their infantry, and together they greatly outnumbered the Nubian horsemen. In the end, the Nubians had to withdraw, and war for that day came to an end when the sun began to set.

The Nubians may have lost the battle, but in the end the Assyrians had paid an extremely high price for the victory. They lost more men that one day than in all the previous days of fighting in the war effort. King Ashurbanipal was furious when his generals reported their losses.

The Nubians had moved into the city of Memphis by the next morning, and the Assyrians were prepared—they had thought ahead and built battering rams and siege rams large enough to scale the city's seemingly impregnable walls.

⁘

A guard came into the hut where Naamity was being held and said to one of her caretakers, "Ready her. We are taking her back to the village."

There were two women who had stayed with her at all times to insure her wellbeing. The women made sure she was fed good meals regularly, her hygiene kept up, and was chaperoned whenever men were present. The captain wanted Ramtouses to have no ill feeling about her treatment upon her return.

"Where are you taking me?" she asked. "Are you releasing me to Ramtouses?"

The guard answered, "We are taking you back to the village, and that is all I know."

She began to quickly gather her things and was escorted to a wagon where she joined the Nubian soldier already there. It took the rest of the day traveling before they emerged from the dense growth of vegetation and trees. The two women sat near her the whole time.

When they finally arrived at the village, the captain folded his hands behind him and greeted them with a smile.

He said, "Naamity, so glad to see you again."

Naamity's face changed to anger. "You have the audacity to put me through this in the name of war?" She climbed down from the wagon, refusing anyone's help, and walked around, stretching her cramped legs and in deep thought.

Finally, she said, "Even though I understand your position as a soldier, I was treated very well, a credit to the fine women you sent with me, but I hate war and what it does to good people." She looked up into the sky. "My Lord teaches me not to hate anyone."

The captain released a sigh of relief and nodded briefly to the two women. "I thank you for saying that regarding the women. It is good to know you were cared for properly. After your long trip we have a meal prepared for you and fresh clothing also."

He pointed to a nearby building, and the women and Naamity walked over to it, the Nubian prisoner to another. The women fed, bathed, and dressed her in fine clothing.

When they had finished, the captain said, "You are amazingly beautiful. I can see why General Ramtouses is willing to fight for you."

She responded, "Think not of my appearance. I am first a child of God."

The Nubian soldier was brought out by two Egyptians rebels. They joined Naamity and the captain and everyone headed down toward the bridge together. It was mid-day, very sunny. Naamity was dressed in a white gown with a long black shawl that covered her head and shoulders and wrapped around her waist. She wanted to look plain and simple, yet her beauty stood out even in the modest, unadorned clothes.

They stopped near the crossing point of the bridge, no one waited on the other side. Naamity anxiously eased closer, her gaze sweeping the area. A few more moments passed, and she impatiently released her emotions, whispering. "Come for me, Ramtouses."

She covered her mouth after she said it as if the plea was unintentional. At that moment, she saw a figure moving very fast within the trees. She raised herself on tiptoes to see better, her hands shielding the sunlight from her eyes, and knew in an instant it was Ramtouses. Three others rode with him as they approached the bridge. She watched him dismount and walk normally to the bridge, one hand resting on the railing.

"You are free to go to him," said the captain.

She nervously placed one foot in front of the other, never taking her eyes from him nor he from her. As she started across the old wooden structure, he released the rail and stood up straight. Her eyes began to fill with tears. *Stop it. Don't cry.* She told herself. *It is the Lord's strength in us both that has brought us this far. Thank you, dear Lord—thank you, dear Lord—thank you, my glorious Lord.* She repeated her thanks, over and over, as she walked across the bridge to within an arm's length from Ramtouses, and stopped. For a moment neither spoke a word.

Her mind was a jungle of concerns and questions, each needing answers, and many focused on all the trouble she had put herself and this man through.

Will we regret ever meeting? Can I live up to what he might expect of me?

After all that has happened, do you still want me? I have caused you nothing but grief from the day we met.

Naamity looked into the face of the man who saved her, the man she loved, whose eyes sparkled while his smile absolutely filled her heart with joy, and who reached out, taking her by the hand. The warmth of his large hand guiding her gently toward him comforted her, and she closed her eyes, as he continued to nudge her to him. *Don't awaken me. I am not dreaming,* she thought.

Then he wrapped both arms around her and said, "Your God has shown me that if I really want you, I must learn how to hold onto you." And suddenly, those nagging concerns and questions about the trouble she brought to their lives simply faded from her mind, into nothingness; they were gone. What remained was just the two of them.

They stood there, in the middle of the bridgeway, embracing as the Nubian soldier came across to join Ramtouses' other comrades, and no one hurried them.

The captain called over to Ramtouses. "Be truthful. If your king had not sent Prince Psamtik to the Assyrians, would you have carried out the order to burn down and kill the people of all the nearby communities?"

Ramtouses answered, "The gods only know the answer to that question. Let's pray we never have to make a decision like that."

He called to the general again. "Perhaps I can do something courteous for you and Naamity for all the trouble I have put you both through. It has come to my attention there is a holy man living in a village about a day's ride from here. As I understand it, there were a few groups of Hebrews many generations ago who earned their freedom and established a few settlements. This is the only one my people know of."

He pointed toward some high hills in the distance. "Go in that direction toward the hills. When you come to a stream, follow it south, and you will find their village."

Ramtouses looked at him hard. "How can I trust anything you say?"

He opened his arms to Ramtouses. "What would I gain by deceiving you now? Naamity is Hebrew, and if you are not going to take her back to Jerusalem, according to her beliefs, you need to marry her under her customs."

Ramtouses said nothing, only listened. "We are honorable men even if our countries are at war." He looked at Naamity. "What do you think?"

She responded, "You know I want to marry you. I will never love another man as I love you. The only way I can feel respectful in the eyes of my Lord is to marry according to my custom—my God must bless our union."

Ramtouses lifted her up onto his horse, then mounted the big steed behind her. "Thank you for the information of the holy man," he called. "Good fortune in your endeavors."

When the general turned to ride away, Naamity whispered in his ear, "The Lord has soaked my heart with love for you."

She held his waist tightly. When they reached the camp, his men were very happy to see her again. It was the dinner hour, so everyone sat down for a celebration meal.

After the dinner was over, Ramtouses said to his age-group brothers, "We are not returning to the war. We are heading south for Napata. Those of you who wish to make your home in Nubia . . . I have no objection to your desires. But I will be at some point making my home in Tungul with our families, a comfortable place for Naamity to raise our children."

Everyone bedded down for the night and Naamity fell asleep in Ramtouses arms. Early the next morning when preparing to mount up, the general spoke first to the soldier taken hostage with Naamity.

"I do not blame you for the misfortune that transpired. You were deceived as I, and to be fair, you should receive your reward as promised. I am a man of my word. I understand your only request was a promotion and duties serving with my men. Is that right?"

The soldier maintained a bowed position as he spoke. "After what has happened, I expect nothing."

Ramtouses continued. "Stand straight. I am making you a comrade. You will be as a brother, equal to my other comrades including a higher ranking."

The man responded, "I don't know what to say."

Ramtouses added, "Say nothing. Ride with my men. They will tell you what is expected of an age-group member."

The general then turned to his people once more. "I need only you three to ride with me."

He pointed at the same three who had accompanied him before. "Those of you who remain will wait for us at the Nubian territory boundary. We"—he looked at Naamity—"have a duty to perform with the Hebrew holy man. I don't want to frighten the whole village with an army of men, so I think it best if only a small group appear there. So, may the gods be with you, and conceal yourselves as much as possible, you don't want to encounter Egyptian rebels."

The two groups departed in different directions.

At Memphis, behind the walls, the Nubians felt protected by the network of ambushes awaiting the marching Assyrians. Within days, four huge siege towers moved slowly toward the walls with the Assyrian forces gathered around them. The giants, in full view from the high walls, were horrifying.

King Ashurbanipal commanded his generals to use the catapults to "Pin down the Nubians who flock as a crowd atop the walls. They aim to stop our towers from reaching them, but they will not succeed."

His generals gave the catapult operators orders to attack. The catapults sent clusters of crushed boulders with sharp edges vaulting accurately toward the Nubians who defended against the approaching towers. Only the men behind the battlement crenel slits were able to shoot fiery arrows at the mighty towers, and that was to no avail. The Assyrian siege towers made it to the walls with none being lit afire.

Pharaoh Tantamani could only watch as the upright gates of the siege towers banged down upon the top of the brick walls and the Assyrians rushed across to enter the city. To their surprise, they were greeted by hundreds of arrows released by an automatic bow. The machine, design by Ramtouses and his generals, could be maneuvered along a track to any position parallel to the wall. The front of the machine was configured with a huge wooden, flat, square surface, with hundreds of small slits in it, each one loaded with an arrow laced with poison. When a coil release was activated, the arrows were fired all at once. Even a minor wound was fatal. The Nubians built five such machines. Four were in place in front of the slow-moving siege towers.

The fifth could be used against a second wave of Assyrians, but after that, the weapon was useless. There was no time to reload the slits before the enemy would be upon them. At each point of contact by the towers, the multi-bow releases easily slaughtered the Assyrian first wave. However the second wave of veteran Assyrians came charging over without that threat.

Tantamani's general signaled for the second booby trap to be triggered, knowing the bow machine had done its job. The Assyrians crowded the long ramp walkways, but when they reached the steps leading down into the yards, it all collapsed beneath their feet. Hundreds fell to their deaths impaled on long wooden shafts that rose from the ground underneath the walkway.

Other Nubian obstacles slowed down the assault but failed to fully stop the Assyrians, and some who had managed to breach into the city were able to set the main gate ablaze from inside the city where the more vulnerable side of the main gate, the unprotected timber, was targeted with flaming arrows. The Assyrian battering ram busted through the burning gate, allowing thousands to flood into the doomed city. By late afternoon, the fighting had escalated until there was one-on-one fighting everywhere.

Eventually, the battle turned to favor those with the better equipment—the Assyrians, with iron swords and shields and superior body armor. King Tantamani realized the end was near, and he and his high command retreated to the escape tunnel King Taharqa had built. They made their way out of the city and exited the tunnel up in the mountains several miles away. With nearly seven thousand men, Tantamani headed south for Nubia, riding all night trying to put some distance between them and Memphis.

The city fell, and King Ashurbanipal slept in the partially demolished palace. He said, "Bring the body of the Nubian king to me. I want it lying before my bed when I awaken tomorrow morning."

But when it was not there he yelled at his officers "I know he was here. How could he have escaped? Send out patrols. Search the countryside—find him. All Nubians must be killed or captured and brought back as slaves. We will not rest until there is no uncontained Nubian left in this country."

Assyrian troops started searching that very day, fanning out in the countryside south of Memphis.

.:.

Ramtouses, Naamity, and their companions now searched for the village where a Hebrew priest was said to live. They headed southwest looking, as the Egyptian officer had described, for a stream flowing rapidly at the foot of the hills. Two days passed before they came upon swiftly running waters which they followed downstream to a place where the waters settled into a large lake. Near the lake sat a small village.

Some people out working their crops saw them and ran to warn others of the soldiers' approach. Ramtouses said to Naamity, "Once we enter the village, you should be the one who speaks."

When they drew close to the village, the party stopped, and Naamity dismounted, slowly walking toward the onlookers who'd curiously come out to see the travelers.

Speaking the Hebrew language, she said, "I am Naamity from Jerusalem. These men with me are here in peace."

A man and a woman stepped from the group to address Naamity. "Come," said the man. "We sincerely welcome you." While his language was foreign, it was somewhat similar to Hebrew, and by listening closely Naamity could discern his meaning.

The woman then spoke, waving her arm. "Come, tell us all about this Jerusalem and your travels and what brings you here to our small community?"

Naamity looked around at Ramtouses with a trusting smile on her face, nodding. Ramtouses and his men dismounted.

The man came toward them. "There is a building for shelter"—he pointed—"over there."

The woman led Naamity off in a different direction. "Your speech is much like ours. We have so many questions for how that can be."

Ramtouses never took his eyes from Naamity. He said, "Wait. I don't want her out of my sight. I will not let her be separated from me."

Naamity turned away from the woman. "He is right. We must stay together. You have no idea how agonizing that has been for us. I will explain later, but for now, we must stay together."

The woman said, "Let's gather for our evening meal—we can talk then."

The man added, "We can eat at the village hall."

Naamity waved her arms, stopped the whole group and said in a fierce voice, "This is General Ramtouses. He has saved my life more than once. He is my hero in life, and I love him with all my heart."

The people smiled and looked at Ramtouses.

The woman nodded. "Let it be as you have requested."

Food was prepared, and the village elders sat down with the visitors to learn whatever they could about the travelers and why they had come to their village. After the meal and a very long discussion in which Naamity was questioned repeatedly and which she answered without hesitation, it was finally Naamity's turn to ask questions.

She had one inquiry. "Ramtouses and I were told there is a holy man here who performs matrimony for the people of the village. Is that right?"

"That is true," answered the man. "We will talk about that tomorrow. Meanwhile you can all get a good night's sleep in the building provided for you."

The woman waved goodbye. "I will come see you tomorrow morning."

Ramtouses held Naamity's hand on the way. "It was good of you to inform them of our situation."

Naamity smiled and swung his hand back and forth in a cheerful way as they walked.

288

When the sun rose, someone knocked on the door. It was the same woman they first met yesterday. Standing aside she said, "I was asked to come and invite our guests to return to the hall for our morning meal."

Three age-group brothers and the couple followed the woman and shared another fine meal prepared for them. When the meal was finished, another man stood, one whom they hadn't seen before.

"You asked after a holy man last night. Yes, there is a holy man here who performs matrimony for our people. However, he often goes into the shrine and may remain there for several days. It so happens he is in a period of seclusion for religious contemplation right now. We can never be sure when he will come out. The good news is he has been in there for four days and might come out at any time."

Ramtouses said, "When he does emerge, is it possible he will do us the honor of making Naamity and me man and wife? Hopefully he will emerge sooner rather than later, and we will wait." He detached a pouch from his waistband, holding it out to the man. "I want to offer in exchange for your hospitality, this pouch with several gold Egyptian coins. We need to get out of the country as quickly as possible."

"We don't want pay," the man said. "We are glad to have new faces among us, to share our provisions with you, and gain information of what happened to our brothers and sisters who left this land so many years ago. The holy man will happily marry you."

Hearing this, Ramtouses felt a sense of relief, and his mind went back to the war effort. He wondered, *Are the Nubians winning the war? There is no way for us to know if the Tungul cavalry successfully offset the Assyrian offense. If they didn't, both our little group and the villagers are in danger.*

As it turned out, King Tantamani was desperately racing for the boundary between the two countries. The Assyrians had numerous patrols scouring the vast territory, looking for the Nubian leaders or any others who might be in hiding. During the search, their trail had been picked up and most of the patrols headed south in an effort to overtake them. When their attempts to overtake them failed, they gave up the chase.

Suspecting still more Nubians hiding in Egypt, the patrols fanned out looking for stragglers who had not been able to find their way back to Nubia and slaves still being held by Egyptians. The comrades of Ramtouses had come from another direction and already crossed into their fatherland Nubia. They set up camp to wait for Ramtouses and their brothers to join them.

After patiently waiting for the holy man for two days, one of the men riding with Ramtouses came to him and said, "Ramtouses, if the Assyrians won the war, they could be looking for Nubians everywhere. Is there no way we can hurry him out?"

Ramtouses had the same concerns. "I will go and speak to the village people."

He and Naamity went to the woman and man with whom they'd previously spoken and explained the situation.

"This whole village could be in danger if they find us here. You must see if you can get the holy man to come out, so we can leave your place as soon as possible."

The man spoke. "I will go to the shrine and call for him. Follow me."

Shortly after they arrived at the sanctuary, the holy man emerged. He wore a white garment that covered his entire body; his long, white hair framed eyes that shone like jewels, and his stare was as if he were in a trance. He raised his arms up to the heavens, uttering in a loud voice, "Give thanks to God of the Heavens, for His loving kindness to time indefinite."

He dropped to his knees and continued as if repeating the words of another. "By the rivers of Babylon we sat. We wept when remembering Zion. We hung our harps on the popular trees. Our captors mocked us and said, 'Sing a song of Zion.' How can we be joyful on foreign ground? If we should forget you, O Jerusalem, let my right hand be forgetful. Let my tongue stick to my palate, if we were not to remember you."

Ramtouses looked at the man in awe. "What does he mean?" He asked Naamity.

"It is prophesy. He said the Lord will always love us. We must never forget our heritage no matter how grim the situation might be—just keep the faith."

The holy man said nothing else, only stayed there for a while before getting up. He walked slowly over to them when the man from the village spoke to him.

"This man"—he pointed at Ramtouses—"and young woman want the Lord's blessing, so they can become man and wife."

The holy man asked Ramtouses, "Are you a believer in the God of Abraham, Isaac, and Moses?"

"No, I am not," answered Ramtouses.

"Then the first thing we need to do is purify your unclean body. We have a ritual called mikveh in which you will be immersed in holy water and consecrated words will be spoken over you, afterwards you must be circumcised. Only then will you be cleansed, and the Lord will bless your marriage." The holy man turned back to the shrine "I will return soon. I must prepare the bath water."

In a short time he returned and approached Ramtouses. "Follow me."

With his host leading the way, Ramtouses looked over to Naamity. "I will be all right," she said. "I will stay close to your comrades. This has to be done if we are to marry."

Ramtouses followed the holy man into a building. Naamity stood near his three age-group brothers and patiently waited. Eventually the general reappeared, wearing a robe and carrying his clothing. He wore a smile on his face.

The holy man said to Ramtouses, "It is up to you to cleanse your soul. I can only wash the flesh. Let Naamity bring the

291

true God of Man into your heart with her teachings. I will now perform the ceremony that will make you man and wife."

Naamity and Ramtouses stood side by side with the holy man facing them as he read the words that would unite their lives and love for each other.

After the words were spoken, Naamity turned and gripped Ramtouses' hands as she looked steadily into his eyes. "There is no one like you in all the world. I love you. I love you."

He slowly lifted her hands to his lips and gently kissed each palm. "And I love you. Let us hold on to our love and to each other until life slips away."

She nodded, and with tears of great happiness filling her eyes, she repeated his words. "Let us hold on to our love and to each other until life slips away."

The reality of their situation closed in, and Ramtouses reiterated the danger to the village if the Assyrians should find them there, and thus, skipping the celebratory gathering for them, his party prepared to leave.

It was early evening, but they could not chance another night there. Before mounting up, Ramtouses went to those who had gathered to wish them farewell. Approaching their host, he put the pouch of gold coins in his hand and closed his fist around it before turning quickly and mounting his horse. They waved as they left and rode well into the night before bedding down.

Egypt, South of Memphis to Napata

They rode hard the following day and around noon Ramtouses called for a rest. It was short-lived, for almost immediately, one of the age-group comrades who'd been standing guard ran back from his post.

"I can see dust in the distance," he yelled. "It can only be a company of Assyrian soldiers headed this way."

They all mounted and rode off swiftly. After a long while of prolonged galloping, Ramtouses said to his party, "We must be smart about the care of our horses. We can only ride them hard for so long. We must slow down to give them a rest."

He surveyed the countryside as they rode. "We cannot conceal our tracks," he said, and pointing toward a wooded area, he added, "but we can make it more difficult by riding in that thick brush."

They camped that night without making a fire. In the early morning they hurried to continue their flight south. For the next two days nothing changed except that the ground became rockier, which put stress on the horses and they rode much more slowly. But by the third day one of the comrades said, "Ramtouses, my horse has become lame."

It was not surprising considering how hard the horses had been pushed, and Ramtouses shook his head with regret as he inspected the animal's leg. "I had hoped we could get closer to Nubia before this happened."

His companion asked, "What do we do with him?"

"If we put him down, the Assyrians will surely find him. If we just release him, other animals will attack him for food."

He looked up into the sky. "It will be night soon. We passed a small stream not too far back. Make camp here. I will take him downstream and return before dawn."

When Ramtouses returned with only the horse he was riding, everyone but the guard was asleep. He lay down beside Naamity. She woke up. "What did you do with the horse?"

"I had to destroy him, sadly. I did not want him to die a painful death being eaten alive by other animals. If the Assyrians find his body, they might think some of us went downstream."

She thought of their situation, newly married and on the run from the Assyrian army with a small group of soldiers. "I never imagined beginning a marriage filled with fleeing and so empty of passion."

Ramtouses answered, "Neither did I, but we will make up for lost time." He kissed her gently and cuddled up close, their heads touching. "The good news is I am almost healed." He kissed her again.

As they looked up into the heavens, Naamity whispered, "The heavenly bodies are so bright tonight, covering the whole sky. It is wonderful to behold God's endless kingdom."

Ramtouses whispered back, "Soon we will make love under a sky like this."

They lay still for a few moments before Ramtouses added, "Do you remember when I went into the shrine with the Holy man?"

"Yes." She held on to the 'yes' in her reply to indicate a curiosity, and Ramtouses continued his thought.

"Before we came out, he said to me, 'Because you are clean but ignorant of our belief, let your wife teach you the way of our Lord God that you may learn and come to follow the Lord in all His ways. Your prayers will be heard, and the door will be open for you to enter the Kingdom.'"

Naamity smiled, and they both fell asleep.

At the new day's dawn, Ramtouses spoke as they quickly prepared to ride.

"Naamity will give up her horse. Since she is the lightest, she will ride with me. However, to keep the weight from being too much for one animal, over a period of time we will rotate the horse Naamity and I ride. Now, let's get going."

After two long days of traveling at an extraordinary pace, they recognized agriculture in the area near them. Ramtouses had his party come to a halt.

"Wait here, I think I see huts off in the distance."

He rode further, concealing himself when possible. At last, he dismounted and lowered his body, watching the activity. He saw only seven men, and they all were unarmed. With his skilled fighters, they could easily overcome them if the need arose, but Ramtouses saw the place as peaceful, and he made the judgement to bring his tired horses and riders in for a rest.

He returned to his group. "Naamity and I will ride up front—you men lag behind. I will do the talking."

The seven men moved together as they rode closer.

"Who are you? What do you want?" called out one of the men.

"We mean you no harm—we need food and to know the best route for traveling to Nubia."

One spoke to the others in a low voice. "These men are Nubians and may have an army nearby." Then in a louder voice, "We humble ourselves to the Nubians. We have plenty of food for you and water and hay for your horses. You all look tired."

"Thank you for your hospitality. We can stay for a while to give our horses a rest."

Another of them asked softly, "If you hate the Nubians, why act as if you are their friend?"

"I have a family to think of—as do you."

They sat and ate outside a small communal hut while the horses were walked, rubbed down, and fed. One of the farmers joined them. "The best way to get to Nubia is to cross the dunes. A half-day's ride from here and you will reach the forest. To enter the forest you must cross a stream. By following the stream south, you will reach Nubia. However, if you want a shorter route, pass through the woods."

Out of caution, Ramtouses told the Egyptian farmers, "We will travel downstream and avoid the hazards of the forest."

Thinking the Assyrians could show up here in a day or two, Ramtouses looked toward the horses. He spoke to his companions. "Go get our horses. I will talk to these people a little longer."

While the men were getting the horses, Ramtouses said, "We want to buy one of your horses. What is a fair offer?"

The man said, "Take any one you like."

Ramtouses answered, "That would be unfair. I am not a thief."

The general opened a pouch and handed the man a gold coin with the head of Taharqa on it. The man took it gladly, and in a few minutes they had remounted and were ready to ride, waving as they rode toward the dunes.

Ramtouses called out, "We need to cross the dunes before nightfall. I don't know how far behind us the Assyrians are."

The sand proved to be much deeper than he'd thought, and they had to slow the horses to a fast walk. But still, their mounts sweated and snorted heavily, showing signs of exhaustion.

He finally said, "We cannot ride them any farther. Let's make camp here."

The general scanned the terrain around them then pointed. "See that high mound? We will position a lookout there overnight."

Ramtouses appointed three of his companions to the first, second, and third watch through the night. Early the next morning, with the sun lighting the horizon, the last soldier on guard came to Ramtouses.

"There is a faint cloud of dust visible off in the distance, perhaps a half-day's ride behind us."

Ramtouses shook his head. He brought his hands up and knotted them in his hair, then suddenly dropped his arms, releasing a heavy groan. "All is right," he said. "We can do this but we must reach the forest today. We can't defend ourselves in the open."

Naamity's voice sounded sad. "It seems misfortune pursues us. I have prayed to my Lord, but things only get worse. I keep remembering the words of the holy man, 'Never abandon your love for the Lord.'"

"We are not at fault," said Ramtouses. "War is responsible, and because of all this hardship it brings, the rewards of peace will be appreciated to the fullest."

Naamity lifted his hand to her cheek, caressing it as she spoke. "You are a champion among men. Your heart is so broad, which is why I love you so."

They all mounted and galloped away, watching as the sands became hard soil that then gave way to a grassy plain. By evening, they saw trees and a forest in the distance. The wooded area grew larger, and eventually they saw the stream.

Ramtouses yelled, "Keep riding until the horses are in the water."

Ramtouses climbed down from his weary stallion. "We will walk downstream and let the horses cool off and have a drink."

After quite a distance, they came upon an area where the woods ran close along the bank.

"Let's enter the forest here and find a place to sleep."

Just before sunset they located a place to make camp for the night, and at sunrise they traveled west again, through the woods as the landscape gradually became thicker with bushes and trees, rocks and large boulders, small cliffs and drop-offs.

Ramtouses consulted with his men. "Do we want to abandon our horses?" The men agreed. "The horses are no longer useful. If anything, they are slowing us down. We can move more quickly without them."

They stripped the horses bare and sent them on their way, moving ahead on foot, picking their way through the bush. Eventually they found some wild berries which they harvested, eating some but storing most away.

When dusk fell, Ramtouses said, "Look, over there. See those very tall trees?" He studied them before commenting. "There is a heavy concentration of branches higher up near the tops. I don't believe it will be safe for us to bed down on the ground tonight. We will climb the trees and sleep up there."

Nubians were generally all good tree climbers. The three comrades each picked a tree from among those close to them— Ramtouses picked one that could harbor him and Naamity.

She said, "I can climb a tree, but I don't think I have ever climbed one as tall as this."

"Don't worry," her husband replied, smiling, "I am right behind you."

She started up then stopped about half-way. "Will you catch me if I fall?"

"Take your time. I am right here beneath you."

At that she looked back, giggled then took off in a flash, and in a matter of seconds she had ascended into the concealment of foliage.

Ramtouses looked up in surprise. "Where did you ever learn to climb like that?"

He continued to climb as she answered, "Hebrew women rise to the challenges of life. Sometimes we would hide in the trees when Manasseh's soldiers came to look for us. As you know, hiding the alter and coming out to worship was no easy task."

The general joined her, lying back among the big leaves and many branches which supported them with ease. Their three companions also attempted to make their areas comfortable but soon discovered they had invaded the home of some aggressive birds. The big white birds cawed loudly and flew about trying to intimidate the newcomers, inciting them to leave.

The soldiers waved their arms in an effort to ward them off, and when that did not succeed, they drew their swords and swung at them. The birds flew away.

Ramtouses said, "This must be their nesting area. If that's the case, they will come back. Make no commotion when they do, and they will share their trees with us."

Soon, the birds returned—one then two and before long, a few dozen. That night, birds and humans cooperatively used the branches and leaves to make their beds as comfortable as possible.

They were awakened early in the morning by sounds unfamiliar to the local woods— Assyrians? The birds appeared oblivious to the presence of people beneath their tree but the human tree-dwellers each woke the next and signaled to be quiet with a finger to the lips.

They looked down only to see Assyrian soldiers searching the woods, speaking to one another, and pointing in different directions. From their treetop positions, they could see several small groups on foot—one of which passed very close underneath the trees in which they hid. One of the comrades moved and some of the berries they picked fell from his waistband.

The soldiers heard the sound of something falling through the leaves and looked up trying to determine what had made the noise. Ramtouses, Naamity, and comrades all looked down cautiously, holding their breaths.

One of the comrades waved his arm at the birds. The birds started to caw again, flapping about then flying away. The two soldiers, content with the idea the sound was made by the birds, walked away, continuing the search with their fellow Assyrians.

After a while, the jungle chatter of animals seemed normal again. Through the heavy cover of trees, Ramtouses could see an opening far off in the distance. He gazed in that direction thinking of home—sweet Nubia—that he knew lay out there.

"Let's climb down," he said. "The Assyrians have been gone for quite some time now, and they may backtrack if they don't find our trail." He pointed in the direction where he had seen the clearing from the treetops to the west. "We will head this way."

Ramtouses took Naamity by the hand, and the group maneuvered through the thick bush with as little disturbance as possible.

By evening, they came to the opening where the grass grew tall—up to their chests in some places. Ramtouses assumed this was the same opening he'd seen from the trees and thinking Nubia might lie across these fields, he said. "I believe Nubia must be within our grasp."

They stayed low in the grass to avoid being seen, even though it slowed them down and they needed to get as far away from the forest as possible before night fall. They came upon a small stream where even the cattail grasses growing around it were tall. While two men ate, the others stood watch. Then the three had their turn to eat. It grew darker and darker.

Ramtouses assessed their situation. "This seems as good a place as any to spend the night." They shared the resting and eating time until it grew dark.

The three comrades lay down to sleep while Ramtouses and Naamity found a good spot to watch over the sleeping men. They sat close to each other. While there was hardly any breeze, the air began to cool, and the stars grew brighter and brighter. The world around them came alive with the sounds of the night.

They looked into the darkness. Ramtouses said, "As long as the creatures of the night are noisy, we are safe. It is when all is quiet that danger is lurking." He leaned his head against hers and whispered to her, "Tell me more about yourself and the God you believe in."

Naamity began to speak in a low voice only Ramtouses could hear. "I was very young when my mother first started taking me to the Temple. Even then I knew my mother was loved by the whole city. She sat me down one day and asked if I knew why so many people honored her as if she were part of the royal family. I said, 'No, I do not know.' And she said, 'Listen to my words, sweetheart.' Then she told me this story.

"An extremely beautiful woman came to her door inquiring of my mother. She asked several questions; she looked my mother over thoroughly and asked her to sing for her. Later, my mother was one of a small group the woman invited to the palace. The woman's name was Judith.

"She dismissed all but my mother and one other. The two of them were told of a task that would endanger their lives and more than likely take them away from Jerusalem, never to return. But it meant our people could be saved if the deed was successful. My mother accepted the undertaking, as did the other woman. The Assyrian army held siege around our beloved city and Judith planned to demoralize their army. There was a sign in the sky. Judith, my mother, and the other woman understood the sign to mean the time for their task was then, so they walked down into the camps of our enemy.

"The Assyrian general took a liking to them and requested they sing and dance for him. The general did not know the power of the Lord. The Lord sent a mighty army that attacked the Assyrians, and Judith and her women companions slew the Assyrian monarch thus saving the city of Jerusalem."

She said nothing more.

Ramtouses gazed out into the night, his pupils fully adjusted to the black of night, the only light provided by a quarter moon and shiny stars. He acknowledged the wisdom of her story and wondered about the timing of his father's army arriving at Jerusalem.

"That was very interesting," he said. "Tell me more."

She went on. "My mother and her companions were returned to the city by these men of the Lord. The people of Jerusalem felt as if their lives had been saved by the deeds of these courageous women, and they honored them as if they had indeed been sent by the Lord. My mother died before my fifteenth birthday. It was a sad time for my family and Jerusalem. My father devoted a great deal of time teaching me the scriptures and the laws of the Torah. I did not realize the long-term benefit of that until now, when I will not be associated with my people perhaps for the rest of my life. To have Almighty God's guidance is a blessing for me and others who are willing to accept the laws of our Lord."

Ramtouses kissed the back of her hand as she continued. "I want you to know of Abraham, Isaac, Moses, and other prophets of our Creator."

She paused for a moment, then, "The beautiful thing about our Lord is that He loves all His followers. A common man or woman can be among the chosen by the Creator depending on the purity of the person's heart and faith in the Almighty.

"Ramtouses, from studying the word of the Lord I can understand some of the Almighty's prophesy. There will be a time of anguish greater than any previous suffered in the many years to come. Yet everyone whose name the Lord has chosen will endure, even those whose souls have vanished and who live no more, their bodies lying asleep in the earth. Even those who do not know His name will He remember—some to everlasting life and others to reproach indefinitely."

She paused again and looked up at the glittering stars as if in awe. "The people having insight will shine as brightly as a sun's brilliance. Those who are bringing many to righteousness will sparkle like renewed stars to time indefinite, even forever."

Ramtouses said, "You must teach me His word. I understand none of it."

Naamity chuckled a little. "In the last days, only the ones having insight will understand the full meaning of the Lord's expressions. When the word of the Lord has spread to all parts of the Earth, he has promised that at the end of a selected number of days, the end of these times shall come. You must have faith and love for the one God with all your heart and soul to be counted as His."

They said little after that and finished their watch with no sign of danger. They held each other, trying to find sleep in a precarious situation.

Early in the morning the comrade on watch shook Ramtouses gently, holding his finger to his lips. Ramtouses and Naamity awoke, and the companion woke the other two.

"A soldier," he whispered. "I only saw one coming straight this way. They may have separated to search this whole area."

The five of them knew the stream of water was nearby. Ramtouses waved his arm indicating they should follow him. They crawled so low their bodies rubbed the ground. No one looked back. Their only hope was reaching the water and doing so without disturbing the high grass tops around them too vigorously and revealing their location.

They lowered themselves into the cool water. The morning mist covered the water's surface. The water was not deep, so they flattened their bodies parallel to the bottom to become submerged. The only thing now was to be quiet and wait.

The Assyrian soldier walked toward the bank noticing the grass looked flattened. He brought up his horn to blow and alert the others but then hesitated, looking intently at the ground. *Wait. This looks more like the movement of animals— large turtles or badgers. I should be certain before alerting the others. I dare not incur the captain's anger again.*

He followed the indentations left on the disturbed grass. At the water's edge he looked around, but there was nothing— neither upstream nor downstream—no movement, no sound.

Ramtouses and one of his men saw a shadow flickering in the water between them. As the man drew closer, the reflection grew larger. It shifted toward the general.

Wait, thought the soldier, *something is not quite right here.*

A man lay in the still, clear water just to his left. The Assyrian raised his horn to blow it just as Ramtouses' comrade leapt at his back, grabbing his arm and pulling the horn away with one hand, while covering his mouth with the other. The only sound was the initial splash as the two men went down into the water. After a few brief moments of struggle, Ramtouses' comrade came up alone, and the waves settled down.

All of them then came to the surface, gasping for air.

Ramtouses said, "It is over. We must run—stay together."

They waded quickly to the other side, climbed out, and started running. They ran until exhaustion nearly collapsed them, one by one, and their run became a feeble trot.

As they started to enter another wooded area, Ramtouses held out a hand to stop them. In a soft, breathless voice, he said, "This forest must be Nubia. We've made it."

Depleted of energy, they sank prone upon the ground, eyes closed, breathing in and out, allowing the earth to cool their hot bodies, feeling the lift of life only Earth's soil can give.

Ramtouses and Naamity lay together on the fields of Nubia, holding hands.

He said, "Assyrians will not venture into such a vast area as Nubia, not wanting to thin out their patrols, and it's too far to communicate with their higher command."

They rested for a short time, and then rose to begin the walk south toward Napata. Come evening, they made camp and cooked fresh game for the first time in many days.

"Tomorrow we will try to make it to the meeting place. It will be good to see our brothers' faces."

They arose early and made steady progress well into the day. Feeling safe, they were all relaxed when without warning a huge lion, a monster male, rose up in front of them, giving a ground-shaking roar before threatening to leap at them. The four men all drew their swords and raised their shields

Ramtouses ordered, "Stand back."

He stepped forward. Foremost in his mind were his father's stories about his days of hunting and slaying lions.

Look the beast in the eyes, show no fear. If he charges, drive your sword into his belly and use your shield as protection from the impact.

Naamity and his companions stayed back. Ramtouses waited, but the lion didn't growl or move, only crouched where he was, looking straight at Ramtouses who kept his eyes also fixed on the vicious animal, ready to react in an instant.

Strangely, the lion turned his back to them, lowered his rear end, and defecated. When he finished, the huge cat strutted away, never looking back. Ramtouses and the others sighed in relief.

Naamity hurried over to him. "What were you doing? You could have been hurt or even killed."

Ramtouses smiled. "Your God would not let that happen."

Naamity shook her head. "Don't be certain of that."

They hugged and continued on their way, and before the end of the day the comrades' camp could be seen. It was a pleasant sight, and the group ran, waving their arms in the air. Ramtouses' comrades likewise came out to greet them, glad to see their leader and friends alive, happy to be together again, yet mourning the many Nubians who had been killed fighting the Assyrians.

"The war effort is lost," said someone.

"Yes, it is," said another, "and we must prepare food, eat, and live. That's our task on this very warm evening."

Ramtouses nodded agreement, his face was set firm, it gave no hint of the sorrow that clung to his heart—only his far away stare hinted at unease. Naamity shifted beside him, she put her hand in his. "That looks like a lake down there."

"Yes, it is," came the quick response from one of the comrades.

Ramtouses pushed aside his thoughts of war, of Tantamani and betrayal, of what might have been, and said, "Naamity and I are going for a walk. No one need accompany us. We desire privacy."

The men understood and retreated away from the lovers.

As they walked, Naamity displayed a big smile. "It's unbelievable. Here I am, married to the man I love. Incredible! Fantastic! Shall I continue?"

Ramtouses walked beside her, making their way to the small lake. "May we always know when and how to pull each other away from the dark memories. Thank you." She leaned into him.

They sat on the bank in soft green grasses. Ramtouses began to disrobe his wife, one item of clothing at a time. He couldn't keep his hands from her soft skin. When she was naked before him, he sighed. "You are so beautiful."

He removed his own garments quickly and led her into the cool water. The change of temperature soothed their weary, hot bodies.

Naamity cooed, "Sooo pleasant. I could stay here forever."

Ramtouses put his arms around her, and she relaxed against his firm chest. The setting sun cast them in a glowing red haze. He buried his face in her profusion of hair, rocking to and fro.

She whispered, "I am happy, so happy. God has strengthened our love to last a life time."

Ramtouses said, "I am going to bathe away all the sorrow and misery laid upon you, including the tarnish collected on your body during your weary journey searching for me."

He led her to a shallow area and washed her body with a soft cloth, every curve and plane, up and down, front and back, leaving no surface unwashed. He cupped his hands and drizzled cool water over her shoulders then watched it trickle down her skin. He pulled her up close until they were face-to-face, flesh to flesh, and kissed her—tenderly, passionately. His kisses moved to her throat, her shoulder, and then her breasts. Over and over, he showed his need for her with his firm lips and wet tongue. When they were both on fire with longing for each other, he lifted her up and carried her to the bank.

The moon and emerging stars were the only ones given the privilege of bearing witness to their love, which rose to fire again and again that perfect night. For Ramtouses and Naamity, it was paradise.

They slept there on the bank, wrapped in each other's arms. In the morning, they walked back to camp.

"My love, I know you must wonder how I kept myself pure for you."

Ramtouses answered, "It wasn't your God who saved you from the many evil men that held you prisoner?"

"Yes." She looked as if in deep thought. "But my Lord works in mysterious ways. He put a wise woman in my life who showed me ways to save myself from the many hungry hands of the Egyptian overlords. Without her I would not have survived, I wonder what happened to her."

Ramtouses voice showed some excitement. "Wait. I met such a woman at the armory depot. She was dying, mortally wounded, and left to die by the soldiers leaving to join the Egyptians fighting my people."

Naamity looked sad and concerned. "She is dead? You saw her before she died?"

"Yes. It was because of her I was able to find you. Her last words were, 'God has kept me alive so I could help her one more time.'"

Naamity's voice was like a melody. "She made it possible for us to be together now."

He responded. "I had no idea."

They reentered the campground and found the tent his men had erected for him and his new wife. After another pleasant day and night, they broke camp and doubled up the extra riders, giving Ramtouses and Naamity their own mounts. The convoy made their way to Napata.

The general rode up alongside one of his men. "Ride ahead and inform the city we are coming."

The town turned out as if he were the king, with throngs of people lining the streets and calling his name. The welcome home gathering surprised him.

Ramtouses informed his comrades, "I will not go to the palace but will locate a place of my own for Naamity and me to stay. The king's relatives occupy the palace, and I understand no one knows for certain where the pharaoh is. I don't want to appear ambitious taking the throne in his absence."

A messenger came to General Ramtouses and said, "The king escaped the fall of Memphis but has not returned as yet. He may be in hiding. The family welcomes you to stay at the palace if you desire."

Ramtouses shook his head. "Express my most sincere thanks to the family of the king, but I have a new wife, and we would like our own home at the time."

He sent word to all his friends, to all those who served with him in war, his companions and age-set brothers who already enjoyed acquaintance with Naamity, announcing a banquet in honor of his new wife.

At the banquet, when she was introduced and stood before them, there was much applause and cheering for her. Following the feast, guest after guest came to speak with her. Ramtouses requested Kobina to stay near him while he watched many people introduce themselves to Naamity, pleased to meet the new wife of their beloved General Ramtouses. Kobina was happy to do so and together, he and Ramtouses witnessed the ease with which she greeted all the new faces.

"She is fantastic," said Kobina. "Yes. She is." Ramtouses agreed.

The next six days were happy ones, but on the seventh day a rider came into the city announcing the king's arrival. The people once again were joyful, although some held resentment deep in their hearts.

A woman said in a loud voice, "Fewer men are returning to their wives, thanks to the war and the love our kings have to rule over Egypt."

Others said, "We are joyful in the return of our beloved king, the living representative of the gods. Nubia will rise again."

A crowd lined the street to welcome him home in spite of their thoughts. He rode on a big chariot drawn by black horses. He wore not the clothing of a pharaoh but those of a Nubian king. Tantamani's family and the aristocrats of the city greeted him at the palace entrance. Ramtouses was not among them. As the days passed, rumors spread of the king's many indulgences at the palace.

Ramtouses began to wonder why the king had not sent for him as there was no doubt the king was aware of his presence in Napata. He imagined Tantamani was secretly exercising his authority on people he despised one by one behind the walls of the palace.

Naamity noticed that Ramtouses seemed to have something on his mind.

"We have been happy. It has been like a never-ending dream, but lately...what is it?"

Ramtouses wrapped his arm around her waist. "Maybe it is nothing. As you may know, I am a powerful man amongst my people. I have been looking forward to meeting with King Tantamani, yet he has not made any effort to have me come before him."

He walked toward the window with her at his side. "War brings out the best as well as the worst in men, leaving deep scars that may never be healed." He kissed her on the forehead. "However, in my case the rewards have been magnificent."

He then kissed her lovingly on the lips.

One morning soon after that conversation, a messenger from the king appeared.

"The king is asking for you, General Ramtouses."

"I will be there as soon as possible."

Ramtouses dressed himself in his best uniform and said to Naamity, "I will return soon. My comrades are always close. You will be safe."

When Ramtouses entered the palace, several officers were there who joined him in seeing the king. None seemed to know what to expect of the meeting.

Ramtouses' second in command general approached him. "Maybe he is having a debriefing about the failed war effort."

"I understand only several hundred men, along with these officers, came back with the king." Ramtouses lowered his head and shook it. "I was convinced with the Tungul cavalry you would win."

The king's chamber doors opened, and the entire group of officers entered. The king stood still, looking up to the high ceilings near the center of the room, his hands folded in front of him. He began to pace aimlessly still looking up. After a while Ramtouses and the others begin to look at one another in wonder.

Finally, Tantamani raised his hand and pointed at a certain area of the ceiling and said, "Look. I see the gods gazing down at us. The cries of your brothers in Ethiopia are loud, asking for help. There are thousands of Nubian refugees fleeing to Nubia to escape death or slavery at the hands of the Assyrians and Egyptians." He continued to pace. "Shall we sit back and take pity on ourselves?"

Tantamani shook his finger again. "We must do all we can to help the flow of traffic into our country. The handicapped, injured, sick, children, the elderly—all will need transportation.

We shall gather all the wagons and horses from our army and townspeople alike. There is no time to waste; we must start today."

He pointed his finger at Ramtouses. "The first general will be in charge of the entire operation." He continued to talk. "We need our brothers and sisters to help once again transform our nation into one of the most powerful in the world. Our male population is depleted. We must become fruitful, multiply, and increase Nubia's might substantially so that everyone will fear us. Furthermore," he said, "we also need to act now in securing our borders against future invasions."

After the talks were concluded, he dismissed everyone but Ramtouses, and when the hall had cleared, he said, "I understand you were able to rescue your concubine from her captors. Is that right?" He walked over near Ramtouses. "I wonder to what lengths you would have gone in order to save her." He folded his arms across his chest. "You deserted your command and ignored my wishes. Is there anything you would not have done for her?"

He looked up to the ceiling again. "Love." He paused, smiling. "What were the gods thinking when they created such feelings?" Tantamani turned his back and walked away from the chief, pounding his fist in his hand. "I considered severe punishment, but that could surely work against me. The military is really your military, and I know the people love you more than their king. So where am I? I ask you."

He spun around quickly. "I know. I will do nothing. It will be as if it never happened." The king moved closer to Ramtouses. "What is her name?"

Ramtouses was cautious and not pleased when he answered, "Her name is Naamity."

Tantamani went on to say, "I understand you have refused to move back into the palace with Naamity. I supposed it would have been somewhat awkward for you to move her into your quarters here. The royal family would be pleased to have her among them. Everyone is curious, wondering how this young woman stole the heart of great Ramtouses."

The general answered, "We are starting anew. I considered it would be well if there were few distractions around us, that we might learn each other's ways."

Tantamani's eyes seemed to hold a subtle, even sly, threat when he said, "I am the king, yet it seems I must ask your permission to see Naamity. After all, she has the power of a goddess, even in determining the outcome of war. Yes, I do want to meet such a woman."

Ramtouses bowed down. "My king, of course you need not ask permission. I will bring her whenever you desire."

The king waved his hand. "No, no. I will come to you to see her, tomorrow."

Ramtouses withdrew, saying, "I will tell her at once. She will be most honored to meet you."

The morning arrived with the king close behind to Ramtouses' compound of dwellings. Naamity was very excited and had dressed in her best clothing. She said to Ramtouses, "How do I look? Is my appearance acceptable?"

Because she arrived in Napata with nothing, Ramtouses had taken his new wife to the markets the day after they entered the city. She purchased a new wardrobe and much of what a new household required. Now Naamity stood before him, finely dressed and as beautiful as the goddess Tantamani had suggested she was. "You are more than acceptable."

One of Ramtouses' top officers greeted the king and several members of the royal family who accompanied him and led them into a large hall where Naamity and the general joined them.

Naamity bowed before the king.

He looked her up and down, and said, "You are a jewel, bright and beautiful."

The king looked around at his constituents and continued, "How could a child like you win over such a fierce warrior as General Ramtouses?"

She answered, "When I heard him speak that day in the assembly at Jerusalem, I felt warmth in my heart that only grew."

The king asked, "You are Hebrew? You have a different belief than we Nubians. Did not this present some difficulty for you?"

Naamity made answer. "What you say is true. However, Ramtouses has opened his heart to learn and understand my beliefs, and that's all I can ask of the man I love."

"Aah," commented Tantamani, "sweet and innocent as well."

While the conversation continued, members of the royal family wandered around her, looking her over, as if making judgement. Ramtouses offered a morning meal for his guests. The king accepted for everyone and later departed.

Tantamani returned to the palace and considered the situation.

I must find a way to rid myself of this Ramtouses. He may have been important when Taharqa was king, but he is no longer needed in my kingdom. He means nothing to me. He brings his Hebrew wife with her belief of a single god into our beloved Napata. I feel as if I have been slapped in the face before our gods. When our country was in desperate need for a victory, he manipulated me into giving the enemy our prize negotiating tool.

Tantamani's heart was engulfed with hatred, jealousy, and a need for revenge. He thought all day of a way to soothe the agony.

"I pray to you, dear Amun-re, grant me the wisdom to carry out a reprisal against this person who cares nothing for you or for me, your servant." He put two fingers to his lips, tapping them softly as he blew out his breath. It was a habit he had picked up from . . . "Yes, that's it!"

The memory of a distant family member who made the same motion while thinking suddenly flooded his mind. He was the kind of man who could accomplish things that needed to be accomplished, in the dark and on the quiet.

When the man came before the king, Tantamani told him of the duty he needed him to carry out. "If you are successful, you will become a wealthy man. You and your family will become residents of the palace. Are you prepared for such important undertaking?"

After receiving an affirmative nod, the king continued. "There are always two or more guards outside the walls at the main gate of his compound. I will arrange a diversion to allow enough time for you to scale the outer wall. Inside the yard you will see a large building with vines hanging from it. Climb the vines to a window and, once inside, find Ramtouses' sleeping quarters. He will be sleeping with his new wife. Kill them both and escape as fast as you can."

The man was pleased to be asked to serve the king.

The assassin came near the compound and waited for the diversion. Four guards in pairs alternated shifts, walking the perimeter of the walls around the estate then returning to the main gate where the other two replaced them, a continuous routine.

An arrow whistled past two of the guards, just missing one. All four of Ramtouses' comrades turned and saw a man running away—two of the guards chased after him. The other two comrades did not leave the gate area.

It was very dark with no moon. The two guards remaining had their backs to the man scaling the high wall. He made it over and silently lowered himself to the ground with the rope he carried. Keen night vision helped him scan the area, and once he saw the vines, he crept toward the building, staying close to the ground. As he mounted the stout vines, a fifth guard standing watch from a camouflaged crow's nest, saw him and came running.

"Who are you? What are you doing?" he yelled. "Get down from there. Now!"

The assassin jumped down with his sword in hand. The comrade drew his own sword and the two men started fighting, their swords clashing loudly.

Ramtouses and Naamity woke up, and three more guards from inside the dwelling ran out. The assassin succeeded to disarm the guard, knocking his sword from his hand, then ran back to the wall, grabbed the rope, and began to climb.

The comrade quickly recovered his sword and chased after the intruder, pulling him from the wall. The assassin was struck several times before he finally fell, dying within minutes.

The general and his wife came out of the house.

"What is going on out here?" he asked.

"We don't know." The comrade was breathing hard. "This man is dead. He put up a strong fight and I regretfully had to kill him. We cannot question him now."

The guard from outside joined them, saying, "There was another one, but he escaped."

They stood in silence for a few moments. "I need to think about this." Ramtouses said, and waved his arm in dismissal. "There is nothing we can do tonight. We will look at the facts and process them later in the day. My wife and I are returning to our bed."

Ramtouses and Naamity disappeared back into their home, but he felt deeply troubled and did not sleep the rest of the night. In the morning, he gathered his age-group members who were quick to verbalize their suspicions that the intrusion was in reality, an assassination attempt.

"Without proof we cannot be certain, but I believe the only person with enough audacity to devise such a scheme would be King Tantamani," said Ramtouses.

He put his arms around Naamity's waist. "I want to assure you, my love, the Nubian people—my people—love me as I love them. There is no place in all Nubia where I am not honored. The generals obey me, not the king. And his jealousy can only be expressed in a cowardly sneak attack. The officers may want to denounce the king for this behavior, but I will not play into his mindless games."

The couple excused themselves and left the meeting to have their morning meal.

The king had no response when he heard of the incident. He kept silent and only later after some thought, he sent a messenger to his aunt, the former High Priestess Amenirdis, requesting her presence in the palace.

Amenirdis entered the king's chambers and gracefully bowed. She could feel his thoughts as she watched him pacing the floor before her, his arms folded behind him. "You sent for me, my King?"

He said nothing but continued to pace. It was clear to her this was not a social meeting. After a while she exhibited a little impatience. "I am here, King Tantamani. Did you wish to see me?"

The king raised his hands in the air. "I cannot understand why it is people assume I will rule as king in the same manner as my uncle. I find myself occasionally needing to correct the error."

He turned and focused his gaze then pointed his finger at her. "You are an example." He paused. "Amenirdis, sounds so charming and powerful. Could you explain the duties of such a person that is the high priestess?"

He waited for her answer.

She began to speak, sure of her words. "A virgin is given to the god Amun-re. Her virginity represents man's loyalty to the gods that they may receive good fortune from them."

"Wait," he yelled. "I don't have to hear more." He advanced toward her, his face a mask of anger. "To break that one law alone could cost the outcome of a battle or a war. A king could pray day and night without his prayers being answered. A king could wonder why the gods do not hear his pleas."

The king threw open his arms. "Yes, the answer comes when he discovers the sacred chosen one, High Priestess to Amun-re, has turned out to be unfaithful, a deceiver."

She stared at him, and lifted her chin while pulling back her shoulders. She became anger itself. Taking a deep breath, she answered Tantamani firmly, her voice low and hard. "Don't you dare speak like that to me. It was I who made it possible for you to be king, and as for our gods—including Amun-re—they had already turned their backs on us when they snatched Egypt from us for the sake of those evil Assyrians. That was before you became king, and you know the truth. I devoted my entire youth to my beloved god, and he deserted me when we needed him the most. We lost everything in Egypt. My prayers meant nothing."

"That's enough." Then, in a softer tone, he said, "So you think infidelity is justifiable? Sometimes the gods test our loyalty in ways that appear strange to us. Perhaps we could have reconquered Egypt if you had remained loyal."

The room was quiet for a few moments before he said, "You have been replaced in Egypt under the new pharaohs. You will be replaced in Nubia also. I will name another virgin from our family to serve the great Amun-re. You, however, must never be seen among the nobles of Nubia again. You must find a new home. I cannot have you bring distress upon our family name, living the life of a promiscuous commoner. You know I could demand your life for this, but even you know it would not be a wise choice in the eyes of the gods or the subjects of Nubia. I want you away from the sight of the people, and perhaps your insults will fade away in time with you."

He pointed to the door. "Leave now. For your sake I hope I shall never see you again."

Amenirdis maintained a straight face, not letting his words bring her sorrow. Returning to her home, she informed Kobina of their situation.

He said, "I love you, very much, and I will never let anything sever us." He thought for a moment. "We could settle near Meroe."

Amenirdis hung her head low, looking out the window opening unto her courtyard.

"The king has made me a true exile. He does not want me near his social network of countrymen. He wants me gone."

Kobina then said, "I shall talk to Ramtouses. Maybe he can help." And he immediately left to speak with Ramtouses.

He arrived at the compound not knowing of the assassination attempt but instantly became aware that something was wrong. Everyone appeared as on alert, shoulders were square and soldiers stood tall. Their eyes darted left and right, missing nothing.

After Ramtouses explained the incident, and though the attack totally surprised him, Kobina now understood Amenirdis' news a bit better . . . the king was threatened by their very presence much as Dafori had been. He informed Ramtouses of the dilemma he and Amenirdis faced.

"I don't want Naamity to live in fear." Ramtouses said as he and Kobina discussed the recent threats to their lives. "In Jerusalem it was King Manasseh, in Egypt the Egyptians, and since she has been with me—one threat after the other. Yes, she is a strong woman, but I want our marriage to be alive, full of joy and happiness, without danger lurking around our next move."

Kobina held his hands open. "I certainly agree. What do we do?"

"I am returning to Tungal where she will feel safe. I know it will not be like Jerusalem or Napata with accommodations such as paved streets, brick dwellings, and nearby drinking water. But once she gets to know the people, she will love it there."

Ramtouses paced around his rooms with his hands akimbo. "Even though I cannot prove it, I know it was King Tantamani who conspired against me. It was not a well-developed scheme. Perhaps he only wanted to warn me of the danger in living here." His tone was angry. "I could make him pay by revolting against his right to be king, ordering the army to attack his government and topple his throne. I could have him exiled or killed then select another son of the royal family to replace him, but he knows I am not going to do that. I am not looking for vengeance. All I want is peace and happiness for Naamity."

The general placed a hand on Kobina's shoulder. "It is best for us to return to Tungul, and I welcome you and Amenirdis to join us as we travel. Manni will be happy to see you."

Kobina smiled. "You are right, and Amenirdis will be thrilled to see her dearest friend, Queen Carnabrara." He departed, hurrying to share his good news.

Egypt, Memphis

Meanwhile, King Tantamani called for the Nubian officers to move the horses and wagons up into Ethiopia where thousands of Nubian refugees were fleeing south desperately trying to escape captivity. The assistance of the wheeled vehicles brought many into Nubian territory, people who might have been captured and enslaved by the Assyrians.

Assyria's Emperor Ashurbanipal moved his army no farther then southern Ethiopia for fear of thinning out his forces over too vast a region.

Among the prizes of war were the women, children, and healthy men for heavy labor. The hunt went on for months. Eventually, Assyria grew tired of their time there, and the need to return home became priority. The Emperor called for Prince Psamtik to come before him.

"I understand the Egyptian people love you as they did your father Necho the First. To attempt a bold task of rescuing you was extremely risky for them. I salute their efforts. I cannot stay here to watch and guard your country. I have my own work to do at home. I need a strong individual to rule over this vassal state of Assyria. Do you think you are up for the task?"

"I am, my Emperor. I want to prove once and for all that Egypt is a powerful nation."

The emperor cut him off. "Wait. I see some things my father could have done before leaving your country. He should have spent more time reinforcing the border wall, and a thousand men in the garrison are not nearly enough men to support the city of Memphis. At your southern border I will tear out the timber in key locations and replace them with bricks on top of the ancient barriers that have been effective for hundreds of years. The garrison near Memphis will house thirty thousand battle-ready troops."

Ashurbanipal placed his finger on his chin as if in thought. "There is one other thing we could do, and that would be to march south and attempt to wipe out the whole of Nubia. That would require a fresh new army willing to fight for years in uncharted lands far away from home. No, it would be too much for my war-weary army. I trust you will have the knowledge to protect yourself against the aggression of the Nubians. Trade is essential. Without it, Egypt becomes a secondary state. Somehow you must build a relationship with all your neighbors, including Nubia. Like all countries, it requires the ability to exchange materials, to offer gifts for peace. I will keep an ear for help if you need it. Only one other thing must be clear—I will not accept excuses for vassal payments."

At the conclusion of their conversation, Ashurbanipal, King of Assyria and Emperor of all its vassal states, dismissed Prince Psamtik. Within weeks, Psamtik was anointed Pharaoh of Egypt, in the year 664 BC.

Nubia and Beyond

Ramtouses first talked with all his age-group comrades.

"Not long ago, I expressed the possibility of returning to the land of our parentage. As I said then, I will not hold it against anyone who wants to remain here in Napata. Nubia is a large country, but only one man should be looked upon as monarch. There is no room for more. I want no questions about who is king or who should be king. If anyone wants to join me, let them make their decision now. We will be leaving in a few days."

The age-set brothers all agreed to leave with their wives. None wanted to break up their union. He also spoke to the remaining tribesmen who'd gone to war as mercenaries.

He sent a messenger ahead to inform Queen Carnabrara and Manni of the move. They were ecstatic. It was like a dream come true for them, and they made ready a welcoming celebration.

Ramtouses and the others arrived a few days before the new moon festivities, so they waited until one day before the new moon to come into the city. Hundreds of people came out to receive them. Thousands more awaited them within Tungal.

Ramtouses came forward and said, "We left Tungul with nearly 70,000 young men, excellently trained horsemen for the cavalry and chariots. Many of them were from your surrounding villages and right here, from Tungal. They were your family and your friends. Sadly, I must say thousands of the brave men who marched off to war with me will not return. Many have died on the battle field. Some others who were not killed in the fighting elected to stay with King Tantamani and build new homes in Napata and other towns throughout Nubia, and others have returned in this group with me. I say, let us give thanks for the bravery of the many men whom we mourn, and also, let us give thanks and celebrate those who returned today."

This particular new moon festival was to honor the ancestors and the people respected their traditions. They

321

feasted and danced, remembering the ancestors long passed. They also feasted and danced in honor of the many brothers, husbands, and sons whom they dearly loved and now missed, those with whom they once feasted and danced, those who died in the war with Egypt and Assyria.

Ramtouses brought Naamity before his mother, the Queen of Tungul, and his father, Manni. He introduced her to the queen who hugged her tightly and immediately started telling tales of the many days and nights her son longed for his lost love. Manni placed his arms across both of their shoulders and thanked the Lord for uniting them. Ramtouses grabbed Naamity and his mother's hands and inclined his head toward Manni. "Come on," he said, "let's dance for joy."

He purposely withheld the information about additional people traveling with them. He'd wanted it to be a surprise, so when he started waving his arms like a bird trying to take flight, Kobina and Amenirdis began to step out from behind his group of comrades.

Suddenly, Carnabrara's eyes grew large and her mouth flew open. She shouted with joy when she saw her dearest friend standing back in the crowd. She took off running, and while Manni was looking to see what caused her excitement, he spotted Kobina standing next to Amenirdis. It was Manni now who looked like a bird attempting flight as he flailed his arms while running toward his friends. There were shouts of delight and hugs all around as the two couples greeted one another.

"You must tell me everything," said Carnabrara with a big smile on her face. Manni and Kobina were together the rest of the day.

"Their happiness seems to create joy in the people around them," mused Naamity, and turning to her husband she said, "Let's have many friends around us, always."

When the food was served, they found seats next to the queen and king. Hundreds of people crowded into the large royal compound to share the feast with the royal family and their guests. At the start of the feast, one of Ramtouses' comrades stood and asked the queen's permission to speak. It was granted.

"I am chosen to represent your son's age-group. We are his comrades. My brothers and I are in full agreement in wanting to express how happy we are to be back among our families. It is a strong and warm feeling to know there are people here who welcome us and love us without reservation. We thank Tungul with all our hearts."

And the people cheered loudly. Someone from the crown shouted, "Did you think we would ever forget?" And the cheers ignited again. It was truly, a welcome home gathering.

Ramtouses and Naamity talked about the new moon celebration well into the night. Most everyone in the village had the wisdom to sleep after all the celebrations but Naamity was full of wonder about the event. She was amazed at the similarity between the Hebrew faith and the tribesmen's ceremony. "All the food and the dancing! Oh, that is so like my people," she said, "Even the animal sacrifice, the burnt offering. This is Hebrew worship."

Ramtouses was a little intrigued now. "Do you remember what I said my great-grandfather told me about people who settled in Nubia long, long ago? Perhaps these rituals could be part of the customs they brought with them."

The new day brought a return to business for Carnabrara. She needed to speak with her son. "Ramtouses, come to my dwelling. I have something to show you."

Ramtouses followed as the Queen led the way.

Once inside her royal domicile, Ramtouses approached business before she had an opportunity to speak. He asked, "Where is Suwanda? Does she stay away because of Naamity?"

"No," answered the queen, and she disappeared into another room.

Ramtouses stood alone, awaiting her return, and when she did, she held a baby.

"Look," she said. "There is good news. I have a grandson—meet the future King of Tungul." She lowered her head. "But there is also bad news. Suwanda died giving birth to him—she wanted so badly to have your son."

The queen gently placed the child in Ramtouses' open arms. He was cautious and held the babe awkwardly, swaying to and fro but without confidence. The baby made a small cry and he said, "Mother, am I frowning at him? Does he not like my look?" She smiled and said, "Hold him like a lamb, not a wild pig. Close to your heart."

He thought of the wonderful moments he had shared with Suwanda and grew sad, his heart grieved for her. "I will not forget your mother," he told his son, "and I will raise you as she would have wanted."

He turned to Carnabrara and said, "Naamity and I will bring the future King of Tungul into the shelter of our home with joy; we will love him and keep him until manhood."

The Queen reached for the boy. "No, my son, the child will remain here with me and Manni to groom for his rightful position, master of our people. You and Naamity will surely have many other children to cherish."

Ramtouses didn't speak at first, but his eyes gleamed as he gazed upon the child.

Eventually, he said, "I told Naamity about Suwanda, but this baby is totally unexpected. I want her to see my son." He hurried away and returned with Naamity.

She tenderly greeted the baby and asked to hold him. "What happiness for you, Ramtouses, that you have fathered such a strong son, but what sorrow for Suwanda that she cannot mother him." Then she turned toward Carnabrara, her eyes filling with tears. "You love him also, I can see he is precious to you and I understand. He is beautiful like his father. Have you taken him as your own?" Carnabrara only nodded.

"Ramtouses, I will give you many beautiful children such as this one. Will you honor your mother? Will you give her your son?"

He took the baby from his wife's arms and placed him into his mother's arms. "I trust you to keep well the future King of Tungul, mother."

Neither Naamity nor Carnabrara bothered to wipe away their tears.

Naamity said, "My mother once told me, 'Keep your tears of joy, girl.'"

She cleared her throat and asked Ramtouses, "May we go to Suwanda's burial site and pray for her?"

Manni and Kobina were happy to be reunited. They walked and talked about the time spent away from each other. Carnabrara shared her delight in her new grandson. Amenirdis explained all the events that led up to her departure from Napata and about the bitter quarrel between her and King Tantamani.

"I remembered the reawakening of love between you and Manni, the complete change in your demeanor, it was a look of mystic happiness. It pierced my lifeless body for I wanted that joy to be alive in me also. I love Kobina—it's as if Amun-re has taken human form to fulfill my life as it was intended. And now I have my dearest friend back as well. Who would ask for more?"

Carnabrara said, "I am filled with joy that now you will have everything you wish. I want to introduce you to another dear friend, my cousin, Lazoka. The three of us will do everything together."

It seemed like the happy ending of a long story until one day as Amenirdis was walking among the people, she heard Manni speaking to a group of elders and other onlookers. She realized he was teaching them that the Hebrew god was the creator of all things.

His words were, "The one God is the creator of Heaven and Earth, and all life. For man he offered a special gift by blowing the breath of eternal life into his nostrils, and thus man became a living soul."

Amenirdis addressed Carnabrara. "Why is it you allow Manni to teach the people of a false god?"

The queen said, "I have not concerned myself with Manni's activity among the villagers. I trust he will not force anyone to believe in his teaching or encourage evil behavior."

Amenirdis went on to say, "You know, as do I, the gods of Nubia and Egypt are the only true gods. Why do you neglect to enlighten the tribesmen?"

The queen pointed her finger. "You must take into account that my people have a faith—they honor our ancestors. In order to maintain stability and settle disputes among villages, the elder shaman receives the laws from our ancestors. These customs were set in motion long before I was born, and I had no problem with them before I found myself in Egypt. The villagers should have a choice in what they believe."

Amenirdis listened carefully, then said, "Carnabrara, now that you have had the opportunity to know the gods of Egypt, what do you believe? What is your choice?"

"It is the gods of course. They control our lives."

Amenirdis took Carnabrara's hand. "If you understand that, then why do you keep this knowledge from your countrymen? Let us open their eyes to the true faith."

"We have no statues to worship or priests to oversee the temples of the gods." The queen laid her own hand atop her friend's. "This shall be your work here, Amenirdis. It will be

326

your responsibility to make the Nubians of Tungal aware of the true gods."

A smile turned up the corners of Amenirdis's mouth, but her tone was unsure. "I don't know where to start. I was not expecting this."

"Amenirdis, I know you will find a way. Ask for what you need." Carnabrara rose to leave. "One other thing—you will not inhibit the teachings of Manni or the shaman. My people shall enjoy free will to how and whom they worship."

Amenirdis arranged for half a dozen altars to be built and several large statues sculpted by Kobina. She oversaw all the work. She also commissioned a place to worship. Many young people began to follow her. Most of the older tribesmen gave a listen to Manni, but no one wanted to totally abandon believing in their ancestors.

Ramtouses watched the new structures being built, and when the temple to give homage to Amun-re was completed, he came to hear Amenirdis speak.

"Almighty god Amun-re, you are so dear. You have found a place in your heart for me. All along you wanted me to come here and teach. You are calling to the hungry ears, which I will gladly fill with knowledge of you. I ask the people to listen to the teaching of the gods."

Ramtouses left feeling angry. *What else?* He knew enough about the one God, the creator of all things, to realize Egyptian gods were not the gods for his Nubian brothers of Tungal.

Ramtouses cared little for the gods of Egypt and knew only what Manni and Naamity had taught him of the one God.

He spoke to Manni. "Why is Amenirdis exposing our people to these hateful gods who love only themselves, unlike the Hebrew God who loves all mankind and only asks that we believe in him? Has she not had enough of being a slave to this kind of faith?"

Manni answered, "I was against it also, my son, but the queen wants the people to have a choice. It is out of my hands. Talk to your mother."

Ramtouses went to Carnabrara. "Mother, you know the gods as well as anyone. They can make unreasonable demands and increase the lust for power. Would not our people be better off without them?"

Queen Carnabrara was slightly taken aback by his comment. "Ramtouses, I know little or nothing of this Hebrew God. Why should our people fall victim to what could be a false belief? Manni teaches them to believe in the Hebrew God only, but I think it is important for them to have a choice."

"Manni must have spoken to you of the one God. Does he not teach you the power and wonder of the Hebrew God?"

Ramtouses humbled himself before his queen. "I do not want to sound like I am trying to tell you how to govern your people?" He spread his hands in question. "I just think Amenirdis's teaching will lead to evil doings."

Carnabrara gave a proper ruler's response. "Manni tried to talk to me about his God, but I refused to let any god or gods control my life. To rule my people fairly, I must listen to their elemental needs, not the will of some god."

Ramtouses bowed, turned, and quickly walked away.

Manni went to his cherished wife and put his arms around her. Seeing she was upset, he said, "Calm down, my love, on my way here tonight I looked up into the heavens. I remembered that this is the time of the year I first asked you to sit with me on one of the hills overlooking Tungal. Do you remember that night many moons ago?"

The queen wiped her eyes and nodded. "You showed me the raining of the stars."

"Would you believe the raining of the stars should be falling tonight? Let us go to the hilltop again."

Manni held her hand as they took a trail leading to the high slopes where they sat together. Carnabrara hugged Manni tightly, and they watched the wonders of the night sky spotted with bright shiny stars.

Ramtouses spent much of his time helping Naamity learn the Nubian language to perfection. She had learned an acceptable amount of words when she'd sung for the Egyptians and Nubians while captured. In exchange, Ramtouses was the recipient of her knowledge of the one God who Naamity so wholly cherished.

Her husband said, "The problem with the worship of any God is that it's much like tossing a stone over your shoulder then hoping it lands in the right spot. It is easy for you to accept your God—you were born into that faith and exposed only to that belief. I am an outsider who has been indoctrinated with many faiths, and each I've eventually accepted as the true belief, and yet each says the others are false. It's as if Nubia dances with the gods and never knows which partner will be the one to save him—a deadly dance that can last for not only his entire lifetime but also for generations to come."

Naamity looked bewildered after hearing these words spoken with intense sincerity, coming from the lips of the man she loved.

"The teaching of the Lord is different in many ways. My God says that all humankind are equal. No belief shall kill the other. Humans shall not lust for power or their neighbors' mates. Above all, humankind shall love God with all their hearts and souls. If you come to God with a pure heart, the Lord will find you and show you the way. Trust me, Ramtouses, the Lord is finding the way into your heart. I can see the growth in your recent behavior."

Ramtouses replied, "I have an idea, Naamity. You have grasped the Nubian language very well. If you speak to the people, it could have a profound effect on the villagers. Would you do it if I get permission from my father, Manni? It should give them some understanding of who God really is. May I talk to my father tomorrow?"

Naamity's eyes grew large from excitement. "Do you mean that, my love?"

"I do." He paused for a moment. "You know much more than my father. I will ask him first thing tomorrow."

Ramtouses saw his father from a distance and called out to him, "Manni, my father and King of Tungul." Manni heard his son and looked up. "Yes," he said, "a king with no dom," and he laughed. "What is it?"

When Ramtouses drew near, he said, "I have a suggestion. Naamity can speak our tongue fluently now, and with her knowledge of the Hebrew God, I believe she can do a great deal to help you teach the ways of her faith. With your permission and at your calling, she has agreed to speak before the people."

"Ah, a worthy proposal. I normally speak to the people on the Hebrew Sabbath, which is a few days away. That will give me time to spread the word," said Manni.

"Amenirdis must be made to understand that the Hebrew Lord is the only true God."

On the Sabbath day when Naamity was chosen to speak, the sky was gray and overcast, blanketed with thick clouds. The air was uncomfortably warm. Still, the crowd was at least four times larger than when Manni taught.

Even Carnabrara, holding her precious grandson, was among the curious. Manni had a small dais built many moons earlier, and that day he addressed the crowd from it, introducing his speaker.

"Someone special has joined us today; Naamity, the wife of my son, has come to share the written law of the one God of which she knows more than I."

Naamity had thoughtfully dressed in a plain and modest gown and wore no jewelry. Today was a day for the Lord's glory, not hers.

Even so, every eye was fixed upon her. She smiled shyly.

"Greetings, and many thanks for having me. This is among the greatest honors of my life. The Lord has placed me here today so that his teachings might be heard. I'm not here to ridicule any other god, but I, like your gracious queen, do feel you should have an option. Knowledge is the light of the world. Open your hearts so that you might hear.

I want to reveal some of the Lord's teaching to you. Believers with insight of the Lord's teaching shall warn the people throughout the many nations, encouraging them to righteousness. On the day when the watchman blows his horn, signifying the end is at hand, they will understand the alarm's meaning. Those who repent will be saved. The people who hear the sound of the horn but take no warning and do not repent, their own blood will come to be upon their own selves. If they themselves take warning and repent, their own souls will escape.

Now, as regarding the people who never receive the teaching of the Lord, when the watchman blows his horn, those people will not comprehend its meaning. For them, it will be the same as if the alarm is never given. Their blood will be spilled by the sword that comes and takes their souls from them. The Lord will ask the watchman to return them to him. Then the Lord will judge them by their worth, whether they be newborn, afflicted mentally, or physically."

Naamity stopped talking as her eyes gradually rose up toward the sky. Some people looked up also. She reached up with her arms, opening herself to the heavens.

"Oh Lord in heaven, please hear our prayers that you will open our eyes and hearts to your forever loving care. Help us to see the gift of your divine Kingdom."

She was quiet and lowered her head, placing her hands in prayer with the palms of her hands together vertically in front of her breast.

Naamity prayed silently for a very long time, so long that the crowds began to disperse in confusion, not knowing if she was finished or even what her words meant. Ramtouses and Manni watched as family members banded together and walked away.

Ramtouses said to Manni, "I don't think anyone understood her message."

"You may be right," answered his father.

Less than the fingers and thumbs on both hands counted twice remained of the crowd. However, these people moved closer and knelt before her.

When Naamity opened her eyes, she saw this small group. Her happiness and surprise were evident in the look she cast on them as she stepped down from the dais. She went to them, each one, and touched the top of their heads with the palm of her hand. Joyful tears filled her eyes. "Blessed be those who so desperately want to know the Lord."

Ramtouses came to her. "Why are you so happy? So very many of our tribesman had no ear for your calling."

"Ramtouses, if only a few cry out in the night, then the door can be opened for all."

Ramtouses said to Manni, "The people of Jerusalem would rather die than to lose faith in their Lord. Is that the same way you feel about this one God?"

Manni said, "I believe each day is given by the Lord, and when Almighty calls upon us, His love will chase away our fears."

Ramtouses asked, "Why is it their God allows their suffering? Are the Lord's followers required to live in poverty and want nothing from this world?"

"No," said Manni. "Life is what we make of it, but we cannot love earthly things more than the Lord."

Naamity came close to her husband, and together they walked home, their arms encircling one another's waists.

The very next Sabbath, Manni came to the house of his daughter-in-law and said, "Naamity, the townspeople want you to come before them again and speak more about your God."

A beautiful smile spread across her face immediately and she asked, "Really?" After a few moments, "Now, right now?"

"Yes. I will escort you as soon as you are ready."

After that day, Naamity often appeared with Manni on the Sabbath, instructing the people in the ways of worshipping the Lord, God Almighty.

Village life remained unchanged for several new moons until the day one of Ramtouses' comrades, the senior warrior who guarded the town, approached him.

"Ramtouses, I went to the queen who said I should come to you."

"What is the problem?" Ramtouses answered curiously.

"There's a traveler I cannot understand, and his dress is different from ours."

"Where is he? Bring him in and let me see this person."

When the stranger came in, Ramtouses looked him up and down. "Who are you? What brings you to Tungal?"

The man's words were so different from common Nubian speech, they could hardly understand what he was saying. After prolonged efforts to understand the man, Ramtouses finally said, "Let us take him to the elders. Perhaps they can understand him."

The village guardians had all the elders assembled to interview the foreigner. Even the elders had difficulty communicating with him, but one recognized his language as the oldest-known Nubian tongue, and that gave him the ability to converse with this man.

When the two men started talking, the elder soon seemed comfortable, almost happy to hear the stranger's words. After a long while, the elder translated his conversation to the others.

"He is from a land that lies beyond the drought and far away sands of the desert, a rich land filled with vegetation and plentiful game."

Ramtouses pointed out, "Why would he leave such a wonderful place to face the drought of the desert?"

"He was found guilty of adultery. His wife, the king's daughter, was the accuser. The king exiled him for life."

The man looked downcast as the elder continued. "He was taken to the middle of the desert and left there, never to return to his village. They gave him one day's water and set him eastward to find his way to the other side. While detained, one of the women who had not accused him concealed a knife in her garment and brought it to him. He would have died on this journey if not for that knife. He knew the ways of the desert, to travel at night, and follow the stars, to cut open the cacti and suck the sap, to hunt small animals for food. He used the knife to survive and eventually made his way here."

Ramtouses pondered the stranger's stories, contemplating the possibility of a new land full of vegetation and an abundance of game. He was captivated by the thought of seeing this new land. Each day he had the man and the elder interpreter brought before him and interrogated him about life far across the drought and mighty desert.

The proud husband of Naamity came to her after such a meeting with the newcomer.

"I need to tell you of my thoughts. This stranger has rekindled the excitement for adventure in me. I am still young enough for one more stirring experience. What do you think of all this talk the foreigner has started?"

"I love you, Ramtouses. I trust you. Whatever your dreams are, I am with you."

334

"Before I make any decisions, I must talk to my age-group brothers."

Ramtouses gathered his age-group comrades and spoke with them.

"My brothers, we have shared our lives from the day of our births. We trained together, learned the ways and rules of life in Egypt, we fought wars, traveled many lands, we have known both victory and defeat, and we are exiled from the only land we called home.

"Tungal is the home of our ancestors. It is the childhood home of our mothers and many of them have now returned to it. They wake up each day to the joy of renewing the bonds of love with their mothers, fathers, sisters and brothers. They are happy—they feel at home. But what about us? You and me? Our wives and children? We are denied the joy of living in our childhood cities, we no longer can see or hear or smell that which was part of our life in Thebes and Napata. We had to flee or be killed.

"What is left for us in life? Do we forget our early days? Do we adopt life in Tungal? Do we have children and accept the truth that we have no history of our own to give them, that what we pass to them is the way of our ancestors only? Do we have a hunger for one more daring adventure, a search for that place which we can name our own and build a home for our families?

"I am contemplating the idea of organizing an expedition that will take us across the desert to this new land the stranger has brought to light. It is in our blood to accept new challenges. We will find this place together with our wives and children and build a city of our own."

The response from his age-group brothers was overwhelming as they all called out their approval to him in rousing voices. All except for one whose wife was soon to give birth. He knew that a trip across the desert was not the place for a newborn.

Ramtouses' excitement was infectious, and as Naamity kissed her husband, she said, "I am thrilled. We will build a new kingdom for Nubia."

Word spread, and the whole town felt the exuberance. As many as three dozen families came forward to join them. The next several days found the town busy helping to launch the large caravan. The donkeys were assembled and loaded down with supplies.

Manni was happy about the undertaking and said, "I wish the queen and I were young enough to join you."

Carnabrara's response was, "I don't want him to go. I will never see my son again." She cried, "Why does he constantly want to leave me?"

She later tried to control her feelings about the matter, but deep inside she was miserable.

It was more than two full moons since the stranger had appeared in Tungal and communication between him and Ramtouses had greatly improved. Ramtouses spent long hours questioning the man about his travels, the land and desert, and the people. He shared his idea of traversing the dessert to find a new homeland for his people.

"You will lead us back across the drought-stricken land."

The visitor looked surprised. "I could never find my way back, while I was there, in the desert, I was delusional. My judgment was affected. Don't you see I was fortunate to make it here?"

Ramtouses added, "Nevertheless, you will lead us. Do you think I would risk the lives of my people on the word of a stranger unless he was willing to risk his own?"

"But they will kill me if I return," replied the foreigner.

"Fear not. When we arrive on the other side, I will see to it no harm will come to you."

Departure day arrived and there were two very dissimilar groups of people gathered at the edge of the village. Those embarking on the journey northwest were ready to move.

Ready and eager to journey out of Tungul and into a drought-stricken land, through the desert, and on to a land of promise, a land of green vegetation and flowing waters, as the stranger had described. They stood by wagons stacked high with provisions, by animals laden with bundles strapped tightly. Children tugged at their mothers' hands. "Let's go!" Their excitement prevented them from standing still. Even the horses and asses bearing the heavy loads were pulling to move.

They had spent yesterday with families, relatives, and friends who opted to stay behind. Extra belongings, items too cumbersome to pack, were given to this friend or that sister. Their goodbyes were said. And hugs shared all around. Sure, tears were spent, some even had second and third thoughts, but it was now time to move on out.

The other group, those not traveling but remaining in Tungal, stood still. They wiped away tears, once, and then again. Yes, the farewells were all made, many times. But today it became real. They were saying their last good-byes, these were we'll not see you again good-byes, and there was no lure of adventure to prop them up. Unlike the first group, they did not feel the excitement of this upcoming journey; they felt finality. It was a sad time for those left behind.

Before the expedition began, last checks of all supplies were made. Plenty of water, check. Extra horses, check. Food, check. Clothing, check. Weapons, check. Cooking supplies, medicinal needs, agriculture tools, check, check, check. What have we forgotten?

Ramtouses sat on his horse and turned for one last look . . . his mother, Queen Carnabrara, holding her grandson, stood next to Manni, his father. "I love you!" He saw Manni put his arm across Carnabrara's shoulders, saw him gently pull her close and then sweetly rub the baby's head, trying to make it better, easier. He waved one last time, then turned back to ride out, to lead this group of more than 400 people away—on a journey toward the unknown, toward the promise of adventure and a better life.

The villagers watched their loved ones disappear in the direction as the setting sun.

⁙

They moved at night, with stars as their guides, and slept during the day. Travel from one new moon until the next was an experience of sameness, that is: walk, set up camp, eat, sleep, arise, walk, eat, and walk again. Night after night, the same. Then, one day the foreigner said to Ramtouses, "I am lost. I do not know where we are." He began to weep.

Ramtouses said to him "You assured us you could follow the stars."

The man answered, "I believed I could, but now I can't tell one star from the next. The desert has perplexed me."

Ramtouses, a leader of men, made a decision and replied, "No. We are not lost. I am a military commander, and we are headed to the other side by following the setting sun." He turned to one of his comrades, "Take the man away. I will send for him if I need his advice in the future."

Half the time from one new moon to the next passed. The sameness continued until one day when the camp was awakened for the night time journey by the screaming and wailing of donkeys. The guards on duty ran to the hobbled animals and found a large pack of vicious hyenas, their eyes dazzling like fireflies in the dark of night. Their yips were like the sound of children playing games. They had attacked the animals for food and unended many of the supplies. The tribesmen shot arrows at the aggressive killers. Some were close enough to use their knives.

Other comrades were awakened and hurried to help. During the battle, one of the men was bitten by the hyenas, the flesh of his arm torn open. After quite some time, the hyenas were driven away.

Ramtouses received the report that the wounded tribesman was resting, but three burros designated to carry water and supplies had been killed. Most all the supplies were retrievable, but water had spilled and soaked into the dry sand. He was concerned about the loss of precious water.

"Our water loss could be critical. We must tighten our rations now. The women and children will take water first, but we lessen the amounts."

Ramtouses tripled the guards of the day patrol around the donkeys and camp. Nearly the same time that evening, the hyenas returned in full force. This time they were met by the guardians and tribesmen standing by in case of another attack, and the hyenas were driven away without a loss or injury to anyone. They did not return.

When several more days passed, the caravan began to feel the effects of intense heat with little water. Ramtouses wondered, *Did I make a mistake leading my people out here?*

As the company of tribesmen prepared to press on, he said to Naamity, "For the first time in my life I feel helpless. It is as if the desert is waiting to swallow us up, and there is nothing I can do about it."

Naamity took his hand and placed it on her belly "We will make it. You must have faith in the Lord. Inside of me another Ramtouses waits to be born."

His eyes opened wide as he realized what she was saying. Questions flooded his mind as did the fear of all the dangers and threats desert travel presented. He stood immobile, terrified. "How long? Why did you not tell me before this?"

She made answer, "I have only just learned of it myself."

He took her in his arms and kissed her, long and tenderly. "We will survive."

Three more days passed, and Ramtouses grew troubled now that the water was extremely low. A few of his comrades were so dehydrated, they'd begun to hallucinate. Ramtouses sat in the shade of a tented cloth, his dry elbows rested on rough knees and his tired head held up by calloused hands. "I am weary and afraid."

Naamity came in. "Stop it, stop it. Yes, you are weary and afraid. Pray to the Lord for help—let Him hear you say you love Him as He loves you. Ask Him for help. You are His selected servant, and if you are sincere, He will save us."

Ramtouses dropped to his knees and placed his hands out before him, entreating. "Oh, great God of all humankind, I know not how to pray, yet I offer myself to You with love. I want to hold You sacred in my heart, not just to call on You when in need but to have You as my guiding torch for all time. Forgive us for the evil things we do to each other and for destroying the world whereon we live, a world You have given us. Reveal Your glory to our feeble minds as we walk on this Earth. Can I be worthy of Your love? If so, put the thoughts in my mind and let them flow from my lips—may Your will be done." After that Ramtouses was quiet.

They walked all that night beside their horses, and just before they were about to make camp, one of the scouts rode up calling to Ramtouses. "I think we've found it." He jumped from his horse and approached his leader.

"Show me the way." Ramtouses and the whole congregation made haste following the scout. They came upon a huge slope leading them to a rocky cliff and, fighting an aching tiredness that threatened success, they slowly climbed to the top. With the rising sun at their backs, an expansive view of green vegetation and shimmering morning dew greeted them. They had no words to voice for far before them set a place almost holy.

Ramtouses and Naamity stood atop the ridge, holding each other up for fear of falling, and witnessed God's promised peace in a distant expanse of thickly wooded areas and grassy plains where carpets of color stretched out and surely, they thought, where there is vegetation so green, there must be water.

It was truly a place of bliss. Ramtouses said, "Control your excitement, and walk, don't run. The animals smell the water—

lead them to it with caution. We don't want a stampede on our hands."

The group walked with renewed buoyancy as the sun rose to its full height, and, by midday, they saw clear brooks and streams teeming with ducks and geese. Flocks of birds soared in the skies, and an occasional herd of animals was seen grazing freely in the long grass.

"Look! Come see what I have found," shouted a child, as he feasted on the berries of low growing bushes in the open field.

Ramtouses slowly raised his arms. His eyes searched the sky.

You actually exist, a loving God. Yet, I cannot help but to wonder why it is that you allow so much suffering, evil, and false gods to subsist. I open my heart to love you as Naamity and trust your will over your children here on Earth.

He then spoke in a loud voice. "You have saved us, oh Mighty God, the Creator of all living things."

He slowly lowered himself to his knees. "I have had my doubts about all gods until now. You have opened my eyes to your loving kindness. It is your will that we have arrived at this paradise to multiply and become many until your desire has come to pass."

Ramtouses' comrades near him lowered themselves to their knees. Naamity placed her hand on his shoulder and kneeled beside him. He continued to speak in a powerful voice.

"My comrades and I will follow your laws and teachings. Make your name be a part of our lives for generations to come. You have brought us through wars and troubled times. You kept my partner in life safe for me, and after near death in the desert you waited for me to seek your love. Your reward is overwhelming. Thank you, my God."

Ramtouses was quiet as more and more of his followers knelt down until all had kneeled to the Lord Almighty.

The Nubians settled into their new home. This was a golden time for these pioneers. Little did they know that after

341

a hundred generations a new danger would emerge, long ships with fat hulls to pack in people like nets full of fish, and, locked in chains, those who once were pharaohs of Egypt would find themselves taken on a faraway journey to become slaves, again—for new masters.

FINI